A CHANCE ENCOUNTER

SUSAN GILLIE

A Chance Encounter
Published by The Conrad Press Ltd. in the United Kingdom 2025

Tel: +44(0)1227 472 874
www.theconradpress.com
info@theconradpress.com

ISBN 978-1-917673-42-6

Copyright © Sue Gillie, 2025

All rights reserved.

Typesetting and Cover Design by: James Sadlier, jamessadlier@me.com
The Conrad Press logo was designed by Maria Priestley.

Printed and bound in Great Britain by Clays Ltd, Elcograf S.p.A

Chapter One

It was his hat which first caught my attention; it was trilby-like (I'm not very good at men's hat styles) and a dusty, donkey brown colour. There were two rather bedraggled pheasant feathers stuck in the hat band, and the whole perched on straggly, shoulder-length orange-red hair. I couldn't see the man's face, but he was wearing glasses whose wide black arms cut a dramatic line across his profile.

The tube was crowded so it was only when we both got off at Camden Town and I was near him on the escalator that I could see his green T shirt and his amazing black leather trousers: they were tight fitting and reached just below his knees. The leather was slightly shiny, and the outside of each leg was ruched as if someone had pulled a drawstring though them.

Once I had taken in these items of clothing, my eyes moved down over his slim, hairless calves to his feet, another surprise for they were clad in beige canvas shoes whose fronts were split into two sections, one containing his big toe, the other for the rest. Japanese, I guessed.

We both turned right as we emerged from the station. I began to speculate about him: was he a stall holder at Camden Lock? That seemed likely. Or a model on his way to a fashion shoot? Or maybe he was asserting his sexuality - surely he had to be gay?

I was so deep in these entertaining thoughts that I barely registered the lively music being played by street entertainers, and walked right passed the turning I should have taken. I was still just a few yards behind him.

Suddenly he stopped and turned round to face me. I hesitated, then continued. As I approached, he looked at me directly with sharp green eyes, almost the colour of his T shirt. It was hard to guess how old he was: around forty maybe.

'Are you following me?' His stance was not exactly aggressive, but definitely authoritative.

'No, I'm not!' I said quickly, embarrassed, and disconcerted by his gaze. 'I was intrigued by your clothes and thinking about them and you and sort of forgot where I was going.'

'And what conclusion did you come to about me?' He still sounded rather unfriendly.

'Er, well, I didn't really.' I'm sure I was blushing. 'Maybe you have a stall at Camden Lock and want people to notice you?' I wasn't going to say I thought he was gay, for all that it seems to be quite okay these days.

'Was that your only thought?' He didn't indicate yes or no to my idea.

'Or a male model going to a job?'

He smiled at that. 'Thanks for the compliment but I think you'll find models look pretty ordinary until they get dressed on the shoot. What else?'

Now I really was in trouble.

'It did cross my mind that your outfit was, well, a bit camp so I thought you might be gay.' I forced myself to say it.

'My, my, you do think in stereotypes, don't you! Maybe I should do some stereotyping on you.'

We were still standing in the middle of the pavement, people pushing past us, occasionally giving us odd or annoyed looks. I didn't know what to say but he didn't wait for an answer.

'Well,' he looked me up and down, ignoring the Saturday crowds, taking in, from the top, my grey hair which was due for a wash and cut, my favourite slightly baggy cardigan. My navy skirt was presentable though not stylish, but my shoes were the pits: old black trainers chosen for comfort trudging London streets.

'OK,' he said. 'Teacher? Librarian? Unmarried. Rather serious, not much fun in your life.'

'Ouch', I said, embarrassed to be so categorised. 'Actually, I run my own successful engineering consultancy, married to a man who thinks I'm the cat's whiskers, three sons at Cambridge...'

He laughed out loud. 'OK, I got that wrong, didn't I – if you're telling the truth. Three sons, all at Cambridge? That's pushing it.'

'Not at all: IVF triplets, full term, IQs 120 plus, all three of them.' I instantly regretted saying so much but I was nettled. 'And as for fun, I've just been to buy the score of an operetta I'm singing in.' I indicated the score sticking out of my large handbag. 'Just because I'm dressed for comfort...'

He grinned a bit sheepishly. 'That will teach me not to jump to conclusions.' He paused. 'Look, my name's Michael and I'm very sorry if I was rude and upset you. Are you in a hurry?' He looked me in the eye.

'Not particularly. Why?'

'At least let me buy you a drink. I think there's an interesting conversation we could have over a coffee – or something stronger. And I'll tell you the truth about me.'

I glanced at my watch, making sure my beautiful sapphire engagement ring was visible above my wedding ring, and thought quickly. There was something intriguing about him, and he didn't seem the type to be trying to pick me up – certainly not, given the way he clearly saw me, and the obvious age difference.

'Well,' I played for time, looked at my watch again. 'OK, just a quick one, I don't have to be home for an hour or so.'

He brightened 'There's a nice café just up the road. Let's go.' I fell into step beside him, following him into an attractively decorated establishment. We sat on opposite sides of a check-clothed table decorated with a single gerbera in a blue vase.

'Tea? Coffee? A glass of wine maybe?'

Feeling this was a mini-adventure, I was tempted by the wine but settled for tea. He did the same. The waitress took our order, not batting an eyelid at Michael's odd appearance.

'Where's the Ladies?' I asked her, feeling that at the very least I should comb my hair and put on some lipstick.

She pointed to the far corner. I excused myself to Michael and made my way over. The lighting was not very flattering, but I used the loo and did my best in front of the mirror.

Emerging a few minutes later I headed for our table then stopped in consternation. There was an entirely different man sitting there – brown haired and balding, no glasses. I went closer then burst out laughing: the trilby and a wig with a fringe of straggly orange-red hair were sitting on the table, black glasses folded beside them.

Michael grinned widely. 'I'd better come clean. Michael Moreton, Professor of Quantum Physics at Cambridge, on my way to a fancy dress party.'

'No, not really? Oh, God, I did get you wrong - or are you pulling my leg? If you're going to a fancy dress party, what's the theme? You seem to have mixed a few ideas: William Tell at the top down to ninja shoes at the bottom – at least I've heard they wear shoes like that.'

'Touché. I didn't have much time to think about it so begged and borrowed what I could. These,' he gestured to the hat and wig, 'belong to my son, the trousers came from my daughter's dressing up box. The shoes I never got round to throwing away once I stopped doing martial arts. But now - you still haven't told me. What's your name?'

'Elizabeth.'

'Elizabeth what?'

Elizabeth Trenchard.'

'I knew it!' Michael slapped his thigh. 'I teach your sons. I guessed it immediately - they're the only triplets at the university. They're always at my lectures – very conscientious, very bright - so of course I know them. Well, well, well.'

Chapter Two

The happy smile on Michael's face was infectious and I smiled equally broadly before we both laughied at the unlikelihood of this encounter. The waitress must have wondered what was causing such merriment as she set the tea things down in front of us.

'Enjoy,' she said, in that automatic way which gets on my nerves, even though I understand it must be hard to come up with a fresh-sounding phrase every time.

The tea, served in mix-and-match bone china cups, was accompanied by two shortcake biscuits which we ate while exchanging a few details about our lives.

'If those are your daughter's trousers, how come they're big enough for you?' I ventured to ask.

'Well, she's very tall - takes after her parents – and, I have to confess, wasn't the slimmest teenager in town. She was very into drama at school and along the way picked up a strange array of garments. I can't remember what part these played.'

It was true that he was tall; he had had quite an advantage over me as we stood in the street, which had added to my discomfort. He was very slim too, so the ruched trousers weren't such a stretch, so to speak.

'Has she left school, then? And how old is your son who sports such a curious hat and wig?' Questions like this would help me gauge his age, I thought. He looked so different bareheaded that I was revising my estimate of 40, and Professorship at Cambridge implied a level of hard-earned seniority – and brilliance.

'Alice is 23 now and working. Toby's 18. He's waiting to

hear if he's got into Cambridge - not to read Maths. Didn't want to follow in his illustrious father's footsteps.' This was said with a self-deprecating grin.

I decided I had better stop probing, but only after one more question:

'And your wife, is she an academic too?'

That cheerful face changed as he looked down and waited a few seconds before answering.

'Anne died four years ago.'

'Oh, I'm so sorry to hear that.' I didn't go on as I find it very difficult to not to sound trite, or at least artificially sincere, in such situations.

We sat in silence for a few more seconds before he looked up and smiled, not brightly as before, but almost as if apologising for introducing a sad note, then continued.

'She was an academic too, but her subject was Classics, speciality Early Greek – didn't make for much work conversation over supper!'

I nodded and offered a potted run-down of my family.

'You know about Angus, Bruce and Callum reading Natural Sciences. I studied engineering – not many women in my cohort back then! – and my husband William is in the City.'

Michael looked suitably impressed, then smiled again. 'Angus, Bruce and Callum; now this is a complete guess, but is that the order they were born in? And might there be some Scottish blood involved?'

My turn to laugh. 'That was quick of you! But talking of quick, I really ought to be going. Let's get the bill.'

The waitress duly presented the modest bill which Michael insisted on paying, and we stood to prepare to leave. As he donned the wig and glasses, on impulse I took out my phone, thinking to take a photo to show William.

'No!' Michael's authoritative mode returned.

'Really?'

'No, absolutely not. These days stuff just gets around on the internet. I'm sure you would find it hard not to show the boys and I'm not prepared to risk becoming the laughing-stock of Cambridge.'

'Of course. Sorry.' I put the phone away. 'But I've had a thought: you would really enjoy meeting William, so I'd love to invite you to dinner one day when you're in London. I don't suppose you have a business card on you?'

Michael looked pleased, and with slight difficulty fished out his wallet, clearly a tight fit in those trousers. He handed me a slightly battered card with his details. I reciprocated with a rather more pristine one of mine.

'I do have to come to town fairly often to give lectures or to confer with colleagues at Imperial. Evenings can be a bit boring so coming to dinner would be a pleasure.'

We shook hands as we left the café, agreeing that, in spite of the unpromising beginning, it had been a very happy coincidence.

'I hope we can arrange that dinner,' he said, looking directly at me before setting off in the direction we had been walking, while I retraced my steps to my missed turning.

I tossed up between a stiff twenty-minute walk or a bus ride, but a bus approached as I was deciding so, recognising that I was already later than I had told William, I got on and was home in less than ten. Those ten minutes were fun, though, as I reflected on my strange encounter. I looked forward to telling William about it, and while I understood Michael's refusal of the photo, I was very sorry I couldn't show him just how oddly Michael had been dressed. One unwelcome thought intruded, however: that final look he had given me as we parted. I hoped it hadn't been a message, more than an acknowledgement of my suggested invitation. Nonsense. I put it out of my mind as I walked the final few yards to the house.

Opening the front door, I called out. 'I'm home, darling, sorry I'm a bit later than intended.'

'No problem, I've been deep in today's papers. Didn't get round to them all this morning - downloading so many on a Saturday, as well as having one delivered, is great, balanced view and all that, but it doesn't half eat into the day,' William called from the sitting room.

I took my comb out of my bag to have a quick tidy up before going through into join him. I was just returning the comb to its pocket when William emerged and gave me a quick kiss on the cheek.

'Had a good day? I see you got the score,' he said, nodding to it still sticking out of my bag. 'Fancy a cup of tea?'

'No thanks, just had one – and thereby hangs a very funny tale.' I replied with a giggle. 'You'll never guess in a hundred years what happened to me this afternoon.'

'Want to tell me now, or over a glass of wine in half an hour or so? I've got a lovely bottle of New Zealand white in the fridge. Read about it in the FT after lunch and went straight out to buy one for us to try. If you like it, I'll get a dozen.'

'OK, let's make it story time over wine. I'll go and change while you get out some nibbles.'

'Actually, darling, I've got something to tell you too,' William called out to me as I went upstairs.

Chapter Three

When I came downstairs, William was ensconced on the sofa, the open wine bottle, glasses and a bowl of cashew nuts on a small table in front of him. He patted the seat beside him and once I was seated, he poured us a glass each.

'Cheers'. He raised his glass to me and I responded in kind. Although I was bursting to tell him of my afternoon adventure, I took the time to savour his special purchase.

'This really is delicious. Well spotted.'

William smiled, pleased, handed me the cashews and said, 'OK, now spill the beans. What happened this afternoon?'

I launched into my tale, describing how I had followed Michael in his extraordinary outfit, not sparing my embarrassment at my guesses as to why he was dressed like that, nor my discomfort as he analysed my appearance.

'I confess I was miffed at his description of me as, to paraphrase, dowdy and boring, possibly an unmarried librarian, and I'm afraid I told him more than I should have done, including about the boys being IVF triplets and at Cambridge. I'm glad I did, though, as he suddenly became much more friendly and persuaded me to join him for a cup of tea in the café we were passing.'

I paused as William's eyebrows had risen enough to show he wasn't altogether happy at this.

'It's okay, darling, it was all very proper.' I reassured him, holding out my glass to be topped up before continuing.

'Nettled at being called dowdy, I went to the ladies to comb my hair and put on some lipstick, and when I came out, he wasn't there.' I paused for dramatic effect. 'In his place was a balding man, much older looking. Then I saw the orange wig, hat and glasses on the table - how we laughed! But that's when he came clean and introduced himself. Michael Moreton, Professor of Quantum Physics at Cambridge - and he knows the boys!'

'What an extraordinary coincidence – well I never. He must be an unusual academic to be willing to walk the streets of London dressed like that.'

'Yes, I think so too. We chatted a bit and exchanged cards as I thought you would like to meet him. Apparently, he comes to London quite often for lectures and meetings. He's clearly quite eminent. Shall we invite him to dinner sometime?'

'Yes, good idea. Does his wife come to London too?'

'No, he told me she died several years ago. But he's got two kids, similar ages to ours.' I paused to take some more nuts. 'But now it's your turn. What's your news?'

William was silent for a moment and turned away, head down. I suddenly froze. What was he going to tell me? No! Surely not, not the William who, I had told Michael, thought I was the cat's whiskers? The very idea he would have an affair was surely unthinkable; I must have watched too many TV dramas. Still, I gripped my wine glass so hard I was in danger of breaking it. The nuts turned to ashes in my mouth.

'Have you noticed anything different about me recently?' William said quietly, still avoiding my eye.

That was not reassuring. I thought quickly. Had he been behaving any differently? Been later than usual back from the office? Been distracted? Secretive phone calls? No, nothing I could think of.

'No, I haven't. Why? In what way?'

'A bit clumsy or shaky, perhaps? Talking more quietly?'

'No, not at all. What are you getting at?' My panic receded;

these didn't sound like the beginnings of a confession to an affair.

At last William looked up at me. 'I've been diagnosed with early-stage Parkinson's.'

All the excitement of my afternoon adventure totally vanished. I put my arm round his shoulders and pulled him towards me. I could see he was trying to stay calm, not upset me with this devastating news, but I could feel him trembling.

'Oh, my darling, darling William. How long have you been concerned? When did you find out? Why didn't you tell me before?' My questions tumbled out.

'I didn't realise myself that anything was wrong, at least nothing that couldn't be put down to ageing – I am almost sixty, after all….

'That's not old,' I interrupted.

'No, but not young either.'

'So, what alerted you? It can't have been very noticeable or I would have suspected something.'

'It was a colleague. Apparently his father had been diagnosed with it fairly recently so he was very attuned to the symptoms. He told me he'd noticed that my hand was shaking when we were going over some papers together, then he saw me hold on to the door frame as we left the room, so he started watching me more closely. Then last week he told me of his suspicions and urged me to see a specialist.'

'You could have told me then,' I remonstrated. 'I would have come with you.'

'I didn't want to alarm you unnecessarily. Although obviously I was a bit worried, I wasn't convinced. I called a consultant friend at the golf club to ask his advice and he said not to hang around but call a Doctor Evans at his Harley Street clinic and see him as soon as possible. So I did.'

'When did you see him?'

'Monday. He was nice, very understanding, did lots of tests. Said I'd have the results quickly, tried to be reassuring.'

'How did you manage to keep quiet about this all week? Why on earth didn't you tell me, share your worry with me? And when did you get the result?'

William sat up straight, took a deep breath. 'I kept hoping it was nothing – convinced myself it was a false alarm. But he called me yesterday afternoon. It is Parkinson's.'

'You knew yesterday and didn't say anything?' I'm sure it showed in my voice that I was upset – annoyed - not just at the news, but that he had hidden his worries and then the diagnosis from me.

'We had the Dentons to dinner, remember. I really didn't want to spoil the evening; we don't often have time to entertain. I did my best to seem normal – must have succeeded as you didn't notice anything.' Now William sounded a bit put out.

'Oh, my darling. I'm sorry I was short with you. It's just that it's such a shock. And a lot to take in. How much did Dr Evans tell you? What happens next?' I released his shoulders and took his hands in mine. I looked him in the eye. 'Do you want to talk about it now?'

'No. I want a nice evening with you, pretend everything is normal. We can talk properly tomorrow. Another glass of wine?'

I nodded, trying to stop tears forming, then gave him a light kiss. 'Yes, please, then I'll get supper ready. Do you mind leftovers from last night? This afternoon's encounter distracted me, and I didn't shop for tonight.'

'Of course that's okay.' William smiled, a slight, sad smile, and reached for the wine bottle.

Chapter Four

I didn't sleep much that night. Although we had had a pleasant enough supper, it couldn't be said it was normal; we had been overly careful with each other, stuck to for neutral topics, and were happy to agree to an early night. As I had watched him head upstairs, I had been acutely aware of how carefully I had observed him during the meal. Had his hands shaken noticeably? Was his speech different? I hadn't seen any difference, but maybe he'd been making a special effort.

My concerns got the better of my wish for an early night. I called up the stairs to say I had to finish something and would be up shortly and headed straight for my computer. I searched for Parkinson's; the results were not reassuring. Though it was clear the progress of the disease might be quite slow, and although far from a death sentence, the strains on both of us were going to be considerable.

William was in bed reading when I went up. I didn't confess to my research and made an effort to behave as he had wished earlier. I had a bath which I usually find relaxing, but my mind was in too much turmoil to linger, and I soon joined him in bed.

Carefully lifting his book from his hands and putting it on the bedside table, I took him in my arms and held him close.

'I love you very much, dearest William. I know it's going to be hard, but I promise I will do everything in my power to help and support you. But right now, please sleep well and we'll talk tomorrow.'

William gave me a rueful smile before kissing me gently. 'I'm so sorry,' he said as he turned out his light. 'I love you too,

Lizzie, you can't know how much.'

All this, plus what I had read, stayed with me as I tried to sleep, to stop myself envisaging the future and what it held for us. There were so many questions: how long before his symptoms became obvious, how would the bank behave, who were the best doctors for Parkinsons, were new treatments emerging and, hitting me like a sledgehammer, who was going to tell the boys – and when - and how would they react.

In spite of this I must have dozed off as I woke to find William setting a cup of tea on my bedside table.

'Good morning, darling,' he said with a smile as he pulled his dressing gown tighter. Although he had kept in pretty good shape for his age – and considering all those business lunches - neither of us could deny his increasing paunch. 'Ready for breakfast?'

This didn't sound like a man facing a traumatic future. I smiled and said I would be down in a few minutes.

I saw no reason to change from our normal routine, so I too donned a dressing gown and went to join him in the kitchen where, as was our habit, he had laid the table and set the coffee to percolate. He was reading the Sunday paper which had been delivered.

Taking my cue from him, I didn't raise the P subject, but busied myself with eating and reading the news in a couple of other papers on my phone. But finally, I could contain myself no longer.

'When do you want to have a proper talk? We have to, sooner rather than later.'

'I know,' William replied. Let's make a start after I've had my shower. I'll feel more up to it then.'

'Okay. Just call me when you're back downstairs. I'll go and get dressed now.'

We reconvened in the sitting room, side by side on the sofa on which we had sat as he told me his news the night before. Neither of us knew quite how to begin, but after a few moments William took the initiative.

'Parkinson's isn't fatal in itself, you may know already, but becomes very debilitating as it progresses. And, I fear, embarrassing too.' He went on to describe in upsetting detail the possible loss of control over movement, loss of balance and, conversely, stiffness which can lead to difficulty walking. Speech and memory can be affected, depression, dementia, incontinence.....

The list went on and on. William was clearly determined to make me understand what both of us had to face. Some of this I had gleaned the night before in my quick computer search, but hearing it spelt out by my beloved William was awful.

'But,' he went on, 'it can progress slowly, and there are things we can do to help, the doctor said. Exercise, diet – I'm sure we'll learn more as we go along.'

'And maybe,' I interrupted, 'research will throw up a cure – it's amazing how medical science advances.'

William shook his head. 'That's a long shot. We've got to live with it now.'

I sighed, nodded acceptance. 'Will you tell the boys, or shall I? And when?'

'Let's wait until the summer vacation when they'll be back home, it's only a few weeks. No point in upsetting them now. And I've been thinking, do we tell other people now or wait until it's more obvious?'

This and the myriad other questions needed thought and lots of discussion. I hugged William again, reassured him that, whatever happened, I would always be there to support him.

'But right now, darling, look, the sun is shining. Let's go

for a walk.' I pointed out of the window. 'Let's go to Regent's Park, the roses will be wonderful already.' I hope I sounded more cheerful than I felt.

'Good idea. Front door in ten minutes.' William smiled his acquiescence and, standing up from the sofa, put out his hand to help me up. He held me in a long embrace before turning away. 'Let's take your car, it's a bit far to walk.'

We set off in my little electric car, so practical in central London. It was small enough to tuck into our front garden while still leaving space for William's big electric Mercedes which we needed to be able to fit in all five of us. I reflected how lucky we were to be able to charge the cars at home – we might be needing them more as public transport became too difficult for William.

It was still only mid-morning and the streets were quiet, but many people had clearly had the same idea as us and the park was busy. The smiles on people's faces as they admired the roses, the cheerful cries of children as they raced around on their bikes, lifted our mood. As we neared the zoo, we could hear the lions roar and were reminded how much the boys had loved visiting the zoo, their favourite animals the big cats and the monkeys and apes who always elicited laughs as they raced around the jungle gyms in their enclosures. By the time we decided to return home, Parkinson's had been briefly forgotten.

But we both knew it was going to dominate our lives from now on.

Chapter Five

We agreed over Sunday supper that we wouldn't tell anyone until we had broken the news to the boys, and then only family and close friends who might otherwise notice something was wrong. The one exception was William's boss, George Davenport, one of the Bank's main board directors, as William wanted to make sure he knew the score before any gossip began to circulate.

Monday morning was much like any other; William took the tube to his office in the City, while I was glad to walk the fifteen minutes to mine as it gave me time to put myself into work mode. The mood among the staff when I arrived was cheerful; my lovely assistant, Melissa, brought me coffee and that day's Financial Times, mentioning with a big smile that there was an interesting message on the website. Various people asked after my weekend, to which I responded that the sunshine yesterday had been lovely.

As I drank my coffee, I opened our website: Trenchant Engineering Consultancy. I was still pleased with the name and its play on my surname, believing it sent the right message of vigorously effective and highly articulate (though it could also mean caustic, but I didn't dwell on that!). The website made it clear we were very environmentally focussed and had expertise in many different aspects of engineering.

The enquiry was indeed intriguing. Signed by one Hamish McCraig (a name to appeal to my Scottish heart), it was seeking advice on a very unusual proposition. He wrote that he had a large estate on which were several rivers, one of them fast flowing. He had recently been on holiday in Bali (lucky man, I thought) and while there had visited the Green School which boasted its eco credentials. One innovation was the diversion of a section of a river through a circular hole, a vortex, in which they had installed a turbine which supplied all the electricity to the school. Would I or my consultancy be interested in advising him if he could do something similar?

Would we just! I immediately Googled both Hamish McCraig and the Green School. Not Mr McCraig, but Sir Hamish, was my first discovery, owner of several thousand acres in the Scottish Highlands. The Green School website was full of interesting information, not only about the unusual electricity generation. In fact, by the time I had finished reading, I sincerely wished our boys had gone to a school like it.

That was a great start to the working week. I replied to Sir Hamish suggesting he ring me. Meanwhile, my mind raced: surely I would need to visit his Scottish estate? Would it be an excuse to go to Bali to see for myself? If William could take time off, we could go together.

An email from Sir Hamish pinged later that morning. He would call mid-afternoon, if that was convenient.

Smiling inwardly, I made the rounds of my dozen staff, checking all were well and busy, offering advice as requested, encouraging and congratulating. I can't say it was luck that I had such good employees as I had chosen each one myself, but they really were a great bunch, mixed in age and discipline, and four of them were women, an unusually high proportion in engineering.

I attended to my emails, then took a break for lunch at a nearby cafe. Inevitably, although excited about this new enquiry, my thoughts turned to worries about William. I texted him to wish him good luck talking to his boss and ended with a virtual hug and a big kiss.

The eagerly awaited call came at three. Sir Hamish proved easy to talk to, his lilting accent music to my ears. He explained he was considering this form of electricity generation as he had some barns far from the house (castle? I wondered to myself) and power lines. He was also thinking of building a couple of rental cottages – no, cabins, he corrected himself – in that area. Both barns and cabins would need power.

We talked for about half an hour, at the end of which it was agreed I would submit a proposal for a study of the possibilities. It would include a visit by me and one of my most appropriately qualified team to see for ourselves.

Judging by the occasional odd looks I got as I walked home that evening, I'm sure there was a big grin on my face.

William arrived soon after me. As we sat in a sunny corner of the garden with a glass of wine. I asked him how it had gone with George Davenport.

'Amazingly well!' William beamed. 'Turned out – another coincidence – that a cousin was two years into his Parkinson's diagnosis and George will put us in touch. Then George was at pains to remind me that the bank's private health cover was very generous, so we need have no concerns on that front.'

'That's reassuring,' I interrupted.

'Yes. But it gets better. He asked me if I wanted to take early retirement and when I said not yet, he was really pleased, said to keep going just as long as felt right for me. Then he added that, as such a long-standing highly valued, senior employee – by this time I was almost blushing! – I should feel free to take time off as needed, whether for medical appointments or just for a break.'

I stood up from my chair and went over to give William a real hug and a kiss.

'Every word of praise was well deserved, darling, you've worked so hard for them, brought in so many high net worth investors and identified such interesting opportunities for them and for the bank, no wonder George wants to keep you as long as possible.'

We then talked about Sir Hamish's enquiry and my Google research. William could sense how interested and excited I was by it, not just the travel possibilities, but also the originality of the Green School and its environmental innovations.

I suggested that, if Sir Hamish accepted my proposal and I would be going on the exploratory visit, William should take a few days off so that he could join me in Scotland for a short holiday. We could visit my sister Fiona and her family in Inverness where her husband was a GP.

'We see them so seldom and I know you enjoy their company. What do you think?'

William didn't hesitate. 'That's a great idea. When might this be, do you think?'

'I obviously can't say for sure, but I would guess sometime in July or August. Depends on Sir Hamish's response and Fiona's plans. After the boys are home at any rate – maybe they would want to come too and spend time with their cousins.'

We were in such good spirits, Parkinson's faded into the background and it stayed there as we discovered in bed that it had had no effect on William's performance and our mutual pleasure.

* * *

Over the next few days I worked with Dave, my specialist on hydro power, researching the vortex idea and also other possibilities such as a small dam or waterfall should the river and its immediate area not be suitable for the vortex solution. Dave, who had never worked on this method of generation before, was intrigued and spent many hours researching what conditions were needed. He asked if he could write to Sir H – by this time I was tired of spelling out his name – to ask for a map reference so he could check the geology of the area, and also maybe a photo of the river at the place Sir H had his barns and planned his cabins. They would not be a substitute for a visit but might help in directing our thinking.

I agreed, and to our delight a response with answers to both requests came within a few days. We were able to put the proposal together quite quickly, allowing for two days on site to do some surveying and water flow measurement. I included airfares, and three nights' accommodation for Dave and me, plus hire car. I dithered over whether we should go by overnight sleeper, given our environmental credentials, but it would be far more expensive, even allowing for saving on two hotel nights. In the end I offered both alternatives.

Imagine my surprise – and pleasure - when Sir H not only accepted the extra cost of the train, but suggested we stay with him for the middle night. 'Save a lot of to-ing and fro-ing', he wrote, 'and I'll send a car to fetch you from the station.' His email suggested I call him to arrange dates.

Dave was tickled pink at the idea of staying with Sir H. 'Do you think he lives in a castle, like Balmoral only a bit smaller? Or maybe he's had an all mod cons house built for him?'

I admitted I had not the slightest idea.

Chapter Six

Work and William were not my only absorbing interests that week: my amateur operatic group convened to start rehearsing The Merry Widow, the score for which I had had in my bag when I met the mad professor (must stop calling him that or it will pop out accidentally at an inappropriate moment).

I loved the singing, a total change from the rest of my life. The members – we were about twenty-five – were a congenial crowd of varied ages and backgrounds. We had a few stars for the main roles; I definitely didn't count myself one of them and was quite content with my place in the chorus. But it wasn't just the company and the music I enjoyed, it was also the exercise; I had learned soon after joining that singing, done wholeheartedly, can be surprisingly energetic.

Our three pre-Christmas performances were always well-attended as the group had built up a good reputation. Our sons had been coming since they were about ten and would sing along sometimes when I was practising at home. Callum in particular had a musical bent and a good tenor voice. William came to performances too, but more out of solidarity than love of operetta. Art was more his scene, and it showed in the crowded nature of the walls at home.

Our sons were, of course, my other preoccupation. They were currently sitting their Part 1 exams and I had been sending them good luck messages at appropriate times. It was interesting to see how, although they were triplets and all reading Natural Sciences, their specific interests were emerging. They had all chosen Physics – hence Michael's knowledge of them - and the compulsory Maths, but their other choices varied across the several options.

I emailed the boys to ask if they had plans for the long vacation, and said I hoped they would spend at least some time at home with us. I mentioned the possibility of their joining us for a trip to Scotland, explaining its connection to the vortex project. Would they like that?

Replies came back, all saying they'd love to come to Scotland with us, that their plans were fluid though they wanted to visit various friends. They added that they hoped to find jobs in local pubs or cafes in London for some of the vacation. I feared it was going to be a complicated balancing act to satisfy everyone while fitting around Sir H and Fiona.

I called Fiona who was delighted at the idea of a full Trenchard visit. Fortunately, it turned out that her family's planned holiday was in August which meant I could suggest to Sir H that we came to do our research in July if that suited him.

Sometimes things just work out right. Everything fell into place with remarkable ease. Sir H was very relaxed about the timing of our visit: 'No plans to go away, plenty to do here', he emailed. Dave was free in July too, still excited about the project and the possible castle stay. The bank was fine about William taking time off, as George had promised. The boys were happy to fit their friends and possible jobs around the Scotland trip.

My next plan was to invite Michael Moreton to dinner to meet William. I decided to do it in the next couple of weeks, before the boys came home, if he could manage it; I wasn't sure how he or they would feel about meeting away from the lecture theatre.

Michael's response to my invitation was prompt and enthusiastic. Love to, he emailed, got a two-day symposium at the end of the second week of June. Was that too short notice?

Not at all, I replied.

William, bless him, was more than happy to go along with all this, grateful for my organising.

I decided not to invite anyone else to this dinner, thinking Michael might not appreciate the explanation of how we had met! We settled on the Friday evening and a simple but good meal at which William could serve a couple of his favourite wines. It was lucky our house had a cellar as it was a running joke between us that he enjoyed buying the wine almost as much as drinking it. We had enough to last us several years, but that didn't stop him buying more.

Promptly at seven thirty on the appointed evening, the doorbell rang and as I went to answer it, I speculated as to what a mad professor in mufti would wear. I was almost disappointed to see Michael was wearing jeans, an open-necked shirt and sports jacket, no sign of sartorial adventurousness.

We shook hands and made standard small talk as I led the way to the sitting room. I introduced William as he emerged from the kitchen, wiping his hands on a tea towel.

William couldn't help a big smile as he admitted I had told him the whole story of our encounter. 'That was very brave of you to walk the streets of London dressed so bizarrely. I'm surprised you got home unscathed – or perhaps you didn't!'

'No, I got away with it, thank heavens. I really should have thought a bit more before setting off. My hosts were doubled up with laughter! But I did treat myself to a taxi back to my hotel afterwards, decided I might be asking for trouble late in the evening.'

'Were the other guests as - shall we say interestingly - attired?' I ventured to ask.

'Er, no. I came in for a lot of ribbing, I can tell you.'

William and I laughed, the ice broken. 'It's a lovely evening, still quite warm. Would you be happy to sit in the garden with a glass of wine before we eat?' I guessed this would appeal.

Michael smiled acceptance and followed me through the French windows to what I called our arbour, a corner well placed to catch the evening sun and warmed by the lingering heat held by the wall of the house. William joined us with a tray of glasses and a bottle of Sauvignon Blanc in a cooler. In anticipation I had already put out a plate of smoked salmon bites. As we sat round the small table, I removed the cloth which had kept insects off the nibbles and invited Michael to help himself.

'This is such a treat after sitting indoors all day.' Michael initiated the conversation. 'I won't go into details about the various papers, mostly about a specific area of research, but it was quite technical. I had to concentrate quite hard at times.'

'Were you speaking too?' William asked.

'Yes, I presented a paper on...' He paused. 'How are you on quantum physics?'

William and I both grinned a little sheepishly and it was tacitly agreed Michael wouldn't go into details.

The wine elicited very appreciative noises from our guest and the half hour until I moved us indoors passed easily, mostly talking about gardening – it turned out his wife had been a very keen gardener and Michael had picked up enough to appreciate the efforts William and I had made in our small patch of North London.

'I hope you don't mind, but we decided the dining room would be too formal for just the three of us so we'll eat in the kitchen.' I didn't expect him to mind, and indeed as he followed us indoors he concurred wholeheartedly that informal was definitely preferable.

Over the lasagne which I had prepared the day before, conversation turned to Angus, Bruce and Callum. He didn't know them well, but enough to be impressed by their evident intelligence and interest in his subject. He asked what other options they had chosen and we were happy to talk a bit about their developing interest in geology, psychology and, for Bruce, the structure of materials, something he had perhaps picked up from my work in engineering.

Michael quizzed William about his work at the bank and was very interested to hear about his venture capital role.

'It must be exciting to be able to help good projects and businesses get off the ground,' he said.

William agreed and talked enthusiastically about one or two of his successes. By this stage we were well into the good bottle of Malbec from Argentina which William had opened, and our chat became less formal.

'And you, Elizabeth. I Googled Trenchant – got the name from your card. Fascinating – great stuff. I really like your environmental focus – it's absolutely vital we take climate change seriously, and fast. In fact, I'm working on something myself which, if it comes off, could be really important.'

'What is it? I asked.

'Electricity storage – we've got to up the game on this.'

I was all ears. 'Tell me more.'

Chapter Seven

My anticipation was well rewarded. Michael's voice was edged with excitement as he told us how he and his colleague, Xi Ling, had been doing some research when they suddenly realised that they had stumbled on a potentially important application for electricity storage. He didn't try to explain the details but said that he and Ling had done lots of maths to refine the idea, and then called in a couple of trusted colleagues to begin some experimentation.

'If it works, this discovery has the potential, maybe not to save the planet by itself, but at least to make a major contribution to our efforts to cut greenhouse emissions. The move away from the need for scarce metals such as lithium – a major plus given China's status as a major producer – is the first advantage, but the really big deal is that the potential storage time and capacity are way ahead of current possibilities.'

William and I immediately grasped the importance.

'You mean you're working on something which would enable us to store the output from renewables in a way that should greatly reduce – maybe even eliminate - the need for gas or nuclear power to supplement the renewable down-times. Is that right?' I wasn't sure if William had been following this aspect.

Michael nodded happily. 'Nuclear is all very well, once in service its emissions are small, but it takes many years and billions of pounds to build each reactor, the amount of concrete needed is vast and production of it is very eco-unfriendly – and, of course, no-one has yet cracked the decommissioning conundrum. It's all very well saying we can bury the nuclear waste under the sea, but it's still there for future generations to deal with.'

'So where have you taken the idea?' William asked, putting on his venture capitalist hat. 'Who have you spoken to? How will you progress it?'

'That's a very important question, and one we'll have to grapple with. But it's early days yet. Far too early to predict the outcome.' Clearly Michael was sensibly cautious.

'Well, don't hesitate to get in touch when things start to develop. I have some useful contacts through the bank.'

I think William was a bit disappointed that he couldn't weigh in with investors right away, but he hadn't been able to resist putting in his professional oar. I also had a few thoughts to share but decided they could wait. I took requests for coffee and suggested William and Michael moved to the sitting room.

I noticed William holding the chair as he got up and moving a little more carefully than usual. I made a mental note to ask him later whether it was Parkinson's related, or perhaps the effect of the wine he had consumed!

When I went to join them with the coffee, I found them standing in front of the portrait of William which I had commissioned for his 50th birthday. We had thoroughly enjoyed the process of choosing the artist from the samples at the Royal College of Portrait Painters, then interviewing the shortlist of three. We rejected the one who kept talking about all the famous people he had painted, and the one who never seemed able to finish a sentence, but luckily got on well with the third. We were sure we had made the right choice when we saw the result, and knew it was a success when William's mother pronounced it perfect.

There were many more pictures and objects to talk about

as we had been collecting over the years, not grand, expensive things, but ones which moved or amused us, and some we had brought back from our travels. However, the coffee was in danger of getting cold, so we sat and moved the conversation to more general topics.

It was such an enjoyable evening that William made a point of suggesting Michael come again before long.

'I would love to, and I'd like to invite you to my house in Cambridge sometime as I've also collected a few things – not up to your standard or quantity,' Martin grinned self-deprecatingly. 'But still interesting, I think.'

'That would be a pleasure,' I said. 'We could perhaps drop by when we're delivering or collecting the boys.'

'Good idea,' William agreed as we moved to show Michael out. 'We'll look forward both to seeing you here again and visiting you.'

'Are you sure you don't want us to call a taxi?' Michael had already said he planned to walk.

No, I really think it would do me good after all that good food and wine. I can always get a bus if I've had enough.'

We stood side by side in the doorway as Michael left. The mild night air was scented by the stocks I had planted in the front garden, and Michael paused to smell the rose by the front gate before turning to us with wave and a smile to express his pleasure and thanks.

'What a nice man,' William said as we returned to the kitchen to tidy up. 'And interesting too – so glad you had that strange encounter, even if you did get assessed as a dowdy, boring, unmarried librarian!'

I laughed, agreeing, then raised the subject of William's hesitancy as he had left the kitchen.

'I wasn't watching for shaky hands over dinner, but I did

notice that you held on to the chair and walked carefully to the sitting room. Was it the Parkinson's or the wine?' I made light of it with a little laugh.

'I didn't drink that much!' William also laughed. 'But, yes, I was being careful about my balance. I hope it wasn't too obvious, I didn't want to have to explain to Michael on our first meeting.'

'You were great, darling, and to be honest, it's been easy to forget the problem as it's really not obvious at all.'

'Let's hope it stays that way for a while.' William's tone was less carefree.

* * *

The week before the boys were due home passed quickly.

William had a helpful call from George Davenport's cousin who turned out to be called Anthony and lived near Guildford. At Anthony's suggestion they had agreed to meet for lunch in Anthony's club. William told me about the call over supper.

'I have to say, I found it reassuring that Anthony, who's more than two years into his diagnosis, didn't hesitate about coming into town by train. I'm really looking forward to meeting him and learning how this ....' William paused, clearly trying to think of the right adjective. 'This bloody illness progresses.'

'I'm surprised your epithet was so mild,' I smiled. 'And as well as telling you what to expect, maybe he'll have good advice as to the best specialist to see.'

'Yes.' William came round the table to give me a hug. 'I really do hope so. I can't help worrying, not just about me, but about the strain it's going to put on you.'

I didn't say I too had been wondering a little about what the future held for me but turned the conversation to collecting the boys and planning our Scottish trip.

Easing the logistics of getting three large young men and their belongings home, Callum had elected to stay with a friend in Norfolk for a few days, coming back by train. We would bring his stuff back with Angus and Bruce.

At work, Dave and I did more research about the area where Sir H lived, and what we would need to take with us in the way of diagnostic equipment, fortunately nothing too bulky. I emailed Sir H to say that I would only be charging the one-way train for me as I would be joining the family for a holiday, but Dave would be returning to London.

The weekend and the boys' return was upon us in no time. We always enjoyed our trips to Cambridge, a mixture of nostalgia for me, and admiration of the colleges for William who had been at Bristol University. On this occasion we took all three boys to lunch – a proper lunch, guessing that if they ate out at all it was more likely to be pizza or a burger. They tucked into the roast beef with all the trimmings as if they hadn't eaten for a week, and followed with sticky toffee pudding and ice cream. I honestly couldn't imagine how they found the space! Over coffee, after they had entertained us with tales of the end of term balls, I told them about the Sir H project, and they were almost as curious as Dave about where he lived and what he was like.

Lunch over, we packed all three's belongings into the car boot, then hugged Callum and waved him goodbye.

Just before William started the car, I ventured a quick question to Callum: 'Is it a new girlfriend you're going to stay with?' I knew he had had a girlfriend the year before, but it hadn't lasted

'Oh, Mum, honestly. Are you trying to get me settled down already?'

We both laughed.

'Anyway, to satisfy your curiosity, no, it's not even a girl, never mind girlfriend. It's a chap, Fred, who lives near Norwich and he's going to take me to a concert in the cathedral there. Also, they have a boat on the Broads so we'll do a bit of sailing. Okay?'

'Sounds lovely, have fun. Look forward to hearing about it.' I blew him a kiss as we drove off.

Angus and Bruce teased me on the way home, joking that surely Callum knew the friend had a sister. William concentrated on driving while I prompted the boys to tell me a bit about their hopes for the exams, the results of which would be out in a couple of weeks. They were modest in their assessments of their chances, but we all knew they would do pretty well. I remembered from my own experience that too much parental questioning didn't go down very well so we moved on to plans for the summer, the Scottish trip and whether and where they would look for jobs.

Initially it was strange having two more large adults in the house, but we soon settled into a routine and looked forward to Callum's return.

Chapter Eight

On Sunday evening I got a cheerful text from Callum. *Concert great u wd have loved it. Sailing tomorrow wp. Plan home Tues eve.*

I went upstairs intending to share the news with Angus and Bruce and ask what wp meant, but approaching Angus's room, I heard snorts and a giggled 'Do you think Mum knows?'

Before I had a chance to knock on the door, I heard Bruce say, 'I bet not. She definitely wouldn't approve.'

I dithered before going in but decided to knock and pretend I hadn't heard. Scuffling noises and a muffled 'Quick!' further raised my curiosity and, if I'm honest, a tinge of concern; I liked to think of myself as a very open-minded mother and, after all, these were young adults, not kids any more. Putting an innocuous smile on my face, I knocked again and waited to be invited in.

'Hi, Mum.' Angus appeared at the door. 'Have you come to tell us supper's ready?' He glanced at his watch. 'Oh, it's only 6.30. Come in. What can we do for you?'

Bruce was stretched out on Angus's bed looking self-consciously relaxed. He swung his legs over and patted the space beside him. I sat down and tried to look as innocent as they did.

'I've just had a text from Callum, says he's coming home Tuesday evening. But he says he's going sailing on Monday wp. What does that mean?'

They both laughed. 'Weather permitting!'

'Oh, of course. I should have known.' I laughed too but

decided to try some subtle questioning. 'Have you heard from him?'

The two looked at each other quickly, which made me even more curious.

Angus took the question.

'Yes, he's enjoying himself a lot. Turns out Fred does have a sister and apparently she's very dishy.'

'Has he sent a photo?' I said casually.

'Er, no, not yet.' Angus paused before continuing. 'But he has sent a pic of the house and garden; a bit posh.' He turned to Bruce. 'Why don't you get your phone and show Mum?'

Bruce slid off the bed and disappeared, returning a few minutes later, phone in hand.

He held the phone so I could see. The house was indeed handsome, not a cottage or farmhouse, but something nearer a mansion. Bruce moved the phone away and swiped over a few frames before showing me a picture of the garden.

'Goodness, that's quite something,' I said, taking in the long sweep of herbaceous border backed by a high wall in warm red brick. 'He seems to have made a friend in high places. Do you know Fred?'

'Not really,' Bruce answered. 'We've met him briefly a couple of times but he's reading politics or philosophy or something. They got friendly through the College choir.'

'Glad he's not only mixing with scientists, good to have a broader range of friends. How about you two? We met a couple of your friends last year, but I confess don't remember much about them.'

It was uncomfortably clear to me that they now felt on safer ground and chatted away happily about the friends they hoped to get together with over the holiday. I then steered the conversation to their plans for jobs as, although we were comfortably off, William and I didn't provide big allowances, wanting them to become as independent as possible. They both planned to find bar or restaurant work which, given the proliferation of fancy – and not so fancy – establishments in our affluent area, shouldn't be hard.

I made a few encouraging remarks then said I must go down and get supper ready. 'About an hour, okay?'

'Fine,' they said in unison. 'We'll be down in good time.'

I refrained from lingering outside the door to catch any further clues but went down to tell William about the odd conversation.

'I shouldn't read too much into it, and anyway, whatever it is, you can't do much about it. He is twenty after all.' William's reply wasn't wholly reassuring.

* * *

I had a busy week ahead at the office and barely noticed the time passing on Monday until towards 4pm Melissa called over to say Callum was on the phone.

I picked up, very surprised that he'd called me on the office number, not my mobile, and asked him straight away.

'Hello, darling. Why the office phone?'

There was a slight pause before the confession came out.

'Er, I've lost my mobile so I'm calling on Fred's. I couldn't remember your number as I only press your name so we googled Trenchant.'

'Oh. How did you lose the phone?'

'Well…'

There was a pause. When he continued, I wasn't sure if he was giggling or trying to sound apologetic.

'Well,' he repeated. 'We were in the boat and the bag with

all my stuff in somehow fell out. I dived in but it sank so quickly and the water was so deep I couldn't reach it.'

Another pause, another question from me.

'What else was in the bag?'

'My wallet – and some clothes. And my train ticket for tomorrow.'

I was silent for a moment as I digested this. My reflections were interrupted by Callum hastening to reassure me:

'It's okay, Mrs Nicholson-Smith - Fred's Mum - is lending me the money for the train fare and the tube home. We can pay her back later, and get a new phone.'

I noticed the 'we' but didn't comment.

'Who else was in the boat?' I couldn't resist that one.

'Just me and Sophia.'

'Sophia?'

'Fred's sister.'

At this point, I began to put Angus and Bruce's giggles into the picture but decided the office was not the place to go into the possibly titillating details of what made the bag fall out. Instead, I resorted to the mundane.

'You can tell Dad and me more about it tomorrow. What time should we expect you?'

'I'll aim to be back by 6.30. Is that okay?'

'Yes. Before you leave, be sure to get Mrs Nicholson-Smith's bank details.'

'Okay. Will do. Bye, see you tomorrow.' And he hung up.

I found it hard to put my mind back into work mode. Callum's casual assumption that we would pay for another phone when it was the second one he'd lost this year really annoyed me. And what had been going on in that boat? Was he really the clever, sensible son we had assumed?

Back home that evening, I resisted the temptation to cross-examine Angus and Bruce about what they knew and what had made them so reluctant to tell me about any photos from Callum. Given today's youth, I was sure he had sent plenty. Over coffee after supper, when the boys had retreated upstairs, I shared the gist of my Callum conversation with William.

'He was so casual, so unapologetic. He said Fred's mother would pay for his tickets home and seemed to assume we would buy him a new phone.'

'It's lucky Fred's mother was happy to pay for the ticket, but there really wasn't any option, we couldn't have got money to him in time. But taking the loss of the replacement phone we had bought him, an expensive one, I remember, so casually, no apology, that's a bit more concerning. I foresee some interesting conversations when he gets back.'

'I can't help wondering what his relationship with Sophia is, and what Sophia and he were up to in the boat, given that Angus and Bruce seem to have access to more information, information they thought I wouldn't approve of.' I shook my head. 'Let's hope it's all innocent fun.'

Chapter Nine

How to describe the expression on Callum's face when he arrived, not at 6.30 as expected, but at 9.30? There was certainly a gleeful element, perhaps a slight hint of contrition, but also a definite air of impatience, borne out by his perfunctory kisses and 'Hi, Mum, hi Dad' as he turned to go straight upstairs.

'Hey, wait a minute!' William was firm. 'I think you can do better than that.'

Callum stopped in his tracks, his expression now more resentful than gleeful, but even more impatient.

'What?'

'How about a proper hallo. And an apology for being late. We waited supper for you until 8.30. What happened?'

William wasn't going to let him off lightly.

'Er, things got a bit busy in Norfolk and I sort of lost track of the time. Sorry. Would have rung if I'd had a phone.'

Callum didn't sound very apologetic and still seemed impatient to head for the stairs.

'That's another conversation we need to have, but it can wait until tomorrow. Please make a point of being around tomorrow evening.'

I had rarely heard William sound so fierce. Clearly Callum's attitude really annoyed him.

'OK, Dad, though I'll be going out after supper.'

I caught William's eye and could read his thoughts. Taking over, I set out a plan.

'All right, let's talk about your weekend, the phone and paying back Mrs Nicholson-Smith at 6.30 tomorrow evening.

Then Dad and I will share some news with you all over supper.'

'Okay. 'Night.'

And with that Callum finally made his escape, his footsteps racing up the stairs. Wondering whether it was because he was impatient to tell his brothers about his exploits – I doubted he would dwell on the concert – I told William I wanted to get my book from by my bed and also went upstairs, though rather more slowly.

There was no sound from either Angus or Bruce's room so I expected to hear chatter and laughter from Callum's but instead I heard what sounded like one half of a telephone conversation. Surprised, I thought quickly then knocked on the door but didn't go in.

'Hi, Callum, just thought, any washing for tomorrow? You must have some after the weekend and Mrs Baker will be doing a wash in the morning.'

A brief pause then: 'I'll sort it and put it out later.'

'Fine. I'll probably not see you in the morning as I've a busy day at the office, so good night.' I kept my tone neutral.

' 'Night again.'

Feeling rather guilty and conspiratorial, I walked away from his door, making sure my footsteps were heavy, and went into our room for my book before walking back more quietly. Yes, there was definitely a phone conversation, but if he had lost his phone in Norfolk, where had he got another one? There wasn't a landline in his room. Curiosity overcoming me, I knocked again and put my head round the door.

'Sorry, Callum, but I was so surprised to hear you on the phone when you had lost yours, I wondered where you got one.'

He put his hand over the microphone. 'I borrowed

Angus's to call Sophia. Okay?' He glowered at me.

'Oh. Of course. Sorry.' I retreated in embarrassed confusion.

Thoroughly chastened, I didn't tell William about my deception.

* * *

Fortunately, work was busy next day. Dave and I planned our Scottish trip to Sir H in more detail and I seized a moment to research train versus flight to Inverness for the rest of the family to join me for our visit to my sister. The huge time saving and much lower cost from flying grated with my eco-conscience; we would need to discuss it.

On my walk home, my mind ranged over how to deal with Callum, and how to break the news of William's Parkinson's diagnosis. Not an evening to look forward to.

When I got in at six, I found William already there. He greeted me with a kiss. 'I came home a bit early as I wanted to talk about how to deal with Callum before we sat down to business.'

'Thanks, darling, let's talk while I get supper ready.'

'No need.' William grinned. 'I've ordered a takeaway from Robertsons for 7.30, thought it might relieve the stress. And let me pour you a glass of wine – also stress reducing!'

I felt almost tearful at William's thoughtfulness, especially given the news he had to impart. I took the glass of wine gratefully and we sat opposite each other at the kitchen table – already laid for five, I noted with more gratitude.

'Oh, one more thing; there's a note for you from Mrs Baker.' William passed me the folded paper which I read with shock, disappointment – and anger.

William saw my reaction.

'What is it?'

I paraphrased: 'Mrs B apologises but says she's known us and the boys a long time so thinks we would want to know that Callum's clothes smelt strongly of cigarette smoke and something else which she thinks might be marijuana.' I paused. 'Marijuana I suppose I shouldn't be surprised about, I guess most students dabble in it, but cigarettes.....filthy habit. Did you have any idea he smoked?'

'No, I'm as surprised and disappointed as you. I wonder how long it's been going on, and if the other two know.'

'I've never smelt it before, but Mrs B must have as she suspected it. Oh, dear, more to talk about with him.' I glanced at my watch. 'Heavens, it's nearly twenty past already. Quick, how do we approach all this?'

'I've thought a bit about it,' William replied. 'I think we have to start very gently, ask him about the weekend, the concert, the Nicholson-Smiths and paying back the train money. Then about the phone. My instinct is that we buy him another, but maybe second hand, not the latest model this time, and get him to contribute to the cost. He's got to learn.'

'That's a good start,' I agreed. 'But the cigarette smoking? We've always been so strongly against it, and I thought they all knew better than to start.'

'I think we play it by ear.'

When Callum hadn't appeared by 6.35, I went up, knocked and put my head round the door. I was surprised to see him lying on his bed, eyes closed.

'Come on Callum, we're waiting for you.'

'Hmm? What? Oh, is it 6.30 already? I must have fallen asleep.' Callum rubbed his eyes and sat up. 'I'll be right down, just give me a mo.'

'Okay but be quick. We'll be in the sitting room.' I retreated back downstairs, my annoyance increasing with every step. However, I forced myself to calm down and resolved to let William take the lead. Halfway down I realised we hadn't given Angus and Bruce a heads-up for supper so I went up again and called through Bruce's door that he should be down for 7.15 and to please tell Angus. He called his agreement.

Five minutes later Callum joined William and me in the sitting room.

'Sorry I'm late. Fell asleep as you saw, Mum.'

'So, do tell us a bit about your weekend.' William opened, smiling encouragingly. 'Did you like Fred's parents?'

'Yes, they're very nice. His mum is Greek, I think from a shipping family and his dad is a director of a big shipping company.'

Might account for the big house, I thought to myself.

'And the concert, what was it?' A safe question from me.

'It was choral, Verdi, Handel and then a modern piece, Britten. You would have loved it, and in such a great setting.'

We went on to ask what else he had done over the few days, leading up to the sailing/phone issue. William broached the subject:

'Sounds as though you got on well with Fred's sister too, if she took you sailing without Fred,' William said with a grin. 'What were you two up to that you rocked the boat enough to make the bag fall out?'

'Nothing, a motorboat went past too fast.' Callum looked down just a second too long for us to believe his excuse.

'Oh. We had imagined perhaps that you and Sophia were enjoying being alone together.' My smile was designed to show no disapproval.

Callum actually blushed.

'It's okay, son, more interesting for us to picture than just a motorboat's wake.' William laughed at Callum's evident discomfort. 'But it does lead us to the question of the phone and the other things that were in the bag. First, did you get Mrs Nicholson-Smith's bank details so we can reimburse her for your travel tickets. How much do we owe her? And how much was in your wallet?'

'She gave me £30 to cover the train and tube, and I had' - he paused – 'about £25.' Callum looked seriously embarrassed as he then confessed that he had forgotten to ask about the bank details.

William's calm demeanour began to crack.

Well, tonight you email her - or Fred if you don't have her address – and get them. Okay? No putting it off.'

Callum nodded.

'Now, the phone. It's the second one you've lost this year. You talked me into getting you a decent iPhone. Because it wasn't a new one, we didn't insure it. If you want another iPhone I expect you to contribute to the cost and the insurance. I propose to deduct £15 a month from your allowance for a year to cover it.'

I looked at Callum to see his reaction. To my surprise he took it very calmly.

'Fair enough, Dad. And I know I've been slow to say it, but I'm sorry.'

Hurdle one over, now for William's news. The smoking can wait till tomorrow.

Chapter Ten

Angus and Bruce came down to join us on the dot of 7.15. Seeing all three boys together I was struck again by the family resemblance. They were all quite tall, though Angus had an inch or two on the others, and all had William's thick once-dark hair. Callum was the slightest of the three, perhaps more my build, while Bruce might not have looked out of place on a rugby pitch. How lucky we were that, although triplets by IVF with all the dangers that entails, they were all not just healthy but highly intelligent.

I know I shouldn't boast, but they had been exemplary kids, hard-working at school, not giving us many worrying moments with regrettable friends or habits, enjoying family life. A couple of incidents are still strong in my memory, however. When they were only seven they went trick-or-treating without telling us. When we found them, I didn't know whether to burst into tears or scream at them. And once, on holiday in Cornwall, they got into a serious fight with some other kids culminating in a visit to A&E in Truro and hugely embarrassing apologies to the other parents. However, we were certainly not prepared for this sudden problem with Callum. Maybe we were over-reacting; I certainly hoped so.

We sat round the kitchen table and William poured us glasses of wine, explaining that we were having a takeaway which would be arriving any minute. Indeed, as he spoke the doorbell rang. Callum leapt to his feet to answer it and called back for another pair of hands. We had to laugh as he and Bruce appeared with a mountain of steaming cardboard boxes accompanied by some appetising smells. William had clearly reckoned on healthy masculine appetites.

William retrieved hot plates from the oven, and we had fun divvying up the chicken, the beef casserole and the various vegetables. The boys took full advantage of the plenitude on offer and there was a happy silence as we ate.

The main course cleared, Willam produced a raspberry arctic roll from the fridge which he sliced and served to an accompaniment of appreciative yums.

'Thanks, that was all delicious.' Angus voiced the general consensus. 'But didn't Mum say you had some news for us?'

Before he could answer, I intervened to say that it was all Dad's idea to have such a feast, partly to celebrate us all being home together, but also to save me slaving over the stove after a long day's work. I stood and went round the table to give William a thank you kiss.

'Yes, I have some news.' William began as I settled back into my chair. He looked around the table at us. 'And it's not great. A colleague at work noticed a change in the way I was walking a couple of weeks ago, mentioned it to me and suggested I see a doctor.'

All eyes were on him. I could imagine what was going through their minds: cancer, heart problems, but not what they were about to hear.

'The doctor diagnosed the early stage of Parkinson's.'

Angus and Callum didn't react, clearly not aware of the implications, but Bruce immediately rose from his chair to give his father a hug.

'I'm so sorry, Dad. My friend Peter's father has it, so I understand what you're telling us.'

William smiled and, with a suggestion of a tear in the corner of his eye, returned Bruce's hug.

'Thank you, Bruce, but I'd better spell it out for the others. Parkinson's is a progressive neurological condition which causes problems in the brain and gets worse over time. I'll gradually lose control over my movements, become twitchy, unbalanced, have some stiffness and, after a while, become very embarrassing for you in public. It's not an immediate death sentence; I may live with it for quite a long time.'

Seeing the shock and confusion on Angus and Callum's faces, William paused a moment to let them take it in, then continued.

'You won't notice much change for a while. I'll still be going to the office – I had to tell my boss, but the bank is being very understanding and helpful – and life will be pretty normal, hopefully for some time. We've not told anyone else yet, and I'd rather you didn't either, but we'll tell the rest of the family as we see them.'

Callum spoke first.

'I'm so sorry, Dad, that's rotten luck, but you know we'll always be here for you, do anything we can to help.'

Angus nodded emphatic agreement.

'Thanks.' William smiled, a little sadly. 'On a hopeful note, I should add that there's lots of research going on, especially around gene therapy for example, so although we can't count on it, there may well be serious improvements in treatment. Let's hope they come in time to help me. But now let's talk about something more cheerful, our Scottish trip. Mum will fill us in.'

Agreeing there was no point in going into more details on Parkinson's then, and guessing all three would be doing Google searches on the subject, I nodded and began.

'I told you over that lunch in Cambridge that Trenchant have a project – a very unusual one - in the Scottish

Highlands. I suggested we should arrange a family holiday around it, and you all agreed enthusiastically.

'So, here's the plan: I'll be going up with Dave from the office on 15th July to see Sir Hamish and do the preliminary survey over two days. Then Dave will come back while I stay on and you all come up to join me. We stay a few days with Aunt Fiona in Inverness - she's thrilled at the prospect, as are your cousins - then you can come home with Dad and me or stay and do your own thing – or things. As you know, it's a glorious part of the world, beautiful scenery, mountains and lochs, lots of walking, swimming, sailing...,' this with a glance at Callum who gave a small grin of acknowledgement, 'and, if you've got no other plans, you could even stay longer and go down to Edinburgh for a few days and catch some of the Fringe events. I know you'd really enjoy that.'

Angus was the first to respond, sounding really excited. 'That sounds great, Mum. I was already planning to do some climbing with a friend from uni who's from Edinburgh. We hadn't fixed a date so hopefully the timing will work for him too.'

Bruce also looked pleased. 'I hadn't planned anything yet, but it does sound good, and we haven't seen Aunt Fiona and Uncle John for ages. I think their kids are similar ages to us, aren't they?'

'Yes, though I think that, like you, they're hardly kids as they're in their late teens, though the third one may be a bit younger. What about you, Callum? Does the idea still appeal?' I turned to him with a smile intended to show we were over the phone discussion.

Callum looked distinctly uncomfortable.

'Actually, I've arranged to spend a couple of weeks with Sophia in Norfolk and then go travelling with her, maybe to Morocco.'

The faces around the table fell.

Angus reacted immediately. 'Oh, come on, Cal. This is a bit special. How many more family holidays are we likely to have as we go our own ways – and, sadly, given what Dad's just told us, how many with him? You can be away as little as four or five days so surely you can work round it with Sophia?'

'But I need to go to Morocco to arrange.....' Callum began but suddenly stopped.

'What do you need to arrange in Morocco?' William asked with genuine curiosity.

'Oh, nothing, I didn't mean arrange.' Callum said quickly but unconvincingly. 'But I'm definitely travelling with Sophia.' He sounded very determined on this.

I didn't want to be too negative so quickly proposed a compromise.

'How about getting Sophia to join you in Scotland at the end of the family stay? Then we could meet her and the two of you could go off for a couple of romantic days in the Highlands before going to Morocco or wherever. Do think again, please, as it would give us all so much pleasure to be the full family, and I know Fiona and co would be really disappointed if you didn't come.'

Callum grunted.

'You could even spend time with her in Norfolk before Scotland,' I added quickly. I didn't ask who was paying for all his travel, we were in deep enough water as it was.

Angus and Bruce made encouraging noises.

'Do think about it, Cal.'

'We'd be really disappointed too.'

William played his decisive card: 'I certainly hope this won't be my last 'normal' holiday, but I can't guarantee it. And apart from anything else, it would be nice to meet Sophia soon, since she's clearly an important person in your life, and before I develop these promised twitches! Please come.'

'OK, I'll think about it and talk to Sophia. When do you need to know?' Grudging acceptance.

'Very soon, I'm afraid, as we need to book tickets. You have to decide whether to come up by sleeper or fly, or up one way and back the other. Up to you. Dad and I will pay for you three – and Sophia, if she can't afford it.' This was generous of me, I knew, but guessed, given her family's business and the size of the house, that money wasn't a problem for her.

Callum stood up. 'Can I please use the landline to call Sophia, Mum? Or your mobile, Angus? I'll ring right away. Then I have to go out.'

Angus fished his phone from his pocket and Callum disappeared upstairs with it, muttering thanks as he went.

Bruce gestured to Angus that they too should retreat and leave William and me to digest the evening's conversations.

'Thanks for the dinner, Dad, and for the holiday suggestion, Mum. It sounds great and I'm pretty sure Callum will come round.' Bruce came round to give us a good night kiss, followed by Angus. 'And bugger the Parkinson's,' he added as they left the room.

William poured us the last of the wine and we sat in silence.

'What do you think?' William finally ventured. 'Is there something going on with Callum and this Sophia that he's hiding from us?'

'I wonder. It could be just young love, embarrassment with aged parents. Let's hope so. But I think I'd better not cross-examine him just yet about the smoking, let's sort out the holiday first.'

'I think you're right. But on the holiday front, you guessed right that I would fly up. Less tiring, I think, as well as quicker – and cheaper! If we really are going to pay all this for everyone and Sophia, we'd better start saving!' William laughed.

We drained our glasses as we stood to clear the table and load the dishwasher. All done, we turned off the lights and William put his arm round my shoulders as we headed for the stairs and a very welcome bed.

'I love you, Lizzie. I hope this all works out.'

Chapter Eleven

When I came down for breakfast at seven next morning I was surprised and delighted to see a note from Callum, written on the back of an envelope he must have got from the recycling bin: 'Yes to Scot'd, S to follow. x C'.

I turned to William as he entered the kitchen and waved the envelope at him.

'Cal's coming! And he says Sophia will join him. Your bit about being nice to meet her before the Parkinson's takes hold clearly did the trick.'

'That's good news to start the day. Now we can plan in more detail – better ensure Sophia comes the day we leave Fiona and John so we don't have the extra double bed question to solve, there's enough of us as it is.' William, thoughtful as ever.

'Good thinking. I'll raise it with him. Now, in the night I suddenly realised we've not yet got the details to repay Mrs Nicholson-Smith, nor have we sorted the new phone problem or got his lost bank card replaced so he has no money.'

'He went out last night without asking for cash; I wonder where he went?' William frowned.

'Maybe he had some left from the loan. Or maybe he scrounged a beer or two off his friends or whoever it was he met up with.' I thought that most likely.

'I agree,' said William. 'I'll call him from the office to make sure he's told the bank about the card and ordered a new one.'

'Remember, he hasn't got a phone!' I laughed. 'You'll have to use the landline and hope he's home. But what about the new phone? I'm no expert, and anyway I can't leave the office today, too much on.'

William scratched his head. 'I'm not clued up on phones either. Could Angus or Bruce help? We could set a price limit and reimburse them.'

'That's probably best.' I paused. 'But I've had a thought, I could ask our IT man at the office how much we should reckon on. He's young enough to be on top of these things and old enough to be sensible! Otherwise, Dave, the one who's coming to Scotland with me. He's a techie.'

'OK' agreed William. 'I'll take care of the bank card, you do the phone research and tell the boys the result so they can get on with buying one. Now I must be going.'

William gulped down the last of his coffee, kissed me goodbye and left. I lingered a little longer, briefly scanning the news on the paper I had picked up from the doormat as I came downstairs. My attention was caught by an article on the increase in extreme weather events, prompted by a hurricane in the Caribbean and floods in Bangladesh. My heart sank. When would governments around the world realise that urgent action was needed, and not just by a few countries? This was a global problem.

Sighing, I tidied the table, fetched my bag and left. I knew there was little point in calling goodbye up the stairs as none of the three was an early riser.

It was a pleasant morning, some fluffy clouds allowing the sun to shine through, but it was quite cool so I strode out, admiring the well-tended front gardens I passed before getting to the main road and the turning to my office.

I wasn't the first to arrive; I was surprised and pleased to see Dave already there, poring over some documents, so I seized the moment to ask him about second-hand phones.

'Morning, Dave, you're early. Something up?'

'No, it's just I needed to check an old report urgently, want to compare data then and now.' He smiled. 'Nice day, huh?'

'Yes,' I agreed. 'Can you spare a few moments to talk about mobile phones, now or later?'

'Now's good, before I go cross-eyed over these figures. How can I help?'

I explained the Callum phone problem, without going into details, and saying we hoped for a maximum of £200, less if possible.

'Are we being realistic?' I asked Dave.

'Sure, even down to £150 gets a decent Smartphone, obviously not the latest but certainly good for any normal use for someone not into competitive phone status.'

'Is there any reason to get an iPhone rather than any other Smartphone? And is it better to buy on-line or go to a shop?'

'On-line is fine if you go to a reputable outlet, and all the big names are good. I would recommend setting the price and getting the best you can for that.'

'Thanks, Dave, that's a huge help. To change the subject, is everything okay still for the Scottish project? Are you finding all the info you need on vortex generation?'

'Yup, there's plenty about, but I think we need to think of alternatives too, in case Sir Hamish's rivers aren't big or fast enough. I'm checking mini dams, though the concrete involved is a negative. Ditto wind turbine manufacture, but anyway he might be against the visual impact, even though that part of Scotland's pretty windy.'

'Good thinking, Dave, great to have all the possibilities to hand. Well done. Now I'll leave you in peace and get on with my own work.' I gave him a big thank-you smile and went to my desk.

Before starting work, I texted William with the encouraging

results of my research, and said I thought we should aim at £150. We didn't need to be involved except to pay as Angus and Bruce could help him with the purchase. He replied almost at once agreeing.

That was one hurdle almost dealt with.

I set to work on my emails, a variety of enquiries, follow-ups, and requests from colleagues, plus a few from business friends. I had been working about an hour when yet another came in. To my surprise, it was from the mad professor, Michael Moreton.

'Written to you at work and home to be sure of catching you,' it said. 'I'm going to be in London the end of the first week in July and wondered if you and William would allow me to return your hospitality. My evenings are free at the moment so do suggest a couple of dates. Hope you can make it. Be great to see you. Michael.'

That was a cheering message - not that I particularly needed cheering just then. I wrote back saying love to come, would send dates when I'd spoken to William.

The rest of the day passed quickly but not stressfully. At lunchtime I went out for some fresh air and did some shopping for supper. I got Melissa to book sleeper trains to Inverness for Dave and me, a return for him. I thought it unfair to ask her to do the arrangements for the rest of the family, and anyway, I needed to know how they each wanted to travel and how long they planned to stay. All for discussion that evening.

* * *

Angus and Bruce were in the kitchen when I got home.

'Not nicking biscuits before dinner I hope?' I said with mock seriousness.

They looked a bit shamefaced, confessed to 'just one or

two', but made amends by offering to help with supper.

'There's not much to do, but you could lay the table for me. And while you're doing that, let's talk about the Scottish trip – oh, by the way, Callum left me a note this morning saying he would be coming to Scotland with us, and Sophia would join us there.'

'That's good news; I was really cross with him yesterday as he's known about the trip for a while.' Angus made a thumbs-up.

'Is he around? Dad and I need to talk to him and you about his replacement phone. Have you seen him this afternoon?'

Angus and Bruce shook their heads.

'He's been a bit odd since he got home, never around, not chatty - a bit secretive,' volunteered Bruce.

'Hmm. Well, lay a place for him for supper anyway and let's hope he comes. We really need to talk to him.'

As they set about their task, the two volunteered their news. Angus began:

'I rang my Edinburgh friend Tom about dates for climbing and it works well for him – but not just that! He said his parents are going to be away for a while and want him to house sit most of the vac. They even suggested he invite a friend or two to keep him company. I said would it be okay if it was me and how about Bruce too – he knows him a bit - and he said yes, of course, good idea.'

Bruce took over: 'After Angus told me about the idea, I started thinking about jobs and we called Tom back and talked about it. Remember you suggested we might stay on in Scotland and go to the Edinburgh Fringe?'

I nodded and Bruce continued.

'Well, Tom said that Edinburgh is so busy then there are

always tons of jobs in bars and cafes, and he knows some people who might employ me. I couldn't have afforded to do it on my own, but with somewhere to stay, it would be perfect. So, I think I'll say yes, please.'

Angus chipped in. 'I might do the same after the climbing, be really fun as we could probably fit in some shows. I love stand-up and Tom says there's loads of it.'

'Well, that sounds as though you two are sorted, though if Bruce isn't climbing, would Tom's parents mind him staying without Tom?'

Bruce's face fell. 'I hadn't thought of that. I'll have to talk to Tom again.'

'I've had another thought,' Angus looked rather solemn.' 'If we stay in Edinburgh and Callum's in Morocco or somewhere, you and Dad won't see much of us. Would you mind very much?'

I confess I had a sudden pang at the thought but put a brave face on it. 'It's something we have to get used to. We can't expect you to be home-based much longer anyway as you might get jobs anywhere or stay on in Cambridge doing Masters. We must make the most of the time you are here now and in Inverness.'

Just then, William arrived home and the two boys filled him in with their plans while I finalised the cooking.

'Supper's ready,' I announced, 'but there's still no sign of Callum. We'll just have to start anyway. It's really thoughtless of him.'

'Especially as we have to sort out his phone,' William added. 'He didn't answer when I rang about it at lunchtime. I fear I'm going to have to have serious words with him.'

Having serious words was not one of William's favourite activities.

'There is one piece of good news for Dad and me, though,' I said to lighten the atmosphere. 'We're invited to dinner with your professor, Michael Moreton, at the end of next week, just before I go to Scotland with Dave.'

'Oh, that's good. I liked him.' William perked up. 'I shall look forward to it.'

Chapter Twelve

It was after 1am when I was woken by the sound of the front door opening and a raised voice. Sliding carefully out of bed so as not to disturb William, I went to the top of the stairs. From there I could see Callum talking on a mobile. A mobile, where did he get that? was my first thought. He sounded angry. I heard snatches:

'Come on, you promised the cash today.'

'No, I won't give you another week.'

'Don't expect to get...

I really didn't know what to do. After a moment's thought, I stepped back from the stairs and called down.

'Callum, is that you?'

After a very short pause and more words which I couldn't hear, he called up.

'Hi Mum, sorry if I woke you.'

'Is everything alright? You sounded upset.' I moved back to the stairs.

'No, no probs. I'll just have a drink of water then come up to bed. See you in the morning.'

'No, I need a drink too, so I'll join you.' I didn't want him to evade us again, so I quickly went down, followed him into the kitchen and poured two glasses of water.

'This isn't the time to go into details, but how did you get a phone when you had lost your bank card and money?'

'Oh, Sophia gave it to me. She wanted a new one anyway, and this is her old one.' Callum was very quick to answer. 'Very kind of her, though her family's so rich they would hardly notice.'

I didn't like his tone but let it pass and agreed it was generous. I didn't want to let him off too lightly, though, and attempted an ultimatum.

'Dad wants to talk to you. He is – we are – a bit concerned about you. Be here before dinner tomorrow evening, please, no excuses. Promise.'

'OK,' this in a very grudging tone. 'But I have to go out later.'

Sighing inwardly, I wished him good night and retreated upstairs. I slipped back into bed, but sleep was evasive. It must have been past three by the time I drifted off having followed too many trains of thought about what was causing this change in our hitherto easy-going son.

Next evening, having armed us each with a glass of wine, William called Callum down to the sitting room.

'Like a glass, Cal?' I asked as he entered.

'Prefer a beer if there is one,' he replied, settling himself in an armchair.

'There's one in the fridge. Help yourself.' I didn't feel like playing waitress.

Callum hauled himself from the chair and disappeared to the kitchen, returning with an open bottle from which he took a slug before sitting down again.

I bit back my urge to tell him to get a glass. I find it an unattractive way to drink, even if it does save washing up. I caught William's eye, inviting him to start the serious talk.

Setting his glass down on the side table, Willam cleared his throat, glanced at me, then began.

'You must be aware, Callum, that we've noticed a big difference in you since you came home. You've been uncommunicative, surly at times - even your brothers have remarked on it. You've been out at odd times, back late, not told us where you're going or have been, not told us if you'll be in for dinner. Your laid-back attitude to the loss of your phone, wallet and bank card was extraordinary.'

I knew this was hard for William but he continued.

'Mum tells me you were on the phone when you got in at one last night, you said it was Sophia's. How did you get it? Did she give it to you in Norfolk?'

Callum nodded. 'Like I told Mum, she said she wanted an upgrade and she'd give me her old one.'

'So why did you need to borrow Angus's phone to call her about Scotland?' William made an effort to sound reasonable.

Callum shifted impatiently in his chair, took another swig of beer.

'I hadn't got it yet. Sophia came to meet me in town yesterday and gave me her old phone then.

I changed tack. 'Since you now have a phone, I guess you've asked Mrs Nicholson-Smith for her bank details to repay her loan?'

'No need. I gave Sophia the £30 to repay her mother.' Callum had a quick answer.

Now it was William's turn to raise an eyebrow.

'How did you manage that, given you'd lost your bank card?'

Callum looked uncomfortable. 'Actually, Sophia lent it to me.'

'So now you owe Sophia £30 instead,' I interjected. 'How will you repay her?'

'I've told the bank I've lost my card and I should get a new one soon. Then I can draw it from my account and give it to her or make a transfer.'

'That's one sensible thing you've done, anyway,' William granted. 'And I'm grateful to Sophia for saving us the trouble of buying a new phone for you – and you, probably, the pain of repaying us.'

I took over the interrogation. 'You've been out both evenings since you've been home. Meeting friends?'

'Yes.'

'Did they fund you too, or was Sophia still with you? I don't imagine you were totally abstemious, given you missed dinner last night.' I couldn't help a sharpness in my tone. 'And I noticed, by the way, that the clothes you put in the wash reeked of cigarette smoke. Taken up smoking?'

At this Callum stood up.

'I've had enough of this third-degree. I'm going out now.' As he reached the door, he turned. 'And, no, I don't smoke. We spent the evening with friends who did.'

He left the house, almost slamming the front door behind him.

William and I looked at each other wordlessly.

Finally, William broke the silence.

'I think we have to accept there's something very wrong and – I hardly dare say it – but I've a horrible suspicion we're talking drugs.'

'Oh, dear, I fear you may be right. It was going through my mind after he came home last night. How do we deal with this? Where has it come from? Sophia? Before that? He's clearly not going to open up to us voluntarily.' I moved closer to William and took his hand. I'm so sorry, my love. It's come on top of the Parkinson's news. It's too much.' I wiped away a tear. 'There's nothing we can do tonight. Let's just have supper and worry again in the morning.'

'Okay. Are Angus and Bruce joining us?'

'Just Angus. They both texted me, bless them. Bruce has gone to meet friends.'

'Do you think Angus will know anything? Would he tell us if he did?'

'I don't know, but I hope so.' I released William's hand and got up. 'I'll finish getting supper and call you and Angus when it's ready.'

Even as I finished laying the table and heating the casserole I had prepared, my thoughts were swirling.

Chapter Thirteen

As I had suspected, over dinner Angus was reluctant to say much about Callum and the apparent change in him. However, we persisted, and I reminded him about the incident with the photo from Callum which Angus and Bruce had been unwilling to reveal.

'I heard you both sniggering and saying I wouldn't approve. When I came in you wouldn't show me, instead you swapped phones and let me scroll through the pictures of the Nicholson-Smith's house in Norfolk. I thought it was odd at the time but wouldn't have mentioned it again if we hadn't become concerned about Callum.'

Angus looked distinctly uncomfortable but didn't offer any explanation. William took over.

'He's been coming in late, not telling us whether he would be around for dinner, offhand. He got very cross, just got up and left when we asked him specifically about a conversation Mum overheard a couple of nights ago. Tell him about it, Elizabeth'.

'It was well after one when I was woken by the slam of the front door, followed by an angry-sounding phone conversation along the lines of 'you promised me the cash today. No, I won't give you another week'. Given he'd lost his phone and bank card, we asked how he got a new phone. He was evasive and clearly lying.'

I sighed before continuing. 'He stormed out leaving us even more concerned. Dad and I admitted we had both had the same very uncomfortable thought: is he dealing in drugs? I've just remembered, too, that he had talked about going to

Morocco with Sophia to sort things out. Morocco does have something of a drug reputation. We hope against hope that we're wrong.'

By this time Angus was looking worried too, not just uncomfortable.

'I honestly don't know,' he said. 'But you're right, he is behaving differently, and he isn't as communicative with us as he always was. I really hope it's not drugs.'

William nodded sadly in agreement. 'I wonder whether you and Bruce could somehow engineer conversations with him, not directly about drugs, but maybe about why he's distancing himself from you – and us.'

'Good idea,' I said. 'And if you do fear the worst, tell us – well, tell us whatever, as it would be such a relief to know whether we were coming to the wrong conclusion.'

'And if it is drugs, we'll have a terrible dilemma, given dealing is a criminal offence.' It was William's turn to sigh. 'But let's not worry about that until we know, and fingers crossed there's a better explanation.'

'I'll do my best. I'll tell Bruce what you've said and see if he knows more.' Angus accepted the task. 'You know, it's weird that the three of us have been so close, and now this – this rift, almost. It's quite recent, but when I think about it, we didn't see as much of him this term as usual, not that we're in each other's pockets, but there's still a change.'

'Thank you, darling,' I said, reaching across the table to touch his hand in acknowledgement. 'We'll keep quiet on the subject, try not to antagonise him further, and wait to hear.'

'Good luck,' William wished him with a hopeful smile.

The rest of the meal passed in relative silence as we each digested the importance of uncovering the reason for Callum's behaviour.

William and I held each other close before settling to sleep that night and resolved to try to think of other things.

'We've got the dinner with Michael coming up, and I'm off to Scotland in ten days,' I reminded William. 'Then you're coming up too. Distractions to help keep our minds off Callum.'

'And luckily I've got some really interesting work stuff on.' William's voice had an anticipatory edge. 'Certainly enough to need all my concentration.'

* * *

William and I breakfasted together next morning as usual before setting off to our respective offices. My day was uneventful, mostly more preparation for the visit to Sir Hamish to which I was increasingly looking forward. I spent some of my lunch break hovering over the supermarket shelves wondering how many to cater for that evening, finally deciding on ready-made meals, spares of which could be put into the freezer.

My phone pinged with a text from Callum as I was unloading my shopping.

'Sorry about last night. Will be in for supper. x C'

Now that was a surprise. I confess it didn't altogether ease my doubts; was he just diverting us from his unsatisfactory replies to our questions, or had we really got it all wrong?

I knew Angus would be home, but texting Bruce to check, I got an instant reply: 'Yes please to supper.'

When Angus came down to join Bruce, William and me in the kitchen that evening, he caught my eye and gave a slight shake of his head which I took to mean he had nothing to tell us yet. Bruce was very cheerful, having spent the afternoon playing tennis with friends. Callum arrived home in good time, gave me a quick hug and a cheerful smile. Good news or more deception?

'Won't be a minute,' he said as he disappeared upstairs.

Conversation over dinner didn't resolve that question, but the meal was more cheerful than I had anticipated, positively jovial in fact, Callum his usual self, and I decided to put my worries behind me, at least until – or if - Angus or Bruce came back with some news.

We were all busy in our separate ways that weekend, William and I gardening, an excellent play at the National Theatre, and lunch with friends in Dulwich, south of the river. It was good to get away from our usual haunts, and the friends suggested a visit to the Horniman Museum in Forest Hill where we had never been before. Mr Horniman must have been very successful in the tea trade to have had the money to gather such a collection and build a stylish museum to house it. The eclectic collection varied from a room of stuffed birds to a fascinating selection of old musical instruments where we put on headphones and heard how they sounded playing music of their period.

Before leaving we walked round the gardens and admired the extraordinary views both north and south from the top of the hill on which the museum perched.

The boys went about their own business but we did notice how much time Bruce was spending at the tennis club. He got teased by his brothers as to the reason, giving rise to the suggestion of a blush and a noticeable lack of explanation. Angus reported on his research on Edinburgh and things to see from Inverness. Callum came and went, cheerful and polite, almost worryingly so, but I determined not to go back on my resolution to leave him alone.

Dinner with Michael Moreton the following week was as interesting and enjoyable as I had anticipated. His choice of restaurant in Fitzrovia was excellent, its booths with padded bench seats making for easy conversation. Naturally we quizzed Michael on his electricity storage project but were disconcerted by his response.

'We're definitely making progress,' Michael said, 'but I've learned there are other groups following the same approach, which isn't necessarily a bad thing as we need to crack this storage problem sooner rather than later. However, one project in China is so similar it raises questions in my mind about possible hacking or other skulduggery.'

'Have you any idea who might be the culprit?' Willam asked.

'It could be government-sanctioned, or a private individual already involved in the research who sees the potential for personal gain.' Michael stopped short of implicating his co-researcher, but we got the impression he had his suspicions. 'I shouldn't be concerned as I'm not in it for the money – or the glory – and it's such an important contribution to slowing climate change, but it still rankles.'

William spoke up: 'In terms of national security it's vital we have manufacturing capability in the UK, or at least in Europe. We can't - mustn't - depend on China. The demand is going to be huge worldwide so there will certainly be investment opportunities here.'

I had to smile to myself at William's investment banking instincts coming into play again, but he was right, there would be money to be made in producing for the UK market.

Michael was encouraged by William's intervention. 'I'm glad you think the same way, and when the time comes, I'll be in touch about how to take things forward.'

We were a bit disconcerted when Michael later raised the question of the boys' exam results. We hadn't talked about them much, accepting that Angus and Bruce had been happy with their marks, which fell in the Upper Second class. Callum – oh, dear, another worry - had definitely slipped this year as his marks were in the Lower Seconds, a come-down from expectations. He had brushed it off saying he hadn't felt well for a couple of the exams and was sure do better the next year.

However, Michael was reassuring: 'These things happen, don't worry, he's pretty much up there with his brothers.'

Other news exchanged and the very good dinner consumed, we thanked Michael warmly and agreed to meet again after the summer holidays. We were already growing quite fond of Michael, he was such easy yet stimulating company, and his interest in things ecological endeared him to me especially.

My Scottish project and the associated family visit were now my focus. It was agreed that Angus and Bruce would go a day or two earlier via Edinburgh to meet Angus's friend Tom and his parents to arrange the house-sitting and maybe sniff out possible jobs. They elected to go by train as they would be able to take luggage to leave in Edinburgh, then travel more lightly to Inverness. Callum decided he would fly up with his father on the Friday afternoon. Got things to do, he said, raising my suspicions again, but I was glad he'd be there to keep an eye on his father, even though I'd had no concerns yet of William's ability to cope. I planned to join them on the Friday evening.

I reminded them all to take stout shoes or walking boots, a warm sweater, and wet weather gear. 'It's Scotland,' I said. 'No guarantees of sunshine'. I took my own advice and reminded

Dave. He would have all the technical gear to carry too.

Having confirmed with my sister, Fiona, that our plans were still as I had discussed with her, I tidied up my desk and emails, had final consultations with Dave, and told Sir H our train arrival time. He said again that we would be met off the train and driven to his house.

On the Wednesday evening Dave and I arrived in high spirits at Euston to find the Caledonian sleeper with its smart dark grey livery ready and waiting. I had blenched at the cost of two cabins, thinking of Sir H's wallet, even though he had generously offered to pay and to put us up, and dared to suggest to Dave that we might share. To his credit, he had agreed, showing no embarrassment at sharing with his boss, and promising he didn't snore.

We found our cabin and Dave was happy to take the upper bunk. We unpacked the few things we would need before heading for the dining car for a light supper and a glass of wine to encourage a good sleep. Retreating to our cabin, we took it in turns in our en-suite washroom (I did allow that small extravagance), wished each other good night and settled in our bunks.

Chapter Fourteen

The gentle movement of the train as it sped north helped sleep come easily and I was surprised to find it was 7.30 when I opened my eyes. Dave had his reading light on, so I called up.

'Morning, Dave. Sleep okay?'

'Morning, Elizabeth. Yes, great, thanks, the motion was almost like a lullaby, and I went out like a light, only woke up at seven. Hope I didn't disturb you at all.'

'No, but I think I'll get up now, so keep reading while I use the bathroom and change.'

'Yes, boss. Promise I won't peep, just tell me when it's my turn.'

We managed our ablutions without embarrassment and set off for breakfast to fortify ourselves for the coming task – it felt more like an adventure. Dave opted for the full Scottish breakfast, but black pudding certainly didn't appeal to me at that time of the morning so I settled for good Scottish porridge, toast and coffee. Our spirits sank somewhat when rain suddenly lashed the windows as we ate, but we reassured ourselves that it might not last.

We were back in the cabin, packed and ready to disembark as the train drew into Inverness Station. Our luggage safely onto the platform, we set off towards the concourse, already scanning the waiting people, guessing which one might be Sir Hamish's driver. That man in the deerstalker hat and plus-fours? Hmmm. The one in a business suit? Certainly not. Maybe that young woman with an empty luggage trolley?

Once in the concourse, we looked around expectantly, but

no-one approached us.

'I think we just wait,' I said. 'I'm sure the driver will be here soon.'

Dave nodded and we stood, surrounded by our luggage, for a good ten minutes before we heard someone calling 'Mrs Trenchard? So sorry, so sorry!'

We turned to see a tall young man running towards us, hand outstretched. He halted, panting.

'I'm so sorry, got caught in a traffic jam. Hamish McCraig.' He shook the hand which I'd automatically proffered. 'You must be Dave,' he said, shaking his hand too. 'Nice to meet you, hope you had a good journey. Apologies again.'

Concealing my surprise at being met by the laird himself, I assured him we hadn't been concerned, were sure we would be met.

'We hadn't expected to be met by you, though, as you said you would send your driver. It's very kind of you to come yourself.' I made light of the delay while concealing my surprise at how different Sir Hamish was from the Sir H I had been emailing and talking to. This Hamish was probably around 30, blond, slim, and distinctly good looking. The accent was the same, though, a reminder that we had woken in a different country.

'Oh, it seemed sensible to meet you myself.' Sir Hamish smiled as he helped us with our luggage. 'I had to see my solicitor here yesterday, so I took the opportunity to stay with an old university friend and have a good dinner with him. I'm afraid we followed it with some very good whisky or I might have left a bit earlier, given rush hour traffic and finding a spot in the car park. I was lucky, actually, that's my car right there by the pay station. Wait here and I'll bring it; the rain's a bit heavy.'

Dave's eyes opened wide as he watched our host run to a gleaming red Jaguar, leap inside and drive it to where we stood.

'Pity about the rain,' Sir Hamish said, holding an umbrella over me as best he could as he held the front door open for me and waited until I was seated and safely belted before returning to help Dave with the luggage.

'Only had the car washed yesterday, not going to look so good by the time we get home.' Sir Hamish grinned ruefully as he got in and we set off.

Once out of Inverness, Sir Hamish speeded up and soon we were driving alongside a loch. On the back seat, Dave had opened a map on his knees and was following our route with his finger.

'Loch Ness,' he said. 'Do people still come and look for the monster?'

Yes, they do. It's extraordinary how it's dug into people's minds. There's one or two places that seem to be engraved on English people's hearts that come to epitomise Scotland. Loch Lomond is another.

To my embarrassment, Dave began to sing, his voice surprisingly deep for such a slim man.

'On the bonnie, bonnie banks of Lock Lomond.'

I turned with a slight frown to suggest this wasn't appropriate, but Sir Hamish laughed.

'It's okay. It's funny how it affects all visitors that way. We get used to it.'

To our surprise he then began to sing it himself, in an attractive light tenor. It was irresistible. Dave and I joined in happily, humming where we didn't remember the words but singing lustily in the chorus.

The atmosphere in the car was now very relaxed so I

ventured to start a more personal conversation.

'So, Sir Hamish, you have a fine voice. Do you do much singing?'

'Er, no, not much singing where we live, though I do let rip in the hymns when I make it to church. But, please, do drop the Sir. Either plain Hamish, or you could even call me Ham or Mish as some of my friends do.'

Dave and I laughed but I knew I would find it hard to go beyond Hamish so set my marker by addressing him again.

'OK, Hamish, it is. Please may I start on a bit of background to this possible project? If I may say so, you do seem quite young to be laird of what I found from the internet is quite a big estate for which you clearly have plans.'

'Ah, the internet, no secrets any more! Well, here goes. My father died about three years ago in a stalking accident – got mistaken for a deer by a novice hunter. Very unfortunate both for my father and the unlucky hunter who, as you can imagine, was devastated, not sure he'll ever be quite the same again, poor man. There was a court case, of course, although it was clearly an accident. All over now. Anyway, that left me in charge with my poor mother and my sister to support.' Hamish was silent for a minute or two.

'I'm so sorry to hear that. Forgive me for having asked.' I was embarrassed at having opened the wound.

'Please, don't worry, you would have heard the story sooner or later, and it gives the background to why you're here,' Hamish reassured me as he negotiated a turn away from the loch.

'Oh, look,' Dave said suddenly, pointing out of the window to our right. 'The clouds are lifting and I can see some hills.'

'Mountains, please,' laughed Hamish. 'We're really getting

into the Highlands now. Some of those 'hills' are what's called Munros, very popular with walkers. They're all the mountains in Scotland over 3000ft – 911 metres if you prefer - and there are about 280 of them. The climbers boast how many they've done. Maybe you'll have a holiday up here sometime and can have a go.'

I knew about the Munros, of course, being Scottish, but Dave clearly didn't and I could sense him thinking ahead to future holidays. I knew his girlfriend was an outdoorsy type who would enjoy the challenges too. I returned to my questions.

'So, can you tell us a bit more about the estate and your plans?'

'Of course, but there's more background to cover first. At the time of the accident we were still living in the castle but it was a real burden and barely in the twentieth century, never mind the twenty-first. After much discussion, we decided to explore other uses for it and, to cut the story short, we leased it to an upmarket American hotel chain - Scotland is very popular with rich Americans. They would modernise it, keeping an apartment for my mother, and there would be a secure income for the family. They've done a good job and it's almost ready to open.'

'But what about you and your sister? Where did you move to? You kindly invited us to stay with you.' I was pleased to have an opportunity to mention this.

'Well, there was still the hunting lodge, and with some funds from the American deal and insurance, we were able to modernise that too. It's quite spacious – used to host sizeable groups of stalkers and fishermen – so you'll be fine. As the hotel's not open yet and there's no other good accommodation nearby, it was the obvious solution rather than driving the hour and a half each way from Inverness.'

Dave hid his disappointment that he wouldn't be staying in a castle and echoed my appreciation of the arrangement.

'To continue the background,' Hamish went on, 'I wanted to diversify the possibilities of the estate and get an income from it to top up the rent from the hotel. It's not only rich Americans who come here; increasingly people are looking for more nature-based holidays and I thought of simple holiday cottages. The scenery is pretty spectacular, as you'll see if the rain holds off, and there's wonderful walking. But as I began to think more practically about what was possible, I realised that many, if not all, visitors these days would expect electricity and hot water, but neither are in ready supply in the areas I have in mind. Problem. Last winter the three of us went to Bali to get some sun and be away from all the business stuff for a while, and we went to the Green School, as I told you. It was a revelation to see what could be done with basic materials. All the buildings were made of bamboo - they claimed their assembly hall was the largest bamboo building in the world - and the electricity was generated by the vortex inserted in the river which flowed through the grounds. The Sayan, I think it was called. Amazing.

'Anyway, we have loads of rivers on the estate, but they may not be strong enough for this, which is why I contacted you about doing a survey. The other problem, of course, is that we don't grow bamboo, but we do have some trees which could be cut to build log cabins, perhaps, or we could provide glamping type tents for people who don't want to be really basic.'

As Hamish paused, a sudden flash of brilliant sunshine bathed the hills in light. Dave and I were transfixed at the beauty set out before us.

'Not bad, eh?' Hamish laughed. He stopped the car. 'We're nearly there now. See that barn over there, that's at the end of the track to the lodge.'

He took out his phone. 'Hi Mac, we'll be with you in ten. Okay?'

We couldn't hear the reply but Hamish set off again and sure enough, ten minutes saw us pulling up in front of a large barn in front of which an older man in overalls stood beside a mud spattered Land Rover.

'All change,' said Hamish getting out and coming round to open my door. 'No way this car is going up there!

Chapter Fifteen

As we swapped from the Jaguar to the Land Rover, I took a moment to look around. Bracken was dominant, bright green against the grey boulders scattered over the hillside and the dark leaves of the abundant heather which was not yet in flower. I imagined that in a month or two the hills would glow purple but now it was splashes of pink ragged robin and yellow ragwort which added colour. There were very few trees in sight, just a few gorse bushes and occasional small pines. It was a far cry from the cultivated countryside of southern England.

The luggage and us safely installed in the Land Rover, which showed signs of heavy country use and had a distinctly earthy smell, Hamish turned the key in the ignition and the engine gave a healthy roar.

'It's not that bad a track, 'Hamish said as the car started to move, 'but do be prepared to hang on.'

The track, steep in places, was stony, with a grassy strip between the wheel tracks. It wasn't quite a bone-shattering ride, but we could well understand why Hamish didn't want to drive the Jaguar up. At one point we hit a serious pothole. Hamish got out and did a quick inspection. No damage, he said, but he took out his phone and called Mac again.

'Hi, Mac, that pothole on the third bend has got worse. Please put it on the to do list – need it in good shape before we get much more rain. Thanks.'

He turned to us as he climbed back into the car. 'Mac's a very important person, mechanic, builder, all round useful handyman. He lives in a cottage on the estate, same as his father did – and his grandfather too. Knows every inch.

Couldn't manage without him.'

Hamish's remark about rain was pertinent as the sun had disappeared behind a very black cloud. The hills – mountains – turned almost black, sudden wind shook the car as the rain arrived, clattering on the roof, so loud we were quite deafened for a few minutes. But as suddenly as it had come, the rain stopped and soon there were patches of blue again.

'That's Scotland for you,' laughed Hamish, who was driving more carefully now. 'Not far to the lodge; it's only just over half a mile from the road.'

We turned one more bend then the track dipped down into a hollow. There, sheltered by some bigger trees and with a small lawn in front edged by blue hydrangeas, was the lodge. It may not have been a castle, but it was still substantial, two storeys with turrets at each corner and enough chimneys to suggest plentiful open fires. Its grey stone walls were blotched with age. It looked thoroughly embedded in its surroundings.

'Welcome!' said Hamish as he tooted to indicate our arrival. 'My sister is expecting us and,' glancing at his watch, 'I hope she has the kettle on for coffee.'

We climbed out of the car and I took a deep breath. The air smelled so different, sweet and fresh with a hint of pine and cut grass. Dave was looking around in wonderment. I turned to smile at him.

'So, Dave, not too disappointed?

Hamish raised an eyebrow and I explained, embarrassed, that when the trip had first been mooted, Dave had had dreams of staying in a castle.

Dave blushed and began to apologise but Hamish interrupted him.

'Not to worry, Dave, you may not be staying in one, but I hope we'll have time to visit ours.'

'Thanks.' Dave decided not to pursue the conversation but when we entered the house through the big, heavy front door, his eyes opened wide. 'Bloody hell!'

I could understand his reaction; the spacious but rather gloomy wood-panelled hall was hung with antlers and whole stags' heads, and a stuffed deer stood guard just inside the door. I was amused to see that its antlers were being used as a hat stand, a couple of deerstalkers, a baseball cap and two woolly hats hanging from the tips. On the window ledges there were stuffed rabbits and several glass-domed cages of various birds.

Hamish hid his amusement at Dave's reaction, clearly making allowances for an English city dweller, and went to fetch our luggage. As we took in our surroundings, a door opened and a young woman came in.

'Hello, I'm Ailsa, Hamish's sister. You must be Mrs Trenchard. Welcome' She held out her hand. 'I hope you had an easy journey?'

'Yes, very pleasant and comfortable, thank you. But, please, call me Elizabeth.' I introduced Dave, now recovered from his surprise.

Ailsa moved to hold the door open for her brother carrying our luggage, and in the brighter light I could see that she was stunningly beautiful, tall and slim like Hamish, with cropped blond hair which showed off her finely chiselled features. She was clearly younger than him, maybe not much older than our boys, and was wearing heavy waterproof trousers and, incongruously, slippers.

She noticed my appraisal of her outfit. 'Sorry about the informality, been out checking on the sheep, our shepherd is in town today so I promised I would. Haven't had time to change, just took my boots off. Now, would you like to see your rooms and unpack?'

We both nodded and, picking up our personal luggage, we followed Ailsa up the wide staircase. At the top, she opened the first door, indicating this would be Dave's room, before turning to the door opposite.

'This is yours, Elizabeth. I hope you'll both find everything you need. Just come down when you're ready. Coffee will be ready in ten minutes or so.'

Dave and I went into our rooms, both emerging seconds later to exclaim about their size, their views, the muted luxury of the furniture and fittings, the spacious bathrooms.

'Do we really only stay one night?' Dave laughed his appreciation. 'This is quite something. I could easily get used to it!'

'Fraid so. But just freshen up now and let's get down for coffee and plan our day's work. See you downstairs in ten.'

I quickly unpacked the few things I would need, leaving the rest in the suitcase, used the bathroom and returned to the hall. Hamish was reclining in a button-backed armchair, a folded map in his hands, his long legs stretched out in front of him.

'We'll have coffee then I'll take you out to show you some of the estate, the places I have in mind for the cabins or tents – and the rivers, of course.'

As he spoke, Ailsa came in with a tray of coffee and shortbread. Setting the tray down on the big oak refectory table which occupied one side of the room, she poured the coffees, offered us milk, sugar and the biscuits.

'I suggest you stock up, it'll be a while until lunch,' she smiled.

We willingly took her advice and pronounced the shortbread delicious.

'One of my specialities; you'll get to try some of the others later.' She sat down with her own coffee.

I took the opportunity to ask about phone signal and wifi. 'I need to get a message to the office, and to let my husband know we've arrived safely – not that he would expect anything different.' I didn't feel it was necessary to say I wanted to check that he was okay.

'The phone signal's okay except the walls are so thick you have to go outside to call. Internet is pretty hopeless, intermittent. If I need to do any serious stuff I go down to the castle – the Americans have got it sorted, of course.' Hamish stood up. 'Now you've finished your coffees, come to the table and have a look at this map.'

He spread the Ordnance Survey map out. It was very large scale and he had outlined the estate in red – it covered a very large part of the map. It was immediately obvious that there were lots of rivers of various sizes, and also two lakes. Hamish pointed at one of them.

'This is one of the sites I have in mind. It's a very attractive spot and there's good fishing. That river,' he put his finger on a line of blue near the lake, 'is pretty fast flowing, coming as it does from quite high up.' He slid his finger across the map. 'Here's another possibility. This river comes over a low cliff, makes a sort of weir, a bit like the river in the Green School in Bali I told you about. I thought it worth investigating.'

Dave, who had done the research on the needs and conditions for vortex electricity generation, was my spokesman on this.

'They both look promising,' he said. 'But we'll need to do various measurements and check the rock quality in those areas. And maybe there will be other places too. Looking at the contours, that river,' he pointed to another line of blue, 'also has good flow possibilities. Do you by any chance have a geological map of the area? And we also need to think about rainfall statistics; not much point in installing a vortex if the rivers run low in the holiday season.'

Hamish looked thoughtful, casting a glance at his sister who had joined us at the table. 'Do we? Where should we look?'

'There may be something in the library here, though most of Dad's books were at the castle,' Ailsa responded. 'I'll have a look while you're out, but I'm doubtful there's much of use.'

'Well, that's a good excuse to go to the castle.' Hamish smiled at Dave. 'Even if the library there doesn't have what we need – they may have got rid of a lot of stuff - we can at least use the internet there.'

Dave acknowledged the reference to his earlier disappointment with a grin.

'But now,' said Hamish, 'let's get off. Got walking boots with you?'

We nodded.

'OK, we'll meet outside in five minutes – and bring rain jackets, just in case!'

Chapter Sixteen

I went quickly up to my room to change into more suitable clothes. As I was about to tuck my phone into a secure pocket, I had a thought. Moving to the window, I opened it and held out my phone. Yes! There was sufficient signal for me to text William. I typed a quick message: Arrived safely, Hamish a delight, the set up interesting, will call later. All well with you? See you tomorrow evening. xE

Picking up my walking boots and rain jacket, I joined Hamish in the hall. Dave appeared a moment later, boots in hand, jacket over his shoulder.

'Those look very new,' I smiled. 'Special for this project?'

'Yep, but I'm already planning to come up here again with Louise, so they're going to get plenty of use.' Dave admitted. He picked up his rucksack with his technical equipment. 'Not sure if I'll need this now or tomorrow, but good to have it with me.'

Hamish took us to the boot room at the back of the lodge where we all changed footwear, leaving our shoes on the rack. I noticed a boot scraper outside the door, and a tap with stiff brushes hanging beside it.

'Looks like you're well set up for muddy outings,' I laughed.

Hamish responded with a grin. 'I think you'll soon see how necessary it is!'

We walked round to the Land Rover, climbed in and set off. The track grew narrower and rougher as Hamish took us further up the hill, but the view became better and better, not a cloud in sight, clear blue sky in every direction. Round one more bend, the track descended quite steeply and there, stretched out below us, was a long narrow loch, the water a startling blue in the sun. The surrounding hills were largely barren, just bracken and rocks, but there was a cluster of trees on one side of the loch, their reflections in the water barely rippling in the still air.

Hamish stopped the car. Dave and I gazed in wonder at the prospect before us.

'This is one of the possible camp or cabin sites I had in mind.' Hamish pointed at the trees. 'Those provide a bit of shelter and also some wood for campfires. Let's go down and I'll show you where the river flows into the loch. Careful how you walk.'

We followed him down, navigating round rocks, tough clumps of grasses and bracken. It wasn't particularly steep, but nonetheless I managed to slip and was just stopped from falling by Hamish's strong grip on my arm.

'Thanks,' I said. 'That was a near thing - I understand your warning!'

We continued carefully and were rewarded by arriving at a clear grassy area between the loch and the trees. Looking up, shading my eyes from the late morning sun, I could see how the surrounding hills formed a protective circle. I could imagine, however, that come evening, the sun would sink behind them, leaving the valley in shadow. Campfires would certainly be needed for warmth.

Hamish led us along a barely visible path a little way along the loch, our boots making squelching noises, the ground wet from the earlier rain. As we progressed, we could discern the sound of running water.

'Is that the river which might take the vortex?' Dave ventured.

Hamish nodded. 'It comes in just round this bend in the loch.'

Sure enough, as we rounded the bend the sound got louder and there, tumbling down the hillside, was a classic mountain stream – a burn - rushing over boulders, carving a route down to the loch. Carefully approaching the burn, I bent down to dabble my fingers in the gurgling water.

'My goodness, that's cold water. Is it clean enough for drinking?'

'Yes, there aren't any cattle or sheep above us, and not enough wildlife to contaminate it.'

I bent lower to cup my hands and lift some water to my mouth. 'Delicious, so different from London tap!'

Dave followed suit. 'Amazing! I didn't know water could taste like that.' He took a second mouthful before standing up and wiping his mouth.

Hamish smiled. 'I can't take any credit for it, I'm afraid, but I'm glad you appreciate it. Now, let's walk upstream a little.'

We followed him, avoiding the occasional boggy patches where the burn had soaked its banks, until he stopped at the point where it became a small waterfall, perhaps a metre or so high, the tumbling noise we had heard as we walked.

Dave took out his camera and took a series of photographs above and below the fall, not just of the water itself, but also of the surrounding land. 'This is one area we need to look at on the geological map, if we find one at the castle - or online,' he said, 'but it definitely looks interesting.'

I nodded my agreement.

'Let's go back to the car.' Hamish helped us retrace our footsteps. 'We've just got time before lunch to look at another site. Up for it?'

Dave and I nodded and the three of us chatted as we walked down past the burn to the loch and up to the car.

'Elizabeth said you had seen the vortex at the Green School. How much of it do you remember? Did they explain how it works?'

'They did tell us a bit, but I'm afraid I didn't take it all in,' confessed Hamish. 'I'm no scientist but I do remember it involved diverting some of the river through a hole, then the diverted part joined the rest lower down so no water was lost. And it didn't spoil the environment, which is another thing I really liked about it, as well as it being sustainable. Perhaps you could explain a bit more in layman's terms.'

'Sure,' Dave replied. 'As you remembered, a barrier is put across part of the river or stream, diverting a good flow of water into a funnel-shaped tunnel with the narrow part at the bottom. Inside the funnel the water turns a turbine creating a vortex whose energy generates electricity just like in a wind turbine but with water instead of air. Once it's installed, there are virtually no emissions and almost no maintenance. As long as the water flows, electricity is generated.'

'It sounds almost like magic – the philosopher's stone!' Hamish looked very impressed. 'Why is it not more known?'

'I think you'll find it is becoming better known, for example in developing countries with remote villages where there's no chance of the national supply reaching them. A plus is that the flow can either be produced by a vertical drop, like the waterfall we've just seen, or by a fast-flowing stream or river. One uses potential energy – the drop in height – the other kinetic energy, the fast movement of the water.'

'If you do a bit of Googling when you're somewhere with good internet speed, you can see it all explained and illustrated with videos,' I intervened, knowing that some people find visual explanations easier to follow. 'Before we came up, I had a look and even found a picture of the one at the Green School.'

By this time we were at the car. We waited as Hamish manoeuvred it carefully between a ditch and some rocks, glad he had warned us to stand back as the spinning wheels sent up spurts of mud and grit. 'OK, safe to get in now.'

Hamish drove us back up, out of the valley and onto a track across the hill and down into a very different valley, this one much narrower. At the bottom, its water sparkling in the sunshine, ran a much wider river. It was fast-flowing, rippling over rocks in places, stony beaches at the sides.

'This is another great fishing spot, trout love it here. In fact, look.' He pointed a little way down from where we stood. 'There's someone fishing now.'

The man stood almost knee-deep in the river, rubber boots up to his thighs, a dark green waterproof jacket hanging open, a long rod held over the middle of the river.

As we walked closer, Hamish waved to catch the man's eye. 'Oh, it's Brad, the American manager from the castle. Hi Brad,' he called. 'How's fishing today?'

The man turned and grinned. 'Hi, Hamish. Look in my bag.' He pointed to a waterproof bag sitting on the stones.

We followed Hamish to the bag which Hamish opened gently to reveal two shiny fat trout.

'Well done, Brad. That'll keep the family happy for dinner tonight.'

'Sure thing, but we've got guests so I'm hoping for one more before I go back.'

'Good luck!' Hamish called as he motioned to us to continue along the rocky beaches until we came to a narrower section with grassy banks. 'This is another place I thought might work,' he said. 'There's space for camping just above us where the land flattens out a bit.'

Dave produced his camera again and took photographs as before. 'This is good too, easier to dig, I suspect, but would need a bit more structure to divert the water into a channel – kinetic energy this time, not potential.'

Hamish nodded sagely and I smiled to myself, guessing he would need time to digest his new knowledge.

'OK, I think we had better get back now or Ailsa will wonder where we've got to. We can talk over lunch about how you want to divide your time between research in the castle library and any measurements you need to do with that kit of yours.'

I realised that, in spite of the shortbreads, I was indeed hungry. The breakfast porridge on the train was a long time ago, and the fresh air had sharpened my appetite. Dave and I followed Hamish to the Land Rover. As we drove back, I caught another glimpse of the loch. I imagined a couple – maybe even William and me – camping there, sitting on camp stools by the loch, fishing rods in hand, then preparing our catch in the evening, cooking it over a campfire whose pine logs would release their heady fragrance as they burned.

Could we? Would we? How long before the Parkinson's would make such an adventure impractical?

My phone pinged. A text from William. 'I'm okay, but v worried about Cal, not himself. Still flying up with me. We need to talk.'

Chapter Seventeen

I was impatient to call William, but as we arrived back at the lodge Ailsa met us with a request to tidy up quickly and come to lunch.

Changing our shoes in the boot room, Dave proudly showed us that his boots were muddy enough to need a rinse before putting them away.

'See, thoroughly baptised' he said with a grin as he brushed them under the tap. 'And no blisters either. Bodes well for future excursions with Louise'.

Hamish and I smiled in acknowledgement. We all three disappeared briefly to our rooms and re-gathered in the hall where Ailsa met us again.

'We're going to eat in the kitchen. Using the dining room seemed too formal,' she said. 'Follow me.'

Obediently, we followed her, Dave and my nostrils twitching at the smell of newly baked bread. The kitchen was big, old fashioned. There was an Aga, a beast I had never mastered though my sister had one, and the big sink was porcelain with a wooden draining board. However, a microwave stood on the long work surface, and a huge fridge-freezer dominated one corner of the room. Against one wall a tall oak dresser displayed two rows of antique plates, while below them hung a line of more modern mugs. A long, scrubbed pine table laid for four took centre place.

We sat down and were presented with steaming bowls of vegetable soup and a big basket of bread, clearly not long out of the oven. A plate with a brick of butter was passed round and we all tucked in. I was tempted to kick Dave under the table as he helped himself numerous times to more bread, but there seemed to be plenty, and neither Hamish nor his sister raised an eyebrow.

'How would you like to spend the afternoon,' Hamish asked. 'More site visits or research at the castle?'

'I think that's been decided for you,' laughed Ailsa, pointing out of the window.

We had been so absorbed in eating we hadn't noticed the darkening sky. Even as we looked, a sudden squall lashed the window.

'Right, it's nearly two now. Let's meet at 2.30 and we'll go to the castle.' Hamish wiped his mouth and put his napkin down by his plate.

'I'll come too, if that's okay,' Ailsa said as she began to tidy away the empty plates. 'I need to pick up a few things in the village shop and I can do it while you're working.'

'No problem.' Hamish stood. 'See you at 2.30.'

Glad of the break, I went up to my room, opened the window which, luckily, was sheltered from the rain, and dialled William. He answered immediately.

'Hi, darling, thanks for calling so quickly. Good moment as I've no meetings for a while. How's things in Scotland?'

I gave him a brief run down without dwelling on details. 'More importantly, what's new about Callum?'

'It's really more of the same only worse. He goes from sullen to charming, abrupt....' William paused. 'But what really shook me was yesterday evening after supper. I walked past his room and he'd left the door open. He didn't see me, but I could see that he was crying. It broke my heart, but I didn't know what to do. In the end I paused and coughed. He looked up, wiping his eyes, so I said, are you alright, what's wrong? And he just shrugged, said it's nothing. I tried to get him to say more but he just clammed up. Said go away, leave me alone.'

'Oh, dear. I wonder what's happened. How was he this morning?'

'He didn't come down to breakfast before I had to leave so I texted him asking okay for Scotland tomorrow? He texted back yes, what time at the airport? I told him Heathrow 3.15 at BA check in and that I had the tickets. He texted straight back, okay see you there.'

'Well, that's slightly reassuring. I wonder if he'll open up sitting on the plane. There's something about being insulated from the world lets people talk more openly.'

'I wouldn't count on it.' William sounded resigned. 'But let's hope that being with the family with things to do will cheer him up.'

'I hope so too. We must try to talk to him about what's going on, though. Oh, dear,' I said again. 'Poor Cal, it must be something pretty bad, I've not seen him cry since he was about ten. Maybe it's to do with Sophia.'

'Maybe. But I fear it may be hard to get him to open up. Man thing.' The nearest William had come to admitting men weren't good at expressing emotions, himself included.

'You're probably right.' I sighed. 'But maybe you could try again gently this evening if he's home.'

'Will do. But you're probably better at it than me. Anyway, there's not much point in speculating now. What are you and Dave doing this afternoon?'

'We're going to Hamish's family castle which they don't live in now – I'll explain at Fiona's – to look in his father's library for info on local geology and rainfall. The weather's turned bad again and we're hoping it'll be better tomorrow to do the rest of the on the ground measurements etc. Must go now, Hamish is waiting for us. See you tomorrow evening – but text me if there's any news on Cal. Bye, darling.'

'Bye, love. I look forward to hearing all about Sir H's set-up.'

Picking up my rain jacket and bag with my laptop and a notepad, I went back downstairs. Hamish appeared almost immediately, shortly followed by Dave and Ailsa.

'I've told Brad we're on our way. We'll take the Land Rover all the way, not worth changing cars for that distance, if you don't mind.' Hamish looked at us for confirmation.

'Of course not,' I spoke for both of us.

The rain was less heavy now, but we were glad not to be out on the hills. It took only five minutes once we got to the road before Hamish turned off into another drive, this one properly surfaced.

'They've done a good job on the drive,' Ailsa commented as Hamish drove between the trimmed verges lined by neatly shaped evergreen bushes. The effect was smart but understated.

The castle wasn't visible until we turned a bend when there it was, its grey stone walls and turrets standing solid and proud above a large lawn. It was big, very big, hard to think of its having been a family home. Hamish drove round behind the house into a large yard bounded by neat outbuildings and parked, saying it seemed odd to him to use the grand front entrance. There were several tradesmen's vans lined up; I noticed an electrician's and a landscape gardening company.

As we walked to the house, I nudged Dave. 'Maybe keep any astonishment to yourself,' I said with a softening smile.

Dave nodded, realising, I think, that his innocence of Scottish land-owning grandeur was already well documented.

Hamish rang the old-fashioned bell-pull by the back door

and, clearly still in some way feeling this was his home, opened the door without waiting for Brad or anyone else to let us in. We followed Hamish though the working part of the house – now, of course, on its way to being a hotel - passing various storerooms and a huge kitchen already fully equipped for serious catering. Ailsa paused a moment to take it in.

'A bit better than ours,' she said glancing sideways at Hamish.

'Well, you did insist you wanted to keep the butler's sink and wooden draining board. Not my choice.' He almost sounded defensive.

'Yes but...'

At that moment Brad appeared, ending the exchange. He shook hands with Hamish, gave Ailsa a peck on the cheek before turning to us.

'You must be the eco-energy guys,' he said with a smile. 'Welcome.'

Dave and I introduced ourselves as we too shook hands with him.

'I guess Hamish knows the way to the library.' He smiled. 'Shall I get some coffee sent in for you all?'

Hamish glanced at us before suggesting perhaps a bit later, and Ailsa explained she was off to do some shopping but would join us in about an hour but hadn't brought the Land Rover keys. Hamish handed her his, and Brad led the three of us to the front hall.

'The interior furnishing people finished earlier this week. What do you think?' Brad waved a hand round the spacious hall. I confess I was the one who had to stifle a comment this time, as the whole effect was a caricature of an American's idea of Scottish baronial. There were heavy tartan drapes at each of the big windows, and groups of armchairs covered in the same tartan. The big mahogany reception desk with computer and monitor had a bell jar glass dome of stuffed birds on each corner. Inevitably several stags' heads were mounted above the heavy wood panelling, and a large Scottish landscape painting hung over the grand fireplace whose grate was filled with artfully arranged logs.

'The guests will love it,' responded Hamish with diplomatic enthusiasm.

'Great, glad you approve.' Brad smiled broadly. 'Now, I guess you know the way to the library - we haven't done much to it, you'll see – so I'll leave you to it. Just give me a buzz, Hamish, when you're ready for coffee and I'll alert Jenny, she's our housekeeper.'

We thanked him as he lifted a hand in farewell. We followed Hamish up the grand staircase and along the corridor. As he reached the end he paused dramatically before opening the door onto the sort of library you see in period films: a long room lined floor to ceiling with bookcases, their contents mostly leather-bound with gilded lettering, some a more motley collection of ordinary hardbacks. A ladder on wheels leant against one case, and in the centre of the room were two long polished tables with green glass-shaded reading lamps at intervals. A side table held piles of magazines which I could see at a glance were the likes of The Field and Shooting Gazette. Leather-seated chairs at the tables were supplemented by big leather armchairs in matching dark green. Three beautiful big windows looked out onto the mountains.

Dave and I were silenced for a moment; it was beautiful but daunting. Where to start? Fortunately, Hamish knew his way around the shelves.

'My father loved the geology and history of the area and had a good collection, though quite a lot of it will be very old-fashioned - not that that matters for geology,' he laughed. 'It's taken a few million years to get this way and ain't going to change for another few million. All the local stuff is in these shelves near the door.' He ran his hand over a shelf at shoulder height. 'Look, here we are.'

'Dave, why don't you start on these while I think about weather and rainfall.'

Dave nodded, put his backpack down by the table and turned his attention to the books.

'Do you know if he took an interest in the weather too?' I asked Hamish.

'I'm not so sure about that, but let's have a look in the same section of shelving.'

A few minutes hunting failed to reveal anything useful.

'I think we're going to have to use the internet,' Hamish said. 'While you get yourself organised, I'll call Brad and get the wifi code for here. I don't know it by heart.'

Within a couple of minutes Hamish had the code for me and I was happily set up at one of the long tables. The sky was still dark and threatening so I was glad of a table lamp. Hamish excused himself, saying he needed to have a word with Brad and left Dave and me silently at work.

Chapter Eighteen

I was so engrossed in my research I was surprised when Hamish appeared, followed by Ailsa bearing a tray with a thermos of coffee and a plate of biscuits.

'Time for a break,' Ailsa smiled, setting the tray on the table. 'Mind if I sit quietly in the corner while you talk?'

'Of course not,' I replied.

She poured coffee for us all and handed round the biscuits before settling in one of the armchairs and taking out her phone.

Hamish installed himself opposite me. 'How've you been getting on, both of you?'

I responded first. 'There's quite a lot on the internet, and what is clear is that rainfall in the Highlands is both unpredictable and often very local – but I doubt that surprises you.'

Hamish laughed. 'Probably doesn't surprise you either, even after just one day!'

Dave and I acknowledged the truth of this, and I continued. 'One thing is reassuring, though, which is that the overall amount of rain in any one year in any one place near here is pretty close to the average over a longish period of records. So, the chances are good that the flow in the streams and rivers is unlikely to vary widely from what we saw today.'

'That's good news.' Dave spoke up. 'But - and it's a big but – global warming is speeding up, more than most people had expected. That's going to change weather patterns, possibly very significantly if the gulf stream gets diverted.'

'Of course, sadly you're right, Dave,' I countered, 'but it's all so unknown I think we have to go on the information we have for now. We're on high ground here, and fairly far west, so hopefully should get what rain is coming – and if it's more rain, more electricity.'

Hamish frowned. 'I see the problem of the unknown, but from what I've read, it's likely the UK will get warmer which will mean holidays in Scotland will become a more attractive proposition. So, if we can be pretty sure of sufficient rain, at least for a few years, I'm inclined to be hopeful of increasing numbers of campers, making it even more worthwhile.'

He turned to Dave. 'How about the geology? What did you find? Are the areas where we were this morning suitable for installing a vortex generator?'

'Looking at the maps, as far as I can see we'd be unlucky to find we're on granite, which is hard to work, but we'd have to do a small amount of test drilling to be sure. By the first stream, it might be quite difficult, but boring a fairly modest hole large enough for the generator should be possible. In the trout river I think it will be easier.'

'That's good, Dave. Now, I think we've done all we can for this afternoon,' I said, looking at my watch. Would it be okay to get back to the lodge now? I confess I'm feeling the effect of the short night and could do with a rest.'

'Of course, I should have thought of that,' Hamish was very apologetic. 'It's already getting on for five. We can talk about tomorrow over a drink before dinner. Six suit you?'

'That sounds very appealing. And again, it's very kind of you and Ailsa to feed us too.' I was more than sincere in this; the thought of having to drive an hour or so back to Inverness or to some unknown local hostelry didn't appeal after our active day.

'You'd have to go a long way from the lodge to get as good

a dinner as I suspect Ailsa will be giving us. She loves cooking and is delighted to have guests to show off to.' Hamish confirmed my thoughts.

Ailsa smiled an acknowledgement, putting her phone away. As we gathered our things and followed her and Hamish down to the car, I could sense Dave was already anticipating dinner, no doubt remembering that freshly baked bread. Brad appeared waving farewell as we set off. 'Hope to see you again sometime,' he called.

Back at the lodge, Dave and I disappeared to our rooms. I treated myself to a long bath, not stinting on the bath essence I found on the shelf by the bath. The scent was so delightful, the water so warmly enveloping, I must have dropped off as my watch, which I had placed where I could see it from the bath, said 5.45.

I leapt out, dried myself quickly on the huge fluffy towel hanging on the heated radiator, slipped into more suitable clothes. It was only just six so I took a couple of minutes to apply some make-up and brush my hair, still a little damp from the bath, before setting off down the imposing staircase.

A spruced-up Dave was already there, talking to Ailsa who smiled a welcome. Hamish appeared a couple of minutes later.

'Let's go and sit in the snug, it's cosier.' He looked at Ailsa for confirmation.

'I've already set us up in there,' she said smugly, and led the way to a - relatively - small sitting room, mercifully free of stags' heads and other trophies of country pursuits. The pictures were totally different too, colourful against the white walls. A low glass coffee table with glasses and a bottle of wine in a cooler stood on an oriental rug whose dark reds and blues reflected the coverings on the two generously upholstered sofas and matching armchairs. There were some tempting nibbles on the table too.

'This is our retreat,' Ailsa said. 'Being with all those stags and stuffed animals can get a bit wearing, but we keep them as hunting party guests expect a bit of appropriate local colour. But, please, sit down and let Hamish pour you a drink.'

We obeyed willingly and held out our hands to receive the glasses of wine, but Hamish suddenly stopped.

'Oh, I'm sorry, I should have asked. Would either of you prefer beer after all that fresh air?'

Dave and I reassured him we were both very happy with white wine. I was delighted with the one he had chosen.

'It's an English one,' he enlightened us. 'I try to buy more local produce, and at least this one didn't travel too far.'

'Going back to our research,' I said, 'if global warming does what seems likely, you may yet be growing vines in Scotland.'

'Actually, there's a bit of experimentation in wine-making in Scotland already, but the wine's not very good yet, only sold in local farmers' markets, if at all.' Hamish was clearly on top of the scene. 'But have some of Ailsa's nibbles before we talk vortex.'

Dave and I willingly complied, agreeing they were delicious, before I began with a summary of where we had got to that day.

'The sites look promising, subject to Dave's further research on the immediate geology, and the outlook is also good for adequate or better water flows. It's definitely worth doing the next stage of research which all comes within my original estimate.

'But,' I added, 'I did a little more googling to see if there were any alternative generating possibilities as I thought it might be useful to have a back-up should either something go wrong or there wasn't enough water. There are plenty of very cheap portable solar powered battery chargers suitable for mobile phones and laptops which you could rent to campers, for example. But I think the vortex, given good water flow, would not only provide more power but would also be an added attraction - and you could be an example to other local landowners.'

'That's a very good point,' Dave interjected. 'We need to move urgently to non-fossil fuel generation, and showing how practical it is even in remote places like this would help wean people off their oil-fired heating – I guess it's mostly oil in these remoter areas, isn't it?'

'Yes, it is,' Ailsa answered. 'But let's stop business talk and just chat for a bit before I go and finish dinner preparations. Hope you're not vegetarian – I really should have asked before.' She giggled.

'No, we're both omnivorous,' I reassured her. 'I hope I would have thought to tell you otherwise - and of any allergies. All restaurants now ask before you order, so it's becoming very normal.'

'Yes, curious,' Hamish shook his head. 'I'm sure even ten years ago no-one asked, and it seems allergies are far more common nowadays. I wonder why?'

'From some things I've read it maybe because we're too clean now. I even saw an article which said parents should let their kids eat dirt - and let dogs lick their children's faces – even on the mouth.' Dave didn't look too happy at the thought.

Dave then surprised me – and probably Hamish and Ailsa too – with his next remark.

'Is that landscape over the mantelpiece by one of the Scottish colourists? It's certainly very like.' He stood and walked over to look more closely at the small signature in one corner. 'Yes, it is - a Peploe! How wonderful. Lucky you.'

Ailsa almost glowed with pleasure at Dave's recognition. 'Yes, it really is. Our father loved his work – and the other Colourists – and manged to buy a couple before they got too expensive. We have this one and my mother has two more over at the castle. But how do you know about them, they're not so well known in England, I think?'

'My mother loved paintings, particularly the late nineteenth and early twentieth century ones. She didn't paint herself, but had lots of books, of the Impressionists, the Fauvistes - and the Colourists - and she used to go through them with me sometimes, and even take me to exhibitions of them – not that there were many. One which made a big impression on me was of the Canadian Group of Seven who also looked at life and nature in a new way.'

'I went to that one! I remember it well - it was at Dulwich Picture Gallery a few years ago. Dad took me down to see it. It was magnificent.' Ailsa beamed. 'Just think, we might have been there at the same time!'

We all laughed happily at this possible coincidence. Hamish refilled our glasses, suggesting a toast to the Colourists – and, he added – to the future vortex. We joined in gladly, feeling that we were developing more than a formal client and business relationship.

Ailsa made her excuses and left, saying she had to finish the dinner preparation. 'Not long,' she said. 'Come through in ten minutes. And, by the way, we're eating in the kitchen again. Hope you don't mind.'

We reassured her with heartfelt honesty that the kitchen was just fine. Given Hamish's prediction that dinner would be good, I made a big effort not to eat too many of the nibbles, delicious though they were, but Dave, with a youth's more elastic stomach, had do such compunction.

I was glad I had restrained myself as, three courses later, a selection of Scottish cheeses appeared, and Hamish opened another bottle of red wine as we had finished the first one with the venison main course.

'Coffee and a wee dram?' Hamish looked at us as Ailsa removed our plates.

I only struggled with my puritan side for a moment before saying yes, please. Dave enthusiastically added his agreement, clearly glad I had accepted. Hamish fetched the bottle and four glasses from the big cupboard, poured the shots while Ailsa made the coffee.

'Let's stay in here, not bother to move back to the snug,' he said.

Ailsa sat down again and we chatted on about our lives, families, plans and hopes.

'We'll sleep well tonight,' I said after a while. 'We didn't get round to making our plans for tomorrow, but I think we'll make more sense over breakfast.'

Dave nodded. 'There's not a lot to decide, and I don't think we'll need very long sessions at the sites. What time do you usually breakfast?'

'Quite early, I'm afraid, but there's no need to come down before, say 8.30. We'll leave breakfast laid so relax and have a good night.' Hamish smiled. 'I'll be at your service all day, but Ailsa will be driving you back to Inverness. It's her turn to do a few errands there.'

We gave effusive thanks for the wonderful dinner and, feeling a little guilty, left them to clear away while we went up to bed.

In my room I took out my phone – six messages! Scanning the list quickly I saw all but one were from the family. The odd one out, to my surprise, was from Michael Moreton. I opened it.

Hi Elizabeth, delighted to tell you my work is bearing fruit. I think it's time to have a chat with William. Please could you give me his contact details,
Thanks, best wishes, Michael.

Smiling, I replied immediately with congratulations, the email and phone numbers, adding we hoped to see him before long, then turned to the other messages. One was from my sister wanting confirmation all was on track for the family's arrival next evening. Quickly answered. William's message was short, just confirming his flight, that Callum would be with him, and hoping I'd had a productive day. Glancing at my watch I saw it was not yet ten so William would still be up. I called home and he answered immediately.

'Hi darling, hoped you'd call. How's it going up there?'

'It's amazing. Sir Hamish is a delight, as is his sister, and they're really friendly and incredibly generous with their hospitality. In fact, I'll ask them if I can bring you to meet them next week; you'd love them and the house and the area. Gorgeous – even if it does rain rather often. We couldn't work outside this afternoon so Hamish took us to the family castle to do research in the library there – it's got good internet which there isn't here in the lodge – an amazing building, very hard to imagine it as a family home. Actually, it's going to be a hotel, but I'll tell you more when we're together.' I'm sure my voice conveyed my excitement. 'How about you?'

'I'm fine. One bit of news, George's cousin – remember, the one who has Parkinson's – has been in touch and we're going to have lunch together after we get back from Scotland. He was very friendly, sounded nice.'

'That's good news. Talking of getting in touch, I've just had a cheerful message from Michael saying his research is progressing to the point where he'd like to talk to you. I gave him your contact details.'

'Great, I hope I can help him. It's a bit of a technical situation, but I should know the right people to get in touch with on the patent side, and maybe there'll be some financing involved. Right up my street.' William sounded really pleased.

'Sounds promising. I'm rather tired so I'll save work news until we see you tomorrow at Fiona's - but I've just had a thought. Do remember to bring your walking boots. If the weather calms down, it'll be great to get out into the hills with the boys. I'll remind Cal too, the other two are already in Edinburgh, I think, so I'll just have to hope they've got theirs.'

'I'll get mine out now while I think of it.' William chuckled. 'Sleep well, darling, and I look forward to seeing you tomorrow. Love you.'

'I love you, very much,' I responded with a sudden rush of emotion as the thought of the Parkinson's future reared its head. 'Sleep well.' I blew him a kiss and, in a moment unlike my usual pragmatic self, imagined it rising to the sky and floating softly down to land on William's lips.

Chapter Nineteen

Unsurprisingly, I slept really well, waking at eight, relieved to find I had no after-effects from the indulgent and, for me, unusually bibulous dinner. I dressed for outdoor work then suddenly remembered I had to remind all three boys to bring their walking boots. I sent quick texts before making my way to the kitchen. I was heralded by the smell of freshly made toast and coffee. Slightly to my surprise, Dave was already there.

'You're up betimes,' I smiled. 'I thought you might be enjoying a bit of a lie-in.'

'Och, no,' he said in a fair go at a Scottish accent. 'Been up a while – went for a run. Built up another appetite.' He grinned, took a bite of toast, liberally slathered with butter and marmalade. 'You should have some of the porridge, it's delicious.'

'I'll have a coffee while I decide.' I poured myself some from the jug sitting in its machine. 'Have you seen Hamish or Ailsa?'

'Yes, they were just finishing when I came down. Ailsa's gone to do something with her horse, muck it out, I think she said. Hamish would like us ready at nine and he'll drive us up to the burn.'

'That's fine – I don't think I could find my way without him.'

'I could – found it this morning on my run! But it'll be helpful having him take us up as he could show us the way to the river. We don't really need him to stay with us all the time – unless he wants to, of course. There's enough phone signal for us to get back to the lodge using satnav.'

'Good thinking, Dave. I did wonder about him having to

spend all day with us. How long do you think we'll need?'

'I think three, not more than four, hours should do it, then we could get back for a bite to eat and be ready for Ailsa to drive us to Inverness when it suits her.'

'If you're sure about the time you need, that's fine by me. I'll check with Ailsa what time she plans to leave. I told Fiona I'd aim for five, and I should let her know if it's going to be much different. How about you?'

'My train leaves at 20.45 and they let us on before then. I can easily kill an hour or two - maybe try some more whisky in a local hostelry!'

'If it's still open when Ailsa drops you at Inverness station, there's an amazing second-hand bookstore in an old chapel quite nearby, which you'd love.' I remembered visiting it myself and being open-mouthed at the book-filled space, open to the chapel's high ceiling. 'But unless there's a left luggage facility at the station, whisky in a bar's more practical.'

'I like the idea, though,' Dave said. 'I'll see when we get there. I've finished breakfast so I'll leave you in peace. See you in the hall at nine.'

I decided I could manage both a small helping of porridge and some toast, both as good as promised. I would have liked to linger over my breakfast but there was too little time. Looking out of the window, I was delighted to see clear blue sky, not a cloud in sight.

Meeting in the hall, Dave said he'd explained our plan and reassured Hamish that we could find our own way once he'd given us instructions how to get from the burn to the river, and that we would ring if we changed our minds.

At the burn, Hamish stood with us for a few minutes as Dave unloaded his gear, asking about the various instruments. It wasn't yet warm, but I could feel the sun on my back. I looked up at Hamish silhouetted against the blue sky, and had a sudden rush of affection, almost maternal, for this young man who had had to take on such a responsibility so young. Trenchant Engineering would do its very best for him and his sister.

Hamish pointed out the route to the river then left us to our work, just reminding us to ring should we need any assistance. He returned from the car a few seconds later however, carrying a small backpack.

'I nearly forgot!' He laughed.' Ailsa's put a few biscuits and a thermos in this for you, keep you going until your late lunch.'

'That's extraordinarily kind of her, please thank her when you get back.' They really were a remarkable young pair. I wondered whether my trio would have been so thoughtful.

'Will do.' This time he really did leave as we heard the car engine revving as he turned back to the lodge.

Dave was the technician here. My task was to record the results of his measurements of water flow, explorations of rock types, and make notes on his observations as he worked. The sun continued to shine, and it was a real pleasure being out in such beautiful countryside doing useful work which, hopefully, would benefit the planet as well as helping make the estate a viable operation.

The burn conditions measured and noted, we had a break for Ailsa's coffee and biscuits before making our way without difficulty to the trout river. There was no fisherman there today; it was totally peaceful, the only sound the gentle tinkling of the river as it rushed over the stones, and the occasional call of a bird. I saw a rabbit peeking at us from behind a clump of grass, but it hopped away before Dave could see it. Towards midday it got very warm in the shelter of the valley. I shared the water from my backpack with a grateful Dave who said he had nearly finished his measurements and only needed another twenty minutes or so.

'Shall we walk back or call Hamish for a lift?' I asked him, hoping for the latter as the thought of a shower and lunch was very appealing. 'It's nearly 12.30.'

'Should only take half an hour to walk,' Dave reassured me.

It took rather more than that as the satnav didn't allow for bogs, streams, small ravines and other obstructions, and I was extremely glad when the lodge came into sight.

'Well done, you two,' said Hamish, emerging from the front door as we approached. 'That was a long morning. Hope you got everything you needed. Ailsa has lunch on the table, all cold so you can freshen up first.'

Leaving Dave's clobber in the hall, we went up to our rooms briefly then met again in the kitchen.

'What time to you want to leave?' I asked Ailsa as we sat down to a generous spread of cold meats and cheese, plus, to Dave's delight, more home-made bread.

'Would three suit you?' she replied. 'Should have you in town by four-thirty easily. Could be earlier if you like.'

I replied for both of us that three would be fine and we tucked in, our appetites well whetted by our morning of fresh air.

Gathering with our luggage just before three, we thanked Hamish and Ailsa heartily for their excellent hospitality.

'You really are a special pair,' I said. 'We will do our very best to get the results of our work analysed and back to you soon with our thoughts. We really admire what you are planning and hope very much that, with our help, you can make your vision come true.' My formal boss-speak.

Dave spoke up. 'I agree. And it's been great, more like working with friends than clients.' He paused. 'Maybe I could even bring my girlfriend to meet you when I persuade her our hiking holiday should be up here.'

Hamish and Ailsa both smiled in appreciation. 'Of course, do bring her. We'd be delighted,' Ailsa said. 'But right now, we must get to you Inverness.'

The luggage loaded into the Land Rover, we shook hands with Hamish, Ailsa climbed in, and we were off. Arrived at the barn by the main road, we switched to the Jaguar and continued in style. Ailsa proved an excellent driver, surprisingly faster than Hamish.

Ailsa opened the conversation. 'We've heard a bit about your family, Elizabeth, but what about you Dave, do you have brothers and sisters? Is engineering in your family?'

'I've just an older sister. She's married, has two kids – I'm surprised how much I enjoy being an uncle! And no, no engineers. My dad's a builder and decorator, has a small business with a partner. I think it's from him I got my interest in how things work. My mum works in a bank, used to be a teller but there's much less call for that now so she's moved to the back office. Misses the people.'

We were discussing how the internet and digitisation of everything had changed life when we saw we were arriving on the outskirts of Inverness. Ailsa drew into a layby.

'Have you got your sister's postcode with you?' Ailsa asked. 'I could drive you straight there before I drop Dave at the station, no problem. I'm meeting friends from uni for drinks and staying with them tonight. Lots to catch up on. Errands tomorrow.'

I gave Ailsa the post code for the satnav. Dave looked around with interest as we drove through the suburbs, into the town and across the river, exclaiming at some of the fine buildings. Ailsa pointed out the castle on the hill above the river, the cathedral on the other bank, as she drove along the tree-lined river. A few minutes up from the river and we were in a residential area, wide roads lined with substantial houses. Ringing Fiona to tell her we were nearly there, I saw there was a text from William, sent just a few minutes before. My heart pounded as I read: *About to board. Callum not here, no message. Coming anyway.*

My mind raced, but there was no time to think or react as Ailsa pulled up in front of my sister's large, grey stone house.

We had barely come to a halt when the front door opened and my sister emerged, waving and beckoning. 'Drive in,' she called.

Ailsa turned the car into the drive and drew up by Fiona who was all smiles.

'Wonderful to see you,' she said, giving me a big hug as I got out. 'Do please introduce me to the others, I'd love to meet them and maybe they'd like a cup of tea after the drive, I put the kettle on when you rang.'

Suppressing my worry, I turned to Ailsa and Dave. 'Will you come in for a few minutes? Fiona would be really like to meet you and she's offering a cup of tea.'

Pleased, they got out of the car and shook hands with Fiona as I introduced them, and we followed her into the house.

'Loo's there if you need it,' she pointed at a door. 'Let's have tea in the garden, it's such a lovely afternoon – must make the most of it. No-one else at home, I'm afraid, John's at work, and the kids are off doing whatever they do with their mates in the holidays.'

I knew Fi was proud of her garden, so I encouraged Ailsa and Dave to follow her while I made the excuse that I needed the loo. Sitting down I called William, but he didn't answer. Probably boarding, I thought, and sent a text saying we were at Fiona's and to please call when he could.

Joining the young people in the garden, I found them admiring the herbaceous border.

'It's beautiful,' said Ailsa, turning to me.

It was true; the border on one side of the lawn was a blaze of colour. Spikes of dark blue delphiniums rose above clouds of white cosmos interspersed with clumps of yellow daisies. The rose bed on the other side was in full flower, tempting us over to savour the fragrances, giving rise to a chorus of mmms and ahhhs as we sampled the different blooms. Ailsa's attention was then drawn to the huge cedar tree at the far end of the lawn, its branches spreading wide over the grass, a child's swing suspended from one, a hammock from another.

'Does your sister have young children? Or grandchildren?' she asked. 'They must love that tree.'

'No, her three are too big for the swing now, but it was certainly very popular when they were young - and with mine too when we visited.'

Our exploration was interrupted by Fi calling us to the table and chairs set out on the terrace.

'Meant to say, Lizzie, had a call from William about an hour ago,' she said as she poured tea. 'The plane is on time, they'll get a taxi, should be with us in plenty of time for a drink before dinner.'

'Have you heard from Angus and Bruce too?' I hoped they had told Fi their plans. I didn't air the concern raised by my recent text from William, but it hung heavy in my mind.

'Yes. Angus called this morning, bless him, to say they'd come tomorrow morning after all, to do with a party or something tonight. I got the impression they're enjoying Edinburgh!'

As we drank our tea and nibbled at some biscuits, I diverted my thoughts by giving Dave and Ailsa a brief summary of the boys' summer arrangement, and my sister quizzed Ailsa on life on the estate before turning to Dave to hear about his work. It would have been easy to sit and chat in such a lovely spot, but Ailsa looked discreetly at her watch before saying she must be getting off to take Dave to the station before going to meet her friends.

Dave unloaded my luggage from the car and took it to the house before our goodbyes. In a moment of pleasure and gratitude, I hugged both Ailsa and Dave - I think he was surprised to be hugged by his boss! They shook hands with Fi again before climbing into the Jag and setting off leaving me almost overcome with worry.

Chapter Twenty

'What nice young people,' my sister said as we walked back into the house. 'Is Hamish like Ailsa? His plans sound interesting, and I hope Dave's researches....' She stopped mid-sentence as she noticed that I wasn't listening and had taken out my phone. 'You okay, Lizzie? You look worried.'

I started to apologise and say I was fine, but my worry got the better of me and I told her about Callum's no-show at the airport. 'I'm texting him, must make sure he's okay. I can't reach William as he's on the plane. I hope he's coped with the flight.'

'Why wouldn't he?' Fi looked at me, very surprised.

Impulsively, I seized the moment to tell her about the Parkinson's diagnosis. 'It was only diagnosed a couple of weeks ago and it's at a very early stage. We decided not to tell anyone except the boys at first, so you're the first to know.' I suspect my voice was shaking.

'Oh, Lizzie, what a shock.' Fiona pulled me to her in a sisterly hug. 'How's he taken it? How did you find out? What's the prognosis?'

I released myself from the hug and wiped an unbidden tear from my eye. 'It was a colleague of William's whose father has it. He noticed William was occasionally a bit shaky and suggested he get checked, so he did and...' I paused. 'It was a huge shock, but William says he feels fine and carries on as usual. Mostly you wouldn't notice anything was wrong unless you knew and were looking out for it. But I confess I was a bit concerned at his travelling alone, so it was a relief Callum agreed to fly up with him. That's why it's so strange he didn't turn up. I don't know whether to be angry with him or worried stiff.'

'Hmmm, I can understand that. But surely there's a simple explanation?'

'But why didn't he call or text William or me? It's not much to ask. Callum has been behaving a bit strangely recently which is why I can't help worrying.'

'Strange in what way?'

I really didn't want to talk about our suspicions right then; one revelation at a time was enough to cope with. I was saved from answering by my phone ringing – it was William.

'Hi, darling, just landed and disembarked. I'm on my way to collect my case and find a taxi. Should be with you in half an hour or so, provided there's no queue for the taxis.'

'Oh, William, I'm so glad you called and you're okay'

'Why wouldn't I be? I'm perfectly capable still.' William laughed.

Although it was good to hear him joking, it didn't ease my worry about Callum, and I had to ask:

'Heard from Callum?'

'No. I've sent texts but no reply yet. Of course it's worrying, but there's nothing we can do until he contacts us. Oh, I've just seen my cases on the carousel, must go. Are you at Fiona's already?'

'Yes, Hamish's sister brought me and has taken Dave to the station. Hope there's no wait for the cab. We'll talk properly when you get here.'

'OK, see you very soon.' William ended the call.

In the hall, Fiona picked up my case and led me up the stairs. 'I've put you in your usual room,' she said opening the door to the front spare bedroom. The boys will share the big attic room, it's got three beds – well, two and the big sofa - all made up already. Why don't you unpack now and then we can talk when William arrives.' She looked at her watch. 'It'll be well past 6.30 by the time he gets here, perfect time for a drink before dinner.'

As she spoke, the front door slammed, and a cacophony of voices reached up the stairs.

'Hi, Mum, we're all home. Is Aunt Elizabeth here yet?'

'Hi, darlings. Yes, she's here, just unpacking, she'll be down in a few minutes.' Fiona called down.

'Come down as soon as you've unpacked and greet the mob, they're so looking forward to seeing you,' Fiona grinned as she turned to go downstairs, 'and their cousins, but they know they have to wait until tomorrow for that.'

It took very little time to sort and stow my things in the well-equipped room and its en-suite bathroom. A quick tidying of my hair was enough to prepare me for the onslaught of three lively teenagers.

And onslaught it was! It was at least two years since we had last seen them all, and I had to negotiate a heap of sports bags, dropped jackets and tennis racquets while being hugged by all three simultaneously.

'Whoa, slow down, careful with your old aunt!' I laughed and kissed each one in turn. 'Were you all playing tennis?'

'No, just Jamie and me,' said Damian, the eldest.

'And I beat him,' bragged Jamie, smirking.

'Only just,' came the rejoinder.

'What about you, Lucy? What were you doing while your brothers slogged it out on the tennis court?'

'Oh, I did some weight training then met up with a friend at the tennis club.' Lucy blushed with a fifteen-year-old's self-consciousness, probably aware that her brothers would rib her mercilessly about her biceps – and the boy they suspected she had met up with – given half a chance.

Fiona appeared at that point, telling them to put their things away and shower before their uncle arrived, thereby forestalling my curiosity about Lucy and weight training. Obediently, all three disappeared upstairs, emerging remarkably quickly, eager to catch up with my family news.

I hadn't got far into telling them that their cousins – at least two of them - would arrive tomorrow from Edinburgh, and about my time with Hamish and Ailsa, when the doorbell rang.

'It's Uncle William!' Lucy rushed to open the door to claim first hug from her favourite uncle. Her brothers were less impulsive but moved to take their turn as soon as he had deposited his case and backpack on the hall floor.

'Hi, you three, it's great to see you! Where's your mother?'

'I'm here,' said Fiona giving William kisses on both cheeks and a hug for good measure.

At last it was my turn to kiss my beloved husband, looking him in the eye as I asked how the journey had been, clearly wanting reassurance that all had gone well.

'Easy as pie, no problem at all apart from...'

'That's good,' I interrupted him, not wanting to go into the Callum question in front of the children. 'More details later.'

'What do you want first? A shower, a drink – tea or stronger – or to be left in peace for a few minutes to catch up with your wife?' Fiona the hostess.

'A few moments with Lizzie and to unpack, I think, then a stiff drink. Got any of that delicious whisky – Glenmorangie, I think it was - you gave us once?'

Fiona smiled and nodded. 'Good memory! Damian and Jamie, please take Uncle's bags up.' She departed in the direction of the kitchen.

William and I followed the boys to our room, thanked them and closed the door behind them. I gave William a proper kiss and held him close before telling him about my conversation with Fiona.

'I'm really worried. I told Fi that Cal hadn't showed up, and I was cross because I'd wanted him to be with you because of the Parkinson's. so don't be surprised if she mentions it. I also said I didn't know whether to be angry or concerned about Cal but didn't go into any details.'

'Well, I'm glad the Parkinson's cat is out of the bag, and they'll soon see I'm still in good shape. Remembered my walking boots! I'm glad you didn't tell her our worries about Callum, though.'

We decided on one more attempt to reach Callum before going down for drinks and dinner, but again he didn't answer so we just left another message saying PLEASE call us and that we're at my sister's.

When we arrived in the sitting room, we were delighted to see John was back from work. He leapt to his feet, embraced me and shook hands heartily with William.

'So good to see you both! It's been too long. Sorry I wasn't here when you arrived, but we had a staff meeting after the surgery closed, luckily not too drawn out. What can I get you to drink?' John was always a generous host.

William repeated his preference for a whisky, while I opted for a gin and tonic, knowing it was a standard in their household and Fi's favourite evening tipple. John turned to get the drinks but was forestalled by Fiona coming in with a tray with exactly the right selection, plus some cheesy biscuits. There were some soft drinks and glasses on a side table, for the kids I guessed.

'They'll be with us any second,' she said, 'but there's no

need to wait.'

We raised our glasses in pleasure at being together again and were just settling in to chat when a thunder of feet announced the children's arrival. It was indeed a happy reunion and the conversation flowed non-stop, there was much news to exchange and weekend activities to plan for when our boys arrived. This, of course, led to the Callum problem, which we sidestepped, saying we hoped he'd be with us soon but not to delay our plans. I did my best to hide my worry, successfully, I think, though Fi did give me a sideways glance.

The family dinner was fun but William and I, tired from our busy days and travelling, as well as being distracted by Callum's absence, made our excuses soon after ten and retired to our room. We were about to get into bed when William's phone pinged. He grabbed it and read: *Sorry sorry sorry*

I immediately rang Cal's number but once again he failed to answer, then another message appeared, on my phone this time: *Sorry again. Love you both.*

William and I looked at one another. What on earth was going on? It took a long time to get to sleep that night.

Chapter Twenty One

I thought I had been dreaming when, disturbed by William getting out of bed, I heard a mobile ring. Assuming he had just gone for a pee I settled again expecting him to get back in. When he didn't, I opened one eye and was surprised to see him just outside the room, mobile held to his ear. Properly awake, I looked at my watch thinking perhaps I had overslept and was very surprised to see it was just past seven. I climbed out of bed and went to join him.

'Who on earth is ringing you at this hour on a Saturday?' I asked.

He held his finger to his lips but his whole demeanour radiated shock.

'Who is it? What's wrong?'

William held up his hand to stop me talking. 'I'll call you back as soon as I've told Mum and we decide what to do. But thank heavens you're there.' He closed the call.

By this time, I was frantic. William turned and held me close.

'That was Bruce,' he said. 'Callum tried to commit suicide, but Bruce and Angus got there in time to get him to hospital. He'll be okay, Bruce said.'

At first I couldn't take it in. Callum? Suicide? No, surely not, not our lovely Callum. I felt as though the bottom of my world had dropped out. I held William tighter, trembling.

Finally, pulling myself together, I asked William what else Bruce had said, what did he know?

'He said that both he and Angus had had very strange feelings about Cal, felt something was very wrong. They rang Cal but he was incoherent, clearly distressed, mumbled something about an attack. He and Angus agonised about what to do but decided that before ringing us they should go and find out what was actually wrong. They caught the last fast train to London and getting near London got a message from him - one like we had - saying sorry, so they were even more worried. They took a taxi straight to the house, got there soon after ten, found Cal comatose on his bed, an empty bottle of whisky on the floor and open packets of painkillers on the bedside table. His face was a mess, covered in blood. They called an ambulance which fortunately came very quickly. The paramedics took charge and let them travel with Cal to A&E at University College Hospital.

'Bruce said they were sitting in the waiting area, panic stricken, not knowing what was going on, debating whether to call us, when a nurse came out and told them they'd pumped his stomach and cleaned him up, moved him to an observation ward, and that it was very likely he'd be okay since they'd got him to hospital so quickly. That's why they didn't ring before.'

'Oh, but they should have done, they should have rung at once, we should be there with them.' I was sobbing now.

'That was my first instinct too. But stop to think,' said William. 'How could we have got there from here that late with no flights, no trains, and a hell of a long drive, mostly in the dark, and anyway, no car? Once they knew he was out of danger, there was less urgency. In fact, there's little lost. We can get an early flight and be there by lunchtime.'

Dear William, always so rational. Sometimes I wished he were less so, but in this case, I had to accept his logic. I wiped my eyes and attempted a smile. 'Let's ring Angus and Bruce back and say we'll be with them by this afternoon. Maybe they'll even have more news, like how long Cal will have to stay in hospital. But let's go back into the bedroom in case John and Fi hear us and want to know what's wrong. We need to think what we're going to tell them.'

We closed the bedroom door behind us. 'You look up flights and trains while I call Angus', I said, fishing my phone out of my handbag.

Angus answered almost immediately.

'Hi Mum.' His voice broke but he managed to continue. 'I'm so sorry. Bruce and I should have picked up things were bad with Cal before, but we hardly saw him these past couple of weeks, and we didn't get this awful feeling we had until last night....'

I interrupted him. 'Thank heavens the intuition kicked in when it did. Bless you both for rushing home. It must have been dreadful, wondering what was wrong, then finding him like that. But you can tell Dad and me more details later. Right now, is there any news? Is he conscious? How long will he have to stay in hospital?' My questions came tumbling out.

Angus started to answer but he must have put his hand over the microphone as I could just hear snippets of a conversation.

I turned to William who was poring over his phone, looking at flights. 'I'll put it on speakerphone so you can hear too', I said.

A moment later Angus came back. 'That was Bruce. He just managed to be allowed in to see Cal. I'll give him the phone.'

'Hi, Mum. I just saw Cal. He's sedated so I couldn't ask him anything, but he looked peaceful though his face is very bruised and cut. I talked to the nurse who said we were lucky to get to him when we did as if we'd been much later he.....'

He went quiet for a moment, but I could hear him gulp and gather control. 'Oh, Mum, why didn't we realise how bad things were before it got to this.'

'None of us did, so don't blame yourselves. But tell us – Dad's listening – did the nurse say anything about what happens next?'

'Not much, except the prognosis is good. She said we'd have to wait for the doctor for more info. She should be coming round in half an hour or so.'

'Have you and Angus had a chance to get some sleep?'

'We took it in turns to doze in the chairs here. It was a bit difficult as Friday nights at A&E are very busy, but we're okay. Are you coming down?'

'Dad's looking at flights now. We should be able to get to the hospital soon after lunch, I think. Is that right?' I turned to William who nodded.

'There's a flight getting into Heathrow just after one, and one into Luton about the same. I'm checking if there are seats,' he said.

'Did you hear that?' I asked Bruce.

'Yes. That's good. Let us know as soon as you decide. I'll call you back if there's any more news.'

'Thanks, darling. Do go and get something to eat to keep your energy up. We'll keep our phones handy. Love you all. Bye.'

I ended the call. 'Any joy on seats? I asked William, who nodded. 'Both okay. I'll book the Luton one, I think, as we won't have any luggage to worry about, and it's so quick by train into St Pancras. More convenient than Heathrow for UCH.'

'Good thinking. While you're booking, I'll decide what we should say to Fi and John – and the kids.'

William returned to his phone while I got dressed and deliberated on how to break our news.

'All done,' said William, putting the phone down. '11.30 departure so we've plenty of time as it's only quarter to eight now. There is an earlier one, but it would be too tight. What do you think about what we say?'

'Is it really only quarter to eight? Feels like much later,' I said before answering his question. 'The boys said Cal's face was battered - on the phone to them he'd said something about an attack. So I think we just tell the family he got rather badly hurt in a fight, no details, except it was enough to have to spend the night in A&E. And that he'd called Angus and Bruce who were so worried they rushed to London and are with him in the hospital.'

'Sounds okay, and we can just stall on more until we've talked to the boys. Hopefully we'll be able to come back up here in a day or two, time enough to decide how open to be. Cal may have views on it.'

I agreed. William shaved and got dressed while I dressed and put on some make up to raise my morale and hide the strain which I could see etched in my face. Before we went downstairs, we had another close hug for mutual support and reflected how fortunate we were that we could just buy tickets without worrying about the cost. Suppose we had been poor when every pound counted but the worry was just as great. It didn't bear thinking about.

The smell of sizzling bacon greeted us as we walked into the kitchen where my sister was putting out a selection of cereals and jams. She showed no sign of having noticed our early telephone conversation and greeted us cheerily.

'Slept well?' she asked as she put a loaf of home-made bread on the table.

William looked to me to answer.

'Well, actually, there's been a bit of a drama. Callum texted last night to say he was involved in a fight and got quite badly hurt - had to go to A&E. He had told Angus and Bruce, and Bruce us called early this morning to say that Cal had sounded very upset so, bless them, they both went down to see how he was. It may not be that serious but Bruce sounded a bit worried so William and I thought we should go too. We're booked on a flight at 11.30. We're really sorry – let's hope it's just a brief visit and that we'll all be back with you in a day or two.'

'My goodness, you must be seriously concerned to fly down when you've only just arrived. Are you sure you need to?' Fiona's face showed her concern.

'I'm afraid so. We'd only worry ourselves sick otherwise. You haven't mentioned any fixed plans for this weekend so hopefully this is just a minor hiccup and we'll be able to pick up on our holiday and enjoy being with you all.' I managed what I hoped was a convincing and reassuring smile.

'Oh, dear, John and the kids will be disappointed as they had actually planned to take you dolphin watching tomorrow, but I expect the dolphins will oblige later in the week, even if John can't be with you.' Fiona made light of the change of plans, but I got the feeling she realised there was more to the sudden change of plans than I had let on.

Chapter Twenty Two

Fi knew me too well to press for more information.

'If you really feel you must go, then John will drive you to the airport and I'll break the news to the kids when they emerge. They'll be disappointed but I'll reassure them you'll be back in a day or two.'

'Thanks, Fi.' I smiled gratefully. 'I'll be in touch as soon as we know what the problem is. Keep your fingers crossed that it really isn't too bad.'

Fiona left the kitchen to tell John about the change of plan while William and I sat down to try to eat some breakfast, though our appetites were thoroughly dampened by our worries.

John soon appeared, commiserated on our news, and said he was happy to drive us when we were ready. Fi hugged us both close before waving us off, hiding her concern as best she could. John thoughtfully didn't probe too hard as he drove. I was sorely tempted to confide in him but decided we ourselves needed to know more first.

At the airport we thanked John warmly. Since we didn't need any luggage as we would sleep at home, check-in was easy and, once on board, we sat in silence, holding hands, too upset to speculate about what had brought Callum to such a desperate step.

At Luton we went straight to the station, caught a fast train almost immediately. William called the boys to say we would soon be with them and was there any news.

'No real news, but the doctor was reasonably positive when she came round, but she didn't say how long Cal would have to stay in hospital. It's clear they take it seriously and we'll have to wait for more information.' Angus's answer was hardly reassuring.

'Where will we find you?'

'Call when you get near the hospital, go to A&E and we'll meet you there as it's a bit of a rabbit warren.'

'Okay. See you there, maybe half an hour or so if we get a taxi straight away. Shouldn't be a problem. Bye.' William closed the call and leant back against the seat. He reached out to take my hand. 'We must look on the bright side. Although this is awful, it's a top hospital and must deal with attempted suicides quite often so Cal's getting the best of care.'

I squeezed his hand. 'I know you're right, but my mind is still racing, trying to come to terms with it.'

We met Angus and Bruce in A&E as arranged, exchanged tearful hugs, and followed them to the recovery room where Callum was being monitored. A nurse appeared and, learning we were Callum's parents, allowed us to go in while the boys waited outside.

He was asleep, peaceful, but even though we had been warned, the black eyes, cuts and abrasions on his face were still a shock. I leant over and kissed his forehead gently, whispering 'We love you so much, Cal, wake up soon and let us help you.'

William, less demonstrative but as deeply moved, stroked Cal's hair and repeated my words of comfort.

The nurse was waiting outside. She introduced herself as Margaret and invited us to sit and ask – and answer – questions. We explained that we had had no prior warning of Callum's state of mind, though he had been behaving rather oddly the past few weeks, withdrawn and not joining in family life as much as usual. She produced the packets of painkillers which, unnoticed by Angus and Bruce, the paramedics had brought to the hospital. I recognised them as ones I had kept in the bathroom cupboard since I had had bad back pain a couple of years before and was able to tell her that one of them had been at least half empty.

'That's good news,' said Margaret. 'Although this is a serious situation, the indications are that it wasn't fully thought through by Callum, and the combination of whisky and painkillers wasn't actually enough to kill him, especially as his brothers acted so promptly. So maybe we can call it a cry for help. We'll need to keep Callum under observation until tomorrow morning, but then I'm very hopeful you'll be able to take him home.' She paused. 'However, we haven't talked about his injuries. His brothers said he had mumbled something about a fight, and his injuries, to his face but there's also considerable bruising on his back and legs which, of course, weren't immediately visible They do suggest a quite vicious attack. Do you have any idea what might have led to such a nasty incident?'

William and I shook our heads. 'No, none at all,' we said in unison, though distressed by this further bad news. The memory of the angry phone call I had overheard flashed through my mind. I didn't mention it, though, as if Callum had been dealing in drugs, that might have had something to do with the fight, but I didn't want to start down that route which would involve police enquiries – and even possible arrest – until we had got the truth from Callum.

Margaret smiled kindly and asked us to wait outside while she had a talk with Angus and Bruce. When they all emerged, she said we should seek some post suicide counselling, and gave us a leaflet with details of where to get good help.

'Callum will wake slowly over the next few hours,' she said. 'If he feels up to it, I'll ask if he would like to call you. I'm on duty until eight this evening. Callum's brothers gave me your home and mobile numbers when they brought him in. I'll call you before I leave to report on his progress and whether it's likely he can be discharged tomorrow morning.'

We thanked Margaret profusely and, with Angus and Bruce, made our way out of the hospital to look for a taxi home. We travelled pretty much in silence, knowing there would be plenty of time to talk in the evening ahead.

Chapter Twenty Three

Although my mind was preoccupied with Callum, I still noticed that William fumbled as he opened the front door for us. Parkinson's or the stress of the day? Not the time to worry about it. Once indoors, intuitively we knew we needed to stay close. I made tea and the four of us sat in silence round the kitchen table. Angus found the chocolate biscuits and we all tucked in, suddenly aware we'd had no lunch.

William was the first to speak, a tremor in his voice.

'You two boys are heroes, responding to your intuition, then staying up all night in the hospital with Cal. Mum and I know that without you he might still have died, even if he apparently didn't take a lethal dose, since no-one would have been there to look after him and he might even have tried again.'

My determined self-control gave way at that point and I burst into tears, tears of relief and gratitude. William reached to put his arm round me and I could see his cheeks were wet too. Angus and Bruce, while not in tears, reacted to the huge strain of the past 24 hours in a close brotherly hug. On impulse, I reached out to take their and William's hands and we collectively and silently shared our tension and relief, our hands clasped together on the table.

Releasing their hands, I cleared my throat and wiped my eyes. 'Let's hope Cal is well enough to come home tomorrow and that he'll ring us this evening, though I fear he may be too upset – even embarrassed – to want to talk to us yet.'

'You may be right, but what do you two think?' William looked enquiringly at the boys.

Bruce answered for them both. 'I hope he feels well enough to know how much we care and want to know he's okay, but we can't count on it.'

Angus nodded. 'We just have to wait and see. In any case, if he's up to it, I think we should get back to Scotland with him on Monday - or even tomorrow. Get him away from whatever's gone so wrong for him.'

'I agree,' said William. 'And we'll have to work out with him what – how much – to tell Fi and John. I really hope he'll agree to admit to the suicide attempt as John, being a doctor, will know what to watch out for, how to care for him.'

'So far, we've said he was in a fight, so at least they won't be surprised by his injuries,' I reminded them.

A silence settled round the table again, broken by William going back to practicalities. 'By the way, let me know what your train tickets cost, you two, and I'll transfer the money to whichever of you paid. Lucky you had enough to cover them, the train tickets are mighty expensive, especially at short notice – hope you got student fares.'

'Silly question, Dad,' said Bruce. 'We do enough train journeys to be on that particular ball.'

'Talking of money, how's the job hunting?' I changed the subject to take our minds off Callum for a minute.

'We've both found bar work, starting 5th August when the Fringe and the International Festivals really kick off. Different bars, but both good places to work and not bad pay – tips too, with luck.' Bruce smiled. 'Means we can enjoy being with you and the family in Inverness until the end of July, very early August.'

'Is it okay with the house-sitting to be away so long?' I asked.

'Yup, Tom is happy to hold the fort as long as we give him

a break at some point,' Bruce reassured us.

'I'm so glad as I'm hatching a plan to take you all to meet Sir Hamish and his sister. It's the most wonderful place and they're really fun.'

'Aren't they a bit crusty to be fun?' Angus raised an eyebrow.

I laughed, for the first time since Callum's strange texts the night before. 'That's what I expected, but how wrong I was! Hamish is a hulk in his late twenties and his sister's not much older than you lot. Plus, she's drop-dead gorgeous and a great cook.'

Bruce and Angus's faces lit up. 'Bring 'em on!' said Angus, grinning.

We all laughed at this, the atmosphere in the kitchen lightening by several degrees.

As we were now more relaxed and knew there wasn't much we could do until the nurse and, hopefully, Callum called, I turned my thoughts to supper. 'There's nothing much in the house in the way of food, so shall we just have a take-away?' I asked. 'And if so, what do you fancy? You men discuss it and make the order. I'm going up to relax in a hot bath.'

They all nodded as I left them to their deliberations.

Coming down a luxurious bath later, I found William laying the kitchen table.

'So, what are we having?' I gave him a quick kiss.

'Hmm you smell nice,' William said. 'That fancy bath oil I gave you for your birthday?

'Yes, it's gorgeous, and still lots left. Thanks again. But supper?'

'Not a takeaway after all. They didn't fancy the usuals, then Angus remembered that new shop in the high street that does frozen ready meals and desserts so they've popped down there to choose something. We thought we'd eat a bit early. We did have the biscuits, but you know the boys' appetites.'

'Yes, they've always had hollow legs.' I was just going to enlarge on their appetites when we heard the front door open. Angus and Bruce appeared with a bulging bag.

'Oven on,' instructed Angus, unloading the bag onto the counter. 'Some of this can heat through, some we microwave. Go and sit down, you two, Bruce and I will look after it and call you when we're ready.'

William and I smiled our gratitude, and William, taking a bottle of wine from the fridge and two glasses, led me to the sitting room. We sat side by side on the sofa in another moment of silence while William opened the bottle and poured the wine. 'I think we need this,' he said, passing me my glass. 'What a day.'

I could only agree as I took a sip. 'Shouldn't we give the boys some wine too?' I stood up and took the bottle to the kitchen only to find they were ahead of us; an open bottle of red wine stood on the table, clearly no longer full.

'Thanks, Mum, but we fancied red and bought a bottle from the off licence on the way back from the shop.' Angus acknowledged. 'Dinner in about half an hour, okay?'

'Perfect, thanks, sweetheart.' I returned to the sitting room where I found William leaning back against the cushions, eyes closed. He opened them as I sat down again.

'A bit tired, I confess,' he said. 'Mind if we don't talk for a bit?'

'Of course not. I'll move to a chair so as not to disturb you.'

'No, don't move. I like having you close.' William reached out to touch my hand.

My love and concern for my husband threatened to make

me tearful again but I smiled and squeezed his hand. 'Have a little doze and I'll wake you when dinner's ready.' I reached for the book I had left on the side table and tried to read but I couldn't concentrate so closed it and shut my eyes.

It seemed no time before I was roused by Bruce laughing. 'Wake up you two, dinner's ready.'

'I wasn't asleep,' I protested, 'but Dad may be.'

'No, I'm awake too!' William stood up. 'Lead on, McDuff, dinner smells good.'

It was indeed good. We finished both wines and had a cheerful meal. All cleared away, I made coffee and we all four returned to the sitting room. It must have been nearly eight when, in a lull in the conversation, the landline rang, a shock in the silence. We looked at each other, the tension palpable. I reacted first, going over to pick up the phone.

'Hi Lizzie, How was the journey? How's Callum?' My sister's voice was loud enough for the others to hear, and they relaxed back into their seats, disappointment as clear on their faces as it must have been on mine.

I answered both questions without going into detail about Callum but added that I would soon know more as we were expecting him to ring any moment.

'I'll call you back when we've talked to him. We're hoping he'll be okay to come back to Inverness with us in a day or so. Must keep the line free so let's not chat now. Love to you all.' I hung up.

I had barely sat down when the phone rang again.

Chapter Twenty Four

This time it was William who leapt to his feet to answer the phone.

'William Trenchard.' There was a pause. Wiiliam's face fell, but his expression lightened as he listened.

Speakerphone! we all mouthed at him, desperate to hear. He lifted a finger to show he had understood.

'Thanks for reassuring us. We'll call mid-morning about when he should be able to come home.' William's voice held a smile. 'But do you think Callum will be up to talking to us this evening?'

Now we could hear.

'I'm not sure, but she's left a message for the nurse who will be on this evening's shift. I'm sure she'll call you.'

'Please thank Nurse Margaret for us, and we look forward to hearing from the new nurse. Thanks for calling.' William hung up.

'What did we miss?' I asked anxiously. 'What did they say?'

'Margaret, the nurse we met, had to attend to another patient so couldn't call as planned but she asked the ward receptionist – that's who just rang - to say that she thought Cal would be okay to come home sometime tomorrow. Also, that she's left a note for the night shift nurse to call once she's had a chance to assess how he is. So now we're in limbo until she does.' William sighed. 'At least that's some good news. Perhaps we could even start planning what to do, stay here or go to Fiona and John's.'

Angus spoke up to remind us we needed to know how Callum felt about both travelling and being with people. 'It's really frustrating, but we do need his input and we still have no idea if he will call.'

We sat in silence for a few minutes. How to fill the time, to distract ourselves until we had more news? I looked at my watch. It was still only 8.30.

'Well, there's no point in just sitting here staring at the phone. I'm going to watch one of the David Attenborough programmes we recorded. Anyone join me? There's one on oceans, I think and one on animal parenting.'

The boys shook their heads and took out their phones, scrolling through the messages they hadn't looked at in the stress of the day. William nodded, however, and switched on the TV. We chose Blue Planet and leant back in the comfort of the sofa to watch. It was very absorbing and quite a shock when the phone rang for the third time. William put the TV on pause while I picked up the phone and, with a grin, pointedly put it on speakerphone immediately. The boys looked up expectantly from their screens.

'Elizabeth Trenchard.' I tried not to sound too eager after the last two let-downs.

'Hello, I'm Belle and I'm looking after Callum tonight. Margaret asked me to give you an update.'

'Oh, we're so pleased to hear from you – at least, if the news is good.' I thought if I qualified my pleasure, it might insulate us from another disappointment.

'I'm happy to tell you it is good.'

There was spontaneous punching of the air accompanied by not quite silent cheers.

'Thank heavens for that. We've been very worried, as you can imagine. Can you tell us more?'

'Callum has been awake and having rather a tough time vomiting, as one would expect. He needs a good night's sleep and, all being well, should be able to come home tomorrow, maybe late morning.'

'Is there a chance he might ring us this evening? We would really love to speak to him and reassure him we are here.' I wanted to say more, how much we loved him, how thankful we were that his brothers found him in time, but I guessed she would know that.

'I'm afraid it's unlikely as he's sedated and probably will sleep right through, the best possible thing for him.'

Although disappointed, I mustered a cheerful response, thanked her and repeated our plan to call mid-morning. Call ended, I turned to William.

'So....' I left the obvious unsaid. 'We might as well have a quiet evening.'

Angus and Bruce decided to go up to their rooms, giving us quick pecks as they left. 'See you in the morning.' 'Sleep well.'

'You too,' I responded. 'Shall we finish the programme?' I asked William.

'Might as well, then an early night. It's been one hell of a day and we want to be in good shape and humour for Cal tomorrow.'

We settled back in the sofa to watch the remainder of Blue Planet, and an episode of University Challenge which William loved even though the subjects were often too obscure for us to know the answers. That over, we caught the weather forecast which boded ill for the next day, then retired to bed.

'I'm actually going to take a half sleeping pill,' I confessed to William. 'My head is so full of worries about Cal and how we're going to be able to help him, I don't want to risk not sleeping well.'

'Good idea,' William responded. 'I'll have the other half.'

In bed, too tense for more than a close cuddle, we read for a short while until the pills took effect.

We were woken in the morning by rain battering the window. I crawled out of bed to look. The weather had certainly changed: dark grey clouds hung heavy over us, and wind was lashing the trees which swayed with its force. I could see debris in the street, twigs and even small branches littering the tarmac.

'Well, they did warn us,' said William, rubbing the sleep from his eyes.

'Let's hope it doesn't last long. It's not exactly cheering weather for Callum's recovery.'

'I doubt very much he'll be fussed about the weather,' replied William.

I nodded. 'I guess you're right, but let's hope we can park near the entrance when we go to fetch him.' I paused. 'That's assuming he really is well enough to come home.'

'We have to believe he will be. Come on, let's go down for breakfast. I fancy toast with that delicious marmalade you made this winter.' William swung his legs out of the bed and reached for his dressing gown.

I took some sliced bread from the freezer for the toast and made coffee while William laid the table. Desultorily reading the news on our iPads as we ate, our heads lifted suddenly as the landline rang. 'It'll be Fiona again,' I said as I picked up. 'She'll want to know when we're coming back.'

'Good morning,' I said cheerfully, wiping my mouth on my napkin.

My jaw dropped and my eyes filled as I heard a croaking 'Hello Mum.'

'Darling! Oh, how wonderful to hear you!' I switched to speakerphone as William came to stand close. 'We've been so worried. How do you feel? Vomiting stopped? Can you come home today?'

There was a pause, then 'Mrs Trenchard?'

'Yes.'

'I'm Nurse Henry and I've taken over from Belle who you spoke to last night. I'm happy to tell you Callum slept right through the night and, although he's still rather weak, he was very keen to tell you himself he's okay. He still finds talking a bit hard after all that vomiting but was insistent, so I lent him my phone.'

'That's really kind. Please, may we speak to him, just for a moment?'

'Yes, of course. I'll give him the phone again.'

William and I began to speak simultaneously but I stopped and let him take over.

'Hi Callum, Mum and I are so happy to hear from you. We've been so worried. We love you so much and can't tell you how relieved we are that Angus and Bruce found you and got you to hospital so quickly. We've all been willing you to recover and sending you strength.' William felt me tugging at his sleeve and handed the phone to me.

'Oh, Cal, your call is the most wonderful Sunday morning gift imaginable. We can hardly wait to see you and bring you home; we'll come just as soon as we're told we can. I just have to say as Dad did, we love you very, very much. We'll save any more news until you're home. Please can you give the phone back to Henry now, so we can ask what happens next.'

'Henry here. The doctors will be coming round during the morning, and I'll call you once they're here as it's likely they would want to have a word with you about any further treatment. Do you live far from here?'

I was about to answer when Henry spoke again, and I

could hear him smile. 'Callum just shook his head to say not far which is good. I don't think there's anything more I can tell you right now.'

'Thank you very much, Henry, you've been very kind. Could you give Callum a big hug from us, and tell him we'll bring him home as soon as we're given the word.....'

I was about to hang up when Henry responded. 'I don't think Callum would thank you for a hug just yet, sadly, as his bruises are still very tender, but I'll give it verbally. I hope to see you when you come. Bye.'

William and I sat down again, happiness at the call mixed with sadness at the reminder of Callum's injuries.

'Morning, Mum, morning, Dad. I heard the phone. Any news?'

William filled Bruce in on our exchange with Henry – and Callum – and our plan that we should all go to the hospital when the time came.

'Great, we wouldn't want to be left out.' Bruce helped himself to breakfast.

William and I went to get dressed and came down to find Angus also there.

'Bruce has told me the good news,' he said, looking up smiling. 'We'll be ready when the call comes.'

Now we had to find ways of passing the time until the hospital rang. It was too wet even to go out to deadhead the roses, a mindless but satisfying task, so I made another attempt at my book while William busied himself on his computer but I – and I suspect, William – found it hard to concentrate. Mid-morning, still no call. I made another coffee, indulged in a chocolate biscuit, tried going back to my book, walked round the sitting room, sat and stared out of the window. Finally, I began to think about lunch and went to the kitchen to see what there was. Not much. I would have to shop so, leaning on the counter, I started a list. Distracted by this, I nearly jumped out of my skin when the phone rang just beside me.

'Elizabeth Trenchard.'

'Henry here. Please could you come to get Callum at 12.30. Dr Richards will be here to run through Callum's care and prognosis.'

'Of course,' I replied. 'Thank you, we'll be there at 12.30.'

'Good. I'll be there too in case you have other questions. Good-bye for now.'

'Bye.' I hung up and told the others, lunch receding into unimportance. Thinking Callum's clothes might have been damaged in the fight, I took a bag up to his room and put in his tracksuit, a light sweater and clean underwear.

When we arrived at the hospital, hearts full and hopes high, the rain had stopped and a faint sun glimmered through the remaining clouds. A good omen, I felt. We announced ourselves at reception, then hovered by the desk looking hopefully along the corridor, not sure who we would see first.

We had only been there a few minutes when a young male nurse approached and, smiling warmly, introduced himself as Henry. We all shook hands then walked with him along the corridor as he explained that we would see Callum first, then he would help Callum get dressed while we met with Dr Richards.

Pausing at a door, he turned to us:

'Please be easy on him, no hugs, not too much excitement. He's still quite frail. I think just two at a time, please, maybe parents first.'

Sobered, we stood back as he held the door open for us, saying, 'Your family are here, Callum. Ready?'

William and I stepped inside. In spite of the warning, we were shocked as we took in our son, his swollen face, one side almost black, the awkward way he was sitting holding his arms out towards us. Approaching the bed, I could see tears rolling down his cheeks and I couldn't hold back tears of my own as I leant over him and kissed the top of his head while William held his hand.

'We love you so much, Cal,' I whispered. 'We're here to take you home and help you through this.'

William nodded and added, 'There's no need to talk now, just let us help you back to strength.'

I was very conscious of Angus and Bruce waiting impatiently outside. 'Your brothers are here too, they were determined not to be left out. Dad and I will swap places then we'll go to see the doctor while you get dressed. I've brought clean things.' I put the bag down beside the bed and we stepped outside as the boys went in.

I hadn't stopped to think what their reaction would be, so I was surprised to hear, 'You idiot, Cal, why didn't you tell us? We might have been able to help.' And 'If we see the buggers who did this to you, we'll give them a lesson they won't forget.' In spite of the strong words, their voices were choked with emotion.

Chapter Twenty Five

Without waiting for the boys, William and I returned to the reception desk and told the young woman we were expecting to meet a doctor to hear about Callum's treatment and outlook. We had only been waiting a couple of minutes when we were approached by a young man, who introduced himself as Dr Richards and invited us to sit down. We were joined almost immediately by Angus and Bruce. The four of us listened carefully as the doctor ran briefly through the treatment they had administered and the outcome.

'The x-rays and scan we've done show no serious damage.' Dr Richards reassured us. 'But the bruising is quite severe, and it will be a few days before Callum is up to full strength. He shouldn't suffer any long-term effects, at least physically. But,' Dr Richards paused, 'things must have been bad for him to try to kill himself. Do you have any idea what might have brought him to that point, or know anything about what was clearly quite a serious attack?'

Bruce spoke first. 'Not really, but he's been a bit strange the past few weeks, sort of distant, much less chatty than usual.'

Angus nodded in agreement. 'He was very excited about his new girlfriend, showed us, well Bruce and me, photos on his phone but he's not mentioned her recently. Maybe that's got something to do with it.'

Angus's mention of the photographs reminded me of how odd Callum had been then, not wanting me to see, just showing me pictures of Sophia's family home instead.

I added what I knew. 'But he has been seeing her, I know, because she – or her family – lent him some money when he lost his wallet, and he met her in town not long ago when she gave him a replacement phone. He's been coming home late, too.' I didn't want to mention our suspicion about his possible involvement in drugs. I felt we should get more from Callum himself before going down that path.

'Can you add anything, Mr Trenchard?'

William shook his head. 'No, sadly not. I'm hoping that he'll soon be well enough to come up to Scotland with us, well away from whatever the problem is. Maybe he'll relax then, perhaps feel safe to tell us more.'

'I certainly hope so,' said Dr Richards, 'but please don't hesitate to get professional advice if he still seems withdrawn and unhappy. Did the nurse give you our leaflet on where to get help?'

'Yes, she did, 'I responded. 'When do you think it will be okay for him to travel? We will be staying with my sister and brother-in-law in Inverness. He's a doctor, a GP, so hopefully will be able to give us some support too – that is, if Callum allows us to confide in him.'

'With luck, maybe as soon as Tuesday. Will you drive, fly, or take the train?'

'Definitely not drive,' said William. 'I imagine there's no medical reason why we should choose train over plane, or vice versa?'

'No, entirely up to you – and Callum. If you've no further questions, I think you can safely take him home now, but do be gentle with him, not too many questions, and it will be a while before he joins you on the tennis court.' Dr Richards smiled at Bruce and Angus. 'I think the change of scene is an excellent idea and hope you have as good a holiday as possible in the circumstances.' He stood up and shook hands with us all.

We thanked him warmly for his reassurance, before returning down the corridor to Callum's room and knocking on his door. Henry opened it and we were delighted to see Callum dressed and sitting in the chair by his bed.

'All ready to go,' said Henry, holding out the bag I had brought. 'Here's the clothes he came in.' He turned to Callum. 'It's been nice meeting you, and I hope whatever has been troubling you so badly will one day be a distant memory.'

'Thanks,' croaked Callum, climbing gingerly out of the chair and making his way slowly to us while we resisted the longing to clasp him to us in big bear hugs.

Angus put his arm gently round Callum's shoulder and steadied him as we made our way to the car, fortunately parked very close to the hospital entrance.

We eased Callum into the front passenger seat, and I sat in the back between the boys. William drove the short distance home, careful on the bends and not using the car's power to forge ahead at the traffic lights. We didn't talk much, just repeated how pleased we were to have him coming home. Then I had a sudden thought.

'We've nothing at all at home for lunch,' I confessed. 'We'll have to do a bit of shopping once we get home. Are you hungry Cal? Can you eat normally or is your throat too tender? I could get some soup if it is.'

'I don't know,' Callum admitted, but I don't think I had any breakfast. I was a bit woozy so don't really remember.'

'Well, once we've got you settled at home, I'll pop round to the supermarket and get soup, and bread and cheese. That should keep us going. We can think about supper later.' I didn't fancy a takeaway supper and hoped inspiration would strike.

'We're nearly at the deli, it's open. Why don't I hop out and get stuff, be very quick. It's Sunday so no parking restrictions, and it'll be less busy than the supermarket,' Angus suggested.

'Good idea, got money?' William replied, slowing down.

'Yup. Bread, cheese, soup no prob.' Angus, sitting on the pavement side, was able to slide out quickly as the car stopped. He disappeared into the shop and emerged five minutes later with a plastic bag from which a baguette poked and, as he climbed back into the car, a distinctly French cheese smell emanated.

'Well done, m'lad. I'll settle up when we get back.' William started the car.

At the house, we helped Callum out of the car and, having ascertained he didn't want to go to bed, settled him on the sofa in the sitting room. I took the shopping to the kitchen and put the soup to warm. When I returned to the sitting room, I was surprised to see Bruce taking a photo of Callum's face.

I heard him say, 'Lucky you're not a hairy type, you don't want to look in a mirror for a day or two as you're a right mess, but later you'll maybe want to see what you looked like in your prime.' It was said with a smile and once again I admired the boys' closeness and care for each other. Okay, they had had their spats – and fights – when younger, and occasionally driven me mad with their bickering, but now they were a remarkable trio, only disturbed by Callum's recent change.

I reminded them of the time I had tripped on a broken paving stone and fallen on flat on my face. 'I looked awful for a couple of days, remember? But it was extraordinary how quickly the black eye faded, and even the bruising and swelling were soon barely noticeable. Sunglasses were a great disguise too.' I hoped that might reassure Callum that he didn't have to hide away. 'Lunch is ready, so let's eat.'

Bruce helped Callum off the sofa, and we all sat down to eat. I poured some soup for Callum and cut the crust off a slice of baguette so it would be easier for him to eat.

'Bon appetit' seemed appropriate given the food, and we helped ourselves. Callum approached the soup with caution, but after a couple of sips, grew braver.

'I am hungry,' he said smiling for the first time since we had picked him up from the hospital.

We relaxed a little, but still avoided the topic uppermost in our minds.

Lunch over, Callum confessed he was tired, so I helped him up to his room. As I tucked his duvet round him, he yelped.

'Sorry!' I apologised. 'You'll need to tell us where to be careful. Let's not talk about it now, but we do hope you'll feel able to tell us more tomorrow so we can understand better and maybe even help.' I kissed his forehead and left the room, not waiting for an answer.

Back downstairs, life returned almost to a normal Sunday. Angus and Bruce went up to their rooms, William and I settled down with coffee to read the news and, perhaps not surprisingly after the stress and the travelling, dozed off for a short while.

Around four, I announced that I would go shopping for supper.

'Why don't I come with you,' said William. 'I feel the need of some fresh air and exercise, and the sun is shining.

I really welcomed his suggestion and, armed with shopping bags, we set off hand in hand – not something we often did, but it felt right that day. As we walked the fifteen minutes to the supermarket, we discussed what to tell my sister, and, given Callum was unlikely to be strong enough to travel next day, whether we should all stay behind with him. We failed to come to any decision, knew we had to ask the boys. Would Callum prefer his brothers to stay with him, or me? Or his dad?

As we went into the supermarket, William surprised me with an unexpected offer: 'It may be many years since I was a student and then lived in a bachelor flat, but I do remember how to cook spag bol. Let me do that tonight, I'll get what I need.'

I accepted gratefully, and cheated for dessert by buying frozen profiteroles with chocolate sauce which I knew they all loved. We bought what we needed for breakfast and were out of the shop and home before we had even been missed.

I phoned my sister, again avoiding any details, apologising that we still weren't sure when we could return to Inverness, and warning we might not all come at the same time. She was very understanding, intuited that perhaps she shouldn't press for more information. I promised to ring again as soon as we'd made a decision.

It may have been the smell of onions frying that brought Angus and Bruce downstairs. They were very cheerful, said they'd peeked in at Callum, seen he was awake and sat with him for a while.

'Did he say anything about the suicide or attack?' I asked.

'No, and we didn't push him at all. He still seemed quite frail and didn't talk much, though he seemed reasonably together. We got him a glass of water and he said he was hungry again.' Bruce smiled.

'Well, why don't you see if he'll come down soon and we

can sit together for a while before supper. I can tell you more about my time with Sir Hamish.'

I don't know whether it was that or the thought of William's spag bol which made Callum decide to come down almost straightaway, but we had a convivial evening, with Callum getting noticeably brighter as time went on. He sensibly decided to go to bed early and requested a couple of paracetamol to lessen the pain from the bruising. When I went up to say goodnight, I ventured to ask him more about it and he showed me the cuts and bruises on his calves and back. Whoever had attacked him had clearly been quite brutal, and one at least had worn heavy shoes. I didn't question him more but gently kissed him goodnight.

'You'll probably already be feeling a bit better by tomorrow morning and we can talk about going back to Inverness then. 'Night, darling.'

'Night, Mum. And sorry.'

Chapter Twenty Six

Next morning, I was putting out the breakfast things when Callum appeared. I tried hard not to react to the sight of his poor face, swollen and with big purple bruises round his eyes.

'Morning, sweetheart. Feeling a bit better?' I said as gave him a very gentle hug.

'A bit. But I am hungry.' He smiled a rather wan smile.

'Good, muesli as usual?

As Callum began to eat, I sat down beside him, wondering how to begin with the many questions we had and the decisions we needed to make. I wanted to ask before the others joined us and started chatting. I decided to come straight to the point.

'You must realise how devastated we were by finding you had tried to kill yourself. We had had no idea you were in such trouble. I – we - understand you may not want to talk about it now, though we hope that before long you'll be able to tell us what brought you to such a terrible point. But right now, we have to decide what to do about our holiday in Inverness.'

Callum kept his eyes on his plate.

'Dad and I thought that you might want to get away from whatever has troubled you so badly and that maybe going up to Inverness as we had planned would be a good way. We just told Uncle John and Aunt Fiona that you'd been involved in a fight and were so badly hurt you had to go to hospital, nothing else, so your injuries wouldn't be a surprise. What do you think?' I held my breath waiting for Callum's response. Had I spoken too soon?

Without looking up at me, Callum muttered, 'Maybe

that's a good idea, if you promise not to tell them anything more without discussing it with me first.'

I breathed a sigh of relief that he hadn't closed the door on the plan.

'Of course, I promise,' I replied, though I would dearly have liked to have my sister's, and especially John's, insight in how to cope with such a traumatised son. 'We must leave it to you how much you are willing to share with them. Remember, Uncle John is a GP and may be able to help in ways that we can't.'

Callum nodded non-committally.

'The next thing is when do we go, and that depends on how you feel. We don't all have to travel together if you don't feel up to it yet; Angus and Bruce could go ahead, Dad too as he needs his holiday. And when you are ready, we could fly or go by train, whichever you think would be more comfortable for you.'

At that moment William came into the kitchen. I smiled up at him. 'Morning, darling. Sleep well?'

'Like a log. Thanks for getting up so quietly, I didn't hear a thing. Morning, Callum, good to see you up.'

'Hi Dad.' Callum turned back to look at me. 'Mum and I were just talking about us all going up to Inverness. I think it's a good idea. How about tomorrow?'

I almost spilt my coffee in my surprise, rejoicing inwardly at his decision. 'That's great darling, but are you sure you'll be okay by then?' I wanted to make sure he didn't feel pressurised.

'Mmmm, I think so, and if we fly it won't be too tiring.'

'That's wonderful, Cal, I'll get onto flights right away.' William beamed. 'Shall we all go together? Maybe better wait to book until Angus and Bruce come down. They may have views, though I suspect they'll say all together, brotherly solidarity and all that.' He grinned at Angus and Bruce who just then arrived for breakfast.

As predicted, the boys elected to travel en famille and William set about finding a suitable flight with enough seats. Once again, I thanked our lucky stars that we could afford all this.

William returned to say that there was a flight from Luton at about 2pm with enough seats for us all. 'There is one at 9.30 but it would mean leaving home soon after six which is too early, I think. Do you agree?' His view was reinforced by the emphatic nods from all three boys – and me.

When the boys returned to their rooms, William and I sighed with relief that it had been so straightforward. But then a thought struck me with uncomfortable force.

'Were we negligent not to check on Callum in the night? Just suppose he was in pain – or had even tried again...' I didn't need to go on.

William looked at me, a worried frown on his forehead. 'Oh, dear, how thoughtless of us, what a stupid risk to have taken. Still, he did seem more or less okay at supper, and now he's agreed to come to Inverness, I think we can hope the immediate crisis is over. Since we're definitely here all day, I'll go and book that flight, then call the office. I might use Callum's drama – the fight, that is - to suggest a couple days more holiday. George was very easy on my taking time off, if you remember. Then I'll catch up on emails. Is that okay?'

'Of course,' I replied. 'I'll call Fi first to tell her to expect us about teatime tomorrow afternoon, then I might call my office, find out how Dave's getting on with the research for Hamish, see if I can be spared for an extra day or two. Apart from that, there's just food shopping to do, so an easy day, time to sit with Callum if he feels like company.'

'Angus and Bruce will need to get back to Edinburgh for their jobs in about a week, but if we do have more time and Callum is happy to stay with Fi and his cousins, and if they're happy to have him, maybe I could spirit you off to a nice hotel for a short break, just the two of us.' This was said with a distinct twinkle.

'Lovely idea,' I replied, 'but let's not think about it now, too many ifs.'

We went to our study to make our calls but I went to Callum's room first.

'Alright darling? Here's some more paracetamol in case you need it, and also a bruise pain reliever the chemist recommended for me once. Anything else you want?'

Callum, propped against his pillows, looked up from his book and shook his head. 'I'm okay, thanks.'

'Reading anything special?' I was genuinely curious to know.

'It's the first of the Master and Commander novels; a friend said they're really good.'

'Yes, they are, and fun, I remember, though it's a while since I read them. I found them quite addictive – and an easy way of learning a bit of history. Just come and find me if you feel like some company, I'll be in the study.' I left his door open, remembering we should be a little vigilant, though I thought William was right, that the crisis was over.

My first phone call was to my sister, reassuring her that Callum, though quite badly hurt, was on the mend already, and gave her the good news that we would be back with them the next afternoon.

I then spoke to Dave who reassured me that he would be fine with his research. 'I only got back to the office this morning, remember!'

That hadn't registered; it felt like a lifetime since I had left him at Inverness station on Friday, just three days ago. 'OK, but you can call me on my mobile if you want to discuss anything.' I didn't say I was in London.

'Thanks. Enjoy your holiday. Remember me to Hamish and Ailsa if you're in touch with them, tell them how much I enjoyed meeting them and that I've started working on the turbine possibilities.'

'Will do, bye.'

The day passed quietly. I did the shopping then a bit of gardening, watering the tubs and dead-heading the roses. I was relaxing with a coffee when William came in beaming again.

'A bit of good news! Going through my emails from the end of last week I found one from your mad professor saying he would be in London this week and was there a chance of meeting up to discuss investors for his battery project. I called him back and we're going to have a preliminary meeting at my office this afternoon.'

'That's great – but do remember not to call him a mad professor in public! Michael clearly has a sense of humour, but the origin of mad professor might take a bit of explaining to others.' I laughed. 'Anything else of note?'

'Not of interest to you except that after I spoke to George about meeting with Michael, I mentioned the couple of extra days holiday. He was very sympathetic about Callum's injuries and quite happy for me to take the time off. I've also booked a car from Inverness airport, we can't expect John and Fi to drive us everywhere, and anyway, we wouldn't all fit in one car and John will need his to get to work.'

'Good thinking about the car. One o'clock lunch okay? Could you give the boys a shout then, please.'

'Will do.' William disappeared upstairs again. Just before one I heard the requested call for lunch followed by the chatter of the boys as they came down to eat with us.

William declined a post lunch coffee, saying he would have some at the office. I waved him off with strict injunctions to remember me to Michael and to say we'd invite him round again when we were back from Scotland, if he'd like to come. After organising a taxi to the airport for us all the following morning, I sat with Callum for a bit while Angus and Bruce went for a game of tennis, saying they needed to get some fresh air and exercise after so much tension and sitting around. I heartily agreed and suggested they get rid of some of the stress by giving the balls a good bashing.

That evening, as William and I enjoyed our usual glass of wine before supper, he filled me in on his meeting with Michael.

'It was a very useful afternoon,' said William. 'I introduced him to George who was very encouraging, then Michael and I had a separate meeting with a couple of the more techie investment gurus who were intrigued and hopeful we could help him get the necessary investment to get his batteries to the next stage and into production if all goes well. I don't pretend to understand the science but with my and the techies' connections, I'm very hopeful we can help him take the next step. One big question is patenting, and I've arranged for him to talk to one of our specialists.'

'Well done, darling, very satisfactory use of an unexpected afternoon. I've really nothing to report except I've ordered a taxi for 11 tomorrow. We can snatch a bite of lunch at the airport. There's hardly any packing to be done, just Callum's things and I'll help him with that in the morning.'

Over supper Angus and Bruce had us all laughing, even

Callum, regaling us with stories of their afternoon at the tennis club. They'd played a few games of singles before joining another couple of lads for a doubles match in which many balls left the court, a few windows were narrowly missed, and various bits of anatomy (on both sides of the net) were likely to show bruises next day.

Tuesday morning the sun was shining strongly as we left for the airport. Callum's baseball cap and sunglasses were remarkably appropriate for the weather, disguising his face well, and no eyebrows were raised that we noticed at the airport - or even on the plane where he kept his head lowered over his book. As we had no checked luggage, we were out of the airport at Inverness very quickly, picking up the rental car with no problems.

I called Fiona from the car and, as we drew up outside the house, a reception committee poured out; everyone was there except John who was at his practice. There were hugs all round and exclamations of delight at having us back so soon, but no yelps of pain from Callum. Fi must have warned the cousins to be gentle with him. As soon as we were in the house, however, they insisted he remove his cap and glasses, eliciting both horror and sympathy.

'It's not really warm enough to sit outside so let's go indoors and relax with a tea or coffee and whatever the boys would like. Callum, are you up for sitting with us, or would you like to go to your room for a rest?' said my ever-thoughtful sister.

Callum elected to retreat upstairs, his bag carried by Damian, his oldest cousin. I followed to see him settled, my heart saddened to see the care he took at each step.

'Do you think you'll come down for lunch?' I asked. Callum nodded, clearly keen to avoid any questions, leaving me to fill the family in with such details as I was allowed to reveal.

Chapter Twenty Seven

I rejoined the family in the sitting room where Fi was pouring tea and Lucy was cutting slices of chocolate cake. Fi and the cousins waited for us to raise the topic surely uppermost in their minds, sticking to anodyne subjects: how was the journey, is the car okay? However, I knew we couldn't put off the questions for ever, so took the opportunity of Damian's return downstairs to raise Callum's injuries.

'Did Callum tell you much?' I asked Damian, smiling to make light of the question.

'No, nothing really, said he was tired and wanted to rest. I asked if he needed anything, painkillers or whatever, but he said no, only a glass of water, and just sort of clammed up, closed his eyes, so I fetched a glass from the bathroom and left him to sleep.'

Angus and Bruce looked at me questioningly, but I indicated that William should tell them what we were allowed to say we knew.

'Callum has been very reserved on how he got into this fight, so we can't enlighten you much, I'm afraid. It was on Friday evening. Angus and Bruce had disturbing texts from him, as did we. He was clearly very upset about something, but he didn't say what. Fortunately, Angus and Bruce sensed something was very wrong, rang him and he was almost incoherent. They realised he must have been in a bad way which is why they rushed down from Edinburgh. When they arrived they found how badly hurt he was and got him to hospital. Honestly, that's all we can tell you until Callum fills us in as, so far, he's been reluctant to talk about it.' William gave nothing away.

Frustrated but understanding, my sister turned the conversation to plans for our stay. The proposed dolphin watching plan was approved, and a visit to the extraordinary bookshop in town. I wanted to go to Cawdor Castle as – and Fi confirmed - we were distant relations of the Calder family whose home it had originally been, and which had lovely gardens. The boys pushed for more adventurous trips but understood that might not be possible unless Callum was stronger or didn't mind missing out.

I then outlined my plan to take William and our boys to meet Hamish and Ailsa, if they were happy to have us. It would be a day of beautiful lake and mountain scenery, weather permitting, and an opportunity for a hike on the estate.

'I don't think we could all go,' I said. 'It would be too much of an imposition for all ten of us to descend on them.'

Reluctantly the others agreed, and discussion continued.

'We must have some tennis, we've got spare racquets,' Jamie announced.

'And can we go to the modern dance show at the theatre, please?' added Lucy. 'It's had terrific reviews.'

Angus and Bruce didn't rise to this bait, to her disappointment, but tactfully asked her what else she would like to do.

'Just hang out with you lot,' she laughingly admitted.

'It's still light quite late at this time of year so how about getting some of your girl friends to come us and watch us slug it out on the tennis court one evening and maybe go to a disco after?' Damian clearly knew what would appeal to all youth present.

At that moment, John appeared, greeting us all warmly

and apologising for not having got home earlier.

'A few dramas at the practice this afternoon, a violent altercation in the waiting room, then a call to an attempted suicide. I had to take charge of that one. Tough, a young man – not much older than you lot – cut his wrists, but not fatally. Very sad, we don't yet know why he did it.'

William and I and the boys tried hard not to exchange glances but failed. I suspect Fi and John noticed our discomfort but said nothing.

'I'll go upstairs, freshen up, and ring Sir Hamish. If my plan is okay with them, find which day would be possible, then we can fit everything else round that.' I left the room and went upstairs to our bedroom, vacated in such a hurry on Saturday. After a quick shower and change of clothes, I sat down to ring Hamish.

To my delight, he answered immediately. 'How nice to hear from you so soon. Are you still planning to bring the family to visit?'

What an opening! 'Yes, please, if that's okay with you and Ailsa. We wouldn't impose on you for lunch as we'll be exploring on the way and have lunch in a pub somewhere. Would later this week suit you both?'

There was a pause and I heard Hamish calling to his sister.

'She says how about Friday. Nothing in our diaries.'

'Perfect,' I replied, not having expected it to be quite so easy to arrange. 'Let's say about 2.30. I know William and the boys would love to do a bit of a hike, see where the turbine might be, though Callum got rather badly hurt in a fight last week so he might not be up for it, and I would stay with him.'

'Sorry to hear that, but maybe a little walk will still be on the cards – a shame not to see what this estate is all about. Anyway, I'll check the weather forecast beforehand. I think this cool spell is due to end soon so you should be in luck. Fingers crossed.'

'Thanks so much, Hamish. They're really looking forward to meeting you both.' I didn't mention that telling them Ailsa was drop dead gorgeous and a great cook had predisposed them to the visit. 'Just drop me a text on Thursday to confirm it's all okay. I may even have some news from Dave on the turbine front by Friday. No promises, though.'

'Understood. Until Friday. Bye.'

I repeated my thanks and closed the call. Returning downstairs, I found the cousins had gone into the garden for a game of croquet before dinner. William and John were sitting comfortably with a glass of wine, Fiona was busy in the kitchen. Eschewing a proffered glass of wine, I went to help her. It was so comfortable, working side by side with my sister, such a rare treat. We slipped into family gossip – news of our aunts, cousins, old school friends.

Callum came down in good time for dinner which was dominated by discussion of plans for the rest of our stay. Having two cars, three counting John's, at our disposal meant we didn't all have to do the same thing, so it got quite complicated. It turned out that Damian had passed his driving test a year before and was considered a safe and fairly cautious driver by his parents, so using his mother's car, the youngsters could do some outings without us.

'Sadly, we need to get back to Edinburgh, ideally Sunday evening, latest Monday morning, as we start work Monday evening and there'll probably be some training before then,' Angus and Bruce reminded us. 'Be good to get settled in again and tidy up – we did leave in rather a hurry on Friday.'

Finally, although some decisions were deferred, dolphin watching was decided for us all on Saturday so Angus and

Bruce could be sure of coming and John could join us. Callum, though clearly keen to join his cousins in more lively activities, said please could he defer his decisions until he knew how well his wounds were healing. He did say he would watch the tennis battle, however, and go with them to the disco, even if he couldn't dance.

After dinner, the young disappeared to chat upstairs while we lingered over coffee and John's favourite whisky. I told Fi and John that William had been given an extra couple of days off, but we hadn't decided what to do.

'Lizzie and I could perhaps have a couple of nights away in a nice hotel, not impose on your hospitality too long.' William kept a straight face.

'Don't be silly, it's no trouble, and we see you so seldom,' was the instant response. 'But on the other hand, I can see the attraction.' This time it was John who twinkled. 'No need to decide now – and of course Callum can stay on here if he doesn't want to go to Edinburgh with his brothers or back to London on his own. The kids would be delighted.'

We thanked them warmly before retiring for an early, less troubled, night.

Wednesday dawned drab but dry. John left early for work. William and I decided we would walk to the city, a pleasant stroll through leafy streets then along the river. Fi couldn't join us as she was volunteering at the local hospice that morning, but we agreed to meet for lunch in town. The youth, who had not yet appeared, could please themselves; there was plenty of food in the fridge, fresh bread, eggs, and lovely Scottish cheeses.

'I filled the fruit bowl, too,' said Fi. 'I've got a big casserole ready cooked for tonight and lots of ice cream, so no worries there.'

After so much sitting around, the walk was invigorating. Gardens were full of roses and other colourful summer flowers, the leaves on the trees hadn't yet lost their freshness, and as we reached the river, sporadic sunshine caused the water to sparkle cheerfully. I took William to Leakey's huge second-hand bookshop in the converted church. He was stunned by its scale and rapidly became so immersed in the thousands of books that I feared we would be late for lunch. While he browsed, I bought a large-scale copy of the Ordnance Survey map of the area round Hamish's estate, and another of the route we would be taking along Loch Ness and into the mountains.

We met my sister for lunch as planned then, at her suggestion, William and I went to the art gallery and museum. I had visited the Highlands exhibition many years before, but it was a good introduction to the history and culture for him. Tired feet – and backs – sent us in search of a taxi back to the house in time for tea and more cake. The boys and Lucy were nowhere to be seen so all was peace and quiet. William and I looked in on Callum, but he was missing too. Delighted that he had felt well enough to be out and about with his brothers and cousins, we seized the opportunity for a recuperative snooze.

We were woken by the thud of feet on the stairs and shouts of laughter. Getting up to investigate, we learned that all six of them had gone to the cinema to see a newly released comedy and were happily repeating its jokes in ever odder accents. Callum appeared more muted than the others but had a big grin on his still-bruised face. Angus and Bruce threatened to tell us their favourites over supper. William and I wondered sadly whether we were too old to appreciate the style of humour which would appeal to late teens. No doubt we would be finding out.

John appeared in good time for the pre-prandial glass of wine, and the cousins came down too. He announced he had to change our plans. 'I'm really sorry, but I'm going to have to miss the dolphin outing we'd planned for Saturday, be standing in for one of the other partners who's got to go to a niece's wedding – three line whip apparently. I'll have tomorrow off instead.'

'Well, we could do the dolphins tomorrow, no? Or have you young people got different plans already?' Fiona spoke up immediately.

Heads were shaken, 'No plans, we were going to decide this evening,' said Damian. 'So tomorrow's fine.'

'Thanks, that's marvellous. I would have hated to miss it; it's not just the dolphins, but that lovely huge beach too, great for walking.' John took out his phone. 'Hmm, the weather forecast's not brilliant, but not too bad. Let's take a chance.'

We all agreed and, well satisfied by Fi's casserole and generous helpings of ice cream, we went to bed in happy anticipation.

Chapter Twenty Eight

By ten thirty next morning we were driving in convoy down the narrow road towards the dolphin viewing beach. We parked in the informal grassy car park and unloaded a surprising amount of gear. My sister produced a small hamper; she had clearly been busy.

'Coffee, biscuits and soft drinks,' she said smiling as I raised an eyebrow. 'Could you bring the rugs and groundsheet, please, boys.'

Jamie had brought two kites and, laden, we made our way down to the stony beach.

We were glad John had warned us it might be chilly and to bring anoraks and sweaters as, turning past the white-painted lighthouse, the strong wind hit us full on, chilled as if it had come straight from the Arctic. I had been dolphin watching here as a child, so recognised the long beach with its strips of yellow sand by the water's edge and close to the small dunes behind, but was newly impressed by the huge curve of the Firth, opening out into the North Sea. There were piles of kelp on the sand, stranded by the receding tide and twisted into works of art. Knots of people were dotted along the beach, looking hopefully out to sea.

We made camp on the scratchy grass above the beach, then went for a walk to stretch our legs. There were no dolphins to be seen so, back at the camp, we fortified ourselves from Fi's hamper and watched the boys driving the kites in the strong wind. Lucy was less interested and wandered off, searching the stones for interesting specimens. Suddenly, we heard her shout:

'Dolphins!' She pointed back down the beach.

Sure enough, the knots of people had coalesced into a larger group standing at the water's edge watching a school of dolphins cavorting quite close to the shore. Kites grounded, we all joined them, thrilled and laughing as the dolphins leapt out of the water, landing in big belly-flops or on their backs. Someone threw a child's coloured beach ball into their midst; it was immediately turned into a plaything, nosed from one to another, tossed into the air.

We watched for quite a while before returning to the hamper for more refreshments.

'Time to head back,' said John, pointing at the sky. 'Look at those clouds!'

The previously grey clouds had turned so black they were almost purple, threatening. Wasting no time, we packed up and returned to the cars.

'See you at home,' said Fi as she climbed into the passenger seat beside William to act as navigator. Angus, Bruce and Jamie filled the back seat.

I joined John and the other three in his car. I was interested to see how both Damian and Lucy seemed to have formed protective bonds with Callum. Lucy, as the youngest cousin and the only girl, brought a different dimension to his life and family for which I was very grateful. His life had been very male-dominated, as far as we knew – or had been until Sophia came on the scene.

As it happened, the rain held off and after lunch Lucy went to see friends to round up some for the tennis and dancing evening now set for Saturday. The boys disappeared to do their own thing. Given the next day would be a long and active one, William and I decided on a quiet afternoon. He and John sat on the terrace with their coffee, no doubt to talk over world affairs and, probably, the political landscape. Scotland's mooted independence was still a hot topic.

My sister and I went into town to buy things for dinner that night and the next.

'Although I suspect Ailsa will produce tea tomorrow, we'll have had lots of exercise and fresh air, and the boys will eat like horses.' I laughed. 'On Saturday William and I will take you two out to dinner, no question. The youth will be at tennis and probably the pub before the disco, so it will be just us.'

Fi gave in gracefully. We had time to spare so we wandered around the town centre. After exploring the handsome Victorian market, we dropped into several art galleries and enjoyed the variety of styles on offer. As we browsed, I had a text from Hamish saying the weather forecast for the next day was good, a warm front having driven the rain further north. He suggested a couple of places for lunch on the way to the estate.

Before dinner, which I again happily helped prepare, William and I, with input from Fi and John, planned our excursion, poring over the maps we had bought.

* * *

Friday dawned promisingly bright, the clouds were light, scudding before a stiff breeze. The five of us set off in good heart, stopping whenever we felt like it. As William drove along Loch Ness, we kept a - sceptical - eye out for the Loch Ness monster. I remembered the fun Hamish, Dave and I had had singing in the car the week before: 'Ye'll take the high road, and I'll take the low road, and I'll be in Scotland afore ye' I sang quietly - to myself I thought.

To my surprise, 'I know it,' said Callum from the back

seat, and broke into song, his clear tenor filling the car. It was beautiful and my heart lifted, hoping this was the beginning of his return to his old self. The others didn't know all the words, but when it came to the: 'On the bonnie, bonnie banks of Loch Lomond' a boisterous chorus erupted.

We laughed in pleasure, then resumed our monster watch until we stopped for lunch.

I recognised the turn to the hunting lodge, marked by the barn where Mac had been waiting for us. William drove carefully up the track and parked in front of the lodge. We didn't have to use the old-fashioned bell pull as Hamish emerged from behind the house.

'Heard the car. Welcome,' he said with a wide smile and a warm handshake. 'Great timing.'

He shook hands with William and the boys as I introduced them. I could see they were immediately taken by his relaxed manner, but I noticed the boys casting covert glances at the front door, hoping, I suspect, for their first sight of Ailsa. They didn't have long to wait as she soon emerged, looking just as gorgeous as I had related, her graceful figure set off by a tight-fitting blouse tucked into her jodhpurs.

'Hi,' she said. 'So nice to see you again, Elizabeth, and to meet your family.' She paused, turned to the boys. 'I knew you were triplets, but I'm glad you're not identical or I'd never get right who was which.' She counted them off: 'Angus, Bruce, Callum.'

This broke the ice, and we followed the brother and sister into the house. There wasn't the same expletive-laced reaction to the hunting trophies adorning the walls and window sills by the boys as Dave had had, but their eyes did open wide as they took it all in.

'Can I offer you tea or coffee or something before we set

off for our walk?' Hamish asked. 'The weather is lovely so we should take advantage of it, but there's plenty of time.'

We declined, saying it wasn't long since our lunch and we'd had a drink there.

'If you don't mind, I won't come with you,' said Ailsa. 'As you can see, I've been out with the horse, and I have a few things to do.'

We changed into our walking boots - I had forgotten to bring Callum's from London but Damian had lent him a pair - and set off in the direction of the stream we had first visited, Hamish leading the way.

The weather was indeed glorious, the hills and more distant mountains as alive with colour as they had been on my previous visit. I could sense William drinking it in, and the boys too were clearly impressed. However, by the time we reached the stream, I could see that Callum was tiring. I explained the principle of the vortex hydro scheme we had in mind that Dave was researching which the boys, as engineers and scientists, had no trouble understanding, then suggested that Hamish, William, Angus and Bruce continue to the river.

'Callum and I can sit in the sun on that nice flat rock we passed and admire the view until you come back,' I said, looking meaningfully at William, not wanting to draw too much attention to Callum's weakness.

'Are you sure?' said William. 'I could wait instead then you can explain again at the river.'

'No, the fresh and exercise will do you good, and I had plenty last week. Hamish knows the theory now'. Hamish looked disconcerted but I reassured him: 'You know it's straightforward, you grasped it really well.'

The five of them set off at a brisker pace while Callum and I returned to the rock I had picked out and sat down side by side in comfortable silence, gazing at the view. Instinctively, I put my arm round Callum's shoulders and pulled him gently closer. Rather than relaxing into me, to my consternation he went rigid and pulled away from me, then folded down on himself and burst into body-shaking sobs. I didn't know how to react. After a few seconds, I reached tentatively for his hand.

'It's okay, Callum, it's okay. Hush, I'm here. Tell me if you can.'

But he continued to sob uncontrollably. Then suddenly he sat up, put his arms round my neck like a child and buried his head in my shoulder.

'Oh, Mum, I loved her so much,' he wailed.

Chapter Twenty Nine

I held Callum and stroked his hair as if he were indeed still a child. But the implication of what he had said suddenly made me freeze.

'Oh, Callum, my poor darling. When did it happen? Was it an accident? A car crash?'

He pulled away and looked at me, his face wet and puffy. 'What are you tal....' He paused mid-word and looked away before continuing. 'I don't know, last week sometime. Just got a brief message from her brother, no details.'

'Isn't that a bit strange? He must have known you two were so close.' I was puzzled, though very upset for him.

'Yes. It is strange, but I wonder.... maybe, something odd.... if there...... I don't know.' He began to cry again.

I really didn't know what to say, just held him close. Looking up, I saw Willam, the boys and Hamish appearing round a bend in the track, sooner than I had expected. I alerted Callum, guessing he would be embarrassed to be seen so upset.

'Here come the others. Do you want a tissue to wipe your face?'

He nodded and I took one out of my pocket. As I turned to give it to him, I saw the men were much nearer, close enough for me to see that William was limping badly and was being supported on either side by Bruce and Angus. And even at that distance, to my horror I could see there was blood on his face and on his trousers.

Muttering a quick sorry to Callum, I sprang up and ran towards William.

'What's happened? Are you okay, William? What have you done?' I called, my heart pounding.

William gave a feeble grin. 'I think so,' he said weakly. 'Just tripped over a rock.'

I didn't dare hug him but turned to the boys. 'Tell me, is it serious?'

Before they could answer, Hamish spoke.

'I feel very bad about this, but I didn't know about his Parkinson's, the boys told me after William fell. If I'd been warned, I'd have taken a different path, a smoother one. I'm so sorry.'

'If you didn't know, you're not to blame.' I turned to the boys. 'How could you let Dad .....'

William interrupted. 'No, it's my fault. I've felt so well recently, not had any wobbles, I forgot about being careful. No one else is to blame.'

Callum had joined us by this time, shocked out of his misery by his father's plight.

'Come and sit down here.' Callum pointed at the rock he and I had been sitting on.

Angus and Bruce helped William onto the rock and I sat down beside him, taking his hand.

'Are you really alright? Did you hit your head badly? Is anything broken?'

'I think – hope – it looks worse than it is.' William attempted another smile. 'I've certainly twisted my ankle and managed to gouge my knee, even through the trousers, as you can see.' He pulled up his trouser leg to reveal a long gash, still oozing blood, and an already swollen ankle.

'But your head, did you hit it hard?'

Hamish answered for him. 'I saw him fall and I think it was only a glancing blow on a sharp rock as he slipped to the ground.'

'If you're sure, that's a relief, otherwise we should get William to hospital for a scan in case there's bleeding on the brain.' I was really worried by the prospect and turned back to William. 'Did you lose consciousness?'

'No, I promise you I didn't. I honestly think the damage is pretty superficial, though the ankle may be a problem for a while.'

At this point Angus laughed to confirm William's view. 'If you'd heard his scream, you'd have known he wasn't unconscious!'

This lightened the mood somewhat. Hamish got out his phone. 'We walked up from the house, but I think William should get a ride back. I'll call Mac to come up with the Landrover to collect him. The rest of you can walk as it would be a squash for all of us - you boys are not exactly small!'

'That's kind of you,' I said,' but I think Callum and I should ride too if you're happy to guide Angus and Bruce home.'

'No problem. I'll call Ailsa to get the first aid kit out. She's pretty good, took a course so she could cope with visitors' mishaps.' He made both calls while William and I sat on the rock and the three boys wandered off to explore a bit more.

'Don't go far,' Hamish cautioned. 'Mac won't be long.'

They nodded acceptance before disappearing in the direction of the burn.

'I'm so sorry to be such a nuisance.' William was clearly embarrassed at disrupting the afternoon's expedition. 'But I think the ride back is needed, this ankle is very painful.'

'Do you think it might be broken?' I asked Hamish, thinking we might need a hospital visit after all.

'I doubt it, but Ailsa will probably be able to tell us.'

The three of us waited in silence, digesting the turn of events. It wasn't long before we heard an approaching engine. Hamish called out to the boys who returned just as the Landrover came into sight. Hamish and the boys manhandled William into the back seat, not an easy feat as the step was high and there was a hefty lift required to get him comfortably onto the seat. I climbed in beside him and Callum sat next to Mac.

'Lucky Hamish rang when he did,' said Mac. 'I was about to drive to the agricultural supply store, wouldn't have been back for at least an hour.'

He drove gently down the rough track and deposited us by the front door where Ailsa was waiting, clearly having been listening for our arrival. Mac, Callum and I helped William slide down, easier than getting him in but it still caused several yelps of pain. To our surprise, Ailsa had brought out a sturdy wooden chair with arms.

'Mac, please could you help William to sit and between us we'll carry him into the kitchen.'

We must have been an odd sight, and William laughed saying he felt like some sort of pasha but without the rich drapes and clothes to complete the picture. The kitchen safely reached, Mac made his farewells and wished William a good recovery.

Ailsa disappeared briefly, returning with a padded stool onto which she gently lifted William's leg. Callum and I watched nervously.

'Your trousers are very torn but I'm afraid I may have to make it worse to dress the wound and look at your ankle properly. Is that alright? I would offer you a pair of Hamish's but I fear they wouldn't fit.' Ailsa said this with a smile to soften the obvious difference in girth between William and Hamish.

'Go ahead,' said William. 'In fact, if it helps, cut that trouser leg off above the knee. They won't be any good in the future, and I do have another pair back in Inverness.'

Taking him at his word, Ailsa opened her first aid box and took out a large pair of scissors which she expertly wielded to reveal the full extent of both the wound and the swelling. 'I'll clean the cut first and put some antiseptic on before I dress it. It'll sting like hell but I must do it.'

She was as good as her word, and we winced involuntarily as William failed to suppress a tortured 'Ow!'

'I think this may need a few stitches; is there a GP surgery you can go to? Actually, hospital might be better.'

I explained that my brother-in-law whom we were staying with was a GP and would certainly be able either to stitch it himself, or get it done promptly at the surgery or hospital.

Cleaning and dressing completed, Ailsa turned her attention to his face. 'I think this is very superficial, fortunately, mainly a scrape though there will be some bruising. I'll just clean it up.'

William's 'ow' was more restrained this time.

'Now let's look at your ankle. I'll be as gentle as I can, but I need to see if it's broken or just a bad strain.' She lifted his leg at the calf. 'Can you move your foot?'

William obediently wiggled his foot, grimacing. 'Seems to work,' he said in relief. 'But it does hurt quite a lot.'

'I think you should get it X-rayed, just in case. I'll bandage your ankle firmly for now, but please be very careful until, hopefully, you've been given the all-clear.'

'Are you really okay, William?' I asked. 'You're very pale.'

'I admit I do feel a bit wobbly, a bit faint.'

'It's probably the shock,' Ailsa reassured him. 'Callum, please could you fill the kettle and put it on.' She indicated the big kettle on the Aga. 'I know it's a bit of a cliché, but a good strong cup of tea can work wonders.' She carried on with the bandaging.

As Callum busied himself with his task, we heard footsteps and voices. Hamish came in, followed by Bruce and Angus. Ailsa responded reassuringly to their anxious questions then enlisted Hamish's help.

'Please can you get out the tea things. The cakes and scones are in the larder. I've just about finished so I'll make the tea.'

'Is there anything I can do to help?' I asked, feeling a bit fifth wheel-ish.

'Not really, thanks, except maybe you could set the table when Hamish has brought everything, then sit down and relax.'

Angus and Bruce had been cast admiring looks at the lovely Ailsa but were soon diverted by the appearance of a large sponge cake oozing jam, and an almost as big chocolate cake. Hamish popped the scones into the microwave for a few seconds before adding them to the feast on the table.

'Tuck in, boys,' he said with a grin. 'But first help me move your father to a better position so he can reach the table.'

In spite of the accident, it was a happy feast and the boys chatted away between mouthfuls.

I looked at my watch.

'Heavens, it's nearly five o'clock. We're going to be late back to my sister's. I'd better ring to alert her.' I stepped outside and called Fi, explaining briefly what had happened. 'Will John be home to advise us when we get back, probably about seven, all being well? Or should we go straight to A&E?' She said to come home first as John would be there and was best placed to decide what we should do.

Returning to the kitchen, I reported on Fi's advice. 'I really think we should be off very soon as it's quite a drive. I'm really sorry we've caused such disruption, and we're hugely grateful to you both for all your help.'

'And for the tea,' Bruce spoke for all of us. 'It was really wonderful. In fact, I might ask if I can come and have cooking lessons from you, Ailsa!'

Angus looked as if he wished he had thought of it too; the idea of a beautiful young woman teaching them cake-making was enticing. Ailsa laughed but looked pleased, an expression noted hopefully by the boys.

We made our farewells, with hugs and repeated thanks. We got William into the passenger seat of the car without too much difficulty, and I took the wheel. At the last minute, I remembered the vortex research. I wound down my window.

'I'll be in contact as soon as we have the results of Dave's research,' I called to Hamish before putting the car in gear and setting off to an accompaniment of enthusiastic waves from the boys and our hosts.

CHAPTER THIRTY

I was very glad the traffic was light as I drove back to Inverness, my head was so full of worries about William and Callum. The boys in the back chatted for a bit then turned to their phones. William very soon closed his eyes and seemed to be asleep. In fact, he was so quiet I became worried and reached across to prod him lightly and was reassured by a slight grunt.

Nearing the city, I called to the back seat to ask one of the boys to ring my sister and say that, barring heavy Friday evening city traffic, we would be back in about half an hour, but we were lucky and made it to the house before seven. William had woken by then and the boys helped him out and to the house, Angus and Bruce again supporting him as he made his way painfully to the front door. Callum had already reached the house and rung the doorbell, John and Fi emerging almost immediately.

'Oh, poor William, what bad luck,' said Fi as she led the way inside while John came up to me.

'How did it happen? Fi didn't have any details.'

'He, Bruce and Angus went with Hamish to look at the river which might be a site for electricity generation. William says he forgot to be careful as he'd not had any serious Parkinsons symptoms for a while, but he slipped or tripped on the stones. I don't know any more than that myself. Hamish's manager drove up to us with the Landrover - not easy to get an injured man into a Landrover, we discovered! Ailsa - Hamish's sister who had done first aid training – cleaned him up. She seemed very competent but said she thought his leg needed stitches and, as he had banged his head, maybe he should have a scan. I explained you were a GP and would know best what to do.'

'Come inside and let me examine him, then we can decide what's needed.' John tuned to the slow-moving trio. 'Let's go to the kitchen, the light's very good there.'

Fi and John's three had joined the procession by then, trying to hide their amusement at William's truncated trousers, and followed us into the kitchen. It was very crowded as all nine of us gathered round William who had been installed in a chair by the big glass door to the garden.

'I think you should all – except Elizabeth - wait in the sitting room or the garden while I have a look at William. Oh, and Fi, maybe you could offer tea or something.'

All six cousins left the kitchen followed by Fi whom I could hear taking orders for drinks. When she came back, she suggested that, in the circumstances, something stronger might be in order for us adults. 'Is it okay for William to have alcohol right now?' she asked John, who nodded.

'Yes, indeed, a neat whisky would be a good stimulant,' he laughed before turning his attention to William. 'Headache? Nausea? Dizzy? Pain?'

'I did feel very shaky for a while,' Willam admitted, 'and I slept most of the way here, according to Lizzie, though I don't remember. My ankle and leg are certainly painful; I can't put any weight on that side.'

John produced a stethoscope and medical torch. 'Fi called me at the surgery just before I left,' John explained as he looked into William's eyes and checked his pulse and heart. 'Certainly nothing obviously wrong there, though the heartbeat's a little bit erratic, but we should still take to you the hospital; it's always good practice to have a brain scan as soon as possible after such a fall. And I'm sure you should have that leg X-rayed.'

'I can drive him, if someone helps me get him into the car,' I volunteered.

John immediately overrode me. 'No, I will. They know me well there – I sit on a couple of their committees – so I can pull a string or two to avoid the usual triage. And the sooner we go the better as later A&E will fill up with drunken Friday night brawlers.' He grinned ruefully. 'When will they learn!'

'But what about dinner?' said Fi as she handed the three of us whiskies.

'Honestly, William and I are fine as Ailsa and Hamish produced a huge tea before we left, though I dare say the boys' capacity is undented. But I'll come with you to the hospital, John.'

'Then bring something to read, as even I can't guarantee instant treatment. And although the X-ray will show an immediate result, they'll probably want to put a cast on if there's a serious break, and we may have to wait a bit for the result of the scan.'

As I left the kitchen, John added quietly: 'Might be a good idea to pack some night things and washbag, just in case – and maybe another pair of trousers too.'

My heart sank, but I knew it was sensible advice.

When we arrived at the hospital, I went to the reception desk to request a wheelchair. A porter arrived quickly and took us to A&E where John disappeared into an office while we waited in the reception area which, fortunately, was not yet busy as John had predicted. John emerged smiling after a few minutes.

'All set for the scan and Xray.' But then, 'Are you okay, William? You look very pale.'

To my shame, I hadn't noticed.

'I do feel a bit odd,' William admitted. 'Not sure if it's still the shock, maybe it's the whisky!' He attempted a grin.

Another porter arrived to wheel William to the imaging department. John and I followed and sat in the chairs outside. He turned to me.

'I'm going to suggest they take William in at least overnight. I know they've got free beds at the moment, and although I doubt there's anything serious wrong, I would just feel happier if he was being monitored.'

I had to agree it was a wise precaution, though I feared it might be because John suspected more damage than he had suggested.

'Give me the overnight things – and the book – and once William comes out from the scan, say good night and get a taxi back to the house. I'll wait until I know what's happening.'

I remonstrated, but John insisted. He was kindness itself and I was very grateful as the stresses of the day were certainly taking their toll on me. As I thanked him, William and wheelchair emerged.

'They said to go on to Xray and they would get the results to me a soon as they could,' he said.

Clearly John's intervention had paid dividends. I explained to William that I was going home but John wanted him to stay overnight, just in case, and would stay until he was settled.

William accepted the plan gracefully and thanked John warmly. I kissed William goodbye and gave John a hug. 'Thank you again. Please call if there's anything I need to know, and I hope you don't have to wait too long.'

'See you later,' said John, reciprocating the hug.

There were taxis outside the hospital and I was back at the house very quickly, surprised to see it was almost 10pm.

Fi pressed me to eat something but I really didn't feel like it so just accepted coffee and a biscuit in the sitting room. Our three and their cousins joined me to hear the news but there wasn't really much I could tell them.

'You'll have to wait until Uncle John calls, I'm afraid. But tell me, did you have dinner? What have you been doing? How are your plans for the tennis and fun tomorrow?'

As they filled me in, Bruce's phone pinged. 'A text, will just read it quickly.'

'Oh, it's from Freddie – Sophia's brother,' he reminded me, but turned to his brother. 'It's really for you, Cal. He says Sophia wants to know why you've not been replying to her messages all week and will I find out and get you to text her.'

I looked at Callum who threw one look at me and fled the room.

Chapter Thirty One

'I think Cal is upset about Sophia,' I said without further comment, and left the room, trying not to seem unduly worried.

I went straight up to the bedroom he was sharing with his brothers. The door was shut so I knocked but there was no answer.

'Please Cal, we need to talk. I'm not angry, just very worried about you.' Still no answer so I opened the door. He wasn't there. I checked the other bedrooms, including ours. No sign of him.

'Cal, where are you?' I called. Maybe he was in the bathroom. I went to the one the boys shared but it too was empty. Back downstairs I checked the dining room; I even looked in John's study.

I stopped by the sitting room to ask if anyone had seen him or knew where he had gone. They were all kneeling on the floor playing some sort of card game. Heads were shaken in denial. Increasingly concerned, I went to the kitchen where my sister was tidying up after dinner.

'Have you seen Callum, Fiona? Did he come through to go into the garden?'

I guess it was partly my expression, but also that I was talking so fast and that I almost never called her Fiona to her face that made her look up sharply.

'No, why?' She put down the tea towel she had been drying the glasses with and turned to me.

'I'm worried about him. He got very upset this afternoon, really desperately upset, something to do with his girlfriend

Sophia.' I tried to keep my voice steady but wasn't entirely successful. 'And just now Bruce read out a text he'd just received from Sophia's brother and Callum gave me a strange look then ran out of the room. I can't find him. I've looked all over the house.'

Fi came up to me, put her hand on my arm and gently pushed me to sit in a chair. She sat next to me and took my hand in hers.

'Look, Lizzie, it's been clear there's something going on with Callum and that you didn't want to talk about it. John and I were concerned but decided not to press you, to wait until you told us. But it's obvious now this is not an ordinary worry. Tell me so we can decide what to do.'

I fought a brief mental battle, remembering my promise to Callum not to tell them about his suicide attempt without his permission, but my worry won. I also told her he'd implied that Sophia that had died, but it was clear from the text to Bruce's that she hadn't. I didn't mention our fears that he was involved with drugs, though.

'So, I'm desperately worried in case he does something silly, even tries to commit suicide again.' Now I was in tears.

'Now, Lizzie, don't fix on the worst. Maybe he's just gone for a walk to clear his head, to think about this text.' She paused. 'If you think it's a good idea, we could make up a search party, look in the street for him.'

I leapt at the idea. 'Oh, please, yes. Maybe the boys could help. It's not that late yet, only just dark.'

I could see Fiona thinking. Then: 'OK, we'll split up. Let's send two of the boys to walk one way from the gate, and the other two in the other direction. You take your car to go a bit further - after all, it must be twenty minutes at least since he left so he could be a mile or more away. I'll stay here with Lucy to field calls from you all and to tell John what's happening.'

'Oh, Fi, you're a star,' I said with heartfelt thanks, wiping my eyes. 'I know I may be panicking unnecessarily, but Callum's suicide attempt came out of the blue – we don't know what is really going on in his life, but it must be bad for him to do such a thing.'

We stood and Fiona led the way to the sitting room.

'Very sorry to disturb your game' she said, 'but we're worried about Callum who seems very upset about something and we need to find him and need your help.'

They all looked up, Damian, Jamie and Lucy concerned and confused, but I could see my two understood why we were worried, even though they weren't privy to Callum's attempt to say Sophia was dead.

'We've come up with a plan,' my sister continued. You four boys split into two pairs, a Trenchard and a Haig, and look along the road in each direction. Make sure you have your phones on. Elizabeth will drive to look further away, while Lucy and I will stay here to receive and send messages and be here for Callum if he comes back under his own steam. We hope we're overreacting, but it's better to be safe.'

All five were on their feet almost before she had finished speaking, but Lucy objected to her role in the plan.

'Why can't I go out to look for him too?' She sounded petulant.

I thought quickly. 'Maybe, if your Mum agrees, you could come with me in the car as lookout. Two pairs of eyes might be better than just the driver's.' I looked at Fiona who nodded agreement.

'OK, off you go,' she said. 'Phones on – and you might need torches if you get to the park.'

'Got them on our phones,' retorted Jamie smugly.

'Take sweaters, it's not so warm now,' Fiona called as the boys disappeared, their sense of purpose tangible. 'You too, Lucy and Elizabeth.'

In a very few moments the house was empty except for Fiona. Lucy and I got into my car and, after a second's thought, I turnout out of the drive in the direction of the city. I didn't want to say it, but if Callum really were thinking of killing himself again, the river would be a possible destination. In a couple of minutes we overtook Angus and Damian. I flashed my lights to show we had seen them and continued, driving fairly slowly so that we could see into front gardens and side roads. Even as I drove and searched, my worry about William surfaced. I was glad he didn't have this on his plate as well, and hoped John would soon see him settled in hospital for the night and be able to return home to Fiona.

Lucy's phone rang. She put it on speakerphone so I could hear.

'Hi Lucy. Dad's just called to say he's on his way home. I told him we were looking for Callum and he said he'll keep an eye open too. No news from the boys.'

'Thanks, Fi,' I called into the phone. 'Did you give him the background?' I was careful not to say suicide attempt in front of Lucy.

'Yes, I did. Bye – good luck.' She hung up.

Getting ever more concerned at the failure of our search so far, I made the decision to turn towards the river and its park-like banks. Luckily Lucy didn't question our route.

Her phone rang again, loud in the silence of our concentration.

'Lucy, it's Dad. I'm with Callum. Tell Aunt Elizabeth to drive to where the road runs alongside the river below the castle. Park near the end where the steps go up. I'm sitting there with him. See you in a few minutes.'

I burst into tears of relief. 'Oh, Lucy' I sobbed, briefly lost for words. Unable to see for the tears, I pulled into the side of the road. I knew exactly where John meant and, tears staunched, I drove there as fast as I dared. I told Lucy to ring her Mum so she could call the boys right away with the good news.

Fiona was tearful too as Lucy told her. 'Thank heavens,' she managed to say. 'Bless John, what extraordinary instinct. Call me when you're on your way home.'

It was only three minutes' drive to the riverside. I saw John's car and parked behind it. Lucy and I leapt out of the car and began to run to the steps, but I put my arm on hers.

'Let's not seem too panicked, we don't want to upset Callum by showing how worried we were,' I said, remembering that Lucy didn't know the background to my fears. But I found it hard to obey my own instructions as we rounded the corner and saw John sitting beside Callum, apparently admiring the view. Callum was staring at the ground, didn't look up as we approached.

John spoke as we neared.

'I happened to come home this way – the river's so nice at night with all the lights reflected in the water – and was surprised to see Callum admiring them too, especially on his own at this time of night, so I stopped to offer him a ride home.' John looked me in the eye as he said this.

'We're really pleased you did,' I replied. 'Callum went out without telling us where he was going and we couldn't help wondering where he had gone.'

In a repeat of the protective role she and Damian had been showing towards Callum, Lucy pre-empted my move to sit beside Callum by taking that place herself and leaning down to speak.

'You mutt,' she said. 'Why didn't you tell us you were going for a walk? I would have loved to come with you as I hadn't seen you all day. And because you had seemed upset, we all worried when we couldn't find you.' She put her arm round him.

I blessed her for her tact – and was impressed at how, in spite of my reactions in the car, she had managed to make it all sound quite humdrum. I waited just a moment before adding my concern, forcing myself to tread as lightly as she had.

'I'm sure you didn't mean to worry us, Callum, but it was so strange that you ran off without saying where you were going. Are you okay?' I kept up the pretence that no-one else knew about his attempted suicide.

Callum didn't answer, just nodded.

'Let's go home now. You come with me and Lucy, Callum. We'll see you at home, John.' As the three stood up, I took the opportunity to touch John's hand and mouth a heartfelt 'thank you.'

Chapter Thirty Two

Lucy and Callum sat in the back of the car, the silence as I drove broken after a minute or so by Lucy asking me to turn on the car heater.

'Callum is really cold. I know it's not far, but I think it would help him.'

I could see her concerned face in the rear-view mirror.

'Of course,' I said, turning the heater to 22 degrees. 'It was really lucky that Uncle John spotted you, Callum. It's not just a cool evening, but it's starting to rain.'

A sudden burst of rain lashed the windscreen as I spoke, and the drumming on the roof precluded any conversation, giving me time to think how to behave, what to say. Callum didn't know his father was in hospital for a brain scan; when should I tell him? Hopefully John would have some news to report before telling everyone, not just Callum, but I would have to account for William's absence almost at once. Dilemma.

In the event, I didn't have to worry as John pulled into the drive just behind me and, while Lucy and Callum went ahead into the house, we stood in the shelter of a tree and thankfully he was able to tell me that the scan showed no signs of bleeding on the brain. However, the leg was indeed broken and would need a plaster up to the knee. The hospital was happy to keep him in overnight, leg bandaged for now, and would do the plaster tomorrow.

'William was very sanguine about the whole thing and was feeling more himself by the time I left. He says thanks for the book, and he'll call in the morning to report on progress. I think he should be home in time for lunch.'

I gave John a quick hug, and his reassuring smile told me that, so far at least, all was well.

'I'm just glad I was able to help. We can talk more about Callum tomorrow, perhaps. Hopefully soon he'll feel ready to open up, but don't push him, let him take the lead. And don't assume this evening was prelude to another attempt.'

We went in to join the others and found the cousins, including Callum, already in a huddle over another card game, the picture of normality. I interrupted long enough to tell them the good news about William, and that he would be staying in hospital overnight. Fiona soon came in carrying a tray with six mugs of hot chocolate and some biscuits.

'OK, you lot, it's getting late and Callum at least must be tired after all that walking. So, drink up. You can finish the game tomorrow.'

There were a few groans but actually very little resistance. After enjoying the warming snack, they hugged us goodnight and set off upstairs, the Haigs leading the way, Damian and Lucy either side of Callum conveying cousinly solidarity.

Bruce and Angus held back, however, and once the others were out of earshot, asked us about how we had found Callum.

'We were very worried, like you, and were so relieved when Aunt Fi called with the good news. Did you tell her about....'

I interrupted Angus. 'Yes, we did, and she told Uncle John who made a point of coming home via the river and saw Cal by the steps to the castle. He was so kind and very careful about not letting on he knew. And thank you both for the search parties - lucky you got back before the rain! We'll have to think what we say and how we behave tomorrow as their three don't know. Now, off to bed so Fi, John and I can unwind after the tension – and don't press Callum about it, not tonight.'

'Of course not. 'Night, Mum.' They gave me a peck on each cheek. 'Sleep well.'

My sister, John and I were glad to sit quietly to digest the evening's events. John produced whisky. 'Help you sleep' he said with a grin. 'I reckon we all need it.'

I raised my glass to them before taking a sip. 'Thank you both so much, you're real bricks, I don't know what I would have done if I'd been on my own. And, John, you've had to deal with young people on the edge, you said, so I'd really appreciate any guidance on how to cope with Callum.'

'As I said outside, just take it gently, no assumptions or accusations. Hopefully, he'll soon be ready to talk. It's not an easy situation, balancing your real concerns and worries against his wish to keep his worries private. But he's an adult now, you can't force him. Just say if you need to talk to us.'

'Thanks, John and Fi. Here's to a happier time...'

We drank our whisky but didn't linger before saying our goodnights and retreating upstairs.

My bed felt huge and empty without William beside me, and it was really hard to stop my thoughts going round and round over the events of the day, but finally I did drop off and slept right through, no doubt helped by the whisky.

* * *

The rain had stopped, I saw as I opened the curtains in the morning, noting it was already past eight o'clock. I opened the window and took a deep breath. The air smelled sweet and fresh, and although there was no sun as yet, the clouds were light and fluffy, holding promise of another fine day to come. I was dressing ready for breakfast when my mobile rang. William!

'Hi, darling, how are you? Did you have a good night?'

'I'm in great shape, no pain from the leg, thank heavens, and I slept like a log until the inevitable early breakfast delivery. Sorry to ring so early. Hope I didn't wake you.' William sounded very much his normal self.

'No, you didn't, and I'm relieved to hear you so cheerful. Any news on when they'll do the plaster?'

'Not yet. I doubt it will be very soon, but I'll call as soon as I know. Any plans for today?'

'Only taking Fi and John out to dinner as we proposed. We'll have to wait and see if you feel up to it.'

'I'm sure I shall – didn't get much dinner last night!' He paused and I could hear someone talking in the background. He continued after a moment. 'That was the nurse saying the doctor will come round soon and she will have an idea of what and when comes next.'

'Good,' I replied. I decided it was not the time to talk about Callum. 'Call me as soon as you know when I can come and get you. Bye for now. Love you.'

'I love you too and I'm just really sorry to be such a nuisance – I promise I'll be more careful in future. Bye.'

I finished dressing and went down to the kitchen which was empty apart from Fiona who was sipping coffee while reading the news on her laptop.

'Good morning,' she said, looking up. 'Everything alright?'

I filled her in on Wiilliam's call while helping myself to breakfast, then turned to the day to come. 'Any good ideas on a good restaurant for tonight?' I asked.

'I'll give it some thought. There's quite a few to choose from - cooking in Scotland has improved by leaps and bounds in the past few years. I'll check with John too – he left for work early but I can call him. Any preference on type?'

'Not really, just somewhere without loud music!' I grinned as I said this, a recurring restriction on our enjoyment of the foodie scene. 'I leave it to you two and remember, it's our treat to say thank you for having us.'

After breakfast, I retreated upstairs to wash my hair; I wanted to look good for William - and the dinner. I was just putting away the hairdryer when there was a tentative tap on the bedroom door. I went to open it, pulling the bedclothes straight as I passed.

To my surprise, Callum was standing there, still in his pyjamas, barefoot.

'Can I come in?' He spoke quietly, his tone tentative.

'Of course.' I opened the door wider and, after a quick hug, led the way to the chair by the window. I sat on the corner of the bed, close but not so close as to demand confidences. I waited for him to speak.

'I've come to say sorry. Sorry about last night.'

'Oh, Callum, you did give us a fright, and we were so very happy that John saw you.' His apology really took me by surprise. 'Do you understand why we were almost panicking?'

Callum nodded, avoiding my eye.

'Can you tell me, were we right to be so worried?' I didn't need to spell it out.

'To start with, yes.' He raised his head to look at me. 'But as I walked, I began to think about you and Dad, Angus and Bruce, how you felt last time, whether I could really do that to you. I found I couldn't.'

'Oh, darling, thank you, thank you for changing your mind.' I couldn't stop myself but slid off the bed onto my knees in front of him, took both his hands in mine. 'We would have been even more devastated than before - and felt so guilty. Why hadn't we understood how you were feeling, what clues had we missed? Had we ignored you, put your troubles on one side because of Dad's fall? I was still reeling from our talk on the walk yesterday, had had no idea how Sophia had affected you so deeply.

'You are such a special person, clever, hard-working, talented, loving and ...' I reached up and cupped my hands round his face, '...very beautiful, even when you're unhappy. Now you have your whole life in front of you and I know you'll make it a good one.' I stood and lifted Callum to his feet, enveloped him in a hug. He was stiff to start with but after a few seconds he relaxed into me and we stood together, as close as two people can be.

Releasing him, I moved us to sit side by side on the bed and, to lighten the mood, said 'At least you must be recovered from your wounds, to have walked so far and so fast. That's really good. Maybe you could even join in the tennis this evening, dancing too, to celebrate!'

Callum grinned. 'Not sure I'm up for tennis, but a bit of dancing might do me good.'

Emboldened by his relaxed tone, I ventured a question.

'Just one thing. Yesterday, why did you let me think Sophia was dead when we learned last night that she isn't and wants to be in touch with you?'

Chapter Thirty Three

Callum looked away, apparently admiring the view from the bedroom window, before taking an audible breath.

'I thought it would be the easiest way out. We had a big row and she said she didn't want to see me anymore. I couldn't imagine life without her, just wanted to end it all. Then when she started texting me again, I didn't want to admit what I had tried to do, and I thought it was better for me to stay away from her in case she hurt me so much again.'

Although Callum's explanation made sense, the way he told it sounded strangely glib, rehearsed, but I soon realised that of course he would have rehearsed it in order to be able to tell me.

'Oh, poor Callum, you really have been in a bad place. I'm so glad you've told me at least the outline of what led you there, and coming in to apologise was brave, must have been very difficult. One day, when you're feeling stronger and ready to tell us more about what caused such a painful rupture, you know Dad and I will always listen and not judge you. We love you so much and believe that you can and will get over this and get back to your normal self.' I gave him another hug before continuing.

'I have to confess that I was in such a panic last night that Aunt Fiona pressed me to explain. She said she and Uncle John had already picked up the tension, that there was something wrong, so I felt I had to tell her the bare outline and she was wonderful. It was such a relief to share the worry. It was Fi who alerted Uncle John and he had the idea of coming home via the river. You know the rest. Obviously,

Angus and Bruce were as worried as I was, but Damian, Jamie and Lucy don't know anything, they just think you got lost somehow.'

Callum nodded. 'I wish no-one knew but I understand. And I am glad I didn't go through with it. I was very happy to see Uncle when he found me. He was so thoughtful, really clever in explaining why he was coming home that way. Lucy didn't suspect a thing – and, honestly, nor did I, though I can see now it was a very strange route for him that late at night.'

Then Callum abruptly changed the subject, to my relief in a way. 'But tell me, how's Dad?'

I told him about the cheerful phone call. 'But I didn't say anything about last night. Do you want to tell him yourself? Or would you rather I told him?'

Callum thought for a moment before deciding. 'You tell him. I think I would find it too difficult. Maybe tell him when you fetch him from the hospital.'

I could understand his reluctance. 'OK, I will. Then while I'm getting Dad, you could plan this evening's entertainment with the others – that is, if you feel up to it. I think they would understand if you dropped out.'

'No, it would be good to be with them, distract me. I think I can put on a good front for them – actually, I already feel better for having told you everything.'

'I'm just so glad you did. And joining in will reassure them that you're alright. Now, why don't you get dressed and have some breakfast. None of the others were up except Fi when I came upstairs so you'll probably have company.' I gave him a quick peck on the cheek before standing up and moving to open the door.

Callum obediently left and I sat on the bed again to digest our conversation. I still had a niggling feeling that he hadn't told me everything, but there was nothing I could put my finger on. After a few minutes, I decided speculation was futile and went downstairs.

Fi greeted me in the hall with the news that she had booked dinner at a restaurant close to the river. 'It's had good reviews and the main dining area has proper tablecloths and padded chairs, none of this hard surface stuff, you'll be glad to hear. It didn't say anything about music on the website so when I rang to book I asked and they promised that although there would be some background music, it wouldn't be loud.' Fi laughed before reassuring me that she had also checked access was easy for poor William. 'The dining room is on the first floor - lovely views over the river - but there's a lift.'

'Bless you. I'm looking forward to it already.' I had a quick internal debate before telling Fi about my conversation with Callum, but I didn't mention my doubts.

'I'm so glad – and John will be too.' Fi gave me a hug. 'And the cousins will have a good time together tonight, I'm sure. Ready for coffee?'

I accepted gratefully and we took our coffees to the sitting room where our chat about old times, friends and relations was interrupted by another call from William.

'All done!' he informed us. 'Gosh, they're efficient here. Lovely people too - except the dour breakfast lady who plonked the tray down and said something in such a strong Scottish accent I couldn't understand a word. Then when the doctor came round, he said I could go home any time after midday.'

I quickly shared the news with Fi. 'Wonderful,' we chorused.

'I'll come at noon. Let me know where best to find you. See you soon.' I blew a kiss into the phone.

There was not much time before I needed to leave. William texted to say he'd be at the main entrance and, sure enough, there he was, grinning from ear to ear and waving a crutch in welcome. It was a bit of a manoeuvre getting him into the car, but no doubt we would improve with practice. Once on the way back to Fi's and my enquires about his brief sojourn in the hospital over, I broached the subject of Callum.

'I think - hope – Callum is getting over his upset, but he gave us a fright quite late last night when he suddenly left the house after a text to Bruce from Sophia's brother had clearly upset him. I got really worried and we sent out search parties, but John found him down by the river. This morning Callum confessed to me that he had intended to kill himself but when it came to the point, he realised he couldn't do it to us, thank goodness. He wanted me to tell you. He also said his unhappiness was because of breaking off his relationship with Sophia.'

'Heavens, I'm so sorry you had to deal with it all without me, but the way your family stood by you is great.' He paused. 'But do you really think Callum'll be okay now?' William asked with a worried frown.

'I think so, but I've a nagging suspicion that he didn't tell me everything. However, John has had to deal with attempted suicide of a young patient and his advice is not press him for more, we just have to wait.'

'Let's hope you're wrong and that really is the whole story. I don't think there's anything else we can do.' said William, gently touching my hand. 'We just have to get on with our lives and he has to get on with his. But clearly we need to watch out for any changes in him, be alert.'

'Of course. When we get back, I think you shouldn't say anything to Callum when the others are around, wait until you get him on his own, then tell him that you know what happened.'

William nodded agreement and the rest of the short journey passed in silence.

The cousins must have heard the car arrive as almost immediately we were surrounded by a welcome committee. I was glad Angus and Bruce were there to help William get out of the car and we all watched as William made his way carefully into the house, negotiating the front step with great caution.

Fiona was inside to welcome him, and apologised that John was at work. 'He'll be back in time for our dinner tonight – did Elizabeth tell you it's all arranged since you were sure you could manage?'

'No, but I'm delighted. However, I confess I'm rather hungry right now. How long to lunch?' William added with a smile. 'Wonderful as the hospital was, the breakfast was very early and honestly not up to much.'

He didn't have long to wait, and lunch was very cheerful, the chatter round the table all very normal. When we had finished, William admitted he was rather tired and would have a rest so as to be in good shape in the evening.

'Callum, perhaps you could help me up the stairs.'

'Sure, Dad, but is one of us enough?'

'Maybe Angus and Bruce could come up behind to catch me if I fall, but I don't think I will, though I'll be very slow, one step at a time, I think.'

Guessing that William intended to have the proposed conversation, I stayed downstairs to help my sister clear up. Angus and Bruce reappeared first. Callum came down a few minutes later and gave me a small smile to indicate that William had indeed told him.

'Dad says, do pop up before he goes to sleep.' Callum said, disappearing in the direction of the sitting room where I could hear the cousins were already installed.

I followed his instructions and, having told Fi I'd have a coffee later, went up and lay down beside my husband, very happy to be two in the bed again. We talked quietly for twenty minutes or so at which point I could sense that he was ready to sleep. I kissed him, then left him in peace. As I got downstairs, I could hear raised voices and stopped to eavesdrop.

To my surprise, there was a heated argument going on between the boys. I heard Angus say he didn't want to partner Rosie if she was the one he saw the other day. 'Her forehand's okay but she's got a lousy serve – and a big bum.' There were titters and Lucy's voice raised in anger chided him forcefully for such a comment.

'You wouldn't like it if I said you – or Bruce – had buck teeth or ugly legs, so shut up.'

There was a mumbled apology, but the argument continued about who would play with whom, Angus and Bruce clearly having different preferences. Damian and Jamie offered various solutions. Callum kept out of it as a non-player. Amused, I retreated to the kitchen to drink a coffee with Fi, and we decided a walk would be a good idea to prepare ourselves for dinner.

It was a mild evening, unusually still, the leaves in the abundant trees in the leafy neighbourhood barely moving as my sister and I enjoyed a quiet walk after the excitement of the previous twenty four hours. We returned refreshed to find William downstairs holding court with his sons and Fi's three.

'How did you get downstairs?' I asked. 'Vertical or on your bottom?' Everyone laughed and assured me he had managed pretty well with his crutches. His sons had hovered below him just in case.

'Have you got the tennis and evening sorted? I overheard some disagreement earlier!' I laughed. They looked a bit sheepish.

'Yup, all organised,' Damian replied for them all. 'We won't leave until about five for the tennis as it doesn't get dark until quite late. Then on to the evening's entertainment.'

'We've said we don't want to be back too late,' Angus said. 'We've got to pack and get back to Edinburgh to be in good shape to start work on Monday.'

'I'm not coming with you to Edinburgh.' Callum announced.

Angus and Bruce looked at him in surprise. 'Why? We thought it was settled,' said Bruce. 'Tom and his parents were happy to have you in the house too.'

'I've changed my mind.' Callum spoke firmly and left the room.

There was a moment's silence.

Chapter Thirty Four

William and I looked at each other but said nothing. It was Callum's decision not to go to Edinburgh. That his brothers were surprised was not so odd if he hadn't discussed it with them. Moments later we saw Callum come onto the terrace. He sat in a chair with his back to the wall and leaned back, apparently admiring the silhouette of the big tree at the end of the lawn against the blue sky.

Bruce, who had organised for all three of them to house-sit his friend Tom's house, looked distinctly annoyed. 'After all that persuasion to get Tom and his parents to agree to let Cal stay too, that's a rotten trick. Come on, Angus, let's go and find out what he thinks he's doing.'

Damian, Jamie and Lucy also exchanged glances. Looking embarrassed, they turned to us and said they would go and get their things together for the tennis and evening, leaving William, Fi and me alone. We were sitting in the armchairs near the open window and were just about to speculate what was behind Callum's decision when Angus and Bruce came onto the terrace, sat either side of him, and began to harangue him. We could hear every word.

'What are you playing at? I made such an effort to get them to let you stay too.' Bruce began.

'So? If I don't come, they'll be pleased.'

'But you should still have told us!' Angus said.

'Why? I don't have to discuss everything with you. And just because we're triplets, we don't have to do everything together. We're not joined at the bloody hip.' Callum sounded distinctly annoyed.

'I didn't say we were. Just you should have told us.'
Angus's voice was also rising.

'Sorry.' But Callum didn't sound it.

Bruce resumed the interrogation. 'So, what are you going to do instead?'

'None of your business.'

We listeners could sense that Callum's abrupt answer raised even more hackles. I felt bad about eavesdropping on their conversation but thought it might give some insight into what was going on with Callum. Fi stood and quietly left the room putting her finger to her lips and indicating she shouldn't be listening. William and I stayed.

'Going to bum off Mum and Dad - or Fiona and John, eh?' Bruce needled him.

'No, though Aunt Fiona did say I could stay on with them.' Callum spoke reasonably, not rising to the bait.

'So, what then?' Angus took over.

'As I said, none of your bloody business. Shut up about it.'

Bruce changed tack 'Another thing, that text from Fred. You haven't told me what to say to him, what he should tell Sophia. Just went off and gave us all a fright. What's wrong with you?'.

'Just tell him to say I never want to hear from her again.'

'But why? You were nuts about her until a week ago. Seemed like you were in it for the long term.' Bruce didn't give up.

'Just shut up about it, will you.'

'Got something to do with that fight?'

Callum didn't answer.

'Come on, come clean. Sophia will want more of an explanation than just no contact.' Angus took over, trying to sound reasonable.

'Look, you two. Just fuck off and leave me alone, will you. Go and knock the little yellow balls to hell and forget about me.' There was a catch in his voice, but I don't think Angus and Bruce noticed.

'Well, fuck you.' Angus responded in kind. 'Thanks for being such fun. Will we see you at the pub anyway?'

'I don't know. Wait and see.' With that, Callum got up and walked away, down the garden towards the big tree.

Angus and Bruce, without saying a word, stood and came back into the house.

William and I sat in silence for a minute before William spoke. 'All's well that ends well,' he said reflectively.

I was surprised at his reaction. 'Ends well?'

'Yes, Cal didn't say he wouldn't join them in the evening, left it open. Deliberately.'

'But they were so rude to each other.'

'I think you're a bit out of touch with the times – and maybe too well brought up! People – well, a lot of them - really do talk like that these days.'

'Hmmm. I suppose if I'm honest, I have noticed there's less of the 'expletive deleted' now, but I don't like it. If you start swearing like that, there's nowhere to go except fisticuffs.'

William nodded. 'Maybe that's what happened with Cal and the fight?' he wondered. 'But until he opens up, we can only speculate. Pointless.' He reached for his crutches and began to manoeuvre himself up. 'I need a cup of tea after that.'

'Stay there, I'll get it. Fi will probably like one too, and she must be wondering how that conversation – if you can call it that – ended.' I left for the kitchen.

My sister was sitting at the table doing a puzzle in the newspaper. She looked up questioningly.

'Really nothing to say. We didn't learn anything, and it was horrible to listen to them swearing at each other. However, William assures me that's not unusual these days.' I smiled ruefully. 'But we feel in need of a cup of tea. Can I make us all one?'

'Yes, do. Lovely. You know where everything is. Oh, and add a mug for John as he may be home quite soon. I'll join you in the sitting room,' she said, folding the newspaper.

I carried the tray with everything through to the sitting room. There was no sign of Fi's three or Angus and Bruce, but just as I was pouring the tea, Callum came in.

'Hi, any chance of tea for me too?' he asked with an engaging smile.

'Sure, just fetch another mug from the kitchen – and put the kettle on again in case we need to top up the pot.' I began to pour the teas, wondering how to raise the subject on all our minds without giving away our eavesdropping.

Callum returned with his mug just as John called hello from the hall. Joining us, he kissed Fi before flopping onto the sofa. 'Ah, tea. Just what I need. Been a long day, interesting, though. Anything new here?'

William responded quickly. 'Callum has just surprised us all, especially his brothers, by announcing that he's not going to join them to find a summer job in Edinburgh after all.' He turned to Callum. 'Can you tell us your new plans?'

I swear Callum smirked as he answered. 'I've got a job here.'

Every adult eyebrow shot up. I was quickest to respond. 'Well done, how did you manage that, and have you checked with Aunt Fiona and Uncle John that it's okay to stay on with them?'

Fi started to repeat their previous offer for him to stay but

Cal held up a hand.

'Actually, I won't need to stay, thanks all the same.' His smirk had turned to a grin.

'Well, put us out of our suspense.' William voiced all our curiosity.

'I'm going to work for Hamish.'

'Good heavens, how did you manage that, and without telling us and what are you going to do?' My face must have been a picture as my questions tumbled out.

'Well, I don't actually know, but I asked if he needed any help on the estate, said I was willing to do anything: gardening, painting, repairs, anything, even mucking out the horses. I told him I'd completely recovered from my injuries and wanted to stay away from London for a bit. I loved where he lived, the air, the views, the wilderness, the peace, and knew it would do me good, be great preparation for getting back to studying.' Callum paused.

I took the opportunity to ask how he had got in touch with Hamish.

'It's really not difficult these days, Mum, but also you left your laptop open and I had a quick look. Promise I didn't read all your emails, just happened to spot yours to him near the top.'

That annoyed me. I frowned but didn't say anything as I had to admire his initiative.

Callum spoke again. 'Actually, it's even better than helping Hamish. I said to him that I wouldn't need more than pocket money if he was happy to put me up, and to my surprise he said straight away that was okay and I would be very useful. Then he added that the hotel at the castle would be opening soon, it was now tourist season, and Brad – the manager - had asked him if he knew of anyone who could either help out behind the scenes or perhaps in the bar and restaurant in the evenings. Hamish had told him he had no ideas, but if I were there, maybe I could split my time – and I would get paid for the work at the hotel!'

'Good heavens, talk about falling on one's feet,' Fi laughed in admiration. 'But you get a sharp rap over the knuckles for reading your mother's emails.'

'I know, sorry, Mum. But it just sort of happened. I should've asked you but the odds against getting this job were so high, I didn't want to let on I was trying.'

'I'm really happy for you, Cal,' said William, smiling. 'But I suspect your brothers may be a bit jealous, so perhaps play it down a bit when you tell them.'

John stood up and clapped Callum on the back. 'Congratulations. I'm so glad you're well enough now to do this, and I think you're right about the fresh air and peace of the Highlands. Now I'm going up to have a shower and maybe a snooze to be ready for dinner. Fi tells me she's booked a really good restaurant so I want to be in shape to enjoy it.' He left the room.

'So, are you going to watch other others play tennis?' I asked Callum, not letting on we had overheard the argument. 'They'll be leaving fairly soon.'

'No, I think I'll pass on that but join them in the pub. I know where it is. I'll go up and email a few friends and check with Hamish when he would like me to start. See you later – or tomorrow.' He left the room.

Fi smiled. 'Well, that's a turn-up for the books. You must be very relieved that he's taken the initiative and is getting away from whatever it is that's troubling him, and I agree with John about the healing power of the countryside. We're happy to have him stay until Hamish wants him to start work. Right now, I'll join John and freshen up for this evening. See you down here about seven.'

'That's fine,' said William. 'We'll be ready.'

Left on our own we took a moment or two to digest Callum's news. 'It must be a good thing,' I said eventually. 'We won't be able to get closer to finding out what's been wrong, but Fi and John are right that getting away from everything must be good for him.'

William nodded. 'And I don't actually think Angus and Bruce will be too jealous as they're so keen on the Fringe activities, all that theatre and stand-up. The opposite of the peace and quiet of the countryside!' He paused. 'Talking of activities, I hope you don't mind but I think the idea we had of a romantic few days away isn't quite so attractive with my leg in plaster. If I'm honest, I would really quite like to go home soon. Would you mind very much?'

'Of course not, darling. It had crossed my mind that perhaps home would be easier for you.' I hid my disappointment and went over to give him a kiss. 'Let's go and freshen up too,' I said, helping him up from his chair and passing his crutches.

As we crossed the hall, the thunder of feet on the stairs announced the arrival of the tennis players.

'Need help getting upstairs?' Angus asked. 'We're not in a hurry.'

William began to demur, but I overrode him and the slow procession, led by William, made it up to our bedroom with no need for their help, though I was still grateful they were there.

The five clattered back downstairs, calling out their goodbyes, promises to be good and not to be too late back.

'Have fun, we responded. 'See you tomorrow.'

Chapter Thirty Five

Wiiliam and I were downstairs just in time to wish Callum a fun evening and give him a peck on the cheek as he appeared, spruced up and ready to join his cousins.

'Up for dancing?' William teased him. 'Must be if you're up for mucking out Hamish's horses!'

Callum laughed. 'Have a good dinner,' was all he said before disappearing through the front door.

My sister and John appeared a few minutes later and we piled into John's car in good spirits, Callum's news having reassured us that his life might be taking a turn for the better.

It wasn't far to the restaurant which, as Fi had promised, had a lift up to the dining room with its lovely view over the river. The menu, highlighting Scottish dishes, was full of temptations: salmon, venison, black pudding, haggis with neeps (I had to remind Wiiliam that neeps were turnips, de rigueur with haggis) as well as more international dishes, and we had a feast. Over good wine, chosen with care by William, and the delicious food, we discussed the events of our week with them, our outing to watch the dolphins, the visit to Hamish and Ailsa, Callum's aborted suicide attempt and his latest revelation. He had been very convincing, but I couldn't help wanting to be reassured that Hamish really did want to employ him. I privately decided to contact Hamish next day with the excuse of telling him about William's broken leg. It would give me the opportunity to raise Callum's news.

Over good malt whisky, insisted on by John - no surprise there – I broached the subject of our return to London. 'I told you we had planned a couple of days on our own somewhere once the boys had left, but with William's leg in plaster, it would be rather limiting, not such fun.' William nudged me under the table with his good foot and twinkled discreetly at me, but I continued as though I hadn't noticed. 'We talked about it briefly before dinner and agreed it might be best to go back to London.'

John nodded. 'It probably would be easier to be in familiar surroundings, quite understandable. When do you think you would go? And fly or train....'

'But don't rush away unless you really want to,' interrupted Fi. 'I hope you'll stay with us at least tomorrow. Angus and Bruce will be packing up for Edinburgh and you'll want to see them off. Then we could have a relaxed evening and you could make your travel arrangements.'

'That sounds a good plan, if you don't mind us around another night,' said William.

'Of course not,' responded Fi and John in unison.

Thanking them warmly, we finished our whiskies and sat back, happy and ready for home. William settled the bill while we thanked the chef, who had come out to meet us, for an excellent meal. Fi drove us home with care, but not so slowly as to arouse suspicion in any observant policeman.

The house was, unsurprisingly, in darkness. We said our good nights with hugs and thanks all round before retreating extra carefully upstairs, guessing that all the wine and whisky might have impaired William's balance. We hadn't been in bed long when we heard the cousins return, laughter and admonitions not to wake the parents guaranteeing we knew they were back. Reassured that all was well, William and I exchanged good night kisses and drifted quickly into sleep.

Sunday morning started late for most of the household. It must have been nearly eleven before all the cousins were down, a couple of them clearly nursing sore heads. Angus and Bruce gulped down coffee before disappearing apologetically upstairs again saying they had to pack. Damian and Jamie also didn't linger but Callum and Lucy sat with us in the kitchen ready to tell us about their evening.

'Let's start with the tennis,' Fi suggested.

Lucy grinned, said it had been fun and they'd only lost four balls in the bushes behind the courts. 'I think Angus was quite taken by Emily – he looked distinctly miffed later when her boyfriend turned up in the pub. But I'm sorry you missed the game, Cal, I played brilliantly!'

'You never know, there may be another chance now I'm going to be working with Hamish – I'll hopefully get a few days off and could come here and show you what good tennis is all about.' Callum grinned. 'But I enjoyed meeting the girls at the pub and the music was good, great beat. It was a bit too crowded, though, and way too noisy to get to talk much.'

'How did your injuries stand up to it all?' I asked, ever the concerned mother. 'Did you dance?'

'Sure, but I did keep it a bit low key, wouldn't have won any prizes.'

'Dancing in our day was a bit more demanding,' John reminisced. 'At school they taught us a bit of ballroom, really had to concentrate when we had those ghastly evenings with the local girls' school. How we hated it! Then, let loose into the real world, we discovered rock and roll and boy, did we have fun. Bet you didn't know your Aunt Fiona was a cracking dancer in her youth!'

Fi laughed. 'You weren't so bad yourself. In fact, I first noticed you when you were dancing with whatshername – Angie – at the Freshers ball at uni. Made sure I got a turn, and that was the beginning. Didn't take me long to see Angie off.' She smiled happily at John. 'Pity we don't go dancing anymore, though.'

'Looks like my dancing days are over,' said William ruefully, 'though it was never my strong point. Luckily Lizzie didn't seem to mind too much.'

Lucy and Callum rolled their eyes at this insight into their parents' youth. Then Lucy confessed: 'Actually, I wouldn't mind trying rock and roll. The music's great and it looks more fun dancing with someone than just jumping up and down in a crowd.'

'Well said, young lady,' said William. 'Couldn't agree more about that dancing together thing, even if I wasn't very good at it.'

The reminiscing was cut short by the reappearance of Angus and Bruce.

'How's the packing going?' I asked.

'About done, we don't have that much with us, left most of our gear in Edinburgh.' Bruce replied. 'Just checked the trains – there aren't as many on Sundays, we've found. The best one is just after 1.30. The next one is quite a bit later and it's half an hour slower, doesn't get in until after seven. I know it's a bit short notice, but if we asked very nicely, might you drive us to the station, Mum?'

'Yes, of course. But what about lunch? There's not much time.'

My sister, ever thoughtful, immediately offered to make a couple of sandwiches. I demurred, saying they could buy a snack at the station or on the train, but she insisted and set to work.

'Go and tell your brothers to come down, Lucy. The boys will have to leave in half an hour or so and they'll want to say their goodbyes.' Fi said over her shoulder.

'No, we've got to up anyway to get our bags. We'll tell them.' Angus and Bruce left the kitchen, followed by Lucy and Callum, only for Angus to put his head back round the door. 'Can you buy the tickets for us?' It came over more as a statement than a question.

'Hmm, they do make assumptions,' I grumbled, a bit cross at being so taken for granted, but recognising we did have deeper pockets. 'Do you want to come to the station, too? 'I asked William.

He shook his head. 'It's such a palaver with the crutches, I'll say my goodbyes here.'

William dealt with the tickets and sent the confirmation codes to Angus's phone. The whole family – both families – gathered at one o'clock, Fi holding a plastic bag with the sandwiches and a couple of apples which she handed over with a smile.

'It's been lovely having you both here,' she said. 'I hope the jobs turn out well and that you have time to enjoy some Fringe events too. There's plenty of choice – I heard there are about three thousand shows this year, if you count everything.' She handed over the bag and gave them both a hug. John echoed her wishes as he shook hands with them before adding a hug of his own.

'Don't get up, Dad', said Bruce as William started to lever himself out of his chair. The two boys leant over to kiss their father. 'Hope the leg heals quickly.'

John stayed with William. Fi, Callum and the cousins followed us out to the car. Lucy kissed Angus and Bruce while the boys exchanged man-hugs and back slaps. After a bit of friendly bickering, Angus won the front seat, Bruce clambered in the back with the bags, and we left to a forest of waving hands.

It wasn't far to the station, and we were in good time.

'Thanks, Mum – for the driving and the tickets – and for the fun day with Hamish and Ailsa. I hope we can see them again sometime.' Bruce spoke for them both and I kissed them goodbye, wishing them luck and good times.

Rather than setting straight off I sat in the car, took out my phone and called Hamish. There were several rings before he answered, and I suddenly realised he was probably in the middle of lunch. I apologised but he said it was only bread and cheese so no worries.

'I just wanted to let you know about William's leg.' I began my prepared opening. 'It is broken, but cleanly, and the hospital in Inverness was great, kept him in overnight, plastered it up next morning and he was home by lunchtime. However, we've decided to go home a few days early so I thought I would go into the office once we're settled back in and get on with the research with Dave. Be good to get the results back to you soon.'

'Yes, indeed. We're not exactly on tenterhooks, but we would love to start making plans. Talking of plans, Callum's enquiry about work came just at the right moment, great timing. There's quite a few jobs waiting for me to get stuck in and having an extra pair of hands will really speed things up. I did worry slightly, though, as you had said he was a bit battered from a fight. Is he really up to pretty heavy manual labour?'

I didn't repeat our doubts about that but told Hamish that Callum had been out dancing with his brothers and cousins the night before so clearly was well on the mend. 'I hope he'll have the sense to tell you if he can't manage something. He also said something about working at the hotel. Is that right? Would Brad really consider employing him?'

'Sure would, as Brad would say,' laughed Hamish. 'But I think Callum will find it pretty tough combining the two jobs as he'd have to cycle over there and back. Still, he's young and seems enthusiastic.'

'That's all seriously good news. Thank you. Callum said how much he loved the Highlands, and I think he's glad to get right away from what was troubling him so badly...' I suddenly stopped, realising I was about to reveal the extent of our worries. Thinking quickly, I added that he'd not been doing so well in his studies, needed to clear his head. 'He's staying with my sister and family for now, waiting to hear from you when you would like him to start. I'll text you his number, and my sister's.'

'I've already got his.' said Hamish. 'Remember, we talked on the phone. It'll be a few days before we're ready for him. The attic bedroom needs clearing for him, and Ailsa and I are going to be away for a couple of nights.'

'It's really good of you to put him up too, and I'm sure he can occupy himself more than adequately in Inverness. His brothers have gone back to Edinburgh, but he gets on really well with his cousins who are around the same age.'

'Looks like a good arrangement all round.' Hamish smiled into the phone. 'Seems like my finding your website has led to several good things. Have a good journey back and give William my best wishes.'

'Will do, and thanks again. I'll be in touch.'

Breathing a huge sigh of relief that Callum had been telling the truth, I pocketed my phone and drove back to the house with a light heart.

Chapter Thirty Six

As I drove, I noticed that the clouds I had seen from the bedroom window were now much bigger and darker. Just as I turned into John and Fi's driveway the heavens opened. The wind was suddenly so strong it almost wrenched the car door from my hands. I made a dash for the front door which was opened by my sister just as I reached the house. Laughing and cursing, I stepped into the hall, shaking the rain from my hair and shrugging off my wet cardigan.

'That was bad luck,' said Fi, 'but come and have some lunch. I'm afraid we didn't wait for you as certain family members said they were very hungry and the rest of us joined them.'

I followed her into the kitchen where everyone was sitting round the big table spread with a variety of cheeses and cold meats, a big bowl of salad, and a basket of crusty bread.

Smiling hello, I took the empty place and was just reaching for the cheese board when Fi intervened.

'Soup? It's tomatoes from the garden, made it on Friday when you were out.

I accepted gratefully. They were clearly good tomatoes as the soup was wonderfully aromatic.

'So, did the boys get off on time?' asked John. 'No problem parking?'

'No, all very straightforward. And after seeing them off, I suddenly thought to ring Hamish and tell him about William's broken leg. He was very relieved to hear it wasn't too bad, and said how lucky it was that you contacted him, Cal. You clearly got him at just the right time.' I smiled across the table at my son. 'Congratulations on taking the initiative and each getting what you wanted.'

'That really was an inspired move, Callum. Well done.' John beamed at his nephew who acknowledged the compliment with a slight bow of the head.

It was soon clear the cousins had finished their lunch and were getting restive. Lucy spoke first.

'Is it okay if I go now, Mum? Rosie, the one with the fat bum you were so rude as to comment on, Angus, has invited me to go and meet the puppy she just got for her birthday. Says it's amazingly cute and clever. We're going to take it for a walk.'

'That's fine. Have fun - be back by teatime, please.'

'Thanks. See you later, guys.' Lucy blew them a kiss and left.

'What about you three?' asked William. 'Any plans?'

Damian responded, casting a hopeful glance at Callum. 'We thought we go for a cycle ride, but we'd need to borrow your bike for Cal, Dad. Would that be okay?'

'I don't see why not. You might need to give it a bit of oil first, I've not used it for a while.'

'Thanks, Uncle John. That's very kind of you. I think the exercise'll do me good – preparation for working for Hamish!'

The three boys made their excuses and left, leaving the four of us to finish our lunch. Fi put the kettle on for coffee and we stayed in the kitchen to drink it.

'I didn't know you had a vegetable garden. When did that happen?' William asked.

'About three years ago, when climate change began to be a bigger issue and there was both talk of food security and an awareness that Scotland was likely to become warmer, better for farming. Mind you, we've always grown the best soft fruit up here, in my opinion. Something to do with slower ripening perhaps.'

'Talking of the veg garden, John, we're going to need some beans or peas or whatever is ready for dinner tonight. Why don't you take Lizzie down to show off your green fingers and she can help you pick.'

'Love to see – and help. Just say when.' I downed the last of my coffee.

William professed a desire for a bit of quiet time. I went with him to the sitting room and settled him in an armchair.

'It was such a relief to hear that Callum was telling the truth about working for Hamish, but how did you manage to bring that into the conversation about my leg?'

'I didn't have to, Hamish did! Said how lucky it was Cal had rung as there were lots of jobs to be done and the help would be more than welcome. And it's true he might work at the hotel as well. No wonder Cal enjoyed giving us the news and seeing our surprise.'

'When does he start?' asked William.

'Not just yet as Hamish and Ailsa are going away for a few days, but Fi and John have already said they're happy to have him stay, and the wait will give his bruises that bit more time to disappear so he should be in good shape to get straight to work. The cycling's a good start in getting him back to full strength.'

'Well, that's all good news. I'll check flight and train options for tomorrow after my nap. By the looks of things, we'll have the house to ourselves all August.' William looked thoughtful before continuing. 'I remember, when we were in Switzerland quite a few years ago, meeting a man with his leg in plaster walking on it. I asked him about it, and he said it was called a gay gips - well that's what it sounded like. I'll see if

I can find out about it. If I could get one, life could be pretty normal – easier to get around, we could go out to dinner or the theatre more. I'll do some research when we get home.'

'Talking of work, I think I'll go to the office on Wednesday, at least for a few hours, if you can cope on your own. Be good to catch up with Dave and his research. I'd really like to have something to tell Hamish before long.'

'I was thinking along the same lines,' said William. 'I've a bit of a conscience about your professor. He wants to talk to someone about patents, plus I said I would fish around for some potential investors. There are several interested in eco projects so I could get on with that. Easy to take a taxi to the office.'

'I'm sure Michael would appreciate it. Maybe we could have him round to supper again too.' I paused before continuing, keeping my tone light. 'There's also your boss's relative – a cousin, wasn't it? – who was going to talk to you about his Parkinson's experience. Be good to follow that up too. We've – probably sensibly – rather pushed the Parkinson's to the back of our minds, but we should do what we can to make it as light a burden as possible.'

William nodded. 'I confess I have spent a bit of time pondering the future, but decided not to worry now, but enjoy normality – or what was normality until this stupid accident.' He laughed ruefully before leaning back and closing his eyes. 'See you in an hour or so.'

Returning to the kitchen I found John carrying a colander and a pile of plastic boxes.

'Thought I'd get on with the picking. You happy to come now?'

'Sure.' I borrowed a pair of gardening clogs and walked with him down the garden, taking the opportunity to thank him again for his inspired help with Callum that ghastly Friday evening. 'You really were wonderful; the intuition about where to find him, then managing to make it seem almost a casual encounter. I don't think Lucy suspected anything, do you?'

'No, I don't – or else she's kept any such thoughts to herself. I'm just so pleased you finally told Fi about his first attempt – a horrible burden you and William were holding, much better shared.' John smiled at me sympathetically.

Once again, I blessed my sister for choosing such a nice husband. We came to the vegetable garden which was clearly no afterthought: four rows of sticks held runner beans and peas, a fruit cage was full of raspberries and currants, strawberries were beside two rows of potatoes. There were onions and lettuces and cabbages and courgettes and broccoli as well as the tomatoes..... I was seriously impressed and told John so.

John beamed. 'It's a great form of relaxation after a day at the surgery; I really enjoy it, get great satisfaction from it, though I confess I do have a few hours a week help from a local chap. Now, let's see what's ripe and ready for dinner.'

It didn't take long to pick a selection of green vegetables. The raspberries weren't ripe, but the strawberries were so we added a box-full to our load and returned to the house and delighted thanks from Fiona.

Going to the sitting room I found my husband busy on his phone. He looked up. 'Didn't sleep long so did the travel research, just finalising booking on the 1pm flight to Luton tomorrow. The train was just too slow - and I did check Inverness airport is broken leg-friendly!'

'That's great, very convenient timing and easy to drop off the car. I'll text Mrs Baker in case she was thinking of coming in. Don't want to give her a fright!' I went to tell Fi and John the news. They were gratifyingly sorry we were leaving so soon but understood our wish to get settled back at home.

Dinner that evening was cheerful, with tales of puppy walking and cycling, and much appreciation of the garden produce, especially the strawberries which were wolfed down, and not only by the youngsters. John said his farewells at bedtime as he would be leaving for work early in the morning, but Damian, Jamie and Lucy – and Callum – promised to be up in time to see us off.

'So I should hope,' I responded, laughing. We won't be leaving before at least 11.'

Texts that evening from Angus and Bruce assured us they were safely installed in Tom's house and would be having bar training all next day.

Monday morning dawned clear and dry. Packing was easy, farewells were warm and contained wishes for quick healing of William's leg as well as many injunctions to come again soon. I confess I was a little tearful as I kissed Callum goodbye and wished him good luck at Hamish's but was brought down to earth when he asked me to send him various items of clothing and shoes suitable for his labours.

As William had learned, coping with the flight was no problem and it was barely four when we arrived home to a tidy house and a small pile of post. I made us a cup of tea before going out to buy provisions for the evening and breakfast and texted my sister to say we'd arrived home after an easy journey. We found we felt at rather a loss, but rather than starting straight onto emails and calls, we decided to relax, watch a film on TV and have an early night. I accompanied William up the stairs which he was managing increasingly well. A snuggle and a good night's sleep set us up for the serious work of the rest of the week.

Chapter Thirty Seven

As we finished breakfast next morning, William sighed. 'You know, Lizzie, what I would enjoy more than anything right now is a hot bath. It feels a long time since Friday morning but with this plaster....' His voice tailed off.

I thought for a moment. 'I've an idea,' I said. 'I'm not sure about a bath, but I can certainly organise a shower.' I went to the utility room and returned with the stool which I used for reaching the top kitchen cupboards, a black bin bag and a ball of string.

'Ready when you are!'

William laughed and set off for the stairs. I followed him to the bedroom where, his pyjamas removed, I pulled the bin bag up over the plaster and tied the string in a neat bow round his thigh then cut the string with my nail scissors.

'Wait here a sec,' I said as I picked up the stool and went to the bathroom where I placed it under the shower head and turned on the water, just extricating myself in time to avoid a soaking.

'Ready, but be very careful as the shower tray is wet and slippery.'

Laughing again, William nodded and went to the shower. I closed the shower door and watched the pleasure with which he let the hot water run over him.

'Call me when you're finished,' I said retreating to the bedroom to make the bed. I had just finished when William called. Extricating him with care, I handed him a towel. 'How was that?'

'Wonderful! Now I'll shave and dress and be down shortly.

I think I can manage on my own.'

'I'll be in the study,' I said, giving him a kiss on his wet head.

We shared the study, our desks against opposite walls, just close enough, back-to-back, to reach across with the phone or address book. My desk faced the window with a view to the street.

By the time William joined me, positively sparkling post shower, and settled at his computer, I had caught up with the few new emails and called the office to say I'd be in next day.

'I'm off to do the shopping. Anything you need?'

'No, I don't think so, thanks,' William replied.

Returning after shopping, I found him still there.

'Well, that was a productive morning,' said William. 'Just listen to this. By chance Michael is coming up this weekend to see his daughter so I got busy and I've already arranged a couple of meetings for him on Monday and Tuesday next week. And I invited him to supper Saturday or Sunday. He said he'll call back when he's spoken to his daughter to let us know which suits.'

'That's really good. Do you really think we should invite his daughter too?'

'I'll ask him when he calls back.' William made a note. 'Oh, and I Googled waterproof covers for plasters. Looking at the illustrations, they don't look very different from your improvised one, same principle, so I don't think I need to buy one. That'll save us all of £20 quid or so.' He laughed. 'I also checked out gay gips, they sounded such a good idea. I've discovered it's German, Geh – walking, Gips – plaster, so walking plasters. But since there's so little about them except in pictures, I think they must have been superseded by these big boots you sometimes see people wearing. Apparently, it's good to put weight on the leg, lessens the muscle atrophy. I've already called the GP to see if I can get one.

'Well, you have been busy. Puts me to shame except I have done the shopping and laid lunch. Hungry?'

'Lunch time already? I was so busy I didn't notice the time, but that shower's given me an appetite. Lead on, McDuff.'

Over lunch we read the news on our laptops as usual, passing occasional comments.

'Right, back to work,' said William, getting to his feet. 'I've still got a few things to get on top of before going in tomorrow.'

'I've had a thought,' I said. 'When Michael rings back, if you do invite him to bring his daughter, remember to say the boys won't be here; she might prefer not to spend the evening with us oldies.'

'Will do. Are you making coffee?'

'Yes, I'll bring yours to the study. I think I'll take mine into the garden. The sun's shining and the roses are out – I might even do some dead heading. I feel like doing something practical.'

Having taken William his coffee, I took mine and my phone into the garden, and settled myself in a sheltered sunny corner. In spite of my good intentions towards the roses I found my eyes closing and I gave in to sleep. I was woken with a start by my phone. Glancing at my watch as I picked it up, to my surprise I saw I had slept at least half an hour. Yawning, I answered, to be greeted by my sister's voice.

'Unlike you to sleep after lunch,' she said, laughing. 'You okay?'

'Yes, I just nodded off in the garden, probably being so relaxed after the past couple of weeks. I was going to call you to say thanks again for having us, and all your support. I don't know how we would have coped without you and John.'

'Well, what is family for if not there when needed? Anyway, we were glad to help. Actually, I had a reason to ring: Callum just had a call from Sir Hamish. I think he may have a date for starting work – oh, talk of the devil. Here he is. Want a word with your Mum, Cal?'

'Hi, Mum, got home okay?'

Yes, thanks, no problems. Is Aunt Fiona right, you have a date to start work?'

'Yup, the day after tomorrow! Hamish and Ailsa are picking me up on their way home from wherever they've been. Remember, I need some clothes from my room. If you could send them tomorrow, that would be great.'

Once again I noted the – probably not unusual - assumption that mothers have nothing to do but attend to their kids' needs on demand. However, I said nothing except to ask what exactly he needed.

'I'll text you a list. If you courier them, they'll arrive in time.'

At this I put my foot down. 'Sorry, Cal, can't do it tomorrow, I'll be working. I'll send them normal parcel post to Hamish's. I'm sure you can manage with what you've got with you for a day to two.

'Oh, okay, I guess.' He didn't sound pleased.

I took a chance with my next remark.: 'Been in touch with Sophia? She seemed keen to hear from you.'

'Don't fucking talk to me about fucking Sophia.'

I could hear a catch in his voice, but I don't think my sister noticed as I heard her tell him never to talk to his mother like that: 'If you were younger, I'd come up with a severe punishment, but as it is, you're old enough to know fucking better, to use your language.'

It was clearly a strain for him to apologise, but he managed it, his voice still cracking.

I eased the situation by wishing him good luck with Hamish and reminding him to be careful not to overdo the heavy work until he was really up to it. 'I'm sure Hamish will understand.'

'Sure. Bye, Mum. Love to Dad.'

My sister came back on the line. 'What was that about?' she asked, understandably surprised by his outburst.

'Clearly something has gone very wrong in his relationship with this Sophia – whom we've never met, by the way - but I honestly have no idea what. He confessed to me at Hamish's that he loved her very much but didn't tell me why he was so upset. We have to wait until he's ready to talk, John's advice, but I think it must be pretty bad to have led to his suicide attempt.'

'I'm sorry, awful for him and awful for you.' Fi sighed. 'I hope for all your sakes they either patch it up or learn to cope with the - I was going to say bereavement, but maybe rift.'

'Thanks, sister. It's great to have you to talk to, but now I'm going to rouse myself and get on with dead-heading the roses. Talk again soon. Love to John and the kids.'

'And love to William. Bye.'

The sky was clouding over slightly so I was glad to get moving and had a very satisfactory half hour dealing with the roses, stopping to smell the various varieties. My favourites were a dark red one whose scent was almost overpowering, and The Poet's Wife, a very beautiful yellow one with perfect blooms and wonderful scent but also fearsome thorns by which I inevitably emerged wounded. When friends noticed my scratches, I told them I had been fighting with the Poet's Wife which always raised an eyebrow.

Returning to my phone, I called Mrs Baker to alert her that we were home and explain about William's accident.

Wednesday saw us in office mode. William took a taxi to the bank while I walked briskly to my office where I was greeted warmly and with commiseration - Dave had clearly told them about the accident. After pleasantries had been exchanged, I sat down with Dave.

'So, where have you got to with the research? I asked. 'Does vortex generation look promising?'

'Well, not really,' he replied. 'Sadly, although a vortex in the burn would be the most interesting option in terms of getting people to take notice and start a trend, I don't think there's likely to be consistently enough water pressure to give meaningful and reliable power. The river is a better bet for that, but the work required would be significantly more expensive. On the other hand, it's a bit nearer the barn Hamish wanted light for.'

'Hmm, that is disappointing, but it's best to be honest up front. But didn't you mention something about cheap solar power for campers?'

'Yes. But it's better than that: there's been considerable advance in small technology in recent years, and if only modest power is required there are simple options, some solar and some water-powered, which require almost no serious installation work. I think that Hamish's best bet is solar for the loch-side camping area. There are quite a few possible models, even the most expensive come in well under £500. They easily charge phones and computers, and the more powerful will run a small fridge. My recommendation for that spot would be for Hamish to buy a solar installation and rent it to the campers – it would be an attraction to put in an advert for camping on his estate and the rent would build up to cover the purchase cost.'

'That sounds good. What about the river site?'

'Well, the solar would also work, but it's a bit shadowed by the hills so sunlight might not be all day. However, there are now small hydro generators which can be installed in the river and can be used to charge the batteries which then charge phones etc. The most expensive ones I found are American and can produce enough power for a small house and also transmit over a reasonable distance. I'd have to do more research, call up the manufacturer in Alaska to get more info.'

'That's really interesting, Dave. Well done. Things have clearly come a long way since I first saw the vortex installation in Bali all those years ago. Write up a preliminary report for Hamish, please, with what you've already found out and do a bit more research on the river possibilities. I suspect Hamish will be disappointed in one way, since he was focused on the vortex route, but he'll be pleased to know the cost won't be nearly as high.' I smiled warmly and patted his shoulder in appreciation before leaving him to his work and making the rounds of the rest of the staff to hear about progress on their various projects.

Chapter Thirty Eight

The rest of that week passed quickly, work and domesticity (and packing and sending Callum's clothes, such an unwieldy parcel I had to relent and courier them in a backpack) were relieved by happy texts from Angus and Bruce in Edinburgh. Both seemed very happy with their bar jobs and enthused about the few Fringe shows they had already managed to fit in - being young, they had the stamina to go to late night ones. Bruce raved about one stand-up he had been to, said he'd nearly died laughing. Although William's and my taste in shows was very different from our sons', I felt a stab of envy and resolved that one year soon we would take ourselves to Edinburgh and indulge in a Fringe binge. Having seen the Fringe programme, I knew it was possible to fit in six or even more shows in one day.

Callum also texted to say that he was safely installed in the Lodge, that Hamish and Ailsa were very relaxed and friendly, but that he hadn't had to do any work yet, that would start on Monday - he trusted his clothes and boots would arrive in time. Ha!

Michael chose Sunday for dinner, but without his daughter who had said she would love to meet us sometime but was busy that weekend. I decided a relaxed supper in the kitchen was most appropriate. I was well prepared, so as I had a few emails to answer I installed myself at my desk while William clicked his way round the kitchen checking wine and glasses.

Glancing out of the window, I saw Michael approach and was just about to get up to go to the front door when he stopped and fished in the bag he was carrying, pulling out – yes! that same wig he had been wearing that fateful day. He donned it, then the glasses and the hat with the feather. I held my breath to see if he changed shoes as well but no, he continued up the path.

Laughing inwardly, when the doorbell rang I called to William. 'Could you answer the door please, I'm just finishing something.'

I heard William's crutches clicking on the wood floor and the door open.

'Sorry, I think you have the wrong house. If you're collecting for charity, we never give at the door.'

'Good evening, William,' said the apparition, by which time I was snorting with laughter and went to join William in the hall.

My poor husband looked so abashed, I felt quite sorry for him as he apologised profusely. 'Very sorry, very sorry, Michael, should have realised.....'

Michael joined me in laughter and held out his hand to shake. 'No problem, I just thought you might be amused to see what had caused your wife such confusion. My daughter got the things out for me but made me promise not to put them on until I arrived.'

'Quite right,' I said. 'I'm amazed you didn't get molested last time. Lucky escape.'

'But I'm glad you did wear them then and got Elizabeth so intrigued; we've made a new friend and possibly a client for the bank as well.' William was all smiles now. 'Come in. Do you want to keep the disguise?'

It was Michel's turn to laugh. 'No, I really think I'm more comfortable as me.' He removed the wig, hat and glasses and replaced them in the bag before pulling out a box of chocolates and handing them to me. 'Just a small offering,' he said with a little bow.

We repaired to the sitting room for pre-dinner drinks.

'White or red wine – or something stronger?' William asked our guest. Michael chose white which I fetched from the fridge.

As I returned, Michael was asking about the crutches which, after the sad tale of William's fall, led to a discussion of my work with Hamish. Michael was very interested, and we learnt more of his involvement with not just batteries but other green initiatives too.

'I've been very concerned about climate change for a long time,' he said, 'and my daughter is a passionate advocate for all things green, would never forgive me if I didn't do everything I could in the cause, even if it's just donating to some of the many organisations pushing for change, or coming up with some useful technical initiatives.'

William mentioned again that he had potential investors in ecological ventures which he and Michael would follow up at the meetings he had arranged for the coming couple of days.

Glancing at my watch, I paused the conversation to announce supper was calling and led the men to the kitchen.

It was a simple meal, largely vegetarian which chimed happily with our conversation, and elicited appreciative comments from our guest. We steered away from work topics and focused instead on our families and other interests. I was surprised to learn that Michael was a keen marathon participant and kept up fitness with Park Runs most weekends. Pressed on his marathon times, he admitted that four hours was his target these days, but he had achieved three and a half two years before. We were duly impressed as we guessed he was over fifty.

Having finished the meal with coffee and the chocolates Michael had brought, as Michael prepared to leave William suggested he came to the bank about ten the next day to prepare for the arranged meetings. 'Suit you?'

'No problem,' Michael replied with a smile. 'Give me a chance to recover from the lovely meal. I've really enjoyed this evening. Thanks so much, and I look forward to reciprocating when you see the opportunity to come to Cambridge, maybe when the boys are back up.'

We shook hands and waved him off, returning to the kitchen to finish tidying up, agreeing what an easy and interesting guest Michael was.

William was very cheerful when he came home from work the next evening, eager to report on the meetings he and Michael had had, both with a potential investor and with a patent agent.

'Obviously, the investor wants to know the patent situation before taking it any further, but if Michael's battery invention really is different and detailed enough to register a UK patent quickly before the Chinese go the same route, it looks promising. I don't know enough about patents to comment so left that with Michael. Tomorrow we'll meet with two more investors with eco criteria. It's all very interesting. How was your day?'

'Nothing special, no more from Dave yet and Hamish hasn't responded to the interim report Dave sent at the end of last week.'

Had we known what was in store for us, we wouldn't have slept so well that night.

Chapter Thirty Nine

In between his various meetings at the bank that week, William arranged to get one of the special boots, the modern equivalent of the geh-gips he had seen and hoped to have it the following week. He also fitted in a Friday afternoon appointment with his Parkinson's specialist who was so encouraging about the new developments in treatment that William came home, earlier than usual, almost singing.

By chance, I had also come home early and raised an eyebrow at his cheerfulness.

'The quack said that I should stop worrying about the future as the current treatments are very good at controlling the symptoms, and within a very few years the new gene and cell-based therapies which are showing real promise may be available.' William reported.

I gave him a heart-felt hug. 'That's great news, and a weight off both our minds. Let's drink to that. Wine or something stronger?'

'Oh, I think this news deserves a good G and T, don't you agree?'

I prepared the drinks and we had barely sat down and raised our glasses to each other when the doorbell went.

'I wonder who that can be? Expecting anyone?' I asked William who shook his head.

Looking quickly through the spy hole I was surprised to see two men standing there. I opened the door cautiously.

Good evening. Mrs Trenchard?' said the nearer man, showing me a detective's badge.

Awful thoughts ran through my mind in those few

seconds: an accident to one of the boys, my family, my staff?

I nodded. 'What's the problem?' I'm sure my voice was shaking.

'May we come in?'

I opened the door wider. As both men entered, the man who had shown his badge introduced himself as Detective Inspector Jones and his companion, a younger man, as Detective Richardson.

Unsure what to do next, stay in the hall, invite them in, I stammered 'What can I do for you? Has something happened to one of our family?'

'No, but we need to ask you some questions. Perhaps we could sit down.' It was a statement, not a question.

Thinking quickly, I wondered whether to take them into the kitchen, or to join William in the sitting room. Deciding that, in spite of the interruption to our celebratory drinks, it was best to bring William into the conversation – if that was what it was to be – straight away. I led them to the sitting room.

'Please excuse my husband not standing to greet you,' I said, indicating William's crutches.

'What's all this about?' William sounded more annoyed than interested.

'Do you have a son called Callum?' DI Jones began.

'Yes,' we answered in unison. 'Why?'

'We would like to speak to him. Is he here?'

We shook our heads. 'No, he's in Scotland, working.'

DI Jones continued nevertheless. 'Have you noticed any change in his behaviour recently? Any change in his habits or spending?'

That threw us, but I wasn't going to answer until I knew more about why they were there.

Nor was William. 'I'm not answering that until you tell us why you're asking.'

'Why, sir, something to hide?' Young Detective Richardson spoke brusquely.

'How dare you!' William began to reach for his crutches as if to stand but I intervened as the Inspector admonished his colleague with a frown.

'Excuse our unwillingness to reply, but until we have some idea of why you are asking, it's hard to answer. However, I can tell you that he told us recently that he and his girlfriend have broken up and he's extremely upset. In fact, he tried to commit suicide three weeks ago. Does that count as a change in habits?' I couldn't help sounding sarcastic.

The Inspector had the grace to express sympathy but pressed his point.

'No, of course that is not what we had in mind. But have you noticed any change in his spending?'

I again responded. 'No. He only came down from university a few weeks before his attempted suicide and we certainly didn't notice any change in spending then. He's been with us, his brothers and my sister's family in Scotland since – well, until a week ago when we came home. He stayed on with my sister until he left to take up a job on an estate in the Highlands a few days ago.'

'Have his brothers mentioned anything?' The Inspector changed tack.

I decided I had to be more truthful. 'To be honest, we had all noticed that he was somewhat withdrawn since he came down from Cambridge, less friendly, less willing to talk to us. But that may have been to do with the girlfriend problem. And he did sometimes go out quite late in the evenings. But nothing else untoward, I can assure you.'

'I agree,' said William. 'He wasn't his usual cheerful self, but we absolutely didn't see the suicide attempt coming, or anything else worrying. And once he recovered from his injuries up in Inverness, he became quite his old self.'

'What injuries might those be?' asked Detective Richardson.

'He got into a fight the night he tried to commit suicide. Some youths attacked him. We don't know why, he wouldn't tell us. Maybe he was just in the wrong place at the wrong time. That's all we know.' Neither William nor I wanted to mention our earlier concerns about drugs, the one odd phone call I had overheard one night when he had demanded payment for something. What would such an admission lead to?

'Hmmm, interesting,' mused DI Jones. 'I wonder, does the name Sophia Nicholson-Smith mean anything to you?'

William and I looked at one another. I responded.

'Yes, Callum's girlfriend – ex-girlfriend – was called Sophia, and I think that was her surname.'

DI Jones looked up sharply. 'What was she like? What do you know about her?'

'We've never met her. All we know is that she lives in a very nice house in Norfolk – Callum showed us a photo of it once. Her father is well off - shipping, I seem to remember – and her mother is Greek. And,' William continued, 'apparently she's stunningly beautiful. Callum was quite besotted.'

'How did he meet her?' Detective Richardson felt the need to partake in the inquisition.

'I believe her brother was a friend of Callum's at Cambridge and introduced them,' I was able to answer. 'But, please, can you give us some idea of what this is all about. If we understood, maybe we would be able to be more helpful.'

'All we can tell you is that we're investigating a drug running group that we suspect is using county lines to distribute the drugs - you've read about county lines?' DI Jones paused.

We nodded, fearful of how this might involve Callum.

DI Jones continued. 'We have reason to believe that this Sophia was actively involved, sufficient reason for us to requisition her mobile. There were many calls to your son, among others, and we're checking on all her contacts. That's why we're here.'

My mind was in turmoil; was it really possible that Callum had been involved? Again, I remembered that late phone call, Callum's withdrawal from us and his brothers. Was it conceivable that he was indeed involved in the drug trade? I shuddered to think about it. I longed for the policemen to go so that William and I could talk.

William spoke up. 'To us it's impossible to believe that our son could be involved and I hope we've satisfied you on that, but we do understand your need to follow up on all Sophia's contacts. I hope this is the end of the matter.'

Although his voice was firm, I could detect an undertone of worry which I hope escaped our visitors.

'I don't think there's anything more we can ask you, but we shall of course be in contact with your son in case he can throw more light on Sophia's activities. You say he's working on an estate in Scotland. We would be grateful if you could give us some details. Detective Richardson will make a note.

My heart sank further. Poor Callum, having regained both strength and his usual cheerfulness, and found a summer job he was thrilled about with such lovely people as Hamish and Ailsa, to be involved in this investigation, whether implicated or not, might well set him back. However, I knew I couldn't escape this so gave the details of the estate.

'You already have his mobile number and he's not changed it – that must show he's not hiding anything,' I said, my fingers crossed behind my back. 'Will you just speak to him, or will you have to go to see him in person?'

'One of our Scottish colleagues will go to question him,' Detective Richardson said, returning his notebook to his pocket. 'More's the pity. I love the Highlands.'

'I think that's all for now,' said the DI, ignoring his colleague's remark and getting to his feet. 'Thank you for your cooperation. I hope for your sakes this will be the end of the matter for Callum and you.'

Feeling weak at the knees and hoping the DI was right, but having a niggling feeling he might not be, I showed the two men out.

Chapter Forty

Returning to the sitting room, I sat down heavily on the sofa next to William and took his hand.

'What do you think?' I asked him. 'Is it really possible our suspicions were well founded?'

'God, I don't know, but it does sound possible. It fits with his behaviour, I suppose, how withdrawn he has been. But I had put it out of my mind when we heard he'd broken up with Sophia and was so upset. That would have explained everything. If he really has been involved, it must be that Sophia who got him into it, damn her.'

'I agree that's more likely than Callum involving her.' I sighed. 'But the immediate question, is what do we do? We have to warn him that the police will be in touch, but is it okay just to tell him by phone? Just supposing he reacts badly…..' I couldn't finish the sentence, but I knew William's mind would be working the same way. 'There's another problem. What – if anything - do we tell Hamish and Ailsa? They'll be very surprised to have the police turn up to question him, and just after he started work with them.'

'I think we have to warn them too.' William said, a troubled frown on his forehead.

'What a mess, what a ghastly situation. Oh, dear, Callum will be devastated either way, to think the girl he loved was involved in drugs and to realise he's under suspicion even if he's innocent, and even worse if he has been involved. And we won't exactly be thrilled if he was either.' I stood up and began to pace the room, hoping it would help me to think but sat down again. 'I think I have to go back, tell Callum in person. Do you agree? Is that the best thing to do, given all the history?'

William sighed. 'There's certainly good argument for breaking the news in person, as you said. If he takes it really badly, at least if one of us was with him, we could make it clear we would support him whatever happens.' He smiled apologetically before continuing. 'And I'm really sorry, but I do think it has to be you, given my bloody leg.'

'Of course. Maybe I could think of an excuse to go to see Hamish at short notice, something to do with his project. Then it wouldn't seem so odd, I wouldn't need to tell him and Ailsa why I had really come.' I thought for a moment then groaned. 'Do you think the Scottish police would go to see him on a weekend? Do they treat such investigations as urgent? If they do, I should go tomorrow – maybe even tonight. But then it wouldn't be realistic to pretend to Hamish that I needed to do some work for him at such short notice – and at a weekend.....'

We sat in silence for a minute digesting the situation and the options.

'I have a plan,' I said finally. 'How about I ring Callum and tell him I've some bad news about Sophia and I want to tell him in person as I know how upset he'll be, say I'll fly up tonight, stay with Fi and come to the estate in the morning. And I'll text Hamish to tell him I'm coming.'

Even before I finished speaking William had his phone out. 'Checking flights. No, nothing tonight. Shall I check sleepers?'

I nodded.

It didn't take William long to give me the depressing news that it was hopeless. 'The only through train tonight leaves at 8.15 and it's already past 7. I really don't think it's realistic to aim for that. None of the others would get you in before midday tomorrow. I think you have to fly up in the morning, if we're sure it's right for you to go.'

He went back to his phone only to report that the earliest flight was 10.55 from Luton, getting in about half past twelve. 'I think you just have to accept that. The chance of the police turning up tomorrow morning must be minimal, so surely it doesn't matter – and it gives us time to think how to play it with Hamish and Ailsa. Shall I book it?'

Sighing, I agreed. Then, with a rueful smile, I pointed at our almost untouched drinks, the ice melted. 'Shall I top them up, get more ice?'

'No, I don't feel like it anymore, no cause for celebration. Have you already got supper sorted? If not, let's settle for a takeaway. While we're waiting we can call Cal and maybe Hamish too. Oh, and I'll book a taxi to Luton and a rental car from the airport right now.'

Once again, I blessed my husband for being so organised and thoughtful. 'OK, what do you fancy to eat?'

'Don't be surprised, but I think I could murder a pizza. '

I laughed. I'll call for pizzas now – your usual with pepperoni?'

'Yes, that's fine, and maybe we could have a glass of red wine with them, I'll come and look out a bottle when I've done the booking.'

Over the meal we agreed what we would say to Callum. I gave up the idea of a work excuse to give Hamish, instead dreamt up a story about visiting an old school friend who was very ill and taking the opportunity to see how Callum was getting on, even though it was only a few days since he started work there.

'Actually, there are some thoughts on the project I can

run past Hamish while I'm there so that's good.' I had had a discussion with Dave during the week about how many campers Hamish envisaged, the scale of his enterprise.

'OK, let's get this call over with. Shall I do it, or will you?' asked William.

'You do it, you're probably better at making the news sound less of a disaster.' I wasn't chickening out, I did think it was best.

William dialled Cal's mobile, putting it on speakerphone. Cal answered after just a few rings.

'Hi Cal, is this a good moment?'

'Yup, fine. How's the leg?'

'All fine, getting one of those special leg braces next week so I'll be able to walk much more easily. How are you getting on with Hamish and Ailsa? Working you hard?'

'Actually, they're being very thoughtful about not pushing me too hard until I'm 100% again. And Ailsa's going to give me cooking lessons.'

'That's good news, but I'm afraid we've got some less good news for you. We had a visit from some detectives this evening, they're investigating Sophia about something and want to talk to all her contacts on her phone, including you.'

'What! Why? What did you say to them?' Callum sounded nervous but William played it down, replying calmly.

'We just told them she had been your girlfriend but that she had broken up with you a few weeks ago and you had been very upset, nothing else.'

'Did they say why they were investigating her?'

At this point William decided to lie. 'Not really, they were very vague. It was all a bit odd. Anyway, they're going to get the Scottish police to come to talk to you, they didn't say when, but we thought we should alert you, not let it come out of the blue.'

Callum was silent. I motioned to William to let me have the phone.

'Hi darling, this is a bore but we really don't have much idea what it's about. But there's another bit of news, sad and happy at the same time. It's sad because an old school friend of mine – you don't know her - is very ill and I am coming up to see her this weekend, but good because I thought I'd pop down to see you. Also, I have something I'd like to discuss with Hamish. Are you free tomorrow afternoon?'

'Can be, I guess, but we planned a cooking lesson. Will you stay over the weekend?' His voice was very flat.

'Maybe, depends on the friend and whether I can stay with Fi and John. It's all very sudden and a bit soon after the last time, but I think I have to come.' It wasn't hard to sound regretful.

'OK, see you tomorrow afternoon. Bye,'

Bye, love you,' William and I said in unison, but Callum didn't respond.

I texted Hamish to say I was coming and gave the same excuse. No problem, he replied, be nice to see you. 'Be in time for lunch?'

'I doubt it, maybe coffee and a piece of Ailsa's cake, though!'

* * *

Picking up the rental car, I drove the now familiar road to the hunting lodge, arriving at 2.30 as predicted. I was pleased to see Hamish come out to welcome me and was about to give him a light hug when I saw the expression on his face.

'What's wrong, Hamish? What's happened?' A cold fear

gripped me. 'Is it to do with Callum? Is he alright?'

'Not what I'd call alright. He's with Ailsa in the kitchen. I'm so glad you're here, he's in a bad way.'

'Is he hurt?' I could hardly get the words out.

'No, but......' Hamish turned to go into the house and I followed blindly, dreading what I would find.

Pausing at the kitchen door, Hamish touched my arm gently. 'He's had what I can only describe as a meltdown. Ailsa found him this morning. She'll explain.'

Chapter Forty One

Tactfully, Hamish left me. As I entered the kitchen my heart was pounding. Concern for Callum mixed with fear about what I was going to find and to hear.

Callum was slumped over the kitchen table, his head resting on his arms. Ailsa was sitting beside him, stroking his back gently. She looked up at me with a careful smile.

'Hi, Elizabeth, I'm so glad you're here, even though it was sad news about your friend which brought you up north again so soon.' She motioned to the chair the other side of Callum who made no sign of acknowledging my presence.

I kissed the top of his head then sat down, as close to him as I could, and put my arm round him. I could feel him trembling.

'Callum, darling. What is it? What's happened?'

He didn't reply.

'Please, Callum, tell me. Whatever it is, I'm here to support you.'

His head moved slightly to show he had heard.

'I think it might be easier if I tell you – right, Callum?' Ailsa spoke very gently.

Callum didn't dissent so Ailsa continued. 'He's told me the whole story and it's probably easier for him not to have to go through it again. It's not a happy one.' She paused before continuing.

'He didn't come down to breakfast as usual this morning, but I wasn't concerned, I know about enjoying a good lie-in. However, when I hadn't seen him by mid-morning I went to see if he was in the stable. He was there, lying in the straw, sobbing, a big kitchen knife by his hand.' Ailsa paused and looked up at me, warning me not to interrupt.

I fought back the urge to cry, to shout out, and involuntarily tightened my arm round Callum's shoulders, pulling us closer together, but he still didn't respond.

'I pushed the knife away and sat down beside him, took his hand and just waited like I would with one of my pupils at school. After a few minutes he calmed down and sat up. He turned away from me and just said 'I couldn't do it.' His voice was husky from crying. Do what? I asked him and he held out his other hand, wrist up. It was all I could do not to cry myself as I saw the cut. Looking over at the knife, I could see some blood on the blade, not much as he hadn't cut very deep.'

'Oh, Cal, thanks heavens you didn't... it's too awful to think of you .....' Now my tears came.

To my relief, Callum looked up at me, a wan smile just touching his lips.

'Shall I go on, Cal?' Ailsa asked.

Callum nodded.

'He told me about your phone call, that the police might come and question him. I asked him what about and the whole sad story came out. As you know, he was deeply in love with this Sophia and devastated that they had broken up.'

'Yes, when he and I didn't go with the others to the river when we were all here, he broke down crying and said he loved her so much... He didn't have time to tell me more as Hamish and his brothers returned. He hasn't talked about it to us since and we didn't want to push him; my brother-in-law who's a doctor said we should probably wait until he was ready to talk.' I began to wonder if John's advice had been right.

Ailsa continued. 'Apparently it all began when Sophia asked him to deliver a packet to a friend in London, which he did, no problem. Then she asked several more times, and he began to suspect he was being used to deliver drugs as sometimes he was given money to pass on to her. He told her he didn't want to do it anymore, but she said that if he really loved her, he would do it for her. He agreed to do a couple more deliveries, always trying to get out of it, but he loved her so much that he didn't want to lose her.

'More and more unhappy about it, he finally told Sophia he would do one final drop, as he had realised she was just using him and didn't really love him at all. Told her it was over, it would be the last one, he didn't want to see or speak to her ever again. That was just before you came up to Inverness. This time, the man he had to deliver to had others with him, and they turned nasty, refused to give him the money they owed. They accused him of cheating them, and they wanted the rest of the drugs – which he didn't have. They didn't believe him and beat him up, quite badly, as you know.

'That evening, back home, he was in serious pain, frightened by what had happened, and deeply unhappy at being taken in by Sophia who he had believed loved him as much as he loved her. He said he was so ashamed of himself and what he had been led to do, and terrified that one day the police would come for him. He couldn't bear the thought that you would find out, the shame brought on you and the family. He thought that if he died, you would never find out. The rest you know.'

At this point Callum sat up and spoke directly to me, his voice trembling. 'I'm so sorry, Mum, really, really, sorry. I know I've been stupid, but I've been so frightened, so ashamed. And after that first attempt to kill myself, when I saw what it did to you, to Dad, Angus and Bruce it made me try to get over it. I ignored all Sophia's calls and texts.

Being with Aunt Fiona and the family really helped, they're so nice. Coming here too was special, the space, the air, and I immediately liked Hamish and Ailsa.

'But then Sophia tried to contact me through her brother and Bruce, that pushed me over the edge again. But when Uncle John and Lucy found me down by the river, I had already decided not to jump. I was so relieved that you all pretended I'd just gone for a walk.' Callum actually managed a smile. 'It was after that I got the idea of asking Hamish if I could come and work for him; I was so happy when he said yes. Life seemed possible again. Then you called last night and I guessed......'

I gently pulled Callum to his feet and we clung together.

Ailsa quietly left the room, 'Just join us when you're ready,' she said as she closed the door behind her.

After a few minutes in silence, we sat down again.

'I'm so sorry, Mum,' he said again. 'I know I've been really stupid, but Sophia was so sweet with me, kept telling me she loved me. We were so happy, had such fun together. It never occurred to me that she was just acting, that she had seen how she could manipulate me....'

'It's alright Cal, I said, taking his hand. 'You know how relieved we all are that you didn't die. We couldn't imagine life without you. But I admit we had been concerned. We had all begun to worry about you as you had become withdrawn, not your usual self at all.

'I have to confess that once, a few weeks ago, when you came home late and I wasn't asleep, I overheard you on the phone, demanding money from someone. I told Dad and we wondered about drugs but decided it was very unlikely and that we shouldn't say anything. Later, when we learned about you breaking up with Sophia, we thought that explained your mood and stopped worrying. Perhaps we should have said something....' I sighed.

'If you had, I would have denied everything – and probably pretended to get cross with you for doubting me.' Callum smiled ruefully. 'But now we have to be realistic, I'm going to get arrested. I'll be sent to prison. I've fucked up my life.'

Chapter Forty Two

We were both silent for a few seconds. My thoughts were racing, from recognition -and fear - that he could be right - and from determination that it must not happen. Finally, I spoke.

'We have to accept that you're in a dreadful place, but you know Dad and I will do everything in our power to make sure it doesn't come to the worst. And we will all support you, no matter what. So, let's think together about the next step.'

I continued calmly: 'We don't know when the police will come to talk to you; there's no point in hiding and hoping they won't find you. I think you should stay here with Hamish and Ailsa who are so kind and where you can continue to be useful, if they're happy with that. What do you think?'

Callum said, nodding. 'I don't know if Ailsa has told Hamish what happened and why, but he needs to know or he'll wonder why the police turn up. It'll be horribly embarrassing, but we've got to do it. If he's okay with it, then I would really like to stay.'

'I agree about telling him. The other people who need to know are Aunt Fi and Uncle John. It would be hard for me to come up from London at a moment's notice if you need support. They are so much nearer, and they know about the first suicide attempt, though not why. Would you be willing for me to tell them the whole story? I'm sure they won't judge you harshly and will be there for you if needed.'

'I would prefer to tell them myself. But it wouldn't be the same by telephone, and I can't ask them to come here, or go there without being a nuisance to Hamish.' Callum sighed. 'I guess it has to be you. Sorry.'

'I honestly don't mind. I'm hoping to see them anyway, and to beg a bed if I can't get a flight tonight.'

'What about your friend who's ill?' Callum asked. 'Don't you want to see her?'

I had to admit she had been a ruse so as not to let Hamish and Ailsa think there was something wrong.

Callum actually laughed. 'Well done, Mum. Good thinking. It worked perfectly.'

I returned to the serious matter in hand.

'When the police come, I think you should be completely honest, as you were with Ailsa. You can't pretend none of it happened. If charged, you will have to plead guilty – of being a mule, but not for dealing.' I paused, two worrying thoughts suddenly occurring to me. 'Did Sophia ever pay you for doing the deliveries?'

'No, not in money.'

'What do you mean?

'Well, she was always extra nice to me afterwards.'

I swear he blushed as he answered and I guessed why, smiling inwardly. I asked my second question, hoping against hope that he would give the answer I needed.

'Did you – do you – use drugs?'

'You can probably guess I've smoked marijuana, everyone does at uni, but not a lot.'

And the hard stuff?' I pressed him.

Callum looked me in the eye. 'Sophia got me to try cocaine, twice, a couple of months ago. I liked it but I knew I didn't want to go down that route, so I refused after that. That's the truth.'

I believed him and was hugely relieved as I had read that

forensics could tell from analysing people's hair whether they were users.

The more I learned, the sorrier I felt for him. Sophia had clearly been manipulating him horribly to drag him into the drug scene, and used him shamelessly. I gave him a quick kiss and suggested we join the others.

They looked up questioningly from the books they were reading as we emerged from the kitchen. I smiled to reassure them.

'Might this be a good time for some tea and cake?' Ailsa said, moving towards the kitchen. 'I guess you could both do with it – in fact we all could.'

Callum and I sat down. I was wondering how to start the conversation when Callum, turning to Hamish, spoke up. 'Has Ailsa told you the whole story?'

Hamish nodded. 'Yes, she did, just now, and I'm so sorry to hear what a difficult time you're having – I was really shocked to hear you tried to cut your wrists. I do hope that telling Ailsa helped, that must have been hard to do.'

'She was wonderful, really kind and patient. I will thank her properly.' Callum's gratitude was evident, tears again not far from the surface.

Hamish nodded before continuing. 'And I'm so glad your mother happened to have to come up today and was here to comfort you. Have you been thinking about what happens next?'

I explained about the police visit in London and that the local police would certainly be coming to interview him, though at present they were just investigating Sophia.

'Unfortunately, there's no guarantee that she won't implicate Callum – in fact, from the callousness with which she's treated him so far, I'm pretty sure she will.' I shrugged.

'There's not much can be done about that except Callum making sure he always tells the truth. We have witnesses – including Ailsa, if she's willing - who can back up his emotional state and huge regrets.'

Ailsa appeared with a tray laden with tea things and a delicious-looking chocolate cake in time to respond. 'Of course I'll help if needed.'

'So, Cal, do you feel you need to be home with your parents now?' Hamish asked as Ailsa set the tray on the table.

'Actually, Hamish, I was going to ask you if, now you know what a mess I've made of my life, would you rather I left? Or might I stay and work for you as we planned?'

'Do you want to leave?' Ailsa asked as she began pouring the tea.

I saw Callum swallow hard before answering. 'No, I love it here, I love being out in the open air, having practical things to do. And you two are the kindest, nicest people I could possibly be with – apart from Mum and Dad, that is,' he added hastily.

'Well,' said Hamish, 'we do still need help and so far – well, until today - you've been helpful and no trouble. So yes, if Ailsa is happy too.'

Callum looked up hopefully at Ailsa who smiled as she handed him a slice of cake and a cup of tea.

'Sure. I was looking forward to giving you some cooking lessons, as well has having help with the horses.'

'Thank you both so much. I'm really grateful.'

I think if Callum hadn't been holding the plate and his tea, he'd have got up and kissed Ailsa.

I added my heartfelt thanks and sat back, relieved to know Callum would be in good hands. I tucked into my cake, suddenly realising how hungry I was, having not had any lunch.

'If you can teach Callum to make cakes like this, our whole family will benefit! It's delicious, and so light.' I smiled before continuing. 'My sister Fiona and her husband, John, live in Inverness. Cal's agreed I can tell them the whole story – they already know some of it, but not about the drugs – so that he can call on them to help if necessary, for example dealing with the police, as I can't promise to come up at short notice. John's a GP and has had some dealings with problematic youth – sorry Cal, shorthand for he may know a bit about police and drugs.'

Hamish and Ailsa laughed, and Callum had the grace to acknowledge my apology with a grin.

'More cake, any of you?' Ailsa asked.

'I'd better not, 'I said with regret. 'I should ring my sister to see if they can meet me this evening, before I get a late flight home. Otherwise, I'll have to stay the night with them. I must call William, too. He'll be worrying why I haven't called before. So, if you'll excuse me, I'll make the calls outside.'

I drank the last of my tea and went into the garden. There was a cool wind blowing but I found a sheltered corner with a decent signal and rang Fi who was predictably very surprised to hear I was at Hamish's.

'It's complicated, but is there any chance I could come over for a serious chat about Callum?'

'Of course, but that sounds worrying. Need a bed? Unfortunately, we're out to dinner tonight so you'd be on your own with the kids – if they're around.'

'Kind of you, but I'd like to get home tonight if I can.' I glanced at my watch. 'Help, it's already past four! But I think if I leave soon and the traffic's not bad, I can just manage to get to you, tell you what's happened and still catch the last flight.'

'I think that's unrealistic,' my sister said firmly. 'It's holiday season so there'll be all sorts of dozy drivers around, rubbernecking as they drive. You'll have to stay.'

My heart sank a little; I really wanted to get back to William – and my own bed – after the stress of the last 24 hours. I was about to concede, however, when my sister came up with another plan.

'Just had a thought,' she said. 'The dinner we're going to is with friends who live out towards the airport, and not until eight. We could meet you at the airport about seven and talk in the café. What do you think?'

What a relief! Calculating I would easily have time to get there and return the rental car by seven, I accepted with gratitude.

'Brilliant, Fi, you're a star. This is really important. I hope John won't mind.'

'I know you wouldn't be up here and wanting to talk unless it was important so I'm sure he won't. You've got me worried so, yes, we'll go with this. See you in the cafe. Drive safely. Love to Callum. Bye.'

With a huge sigh of relief, I returned to the house.

'All fixed,' I said. 'My sister's suggested meeting at the airport at seven as they're going to dinner near there, so the pressure's off a bit. I actually have time for more tea – and I've changed my mind about more cake, if Cal hasn't eaten it all.'

Now having nearly an hour to spare, I was able to relax a little, enjoy the company and seeing Callum also more himself, knowing he could stay. I took the opportunity to raise a work issue with Hamish.

'To change to a less troubling subject, Hamish, Dave and I have been discussing your project and there's one big question which we should have raised with you before, though we have talked about it ourselves, as it will affect what we can recommend.'

'And that is?' asked Hamish.

'What scale of camping are you thinking of? Occasional campers who want wilderness, or perhaps a slightly more formal site with a modicum of amenities? It still needn't be very formal, but could have, for example, a communal composting toilet and maybe an outdoor shower.'

'Hmm, interesting that you raise that. I've been thinking about it myself recently – should have thought before, of course, as obviously it makes quite a difference to power needs. I've been meaning to talk to Ailsa about it.'

'Glad you're not leaving me out of the discussion.' There was a touch of sarcasm in Ailsa's tone. 'It does rather concern me too.'

I couldn't resist a small smile at her intervention but carried on without comment.

'Initially when you contacted Trenchant, Hamish, you said that you hoped to increase income for the estate. A more formal operation would be easier to promote and probably have wider appeal but might have more impact on your lives.' I paused, not wanting to complicate matters further, but felt I should add one more consideration. 'And have you thought about the impact on the wildlife on the estate – and, of course, the hunting?'

Suddenly remembering that his father had been shot in a hunting accident, I wished I had kept my mouth shut but neither Hamish nor Ailsa reacted. To my relief and surprise, Callum then spoke. He had clearly been following the conversation, perhaps it took his mind off his problems for a few minutes.

'Do you remember, Mum, a few years ago, when we were

about ten, you took us to an eco-camping site somewhere in the west country? It was such fun. The tents were all provided, there were only composting loos and outdoor showers like you just mentioned. But I also remember that there were activities like nature walks, plant spotting – they even had a bread making session. I remember I loved that.' He smiled at Ailsa. 'And there were animals to pet as well.'

'Indeed I do.' I laughed. 'It was hard to tear you all away when it was time to leave. But I don't think at this stage it's what Hamish has in mind.'

'I agree, but let's not rule it out. Fun and education and ecology all at the same time.' Ailsa spoke thoughtfully. 'I might enjoy managing that. Lots to think about.'

Surprised at the direction the conversation had taken and aware of the time, I decided this was a good moment to take my leave. I stood and thanked our hosts warmly, not just for the refreshments, but particularly for their kindness to Callum.

'I can't tell you how much I – we – appreciate it. I just hope that the police visit and any follow-up don't take up much of your precious time. And I trust you have lots of good hard work for my son!'

'Don't worry, we can keep him busy,' Hamish grinned giving me a hug, to my surprise.

'Absolutely,' added Ailsa, also hugging me. 'And I'll definitely teach him cake-making. He'll never want for friends if he can master a good chocolate cake!'

Callum followed me out to the car.

'Thanks, Mum. I know this is an awful situation, but it isn't half as awful as it was before Ailsa found me and you came. Thanks a million for coming. Tell Dad I love him and won't do anything silly ever again.' His sad face and drooping shoulders reinforced his words.

We kissed goodbye and I got into the car. Just as I was about to drive off, I had an important thought and wound down the window.

'Are you going to tell Angus and Bruce, or shall I?

A cloud passed over Callum's face and he paused before replying. 'I will. They'll understand.'

I nodded and put the car into gear. Hamish and Ailsa waved from the doorway. Callum turned and went back to them.

As I drove away, in my rear view mirror I saw Ailsa give Callum a hug and knew he was in good hands.

Chapter Forty Three

On my way down to the road I saw Mac leaving the barn and put the window down to say how much Callum enjoyed being on the estate and hoped he wouldn't put Mac out of his job.

Mac laughed. 'No danger, plenty to do!' and waved me cheerfully on my way.

I was about to turn into the road when my phone rang. I pulled in to answer. William. Cursing myself for not calling him after talking to Fi, I answered.

'Sorry, darling, I was about to call,' I lied.

'So I should bloody well think. I've been sitting here all afternoon, getting more and more worried, thinking perhaps the news was so bad you didn't want to tell me.'

It was very rare to hear William so cross.

'I'm really, really sorry. It's been full on since I got here, and I've just left to drive back to Inverness. I'm meeting Fi and John at the airport so I hope I can get on the last flight.' I don't know why I went into that detail rather than telling him immediately about Callum. Nor did he; his response was just as cross.

'For god's sake, woman, put me out of my misery. How is Cal?'

I took a deep breath before starting. 'He tried to cut his wrists.....'

I got no further as William cried 'No!' and began to sob.

'Hush, darling. He's okay. Let me tell you the whole story.'

William's sobs died down as I related how Ailsa had found him in the stable and how exceptionally kind and thoughtful she had been. Cal had told her everything and she, with his permission, had related the whole sad saga to me.

'I'll tell you everything when I get home but, most important, Callum's on a more even keel now, though clearly still very worried about what will happen to him. Hamish now also knows the full story and is happy to have Cal continue to stay and to work for him. Cal was very happy to hear that. He couldn't be in better hands.'

'Phew, that's some relief at least.' William sighed. 'When will you get home?'

'I hope by midnight, but I'll confirm when I know I can get on that flight. I called Fi as I think she and John will be great back up for Cal if he needs support with the police. I've arranged to meet them at the airport - Fi's idea as they're going out to dinner with friends near there. Cal's given me permission to tell them everything.'

'What will you do if the flight's full or you miss it?'

I thought quickly. 'There's probably an early flight tomorrow – though maybe not as it's Sunday, I've just realised. If there is, I'll stay at the hotel I noticed right at the airport, otherwise I'll beg a key from Fi and kip at theirs.'

'OK, but I really hope you get home tonight. I want to know everything. Keep in touch about the flight.'

'Of course – and I'm so sorry I couldn't call before. Bye, darling. Love you.'

'Love you – and I'm sorry I shouted at you. Fingers crossed for that flight. Bye'

I sat quietly for a couple of minutes before starting the engine and turning onto the road to Inverness. As luck would have it, it began to rain heavily and the traffic was slow, so I was very glad I was meeting them at the airport and not at their house. I returned the rental car in good time and found Fi and John already installed in a quiet corner of the café in the terminal.

After exchanging hugs, I explained I needed to check availability at the ticket desk.

'Order me a G&T if they serve them here, please. Otherwise, I'll make do with a strong coffee. Won't be a minute – I hope.' I ran to the desk and was hugely relieved to find I could get a seat in Economy, though I would have paid serious money for business class if necessary.

I rang William to give him the good news before joining the others. I told him not to meet me, I'd take a taxi. He protested but I insisted. 'It'll be late and there may be delays, you never know. I don't want you having to hang around. Be at home - and awake - to welcome me back.' He agreed reluctantly, and I returned to the café.

'G&T it is,' said John smiling as he handed me the tumbler. 'Forgive us for sticking to coffee, but there'll be plenty to drink at this dinner and we've got to drive home. Did you get on the flight?'

'Yes, I did,' I replied, brandishing my boarding pass and taking rather more than a sip of my drink as I steeled myself to launch into the Callum situation.

They listened closely, asking just a few questions. As I finished, I explained tentatively how I hoped they might be able to help if necessary.

'Obviously William or I would come up to help deal with the police, but it for some reason we couldn't get away, do you think you could bear to be in loco parentis, as it were? Callum really likes you both – he was so happy at the way you handled him that evening by the river, John.'

Fi and John looked at each other before John spoke.

'It's a big ask. Although in principle I would like to say yes, given my job it would be hard to prioritise Callum. And my experience with young people, drugs and the police is not that extensive so I'm no expert. What do you think, Fi?'

'I'm not that tied up with other duties so I could probably be supportive to be supportive if he needs a shoulder to lean on, or to be present when he's being questioned. But my knowledge of drugs and the law is pretty much zero.' Fi replied hesitantly, smiling apologetically.

My heart sank at their lack of enthusiasm but I rallied and thanked Fi. 'I sincerely hope it wouldn't be more than going with him when he's summoned for questioning. He'll be scared and very glad of family support. But another thing, we may well need a solicitor. Could you possibly ask around for a recommendation? That would be a big help.'

John readily agreed. 'I'm sure I can get some suitable names, no problem.'

'Thanks, that's very helpful. I fear he – we – are going to have a pretty uncomfortable time, especially if the wretched Sophia tries to paint him as more of a willing accomplice than he actually was.' I sighed. 'We'll just have to take things as they come.'

I took another swig of my drink before changing the subject. 'Enough of our woes. What's new with you two? And the kids?'

'Not a lot since you went back to London. Damian's doing well in the tennis club junior tournament, though. Looks like he might make the finals. Oh, and John's wangled some leave later this month so we're plotting a short trip to France. Haven't decided where yet.' My sister glanced at John. 'We seem to have different ideas...'

Our conversation continued in this light vein for a few minutes when John suddenly scraped his chair back from the table and stood up. 'Hey, look at the time! Sorry, Elizabeth, but we must be going now or we'll be late for the dinner.'

I thanked them warmly for meeting me and we made our farewells. I suddenly felt very alone as I waved them off and sat down again with the remains of my drink. I had barely finished it when I saw the gate for my flight was already displayed. Gathering my bag, I set off for the gate, popping into the Ladies where, as I washed my hands on the way out, the mirror showed a face bare of make-up and I looked very much my age – even older, I thought ruefully. I took out my make up bag and applied a bit of lipstick and eye shadow. The change cheered me up a little and I made my way to the gate, noting there was still a good half hour until departure time.

I sat down and took out my phone to check for messages, but a wave of tiredness struck me. My eyes closed involuntarily as the stresses of the past 24 hours made themselves felt, and I fell asleep. I was woken by one of the check-in staff shaking my shoulder.

'Wake up, madam, we're about to close the doors. Hurry, please.'

Apologising profusely, I dragged myself to my feet, my phone falling from my lap. Cursing mildly, I picked it up and stumbled through the now empty waiting room and onto the plane, curious eyes following me as I found my seat.

Chapter Forty Four

To my relief the journey home went like clockwork. The plane landed at its predicted time, and I didn't have luggage so was able to go straight to the taxi rank where there was no queue, to my relief. Traffic was very light, and it was not yet midnight as my taxi drew up at the house. As I approached the front door, feeling in my handbag for my keys, the door opened to reveal a pyjama-clad William.

'Was watching for you!' he said with grin, holding out his arms – and crutches - in welcome.

I was almost too tired to give him a kiss but managed a peck on his cheek combined with a sigh of relief at being home. William led me into the kitchen.

'Sit down. What can I get you?'

I thought for a second before saying I was exhausted and just wanted to go to sleep, but then relented and allowed him to get me a glass of water.

William started to ask me about Callum, but I stopped him. 'Why don't you run me a hot bath and sit by me while I briefly tell you the main parts of the story. Then bed. I really can't cope with more tonight – I actually fell asleep in the departure lounge and had to be woken to get on the plane.'

That made William laugh. Containing his impatience, he followed me upstairs.

In the bath, I felt some of the tension easing as I told William briefly about Ailsa finding Callum and persuading him to tell her what led to his breakdown. 'I'll fill in the details in the morning and then we can talk about what to do.'

William was already in bed when I returned to the

bedroom. I climbed in beside him and gave him a proper kiss before closing my eyes and falling instantly asleep.

I was woken by William next morning. Looking blearily at the bedside clock, I saw it was already past nine. It took some determination to sit up.

'Brought you a cuppa,' William said, sitting down on the bed and handing it to me. 'Managed not to spill it – tricky with crutches. How do you feel?'

I took a few sips and felt myself returning to the world. 'Much better for the tea. Thanks. Let's have breakfast then I'll go through the whole visit and we can think about what we can do to help poor Cal.'

Breakfast over we stayed at the table and I filled William in, ending with my brief rather disappointing discussion with my sister and John.

'The first thing to find out is the likely procedure.' William spoke thoughtfully. 'Do the police just turn up at Hamish's and ask Callum general questions about Sophia, or do they take him in for questioning straight away. If so, are they allowed to question him without a solicitor present. In either case, should he admit to having delivered the drugs, or say he didn't know what was in the packages, envelopes or whatever they were.'

'I told him to tell the truth, but that might make them think he was complicit. And does it help if he explains he did it for love? Would they believe him? I don't know.' I sighed.

'What we need is professional advice, urgently,' said William firmly. 'Let's hope the police don't have Callum top of their list for questioning – after all, the way they put it to us, his was only one of the numbers they had to investigate. Do we know any solicitors who might have some experience in drug cases – or any at all involved in questioning in a case like this?'

I thought for a moment then shook my head. 'None come to mind, and asking around amongst our friends and acquaintances would mean telling them what it was about.'

'I don't think we should let that put us off. We know Cal was besotted with Sophia and would do anything to please her; we can make it clear to anyone we ask that he was doing it for love not money.' William paused. 'It's Sunday so I don't think we can do anything today except rack our brains about possible connections, but first thing tomorrow I'll get on to Fred Tanner, he's my best contact at Jackson Steiner, and see whether they can help – they're a big practice and probably cover most fields.'

'You're right, but it's frustrating, and worrying being so ignorant about what's likely to happen.'

We sat in silence for a few minutes, then William stood up.

'Right now I'm going to call Cal and tell him we'll do everything necessary to help him. Why don't you call Angus and Bruce and see if he has spoken to them yet.'

I went into my study and rang Angus's mobile. No answer, so I tried Bruce. His phone rang for ages before he answered.

'Hi Mum.' He sounded groggy. ''s a bit early, isn't it?'

'Half past ten. You okay? You don't sound it.'

'Er, well, it was a bit of an evening, actually.' I heard the ghost of a grin before he continued. 'Busy evening in the bar - heaving, it was - then a fab stand-up show and a few drinks afterwards. Got back a bit late.'

'Was Angus with you?'

'Er, yes, I think he was. Must have stayed longer, though. Not here when I got in.'

Maybe I was paranoid, but the thought flashed through my mind that something had happened to him, so I asked

Bruce to check quickly. I could hear his heavy – stumbling – footsteps then, to my relief,

'Yup, he's here. Out for the count.'

'Well, don't wake him, but tell me, did Cal call yesterday?' My fingers were crossed that he had; it would make it easier for me to raise the subject.

'Did, but I couldn't take it, busy in the bar, then it was late. Why?'

I thought quickly. How much should I say? I decided to keep it short, just told him that the police had told us they were investigating Sophia and were checking all contacts on her phone, and that I had flown up to check he was okay. 'It really upset him, as you can guess. So glad I was there. Hamish and Ailsa were real bricks.'

'Christ, poor Cal.' He paused. 'Do you think Angus or I should take time off to be with him?'

'That could be really helpful – but would they let you, given the bars are so busy? You might not want to say why…'

'Hmm, good point. Could lie, say he's ill or something.'

'Don't do anything yet, just tell Angus and wait until Cal calls you – I'm sure he will soon.' The mother in me couldn't resist adding, 'And maybe cut back a bit on the drinking in case you are needed – both of you.'

'Okay, fair do's! Thanks for calling. Love to Dad – and fingers crossed it turns out not to be a big deal.'

'I'm afraid that's unlikely, but we'll keep hoping. Bye darling.' I hung up with a sigh and went to see how William had got on with Callum.

William was sitting staring into space. He turned as I came in and shrugged his shoulders. 'Nothing to report. He sounded down, not surprisingly, but resigned. Hamish has lined up plenty for him to do, he said, which will help take his mind off things. We just have to find out what we can about what's likely to happen and get ourselves some legal support.'

'I've just had a thought. Hamish might know a good local solicitor.' I kicked myself for not thinking of that when I was there. 'If he and John both come up with someone we can choose the most suitable.'

'I think we need a better understanding of what's going to happen before we start choosing a solicitor. I'll search on the internet to see if it's any help. If not, unless we have any brilliant ideas among our friends, we'll have to hope Jackson Steiner come up trumps when I call them tomorrow.'

It was very frustrating not to be able to do anything constructive yet. I turned my attention to tidying the kitchen, but that only took ten minutes. A sudden burst of sunshine made me look out of the window. The recent mild weather and some rain had caused everything to grow rapidly, and I could see, even from the kitchen, that it included the weeds. I called out to William that I was going to do some gardening to distract me, collected my apron and tools and went out into the garden.

The first thing which struck me was how different the London air smelled compared with the sparkling freshness of the Highlands, the freshness which Callum had noticed and loved. Pulling myself away from that train of thought, I set to work. The smell of damp earth mingled with the scent of the roses round the patio, and I bent to smell the different varieties before doing some dead-heading. I tackled the weeds with vigour and felt much better for it, imagining I was pulling the wretched Sophia up by the roots and consigning her to the bin.

Our garden was not big, but it occupied my attention and I was surprised when William called out to say he had put lunch on the table. As we ate, he said he'd not found anything very useful on the internet, but it did seem likely that Callum would be arrested, though whether immediately or after questioning was not clear. Most articles dealt with vulnerable kids caught up in county lines, or with people found in possession of drugs, neither of which applied to Callum.

That hardly cheered me up, but then I suddenly remembered coming across a law charity which helped young people up to the age of 25, including representation in court in drug cases. Lunch over, I googled them and was encouraged by the sort of help they offered. I told William and we agreed I should call them from work next day.

Aware we could do no more, we did our best to relax that afternoon and evening. I wrote a hugely grateful email to Hamish and Ailsa and told them not to hesitate to call me if there was a problem or any news.

Over dinner, William suddenly said that, in all the Callum problem, he had completely forgotten to tell me his piece of good news, that the surgical boot for his broken leg that would allow him to walk without relying on crutches was ready and he was getting it on Tuesday.

'That's wonderful news, darling, it will make such a difference.'

Chapter Forty Five

At the office next day, although I felt well rested, I found it hard to concentrate, my head again filled with Callum's plight. I did, however, manage a coherent discussion with Dave on his researches on Hamish's electricity generation ideas. He said they still indicated that solar panels were the easiest and much the cheapest solution. I mentioned that I had raised the idea of a more ambitious camping project which could include various ecological and entertainment activities. I was just going to expand on the idea when my phone rang.

'Elizabeth, it's Hamish. The police are here.'

'Elizabeth, are you there?' Hamish again.

I must have gone pale as Dave was looking at me, concerned, mouthing 'are you alright?'

I forced myself to speak, though my voice came out as a croak.

'Yes, sorry, Hamish. I'm in a meeting. Hold on while I go to a quieter room.' I mimed an apology to Dave and went to our small meeting room - I don't have a separate office, preferring to be openly available to my teams.

'So, Hamish, what happened?' I held my breath for his answer.

'A couple of police turned up about half an hour ago, showed their ID cards and asked quite politely if I was Callum Trenchard. I introduced myself and told them he worked for me. They said they needed to talk to him, where could they find him. He was chopping wood in the yard, so I took them there.'

'How did he react when they appeared?'

'He was obviously surprised and anxious they had come so soon but collected himself quickly. The police said they needed to ask him some questions and could we go and sit down so I took them inside. They began by checking who he was then asked if he knew Sophia Nicholson-Smith.....'

I interrupted him. 'Did they let you stay with him?' My fingers were crossed.

'Yes.'

I breathed a sigh of relief. 'Then what?'

'He said yes, of course, and when they asked how, told them she was the sister of a friend of his at Cambridge. They then delved increasingly into his relationship with her, and he cracked. He howled 'I loved her so much' and collapsed, weeping. Fortunately, Ailsa heard him and came in. She knelt beside him and comforted him like she did before.' Hamish paused.

I curled up inside as I remembered Callum's breakdown on our walk; I could still feel his trembling and hear his sobs.

Hamish spoke again. 'It was a strange and, I have to say, a powerful moment. The policemen were clearly taken aback, embarrassed but also sympathetic. A lump rose in my throat too.'

I heard him swallow before he continued.

'The men realised that they weren't going to get much further with Callum then, but they had more to ask. As he calmed down a bit they said, gently – good for them – that they would need to question him under caution at the police station, and he should bring his solicitor with him.'

'How did he take that?'

'He nodded his understanding and managed to tell them he didn't have a lawyer yet but his parents or his aunt and uncle would help him find one.'

'Did they give any indication of timing? I think they sometimes do it immediately, but surely they wouldn't if he didn't have a lawyer?' I hoped I was right.

'I asked that, and they said if I would act as guarantor that he would respond to the summons, they could wait a few days for him to get it sorted.'

'And...?'

'Of course I said yes – Ailsa insisted she would too.'

'Bless you both. I can't believe how remarkably kind and helpful you two are being to, effectively, complete strangers who have brought such trouble with them. I can't think how we can ever repay you.' I was close to tears of gratitude.

'Let's not talk about that now. The police are still outside and it might be a good idea if you had a word with them. I'll walk to the car to tell them and then you can take over.'

As he left the house I could hear his footsteps on the gravel and then him speaking to the police, telling them I was in London. I couldn't hear their response, but Hamish handed them his phone and said I should give them my work and mobile numbers, which I duly did.

'I'll close our call now and they'll ring you on your phone. Call me when you've finished.'

It was with some trepidation that I answered the police call. I introduced myself and asked what the next steps were and was there anything I should do. They repeated about getting a lawyer to be with Callum when he was questioned, which would be in Inverness, and reassured me that I or a nominated person could be present at the interview as well.

Greatly relieved, I made a note of their contact details and said I would be in touch as soon as we had the solicitor. I also took the time to say how kind Hamish and Ailsa had been, and mentioned that my sister and brother-in-law lived in Inverness which might be helpful as Callum could stay with them if necessary and could even be with him during the questioning if I couldn't get away from the office in time. They asked me a few questions about where I lived and some general background; I wasn't sure why they needed it, but I guessed it couldn't do any harm to let them know we were a respectable family. I wondered about bringing up Callum's suicide attempts but decided perhaps this wasn't the time or place.

Call over, I rang Hamish who, after asking if the police had had anything important to say – no, was my easy answer – said did we have a solicitor lined up. I confessed not but that we were searching for a suitable one, both in London and, via John, in Inverness.

'At the risk of seeming to take over your lives, we may be able to help. Ailsa has just reminded me she had dealings with a local family whose older son, brother of one of her pupils, got into bad company, and she remembered that they were really happy with the solicitor they used, and she was Inverness-based. Might that be a helpful introduction?'

Had I been there, I swear I would have kissed him. As it was, I asked him to send me the family's contact details and thanked him profusely again.

'We'll keep in touch,' he said. 'And, as you must have seen, we're already very fond of Callum and are only too pleased to be able to help. Bye for now.'

I sat for a few minutes, unable to switch straight back into work mode. So much had happened in the past very few weeks, it was hard to take in: Hamish contacting Trenchant about electricity generation, Michael Moreton changing from mad professor to inventor, bank client and, increasingly, valued friend. Then William's Parkinson's diagnosis, Callum's beating up and first suicide attempt, William's accident and now the whole damnable Sophia and drugs affair was taking over our lives.

My reverie was interrupted by my assistant putting her head round the door to say there was a call from a client and would I like a coffee. Thanking Melissa, I pulled myself to my feet and returned to my desk, passing Dave on the way to say I'd be back to talk about the generation project when I'd taken this call.

Fortunately, the client was easily dealt with and, coffee in hand, I went over to Dave's desk, wondering as I went whether it would be sensible to explain my distraction, or would Callum's plight become the hottest office gossip topic ever. The dilemma was solved for me by Dave opening our conversation by saying he realised there was something wrong, and if it would be helpful to share at least some of it, he promised not to say a word to anyone, in the office or out.

'That's really kind, Dave, and I think helpful as you may well find I'm distracted from time to time, and I might have to rush up to Inverness at short notice.'

I gave Dave a brief outline of Callum's misadventures and explained Hamish and Ailsa's involvement. He said that he had immediately liked them too and was glad to be working on their project.

'They're a very special pair,' Dave said smiling.

It did occur to me to wonder whether it was Ailsa more than Hamish who had taken Dave's fancy, but he and his girlfriend seemed a solid pair, so I put that out of my mind, only for another thought to intrude - Callum and Ailsa? – and be summarily dismissed.

Chapter Forty Six

Dave was very understanding when I excused myself yet again, this time to text William – I didn't want to call when he might be in a meeting – with a very brief account of the police visit and promising to give the full report later. I also texted Callum to say I would call very soon.

I then resumed my discussion of Hamish's camping proposal with Dave who listened carefully as I talked about enlarging the project to include various ecological activities for both adults and children and mentioned that both Hamish and Ailsa had been very open to the idea. Indeed, Ailsa had immediately seen opportunities to get involved.

'It makes a lot of sense,' said Dave thoughtfully. 'It would certainly be a better income generator than the original wild camping idea and might even justify the cost of installing the vortex generator in the salmon river – it would be a real talking point, a considerable local attraction, and a learning experience. There are so many things they could organise, like nature walks, deer spotting, foraging – even outdoor art classes.'

As Dave spoke, I could hear his increasing enthusiasm, but even as he enlarged on the theme my attention went back to Callum. Finally, unable to concentrate, I interrupted Dave to suggest he put the outline of his thoughts in writing. This was a big step we were proposing and would require a much bigger investment for the potentially greater return.

'Very good ideas. Let's talk about it more tomorrow,' I said, standing up. 'I must just have a word with some of the other staff, there's a lot going on even though this is supposed to be the quiet season.' I smiled as I moved away.

I stopped to exchange a few words with the different teams, checking that they didn't need me just then, before returning to the meeting room to check my phone. One message from William saying talk at lunchtime and – wonderful news – one from Ailsa with the contact details for the Inverness solicitor, Catherine Jamieson, and saying she had spoken to her to explain very briefly and in confidence about why I would be contacting her.

I immediately googled Catherine Jamieson and found she was senior partner in a fairly small firm specialising in criminal and family law. There were some very positive quotations from clients and, while acknowledging that no company would put up bad reviews, I was reassured. Glancing at my watch I saw that it was approaching lunchtime but before calling William I rang Callum.

'Good moment, darling?'

'Yes, fine.'

'Hamish rang to tell me the police had come. How did you cope with them so soon and without warning? Was it very upsetting?' I kept my voice calm.

Callum took a breath before confessing he had broken down when questioned about his relationship with Sophia. 'The police were okay though, not aggressive. At the end they said I'll be called to Inverness for questioning under caution and to have a solicitor with me. I told them I didn't have one yet but would soon.'

I told him about Ailsa's suggestion and that I would contact this Catherine Jamieson today. 'Ailsa said the family who recommended her had been very happy with her.'

'When will is the interview likely to be?'

'I won't know until I've spoken to her and the police,

but the police have agreed to wait, and Hamish is acting as guarantor that you won't abscond.'

'He and Ailsa are amazing. I didn't know there were such nice people in the world. How will we ever thank them?' Callum echoed my thoughts.

'I honestly don't know. But soon we have to think about who will take you to Inverness and who will be with you at the questioning if for some reason Dad or I can't come up. But we must try not to impose on them more than we have to.'

'I think there's a bus to Inverness a couple of times a day,' Callum offered. 'If the timing's right, I could take it and maybe stay with Aunt Fi if necessary.'

'Don't let's worry about details yet. We won't know enough about exactly what will happen and when until I've talked to Mrs Jamieson.' I changed the subject. 'Tell me, have you spoken to Angus and Bruce? I didn't tell them much as I thought you would prefer to fill them in.'

'Yes, they were shocked and offered to come up, but I told them not to unless they were really needed. They're enjoying their jobs and the Fringe events, lucky devils.'

I then asked how he was feeling and whether he had recovered from the beating-up sufficiently to do the work Hamish had lined up for him. I was reassured to hear he felt completely fine and was glad of the distraction and hard labour.

'Ailsa has offered to teach me to ride when this is all over – provided I'm not in prison.' Callum managed a small laugh. 'What with work, cooking lessons and riding, I shan't have time to think.'

'Well, we must hope it doesn't come to prison. Over to Mrs Jamieson! But I must stop now and bring Dad up to date, then actually do some work. Bye. Love you.'

'Love you. And sorry again.'

Callum hung up before I could respond.

I then rang William who answered immediately. 'Tell all.'

I went through my conversations with Hamish, the police and Callum. William listened intently.

'This Jamieson woman sounds our best bet; rather have a recommendation than stick a pin in a list. Have you got time to call her? I'm a bit busy.'

'Yes. I've told Dave about Callum in confidence so he will understand if I disappear for a bit. I've left him working on the possible enlargement of Hamish's project - will tell you more later. All well at the bank?'

'Yes, and some good news which can also wait until tonight. Must go, got a visitor. Bye.'

'Bye.'

Crossing my fingers for a positive conversation, I rang Mrs Jamieson's office and announced myself. A very Scottish voice answered and said she would put me through.

'Catherine Jamieson. Mrs Trenchard?' Her accent was also Scottish, but less strong. 'Ailsa McCraig told me you might call. I'm very sorry to hear the trouble your son has got himself into. Miss McCraig didn't give me details. Could you tell me more and I'll see if I or a colleague might be able to help.'

Before embarking on the full story, I questioned her about her practice's experience with drug cases and was reassured to hear it was considerable – and said maybe Inverness wasn't quite as drug and crime free as I had assumed.

She laughed ruefully. 'I think everywhere has drug problems. County lines and all that have disseminated drug-taking into pretty much the whole country. We've had some dramatic seizures here. But tell me more about your son's situation.'

I went through the whole sad story, including his suicide attempts. 'Initially he had no idea what he was delivering to her supposed friends then got suspicious, but she put emotional pressure on him. After the first suicide attempt, the most serious one, he told me he thought that if he died, we would never know he had got mixed up in the drug trade, he would save the family from the shame. Later, I think his humiliation at having been manipulated by Sophia who he had been besotted with and who told him she loved him, played an additional role. He was in a very bad place. Effectively, he did it for love.

'So, Mrs Jamieson, what do you think? Is it a case you would be willing to take on?' I held my breath.

'First, she replied, it's not Mrs –'

I began to apologise but she cut me off.

'No problem, it was a natural assumption, even these days. Just call me Catherine.'

I was glad it wasn't a video call as I could feel I was blushing with embarrassment.

'It's an interesting case, and not clear-cut,' she continued. 'The police are of course suspicious, with good reason, and their questioning will be tough. There's no doubt Callum will need good support and having listened to your explanation I would be happy to provide it. However, I'm afraid ....'

My spirits suddenly dropped to rock bottom as I thought she was going to say she was too busy to take on the case. I think a groan may have escaped my lips but, pulling myself together, I realised she was talking about fees.

'.... as Senior Partner, my fees are considerable. This is going to entail talking to Callum - maybe going to see him - to hear his account, liaising with the police, attending the questioning and, maybe – though of course we would hope not – representing him at a trial. Sorry to have to ask, but is that a problem?'

With a swallowed sigh of relief, I said we were happy to pay whatever it cost. We then got into details of setting a date for the questioning and how much notice we would have – the answer was very little. Checking that someone from the family could be present, I explained about my sister possibly being able to stand in if I couldn't get up from London in time.

'I think that's all we can do for now.' Catherine sounded very business-like. 'I'll get on to Callum this afternoon - you're lucky you caught me at a quiet time – and take it from there. Please give my secretary all contact details before you hang up but let me just say again this is an interesting case and I shall do my very best. I look forward to meeting you at some point.'

I thanked her heartily and was then transferred to the secretary who took down all necessary details and, to my surprise, congratulated me on choosing Catherine. 'She's very good' was the reassuring message. 'I think you'll be very pleased to have engaged her.'

Before going back to my desk, I texted Ailsa to thank her, and Callum to tell him what was happening. Although Catherine had taken some of the immediate worry from my shoulders, it was hard to lay the burden down completely and I had to make an effort to get into work mode. As I sat down at my computer, I suddenly realised, I was very hungry and stood up again.

'Just going to get a sandwich,' I said to Melissa as I passed her desk. 'Could you have coffee ready in ten minutes, please.'

She nodded and smiled, but I could see a tinge of worry in her eyes: the boss seems very distracted these days.

Chapter Forty Seven

My brain was buzzing as I ate my sandwich. The walk to the coffee shop had refreshed me a little and I started making a list of the things I needed to do: text William, Callum and the McCraigs to say I'd engaged Catherine; let Fi and John know we had a solicitor; text Angus and Bruce to bring them up to date; check with Melissa if anything important; check emails; make sure Dave happy with drawing up the ideas for Hamish's possible bigger project; shop for supper.

At that moment, Melissa came over with my coffee and I seized the opportunity to tick her off my list. She said that nothing urgent had come up, just some staff holiday dates to agree, a couple of letters to sign and an enquiry about Trenchant doing some consultancy on a new eco-housing development in Wales.

'But there's no need to think about that just yet,' Melissa reassured me. 'They're going to send the outline of the development and where they would like our input.'

I thanked her and forced myself to relax a bit as I finished my coffee. Before I could start on my list, one of my senior staff came over with a tricky question on his project. Dealing with it took a good hour of discussion with him and his team. I had just returned to my desk, texted William and Callum and was about to ring my sister when there was a scream and sudden rush of feet. I leapt up to find that, in a freak accident, one of the junior staff had dropped a heavy, very sharp knife while slicing a pineapple for her lunch and it had pierced her foot and flimsy sandal, pinning her to the floor.

I did my best to calm her down while someone called an

ambulance and another fetched ice from the fridge which he placed carefully on her foot to help stem the blood and dull the pain. Fortunately, the ambulance arrived very quickly and the paramedic extricated the knife. A colleague accompanied poor Lizzie, still shaking with shock, to the hospital. By then, someone had kindly cleaned up the blood and everyone returned to their desks, a strange silence hanging in the air as I returned to my desk.

Not wanting to share my delayed call with everyone, I retreated to the meeting room again and called Fi. Luckily, she was home and I brought her up to date.

'I hope you and John haven't put too much time into thinking about solicitors,' I said apologetically. 'But having a direct recommendation was too good to pass up.' I told her about my talk with Catherine and the secretary's comment. 'Have you come across her?' I asked.

'No, but I'll ask John when he gets home. She sounds good, though,' Fi acknowledged. 'Let's hope she can get things moving quickly. And, by the way, if you or William can't make it up here when the questioning happens, if it's this week, I'm pretty free and can step in, but next week is busy.'

I thanked her warmly. 'That's a weight off my mind.'

Before going back to my desk and more possible interruptions, I texted Angus and Bruce and got a reply almost immediately from Angus saying he'd talked to Callum at lunchtime and he seemed to be bearing up well, all things considered. Next on my list was Ailsa whom I texted with my gratitude, then Hamish to say the same and that Dave was working up first thoughts on the enlarged project.

On my way back to my desk I stopped at Dave's.

'Got time now for a bit of discussion on Hamish's project? I feel bad not giving you more guidance earlier.'

'No problem,' Dave said. 'But if you do have time now, it would be helpful, there's an awful lot to think about.' He pulled up a chair for me and we set to work.

'How far had you got?' I asked him.

'Not very,' he confessed ruefully. 'I wasn't sure where to start.'

We then spent a very productive hour, listing questions to be answered and ideas to be thought through with Hamish and Ailsa. One question was whether planning permission would be needed, given that the prospective camping area would not be visible from the road. Another was whether a larger site with more people would have a detrimental effect on the wildlife, and possibly be a hazard, particularly in the shooting season, especially if people brought their dogs. What health and safety regulations would apply?

We then moved on to the more practical side: for different projected numbers, what facilities would be needed, could these be ecologically good, for example, composting toilets, solar heated showers and water to supply them, wattle fencing for privacy. Some could be supplied using local companies with experience. Catering: individual or would there be a kitchen and communal meals. Would all this preclude the original idea of wild camping. Would people bring their own tents and/or would the main centre provide tents to rent.

All this began to sound rather daunting, both as tasks for Dave to research and for Hamish to finance and manage. We did, however, spend a few minutes indulging in the fun thoughts on what activities might be a draw: wildflower and animal spotting, learning traditional crafts such as dry-stone walling, coppicing and fence building, art, music – bagpipe lessons? - and cookery. Then, obviously hiking, and possibly fishing, riding, animal petting.

'You know,' Dave said thoughtfully, 'I think we're getting ahead of ourselves and we should put all this to Hamish and Ailsa before we go any further. They need to have some idea of what they would be letting themselves in for.'

'You're right, Dave. It's an interesting idea, and certainly a business which, if successful, could be a real earner for the estate, much more than wild camping, but the implications are huge. However, maybe they could start on a modest scale and build up if it proved a success.'

'I think,' Dave ventured, 'I should put together a summary of our discussion and conclude with your last suggestion of starting slowly. Then they can decide whether, and at what scale and speed, to proceed from there.'

'Good thinking, Dave. There's no need to go into detail and costing until they decide what course to pursue. I leave you to get on with that. How long do you think you need?'

'Only a day or so, if that's soon enough.'

'I'm sure it is. Hamish won't expect anything before next week, in fact, so take your time. Just run it past me before you send it. Now I must go and check my emails – I've barely glanced at my computer yet today. See you tomorrow.'

I returned to my desk and, looking at my list, was relieved to find only emails and shopping for supper remained to do. I checked my watch and saw it was only 4.30 though it felt much later. I skimmed my inbox and was delighted to see there was nothing of great importance, and some of it Melissa could deal with. I then took a moment to ask Emily, who had accompanied Lizzie to the hospital, how she was.

'A&E were great, praised us for chilling her foot and they took it very seriously,' Emily reported. 'She'll probably stay overnight. I called her mother who came to be with her.'

'Thanks, Emily. It was kind of you to go with her and I'm

sure she found it very comforting.'

By then I felt it was legitimate for me to go home so I tidied my desk and said half apologetically to Melissa that I had to leave promptly to shop for dinner. Walking home, I rejected a takeaway, thinking that cooking would help keep our problems at bay. However, standing in the supermarket my mind was a perfect blank. I confess I swore to myself, went to the frozen meals cabinet and picked out a couple of dishes almost at random. At the checkout, I was extricating my bank card from my purse when an arm went round me and a kiss landed on my cheek. Startled, I turned round to find William grinning at me.

'Surprise, surprise!' William laughed. 'I rang the office and heard you were shopping on the way home so thought I might beat you to it. Here, let me pay, I've got my card out already.'

It was only at this point that I realised William was not using crutches, just a walking stick. He saw my surprise and struck a dramatic pose, much to the amusement of other shoppers.

'Ta-da!' he said as he stuck his broken leg forward to show me the surgical boot. 'Got it a day early. It's wonderful. I could almost dance.' He made as if to hold me in dancing pose but thought better of it as he wobbled slightly. 'Whoops, not quite used to it,' he laughed.

We walked home, only a little slower than normal, William using the walking stick for security. It wasn't far so I didn't start on the events of the day except to tell him about the knife accident.

William opened the front door for me and we went straight to the kitchen to put the meals in the freezer.

That done I gave William a proper hug and a kiss.

'I'm so happy for you. Was the boot the good news you had for me?'

'Half of it,' William replied. 'I'll tell you the other half over a glass of wine – or two. There's plenty of time before supper, and those meals only take about half an hour or so. I like your choice, by the way.'

'That's lucky', I replied laughing, 'as I'm really not sure what I bought.'

Chapter Forty Eight

We had barely sat down with our drinks when my mobile rang. Callum! I put it on speakerphone so that William could hear.

'Hi, darling, all well?'

'The questioning is 9am Wednesday morning.' Callum didn't waste time on niceties. 'I hope the solicitor can come then.'

'Goodness. I hope so too. Short notice, but we expected that, and at least it's good to have it fixed. I'll call Catherine first thing tomorrow – in fact, I'll send a text as soon as we've finished talking, just in case she happens to check.'

William chimed in: 'You can have someone with you for support, not just your solicitor. Who would be best for you, do you think? One of us, or possibly Aunt Fiona if she's free?' He paused. 'Whoops, just realised it can't be me as I have an important appointment Wednesday morning. So, Mum or Fi?'

'Or Hamish or Ailsa,' said Callum hopefully.

'Do you really think we should ask even more of them?' I responded. 'They've done so much for us already.'

'But Hamish says he has to go to see his gunsmith one day this week so will drive me there. Maybe he could be with me as he's there anyway.' Callum didn't sound exactly peevish, but it was clear what he would like.

'I'm still reluctant to ask him. It's quite a drive and you would have to leave horribly early to get there by nine. As it happens, I talked to Fi this morning and she offered to step in if it would be helpful as she's not busy this week. After all, she knows all about it. What do you think? I could come, of course, if that's what you would like.'

I hoped he would be happy with Fi. With all the stress and having gone up for the day on Saturday, I was still pretty tired.

'And,' I added, 'if Hamish can go to his gunsmith tomorrow, he could take you to Fi and John's, and you could stay the night with them and only have a short journey to the police station. You would see your cousins, too – they'd be delighted.'

'But how would I get back to Hamish's?'

'Good point – but you did say before that you could take a bus to Inverness, so you could get one back.' I was glad I remembered that.

William spoke again. 'If it's Mum you want, that's fine. She could take time off work and come up tomorrow afternoon.' He looked at me sympathetically before continuing. 'But do think about Aunt Fi; she knows everything, as Mum said, and having someone there is just for emotional support, they don't have to advocate for you or anything. Mum's just going to her study to text the solicitor.' He indicated with a nod of his head that I should go.

I returned in time to hear William ask why Callum had only just called us. 'Didn't you get the message earlier? Seems odd they left it so late in the day.'

'Remember, the phone reception here is pretty intermittent. I had left my phone on charge and gone to help Hamish all afternoon. When we got back Ailsa had tea and cake waiting, then he asked me to help move some heavy boxes. I was hot and sticky by then so went to have a shower and a sit down and fell asleep, didn't wake up until after six. The voicemail and a text were left at 4.30. I called you as soon as I knew.'

'That certainly explains it.' William commented. 'Now, have a think about what I've said about who should be with you and call back in an hour or so, after supper maybe.'

'OK, Dad. Thanks for the offer, will call back. Love and a long-distance hug to you both. Bye.'

'Bye,' we both said as he hung up.

'What did you say to him while I was in the study?' I asked immediately.

'I told him I was a bit concerned about you doing all that travelling again so soon, and about the accident at work adding more stress, said that I thought I could probably move my appointment if I would be an acceptable substitute. He was worried about me travelling alone with crutches but I told him had the surgical boot now so I was more mobile and could manage the journey okay.'

'That was very kind of you. I hope you're right about managing the travelling. But how sure are you about moving the appointment?'

'I think I could fix it. Tuesday afternoon's not busy so I could fly up and stay with Fi and John too. It's not ideal but I can do it.'

'That sounds a bit uncertain. Let's finish our drinks and have dinner while we wait for Cal to call back and decide then. You haven't told me your second piece of good news so how about now?'

'Right, here goes. I got a call from Michael this afternoon. He said he'd had some very useful discussions with some colleagues in the field which in some ways were disappointing. Seems he wasn't as far ahead of the quantum battery storage curve as he had thought – hoped. I began to commiserate but he stopped me and went on to say the discussions had shown that his work so far was already practicable and usable, while not a complete game-changer. He passed this on at his meeting with the possible investors who were very positive and they're wanting to take things further, get him talking to manufacturers and so on.'

'That really is good news.' I raised my glass. 'Here's to Michael, and let's hope it leads to real progress soon.'

William raised his too, and we drank to our new friend. 'Let's have him round to supper again, once we feel on safer ground with Callum,' I suggested, and William nodded agreement.

I was glad I hadn't put much work into our supper as it was interrupted several times. First my phone pinged with a reply from the solicitor. She could manage nine on Wednesday morning and had already called Callum to ask him to come to her office on Tuesday afternoon for a preliminary discussion.

We hadn't got far into our lamb casserole when Callum called to say he'd decided that it was sensible that Fiona would be with him, that he'd called her and she was happy to do it. He'd spoken to Catherine Jamieson and had arranged to be at her office at four. He'd also talked to Hamish who said going to the gunsmith next day was very convenient and he would drop him at Fi's.

'That's really good news, very organised of you,' William said, having heard it all as I still had my phone on speaker.

I added my relief that it was all settled and confessed that I was glad not to be flying up to Inverness again. 'It was kind of Dad to offer to go instead of me, but it would have been a bit awkward rearranging his meeting. I'm sure Aunt Fi will be a great support. I'll speak to her later. Don't lie awake worrying tonight. You're in good hands.'

'All that hard work and fresh air will help.' Callum managed a smile. 'Let's talk again tomorrow. Bye again.'

'Bye, love you,' William and I said in unison.

We returned our attention to our meal, now

unappetisingly cold.

'Let's go straight to dessert,' I proposed.

William nodded agreement and I fetched the apple pie from the oven and some cream from the fridge. We were just finishing when my phone rang again.

'Hi, Mum, you both there?' It was Bruce.

'Yes,' I answered for us both, putting down my spoon. 'On speakerphone. How are you? How's the job? Seen any good shows?'

'All okay, but I wanted to tell you something before Cal hears. I've had a couple of texts from friends, word's getting round about investigating Sophia. Seems Cal's not the only one of our lot who's on her contact list and has been visited by the police.'

'I think that's good news.' William put the emphasis on think.

'Let's hope so, but there's more. Don't tell Cal, but I'm beginning to think he may not have been her only boyfriend. What a cow.'

'Good heavens, that's awful. Poor Cal, he'll be even more devastated if – when – he finds out. It's hard to believe. What makes you think it might be true?' I felt quite shaky at the thought of this bad news coming on top of everything. I refrained from criticising Bruce's language. I might have said something worse.

'He'll not be the only one devastated. I've seen various bits of gossip going round on Instagram and Facebook. Don't know how she found the time.' Bruce snorted. 'I know Cal's keeping off his phone and hopefully not delving into social media. You never know how much is true, but it would be a terrible blow if he read some of this stuff.'

'There's honestly not much we can do,' I said sadly.

'Just hope. He's being interviewed by the police first thing Wednesday and we've found what I hope is a good solicitor to help him. Aunt Fi's going to go to the interrogation with him, bless her.'

'Angus and I will keep our fingers crossed that he doesn't find out, at least for a while. There's nothing else we can do, I think.' He paused. 'Or do you think we should warn him?'

'That's a tough question.' William was thoughtful. 'I suppose we could say that word is starting to go round about the investigation and it's best if he just tells his side of the story, first to the solicitor and then at the hearing, not look at what others are saying that might or might not be true.'

'Yup, that's probably right. Best from you?'

'I think so. We can say you alerted us to some wild tales, and to keep away.' William sighed.

There was a pause as we each digested the news and pondered what to do. Finally, I spoke.

'Just keep us in the loop, let us know what you hear that might be important.'

Chapter Forty Nine

Having thanked my sister for agreeing to accompany Callum to the interrogation, William and I made our weary way to bed that Monday night, knowing there was nothing more we could do or say until Callum had spoken to Catherine the next afternoon.

That didn't stop me – nor, I suspect, William – lying awake for a while running through the possible outcomes of this mess in our minds before exhaustion finally took over and we were woken by the alarm in the morning.

I helped William to put on his boot before we went downstairs, so pleased for him at his increased freedom of movement. That said, I noticed that he was very careful, not just in walking, but in opening and going through the doors. I didn't say anything, knowing he was fiercely independent and determined not to be held back by the Parkinson's, the manifestations of which were, thankfully, still very mild.

Work was busy enough to keep my mind focussed, at least until four o'clock approached when I sent Callum a brief text to say I hope he liked Catherine Jamieson and found her helpful, and to ask him to call that evening. After a moment's thought, I also texted Catherine herself to say I hoped she would have time to call me to discuss how she saw the situation after her meeting with him.

Just as I got home, fretting with impatience, Callum texted to say he was on the bus back to Fiona's and would call from there. William got home soon after, an eyebrow raised to ask what was new. I shook my head and busied myself preparing supper.

When my mobile rang, I almost dropped the potato I was peeling in my haste to answer. It was Callum. Speakerphone on, William and I sat at the kitchen table.

'So, how did it go?' William spoke first. 'Did you find her helpful? Friendly?'

'She got me to tell her everything from the very beginning, listened carefully almost without interrupting, just asked a few questions. When I finished, she was very down to earth, didn't mince her words, said I was definitely in a difficult position but not a hopeless one.' He paused and we heard him swallow before continuing. 'She was very kind, though, and told me not to despair, that she could help me put my best case tomorrow. I liked her and I think she'll be good – I certainly feel much better about the interrogation knowing she'll be there and have my back.'

'That's good news, up to a point,' I said. 'Did she give you advice on how to deal with the questioning?'

'Yes, she said that complete honesty was probably my best approach. Since I couldn't deny that I had delivered drugs for Sofia, I was to admit to being in love with her – even to say besotted – and that she had used emotional blackmail to get me to continue after I got suspicious.'

'I can imagine you'll find that hard, but the police officers who came to see you at Hamish's saw you break down and Ailsa comforting you. I'm sure that will back up that aspect of your case.' I hoped the same policemen would be involved in the interrogation.

'I told Catherine about that, and she said the same thing.' Callum confirmed.

'I don't think we can be any help now, but you know we're thinking of you all the time.' William's voice held all the warmth and encouragement we both felt. 'To change the subject a bit, did Hamish deliver you to Aunt Fi's without difficulty?

'Actually, Hamish took me straight to the solicitor's office as we were a bit late. And yes, I did warn Aunt Fi! The office wasn't that far from their house, so I caught a bus there after the meeting – that's when I texted you. Oh, here comes Aunt Fi. She'd like a word with you. Talk again later, maybe. Bye.'

We heard him hand over his phone and say William and I were both there.

I repeated my thanks for having Callum overnight and for her help next morning.

'How do you find him? In good heart?' William interposed.

'Surprisingly so. I think the solicitor must have been very supportive and done a good job of briefing. By the way, John asked around a bit and heard good reports of her.' Fi was reassuring.

We double checked that Fi knew where and when to go next morning, then asked her to put Callum back on as we wanted another word.

'Hi again, Mum, what is it?'

Taking a deep breath and trying to sound casual, I raised the topic of internet gossip.

'We heard from Bruce that's there's all sorts of speculation beginning to circulate on social media, some of it really weird. We know you've been keeping off it, but we just wanted to say you should stick with that, not be tempted to read any of it as some is apparently vicious trolling.' I sighed. 'I really don't know what gets into some people. So, only take calls from the family until this is cleared up, one way or another.' I hoped I hadn't raised his curiosity more than I'd reinforced his resolve.

'Okay, message received loud and clear,' said Callum, a

touch sarcastically. 'Don't worry.'

'Sorry, of course you're more aware of these things than we are,' William apologised for me. 'But we just wanted to protect you. If you stick to the facts and your side of the story, what's circulating shouldn't affect you.'

At this point my phone pinged to say I had a message, so we said our farewells and promised to call again before the interrogation meeting next morning.

The message was from Catherine asking me to ring her.

'Good evening, Catherine. Sorry, we were on the phone to Callum. My husband and I are both listening now. How did your meeting with Callum go?'

'Very well in that there were no surprises and he's a very nice, intelligent and articulate young man. He was very open with me, and I feel I have a good understanding of how he got into this mess and the effect it has had on him, so I'm in a good position to advise and support him.'

'That's an encouraging start,' William said before remembering to introduce himself and continuing. 'What's your view of the case and how he should answer what is likely to be tough questioning?'

'My advice is for him to be as open with them as he was with me, and not to hide the emotional side of the relationship, even if he finds it upsetting to go through again how he was so vulnerable to being manipulated because of loving her so much. The assault as the final straw and his shame and unhappiness prompting his attempted suicide will weigh in his favour. Also, his insistence that he didn't get paid – monetarily - for it.'

I began to interrupt but she continued. 'Yes, he admitted how he was rewarded. He can show his bank details to back the non-payment, though of course he could have a stash of cash in his bedroom, or some fancy watches. The police may well follow that up with a search.'

'Thank you. Apart from the police search, that feels right to me,' I commented. 'But do you have any idea of the likely outcome for him?'

Catherine paused before replying. 'Given that he admits he was effectively acting as a drug courier, he is likely to be found guilty of drug dealing....'

William and I both gulped and exchanged worried glances as she continued.

'However, his story is so compelling that, if it does come to trial, with good counsel for the defence, his clean record and likely excellent character references, I would hope he would be let off with a caution.'

This time we exchanged hopeful glances.

'Thank you,' we said in unison before William continued. 'Let's hope it doesn't come to a trial, but if it does, we'll ask your advice on appointing counsel - oh, just realised it would probably not be in Inverness as this seems to be a wider investigation. But maybe you might still be able to help?'

'I can't say at this stage. Meanwhile we hope for the best but have to be aware of the possibility of a trial. On a more immediate practical matter, if they do charge him, he will almost certainly be remanded on bail. Are you able to stand surety?'

'Of course,' William replied at once. 'Whatever the amount set.'

'I think that's all I can say for the moment.' Catherine prepared to end the call. 'I'll ring after the interrogation.'

We thanked her profusely, apologising for having kept her waiting, then sat back to absorb what she had said.

Agreeing there was nothing we could do to affect the

outcome, we turned our attention to supper then diverted our minds by watching a couple of episodes of Yes, Minister, one of our favourite series, until bedtime.

We didn't need the alarm to wake us in the morning and were downstairs and breakfasted by eight. Judging Callum and Fi wouldn't have left yet, we rang Callum as promised.

Not wanting to increase the pressure I began with a general enquiry. 'Did you have a good evening - were all your cousins around?'

'Yes, and they were very good at distracting me. We played some silly games after supper – Uncle John and Aunt Fi joined in. It was really fun.'

'That's good,' I replied, 'Nice to know they're not too old for such things. But how are you feeling now?'

'Nervous, what do you expect?'

'Sorry, silly question.'

'Actually, not as bad as before the meeting with Catherine. Her guidance was very clear. She made me understand that to some extent the initial outcome is a given, I was involved in drug dealing so will almost certainly get charged. But she said not to panic as there's a big step - and probably a long gap - between being charged and a trial, and that I would certainly get bail. She also said a judge would be likely to be lenient, given the whole story. I will have to live with the uncertainty, though.' Callum's voice betrayed his anxiety.

William spoke. 'Yes, that will be tough. Do you think you'll be able to continue to work for Hamish, at least until term starts?'

'I've not asked him, but he's been so understanding about all this and there's so much to be done on the estate that I think he'll be glad to have me. I certainly want to stay.' Callum was emphatic.

'Well, good luck, keep calm – and give our love and thanks to Aunt Fi for standing in this morning. Call us afterwards.'

'Will do – oh, here she comes, making signs I should get ready to leave. Love you. Bye.'

We barely had time to reciprocate before he switched off, leaving us to face the morning of uncertainty.

Chapter Fifty

On the fateful Wednesday morning William left immediately after breakfast to prepare for his meeting.

'Obviously I want to hear how the interrogation went as soon as possible, but between ten and at least eleven I'll be with the clients. Could you text Cal to make sure he calls you, not me. Thanks.' William gave me a peck on the cheek as he rushed out of the door.

I did as requested then set off to my office at a more leisurely pace, wondering how long the interrogation would go on for. Walking past the staff to my desk, I greeted everyone cheerfully as if I hadn't a care in the world, though Dave gave me a sympathetic smile. I was deep into editing an important report at ten when my mobile rang.

'Hi darling. What news?' I asked without checking the caller, assuming it was Callum. I endeavoured to keep my voice calm.

'Sorry, Elizabeth, it's Catherine. There's been a major development.'

My legs were shaking as I walked to the meeting room which I knew was free that morning. 'Did they charge him?'

'No. They've suspended the interrogation.'

I breathed a sigh of relief, but it was premature as Catherine continued:

'One of the interviewers was an officer from the wider investigation up from London for the questioning. He got a message to say,' Catherine paused, 'to say that Sophia was found dead in a river not far from her home early this morning.'

I gasped in shock. 'That's awful. Did they tell Callum?' Tears rose to my eyes as I thought of the effect it would have on him.

'Yes. They were very matter of fact, told him just what I've told you and that, in the circumstances, they were suspending the questioning and that he was free to go.'

'Oh, Catherine, how cruel, in public and without warning. How did he take it? I know he had ended the relationship, but he did love her very much...' I couldn't go on.

'He screamed NO! – and collapsed in tears on your sister's shoulder, shaking and sobbing.' Catherine didn't mince her words. 'Thank heavens you had arranged for her to be there.'

I guess I needed to know but it was harsh.

'I'm sorry to have broken the news like this, Elizabeth – but there is an upside. I think it's increasingly unlikely Callum will be charged. Clearly there's something serious going on, and I suspect the police will conclude Callum was not a significant player. My professional opinion is that the most he'll get is a caution, and maybe not even that.'

'Where is Callum now? Is he with my sister? Can I call him? When will we know more?' My questions tumbled out.

'I'm sure it's fine but I'll go back in and check with Mrs Haig. I told them both I would bring you up to date. But, before I do, I must warn you that the police have not ruled out foul play. It will be all over the papers tomorrow. Her father is a major figure in shipping in the City, as you probably know, so it's a story that's going to get lots of publicity. I'm really sorry, but I must alert you that you may get journalists trying to interview you, and the family too, if word gets out that she and Callum were lovers and that he has been taken in for questioning. It depends how much information the Norfolk police divulge as part of their investigations.'

My heart sank at the implications for us all. I finally found my voice.

'This is a real shock. Poor Callum, this on top of everything he's been through these past few weeks. Thank heavens he has my sister nearby, and Hamish and Ailsa are so supportive.' I paused wondering what else I could say, the shock making it hard to think straight. 'I hope you will keep us informed of any news on the case you hear that we won't get from the papers. We shall expect your invoice at some point, of course. And may we call on your assistance again if we feel it's needed?' Something made me retreat into work mode.

'I'm surprised you can think about paying me at a time like this.' Catherine sounded both sympathetic and amused. 'It's a very unusual situation, but I appreciate it. Good-bye and good luck.'

'Thank you again, and maybe we shall be able to meet up sometime.'

It was only a couple of minutes before my phone rang again. My sister.

'Catherine has told you everything,' Fi said. 'What a ghastly turn of events. Cal was understandably shocked and upset, but he's calmed down and wants to talk to you. Here he is.'

'Hi, Mum.'

'Hello, darling. I'm so, so sorry about Sophia. I know you're very upset, are you really up for talking now?'

'Yes. I can't change things, I just need to know what's really happened. She is – was - a very good swimmer so I don't believe it was an accident.'

'I don't know any more than you do. We'll have to wait for more information from the police. It's going to be a tough time.' I told him Catherine's warning about press intrusion. 'We're in for a difficult few days – maybe weeks, I fear. I'll warn Aunt Fi and Hamish and Ailsa. Oh, and your brothers too. Have you spoken to them recently?'

'They both rang last night to wish me luck in the interrogation.' He changed the subject. 'They're clearly having a good time in Edinburgh. Did you know Bruce had a stand-up gig in one of the comedy clubs?'

'No, I didn't! Good heavens.' I was impressed that Callum sounded so normal. 'I'll call them for the full story, maybe tomorrow – no, this afternoon, when I warn them about journalists. The press will only be a problem if your name comes up as one of her contacts who was being investigated, so we may be lucky – if that's the right word. But because Sophia's brother was at Cambridge with you, and he and various friends knew about you and Sophia, the police may be talking to them....' I was thinking aloud as I said this and realised the danger was greater than I had thought.

'Are you going to stay with Aunt Fi now, or what?' I turned to more immediate practical considerations.

'I'd already provisionally arranged for Hamish to pick me up from there later this afternoon on the grounds I was likely to be released on bail if I was charged. He said he needs me for some big jobs on the estate. I think he really does like having me there – cheap labour!'

'That's great as I know it's what you would like. Well done for staying so calm, darling, and please, please tell Dad or me if there's anything we can do, though at this point I'm not sure what it could be. Maybe you would like Dad and me to come up?'

'I'll let you know, but I think being back at work is the best for me. The hard physical work really helps to keep my mind off things. Here's Aunt Fi. Bye.'

'Bye, sweetheart.' Relieved but with a lingering feeling he

was playing down his distress, I turned my attention to my sister who confirmed everything Catherine and Callum had said.

'It was horrible that the police told him about Sophia so bluntly. I think the London man was quite shocked by Callum's reaction, maybe it will teach him – and his colleagues – a lesson in how to treat people,' Fi mused.

'I hope you're right,' I said. 'I don't think empathy is a major part of the training. But is Callum really coping well enough for me not to come up?'

'I think so, and getting back to the estate and out in the fresh air will be very helpful. If necessary, maybe you could come at the weekend if he's not coping very well. I know Hamish is picking him up this afternoon and I'll make a point of putting him in the picture.'

'Thanks again, Fi, it was incredibly kind of you. It's been a tough week one way and another, and I confess I'm tired, but of course I'll be up in a flash if needed.' I had a sudden thought. 'You need to say something to the kids as they're sure to see stuff about Sophia in the papers or on social media and must have picked up Callum's involvement because of your going with him today.'

'John and I will put our heads together as to what to say. But, please, don't panic. I'm sure we'll cope unless something new turns up, and the chance of journalists finding us must be remote.'

'I hope you're right. Thanks, again, Fi, and give my love to John and say hi to the kids from me. Bye.'

I sat at the conference table, head in hands, my thoughts spinning. How will Fi cope if he breaks down again? How will William, Angus and Bruce react when they hear, and I warn them about intrusive journalists, especially if the suspicion of murder comes out? Who else do we need to alert? Hamish and Ailsa obviously. The boys' Cambridge friends will certainly be following the case, and that will surely lead to more social media gossip and speculation. My staff will be agog if Callum is named. Oh, dear. A heavy sigh escaped my lips, and I began to feel sorry for myself as well. I really didn't need even more pressure.

Pulling myself together, I looked at my watch. Unbelievably, it was still not eleven so William not to be disturbed. Desperately feeling the need to talk to someone about this new development, I called Dave and asked him to come to the meeting room.

I think he could see as he came in that I was distressed. He sat down beside me, waited a few seconds than asked straight out what the problem was, and was it to do with Callum.

'Yes. He was visited by police at the weekend, and today was taken in for questioning about possible drug dealing because that girlfriend of his was being investigated for it and they were checking her contacts. That was bad enough. But his solicitor just called to say the girlfriend had been found dead, in a river, and they're not ruling out foul play.'

Dave's eyes widened. 'Seriously?'

I nodded. 'Her father's a big shot in the City so there'll be lots of publicity and speculation which may well name Callum - and any others she was working with – as his friends at Cambridge were already gossiping about their relationship, and possibly the drug dealing too. Callum Trenchard's not exactly a common name so everyone's going to know...' my voice trailed off.

Dave didn't say anything for a while, then sighed. 'I fear you're right. But my advice, for what it's worth, is that, when the story breaks and Callum's name comes up, you call all the staff together and tell them the whole story, even how badly the attack and Sophia's exploitation of his feelings hit him.'

'Really?' The thought of doing that was horrific.

'Yes, I think you'll find that everyone is very sympathetic. They'll see how distressed you are – don't try to hide it – and will be very protective. If journalists turn up here too, we can keep them at bay.' He paused. 'How has Cal reacted?'

I told him briefly and thanked him for his advice before sending him back to his desk. It was now after eleven, time to ring William.

Chapter Fifty One

I called William's PA in case William was still in his meeting.
'Good morning, Elizabeth, good timing. He's just saying goodbye to the visitors. They're all smiling broadly, shaking hands and slapping backs so clearly the meeting went well. I'll get him to call you as soon as they've gone.'

'Thanks.' I sat back, trying to control my impatience.

I didn't have to wait long.

'And?' William didn't waste words.

'They've suspended the interrogation because Sophia's been found dead in a river.' I didn't waste words either.

'What? No! Oh, God, what happened? Was she swimming? Did she fall in?'

'You know as much as I do,' I replied somewhat tartly, 'except that the police haven't ruled out foul play.'

'I don't believe it.' William sighed. 'Where does that leave Callum?'

'They let him go without charging him, thank heavens. He took the news badly in the meeting, apparently, but I spoke to him half an hour ago and he seems to have calmed down now he's got over the shock.'

'I can imagine his reaction, he was so besotted with her. Even though he discovered her duplicity and ended the relationship, he hasn't had time to get over her. Poor lad, he's gone through more in a month or so than most people in a lifetime.'

We were both silent for a moment.

William spoke first. 'Where is he now? What next?'

'He's on his way back to Fi's and then going back to

Hamish and Ailsa's as he wants to stay there, says the hard work and outside life help keep his mind off things. Hamish is going to pick him up this afternoon.'

'Blessings on that pair. What extraordinary luck it was that Hamish contacted Trenchant.'

I could only agree, but then went on to warn William of the possible press intrusion.

'Hell's bells, the last thing we need on top of everything. Let's just hope Cal's mates don't revel in their reflected glory, so to speak, and spread salacious rumours which bring him into the limelight.' William gave another heavy sigh, and I heard a half-swallowed expletive followed by: 'If gossip gets really bad this could even get to the bank. 'Bank executive's son outed as a drug dealer...'. I can see the headlines now.'

I hadn't thought of this aspect of the whole affair. Would it affect Trenchant?

'There's damn all we can do to stop it if the press really go for the story,' I said with sinking heart. 'We must just hope for the best – but maybe you should talk to George soon to warn him, tell him the background and why it might get nasty. I'm going to tell Angus and Bruce next, and I've already warned Fi.'

'Good. With a bit of luck, if we warn everyone to keep stumm, at least the rabid hordes may not find Callum at Hamish's. Even if they discover he's working there, there's plenty of places to hide – he could test Hamish's wild camping ideas!' William even chuckled at that thought before returning to the bank worry.

'I know it's unlikely, but bad publicity could even scupper the deal I just signed off on before you rang. It's a seriously big one, good for the investors, good for the bank and good for me – and you. Fuck.'

'Look, darling, don't panic. We don't know if the police will give more information than the basic facts, and if the on-line gossip does get serious, at least the police already know Callum was hardly a big player in the dealing. If they were really concerned about him, they wouldn't have let him go without bail.'

'I guess you're right. But I will warn George as you said, and maybe the reception desk if it looks as though the press are going for us. At least there's a back door, if needed.' He paused. 'You know, I was always so pleased to have an unusual surname, especially given some of my father's ancestors' exploits, but right now I wish it was Smith.'

'I see your point,' I said with a small laugh, 'but I'm afraid we're both stuck with it. I'm going to warn the staff – Dave said he thought I should tell them much of the background and that they would be very understanding. But right now, I must get back to work. I've a major report to review against a tight deadline, even though it's the last thing on my mind.'

'Me too, get back to work, I mean. Let's keep our fingers crossed that it's not as bad as we fear it might be.' He paused. 'Can you ask the solicitor if there's any way we can find out what's going on behind the scenes, not just what's in the news? Forwarned etc.'

'I'll try, but I doubt she'll be able to help. I'll call you again if there's any news. Love you. Bye.'

'You too,' I heard as I ended the call.

I headed back to my desk and the report. Melissa brought me a coffee and a big chocolate biscuit.

'Dave said you might need some sustenance,' she said with a smile. 'And that you had urgent work so were not to be disturbed.'

I thanked her and, silently, Dave too. He really was a very

thoughtful young man. I hadn't had time to realise how depleted I felt until the sugar rush kicked in and I felt able to tackle the report.

The report, an in-depth assessment of possible sources of power for a big development in Ireland, was thoroughly researched and concisely written and didn't need much amendment. I went over to congratulate Jennifer, who had written it. In her early forties, she was a fairly recent and senior hire. She clearly appreciated that I came to speak to her myself.

'I'm glad it passed muster,' she said. 'It's the first big job I've done for you, and I did put a lot of work into it.'

I was just turning away when she continued:

'This is a good place to work,' she said. 'I'd heard positive things of Trenchant, but it was a big step to take. I'm glad I did.'

'Thank you.' I smiled. Then, realising I had to be available if Callum needed me, I thought quickly: 'It's an important client and a big development. Would you be able to go over to Ireland to present the report in person? If we get this right, there could be a lot more work from them. Good to build up a strong relationship from the beginning and I think you have the qualities to achieve it.'

Jennifer didn't hesitate. 'Of course. I'd be delighted – thank you for putting such faith in me.'

To my surprise, she stood up and came round her desk to shake my hand. 'I'll do my very best to put Trenchant at the forefront of this Irish development. Thank you again.'

Her pleasure and enthusiasm lifted my spirits, at least until I got back to my desk where I heard my mobile buzzing. It was Angus.

'Hi Mum, seen the latest news?' He sounded both anxious and excited.

'No – but I know about Sophia, the solicitor told me. I was about to call you and Bruce to warn you. Tell me the worst.' I took the now well-worn path to the meeting room as I listened.

'Luckily there's not much detail, just the headline 'Shipping magnate's daughter found dead in river' then a brief bit about Mr Nicholson-Smith and where they live. There's a photo of Sophia, probably from her Facebook or Instagram page as it's very glamourous, clearly posed.'

'Thank heavens that's all – though I guess there'll be more as the investigation gets going. Did the news say the police haven't ruled out foul play?' I hoped the answer would be no but was disappointed.

Angus groaned. 'Yes. Yikes! But it also said it could be accident or suicide. I told you there's rumours circulating about her and various boyfriends, so reporters are going to dig for stories.'

I repeated my warnings about not talking to them. 'At the most just say the three of you knew her through her brother and leave it at that, and I know it will be hard, but don't discuss it with your Cambridge friends either.'

'We know from all those TV programmes and news reports that the safest answer is always no comment,' was Angus's rather flippant reply.

'Yes, but also please don't let out any hints at all about where Cal is, not to anyone. In fact, I'm not even going to tell you.' As soon as I said this, I realised that would be almost impossible as Callum would certainly tell his brothers himself. I ended the conversation by adding: 'Do as your father put it to me, 'just stay stumm'. Does Bruce know already?'

'I don't know, not seen him since last night. I think he's gone out already – or he's still asleep.' This with a snort. 'Do you want me to see if he's here and give him the outline, or will you call him?'

'I'll call him but do put your heads together as soon as you can and devise a strategy for if Cal gets named as a boyfriend or, worse, that he delivered drugs for her, though I have no idea how widely known that would have been.'

Angus reassured me that he hadn't heard any gossip on those lines.

I then realised I hadn't told him the good news. 'Callum was released without bail when the news about Sophia arrived while he was being questioned at the police station.'

'Phew, that's a plus at least. Where will he go, to stay with Aunt Fi? Come back home?'

'I just said, I'm not telling you, though I know you'll find out in time. The less you know, the less you can tell. Now I must go, work has to continue, initially at least, as if nothing has happened, though Dave - he's worked with me in Scotland and knows a bit of the Callum-Sophia story - says I should warn the staff if Callum's name gets mentioned.'

'Understood, Mum. I've got to do some tidying up before my evening shift so I must go too. Let's hope the worst doesn't happen and the Trenchard connection doesn't get out. Bye.'

'Bye, darling.'

I then called Bruce but got no answer so left a message to call me urgently, which he did only a few minutes later. He hadn't seen the headlines and was shocked when I filled him in. I repeated the warnings about reporters and that he and Angus should decide on a strategy to keep them at bay.

'On a different matter, Cal told me you've got a stand-up gig. How did that come about? I had no idea you were a budding comedian!'

'Don't get excited, I've not done it before but there's a possible routine been forming in my head. I tried it out on a friend and he was snorting with laughter so I thought I would risk it.'

'So, when is this debut to be? Any chance of a recording?' I confessed I was both intrigued and impressed. What a dark horse!

'Tomorrow night. Will ask a friend to get it on his phone – but I'll only send it if it's not all boos and catcalls! Wish me luck!'

'Will do. And promise me you'll not give any information to anyone about Cal and Sophia, none at all. Right?'

'I promise. Must go. Bye.'

I called him straight back. 'Can you use a pseudonym, a stage name? Let's not mention Trenchard any more than we have to.'

'Hmmm, not a bad idea. Text me if you get any inspiration. Bye again.'

I tried to think of a fun stage name for him as I walked back to my desk, but my imagination failed me.

As I sat down at my desk, a different inspiration struck me: Callum should get a new phone and only give the number to the immediate family, Hamish and Ailsa, Fi and the solicitor. If his friends couldn't call him, tough, they could still go back to old-fashioned email.

Chapter Fifty Two

It was still only lunch time and I realised one chocolate biscuit had not been enough to sustain me. Looking out of the window, I could see the sun was shining brightly but the trees in a neighbouring garden were swaying in obedience to a strong wind. Just what I need, I thought and, alerting Melissa, set out for a brisk walk to my favourite sandwich shop.

I had only gone a few yards when I passed a newsstand where copies of the morning papers' later editions had the dreaded headline in big black letters 'Shipping magnate's daughter found dead in river'. Stopping myself from taking a copy to read, I continued to the café where, instead of taking my sandwich to eat back at my desk, I added a coffee and found a seat at an empty corner table. As I ate, I pondered my course of action.

First, call Fi and ask her yet another favour, this time to take Callum to buy a new phone before Hamish arrived to take him back to the estate. Call Cal, tell him about the phone, warn him the papers are highlighting Sophia's death, though he might have seen already.

Then back to the office to call a staff meeting, get that hurdle over. Hopefully, there wouldn't be press intrusion for a few days at least, if at all, but best to get Callum's side of the story in before any speculation starts.

Feeling better for having a plan, I left the café, only to find the weather had changed; the skies had darkened and rain was clearly imminent. I set off to the office at a brisk pace but was too late to avoid a drenching, the last thing I needed.

Cursing inwardly, I went straight to the Ladies where I

patted myself down with paper towels and did my best to return to respectability. Satisfied I could do no more, I went over to Melissa who commiserated before asking what she could do for me. I said I would like everyone to gather in the meeting room at 3pm. It would be standing room only for the fifteen of us, but no matter. Melissa raised a questioning eyebrow, but I didn't elaborate.

I could tell when Melissa sent out the summons as people were looking at each other wonderingly, receiving shakes of heads in return. One or two cast curious glances in my direction but I studiously avoided their eyes and buried myself in work until the meeting. It was hard to concentrate, though, as I really needed to get the tone of my announcement right. Various approaches ran through my mind before I decided.

Just before three I made my way to the meeting room, greeting people individually as they arrived. Some seemed subdued, others feigned lack of curiosity. When everyone was there, I began by welcoming them and reassuring them that I wasn't about to close down the business – or even sell it. Nervous laughter ensued.

Clearing my throat, I began:

'Some of you may have already seen the breaking news that an attractive young woman called Sophia Nicholson-Smith was found dead in a river in Norfolk early this morning. Until a very few weeks ago she was my son Callum's girlfriend.'

There were some gasps of sympathy which I ignored, going on to say that he had broken up with her when he realised she was being less than honest with him.

'Then, just a few days ago, he was unexpectedly interviewed by the police, and he discovered Sophia was being investigated by the Met who had found he was one of the contacts on her phone, all of whom were being questioned. It seems she may have been involved in something illegal, possibly drugs.'

I had everyone's full attention now. I swallowed before continuing.

'The reason I'm sharing this with you is that it's very likely that the papers will follow the story closely as Sophia's father is a big player in shipping in the City and journalists are likely to latch on to any leads dropped by the police who have said that, although it may have been an accident, they have not ruled out foul play. I sincerely hope that Callum's name will not come out as her recent boyfriend, but there's no guarantee, and with a name like Callum Trenchard it will be easy for them to find both me and my husband who, as some of you may know, is a respected investment banker.

'So, I'm alerting you just in case reporters turn up here. None of you knows anything more than I have told you, nor do you know where Callum is. I – and my family - would greatly appreciate it if you make no comment if approached. Thank you.'

There was a moment's silence before chatter broke out and Dave and Melissa stepped forward.

Dave spoke first. 'Thank you for trusting us with this and of course we will all keep our mouths shut.' There were murmurs of assent round the room.

Melissa said 'Of course, and we will send any pushy reporters away with a flea in their ear. If there are reporters around when you need to leave the office by the front entrance, we'll form a posse to surround you.'

A voice from the back of the room called out 'And we'll fetch your lunch sandwiches for you too.'

This elicited laughter and a relaxing of the atmosphere. Several staff came up to me to express sympathy and to say they hoped Callum was okay. I began to relax too as they drifted back to their desks leaving just Dave and Melissa with me. Dave smiled and gave me a quick pat on the back before he too left the room. Melissa, bless her, gave me a real hug.

'Don't worry, I'm sure – I hope - that it will blow over quickly.'

Kindly meant though it was, it didn't really reassure me, but I smiled gratefully and said I hoped she was right. As I went back to my desk, another thought assailed me: Callum had stayed with Sophia's parents who must have known they were lovers. Maybe he should write to them. Would they notice or think it rude if he didn't? I decided to consult him and William that evening.

The rest of the day passed quickly but I was glad to get home. Over a glass of wine before dinner, I raised the letter from Callum question. William looked thoughtful before saying that they had been very kind to him, paying his fare home when he lost his wallet, and he thought it wouldn't upset them. 'If it was me, I think I would be pleased to hear from him. I'll do something about dinner while you call him.'

'Thanks, it's all set out ready to heat up.' I rang Callum. 'How are you, darling? Safely back at the lodge? Got your new phone okay?'

'Yes, Hamish brought me back, no problem. And no to the phone. I talked Aunt Fi out of it. Honestly, I think you're being unduly paranoid. I'm hardly a big name, not important enough for reporters to be hacking into my phone, even if they got the current number. And I would still want to hear from my friends, even though I might not like what they say or want to reply to them.' Callum spoke kindly but firmly. 'Aunt Fi agreed with me when I explained why I didn't think it would be any help, and so did Hamish when we talked about it in the car.'

'Are you really sure?'

'Yes, sorry to disagree. I don't think I'm hack-worthy, as I said. Maybe you've been reading too much royal gossip in the tabloids....'

'I won't take that seriously,' I said with a laugh, glad he could joke about it. 'OK, if you're certain it's not necessary, but please, please don't let on to your friends where you are, however much you would like to tell them about Hamish and Ailsa. It would be so easy for a reporter to get the information out of them over a drink, for example.' I could well imagine this.

'Don't worry, I understand. I'll be very cagey.'

'But another thought. The Nicholson-Smiths were very kind to you when you went to stay and lost your wallet. They must have known you and Sophia were close so do you think you should write them a short note? You could put our address so that wouldn't give any clue where you were. What do you think?'

There was a long pause before Callum answered.

'I've been wondering about it myself, but yes. It will be hard to write but they were really nice, made me very welcome, and of course they knew Sophia and I were lovers. I think it would be strange if I didn't say anything.'

'Have you got time to do it this evening? Seems right they should get the letter quickly. Maybe Hamish or Ailsa could post it for you.'

'Or I could borrow Hamish's bike and cycle into the village myself if there's a post office to get a stamp. Be nice to explore a bit, not had much time to do that.'

'That sounds a good idea, if Hamish doesn't have work plans for you.'

'I'll write the letter this evening, I'm sure Ailsa will

have paper and envelope, and get it into the post somehow tomorrow. But I must go now, Ailsa's making dinner time faces at me. It will be a relief to sit down peacefully with them after the past couple of days.'

'I can well believe it, it's been a rotten time. Please say hi to them both from Dad and me and tell them how much we appreciate everything they're doing for you.'

'I will. Bye.'

'Bye, darling, keep in touch.'

I reported the conversation back to William over dinner. He shared my concerns about the phone but said we had to trust Callum. 'And let's remember, there's no certainty Callum's name will get out. We may be making a mountain out of a molehill.'

Sighing, I agreed 'Fingers crossed. But tell, me, did you talk to George about all this?'

'Yes. He said it was good to alert him, but to wait and see if there was any publicity which mentioned me and the bank. He doubted very much it would affect the bank -or me – anyway, so not to lie awake worrying.'

'Were you reassured?'

'I think so. It is quite hard to imagine what the press might say that would have any serious effect, more likely just to be embarrassing. So, for now, we just get on with our lives.' William paused before reminding me that it might be worth contacting Catherine so see if she had heard anything via her police contacts.

'Yes, I'll text her tomorrow.'

Chapter Fifty Three

The early editions on the newsstands as I walked to work next day didn't have the Sophia story as the main headline, a political sleaze story thankfully taking precedence. However, checking on my phone, I found an inside page of the Times did have a piece about her, reporting that she had been under investigation by the police for possible involvement in the drug trade. It said the police were not giving out any more information at this stage as it was an ongoing enquiry. I breathed a huge sigh of relief.

In fact, it was a more peaceful and positive day altogether and I was able to get on with my work, check up on my various teams and finalise what Dave was going to report to Hamish. One positive piece of news was the return to work of the poor girl who had pinned her foot to the floor when slicing a pineapple. She was all smiles now, though her foot was still bandaged.

'I'm fine now,' she said, catching my questioning look as she passed my desk. 'It wasn't funny at the time, but I shall be able to dine out on the story for months!'

I laughed with her and checked that she was happy with her work in the sustainable building team. 'They're great,' she said. 'It's very interesting and I'm learning a lot.'

Mid-morning a text from Callum told me he had written to Sophia's parents, using our London address as I had suggested. Ailsa was going to post it for him with a first class stamp that morning as Hamish needed him to help sorting out the storage in one of the barns. I texted Catherine as I had promised William, and she replied promptly that there was no news yet, good or bad. Two boxes ticked.

At home that evening there was a call from Bruce.

'Hi Mum and Dad, just sent you the link to the You-tube video of my gig. I think it went okay. See what you make of it.'

'Thanks, we'll watch it straight away and call you back.'

William and I sat at my computer and clicked on the link. Much of it went over our heads – not just because Bruce was talking at shot-gun speed, but because so many of the references didn't mean anything to us oldies. However, to my relief it wasn't overly expletive-laden. Then, about half-way through the fifteen minutes, he switched to political commentary and was brilliant; he had us in stitches.

We called him back on FaceTime. 'I think you've found your niche,' said William, still laughing. 'The first part didn't grab us but, my goodness, your political satire was hilarious - especially the bit about the Chancellor. Did it go down well on the night?'

'Actually, yes, it did,' Bruce admitted, a grin on his face. 'And it was more fun to write than the rest. As long as our politicians keep on like this, I'll try to do some more. The venue seemed willing to have me back too.'

'Well, congratulations! But I hope it won't be too much of a distraction when you get back to Cambridge.' I couldn't help voicing parental concern.

'Come off it, Mum, that's weeks away. But I promise I'm not intending to make stand-up my career.'

'Well, that's a relief,' I replied laughing. 'Pay's not great and the hours are terrible!'

William then checked that Bruce hadn't been gossiping about Callum and Sophia with his Cambridge mates. 'I hope you've not told anyone where he is?'

'No, silent as the grave on that topic. Actually, although

several have commented, no-one has been overly inquisitive, so it's not been a problem.'

'Good. Seen much of Angus? What's he up to when he's not working, do you know?' I hoped his time in Edinburgh was being as fun as Bruce's clearly was.

'Lots of tennis, I think – and don't let on, but I think he's met a girl, another tennis player. They hang out a lot together when he's not working – and she comes to his bar to keep an eye on him most evenings!'

'Have you met her?' William was a curious as I was.

'Not really, only briefly. But she's pretty bloody gorgeous, and nearly as tall as him. Must be super useful on the court.' Bruce laughed. 'Must go, sorry. Work calls. Lots of love. Bye.'

William and I returned to the sitting room, our faces wreathed in smiles. We had barely sat down when my phone rang again. I didn't immediately recognise the number.

'Elizabeth Trenchard.'

'Good evening, Elizabeth. Michael Moreton. Hope I'm not disturbing you?'

'Not at all. Nice to hear from you. How are you?'

'Very well – and a bit excited.'

'Tell all, we always enjoy good news!'

'Well, first – and I'll call William about it at the office tomorrow – it looks as though the investor he found for my battery project is very serious. Very good news indeed after such a long research and development period.'

Michael did indeed sound very happy. I didn't ask for details but said, if that was first good news, what was the second.

'I don't know if you remember, but my daughter Alice is an aspiring actor – it was some of her prop clothes I was wearing on our encounter back earlier in the summer.

Well, she's landed a prominent part in a play which opens tomorrow. I'm coming down specially to see it and I just wondered whether by any chance you and William are free and would like to join me and cheer her on?'

'That is indeed good news for her – and you. This is a slightly difficult time for us but let me ask William what he thinks. Where is the play on?'

'In north London, not that far from you. To be honest it's a very much a fringe theatre, what you might call off-off Broadway, but it does have a good reputation. I've read the play, it's interesting, quite dramatic but funny in places too. Have a word with William and call me back.'

'It's an unusual invitation. Give me ten minutes and I'll call back either way.' I hung up.

'What was that about?' William asked, eyebrow raised.

'It was Michael Moreton.' I explained his invitation. 'What do you think? Would we be able to concentrate with so much going on with Callum?'

'You know, I think it would do us good, take our minds off all this. It's unlikely anything urgent will come up that we would have to deal with in the evening. And anyway, I like Michael, be good to see him – maybe suggest we eat together before or after, depending on how long the play is. If that doesn't suit him, them at least a drink.'

As William reasoned, I found myself looking forward to it already. What with work, William's accident, and Callum's troubles, we'd not been to the theatre – or done anything sociable in London - for ages.

I rang Michael back. 'Yes, please, lovely idea. it would make a change as we've not done much recently.' Depends what you mean by done much, I thought before asking about where and what time. 'Would there be time to eat together before?

Or would afterwards or just a drink be better for you?'

'It starts at 7.30 and is only an hour and a half so maybe a light meal after and Alice could join us. Hopefully we'll be able to say good things about her performance!'

We finalised arrangements and said our good-byes before going to the kitchen for supper, enlivened by the prospect of a different Thursday evening.

Thursday's Times relegated Sophia to page three, but there was at least real news. 'Shipping magnate's daughter's death suicide'. The article said that the autopsy had found she was alive and uninjured when she went into the water and had drowned. Her car had been found nearby with evidence of drugs which would have rendered her unconscious quite quickly.

At the office I texted William who had already seen the news. Although it was sad that she had been so desperate, we were relieved she hadn't been murdered. I then texted Callum to tell him the news. He rang me straight back, seeming to take the news surprisingly calmly, but I could hear the tension in his voice. I went to the meeting room, listening as I went.

'I think she must have been getting out of her depth with this drug thing and couldn't bear the shame of being found out – a bit like me.' He gave a rueful laugh.

'I'm so very sorry,' I said. 'Although you had broken off the relationship, it's all still very recent and we know how deeply you cared for her. She must have been very unhappy to kill herself. Perhaps it was triggered by the police investigation. Did you learn anything about who or what she had got involved with?'

'No. Nothing came up in the police interview, she never offered any information, and I certainly didn't ask – better not to know, I thought, once I realised what she was getting me to do.'

'Very wise not to have asked. It's all a horrible situation and Dad and I hope that the police will leave you alone now.'

'I suspect that's unlikely as they'll still want to find out what I knew. I just have to hope they believe me when I say I don't know anything.' He sighed. 'I'll text Catherine to see what she thinks.'

'Good idea. Let me know what she says. Must go now, sorry, got a meeting. Bye.'

Callum's voice had a catch in it as he said goodbye. Heartrending.

Pulling myself together and wiping away the tears which had formed, I went back to my desk and let the work day take over.

Later that afternoon Callum texted to say Catherine had confirmed his suspicion that the police would want to interview him again, and that she was ready to accompany him for the questioning. That was a relief.

Home in good time and looking forward to our theatre evening with Michael, we freshened up before driving to the theatre, actually a room above a pub. Michael was at the bar as we arrived and beckoned us over.

'Time for a quick one before curtain-up. What would you like? No need to buy tickets, by the way, I got complimentary ones as father of the bride, so to speak.'

William and I both asked for G&Ts which we drank at a small table in the quietest corner we could find. The noise level was quite high as there were a lot of young people about, many of them clearly friends of the cast, so there must have been some good messaging amongst their circle. We weren't quite the only ones in our age group, I was relieved to see, having feared that, in spite of Michael's description, much of the play would be over our heads.

When the bell rang to call us to our seats, we downed the last of our drinks and made our way upstairs. The room was surprisingly spacious, and the seats tiered as in a normal theatre, but there was no curtain. We found places near the front and waited in curious anticipation. Michael alerted us that Alice was tall with red hair – couldn't miss her, he said with a proud grin.

The lights dimmed and there she was. She delivered a very personal monologue, setting the scene for a domestic drama involving politicians and civil servants. Her delivery was outstanding, conveying the character's sadness, mischief and personal conviction in the importance of good government. I settled in for a good evening and was not disappointed. Humour there was, and satire and drama. I made a note to tell Bruce about it.

The applause at the end was almost overwhelming. Within a few moments, most of the audience was on its feet – including the three of us. Casting a covert glance at Michael, I saw him wipe his eyes before joining in with the most enthusiastic clapping I had ever witnessed.

As the clapping died down and the audience began to disperse, Michael said he had booked a table for four at a nearby restaurant, but that Alice would only join us briefly as she had arranged to celebrate the opening with her fellow cast members. We followed him to the restaurant, an Italian one - safe choice he said, deprecatingly. We ordered some wine but were still studying the menu when Alice joined us, flushed and bubbling with excitement.

She kissed and hugged her father before allowing him a moment to introduce us. She shook hands politely but distractedly before announcing that, unbeknownst to her, there had been a major critic in the audience, and he had come backstage to congratulate her.

'I don't know who persuaded him to come, but it's amazing, said he loved my performance and he knows everyone so.....'

We didn't need to focus on her words which tumbled out with such excited happiness we couldn't help smiling. Her father had a silly happy grin on his face. When she finally stopped and said she really must go, he stood and gave her such a close hug that I could almost feel it too.

'She really was great,' I said, William nodding in corroboration. 'It sounds as though it might be a breakthrough for her. What fantastic luck the critic was there - I hope he gives it a write up. Who knows where it might lead – National Theatre, here comes Alice Moreton!'

We all laughed and congratulated Michael who confessed he didn't know where her talent came from.

'Not from me,' he said ruefully. 'Somehow lecturing a room full of engineering students on abstruse mathematical formulae doesn't quite call for either the dramatic skills or the humour. I'm just lucky if I can keep their attention, never mind make them laugh – though some might be tempted to cry at the difficulty of it all.'

Let's raise our glasses to her success,' said William, 'and order some food. I'm starving!'

Chapter Fifty Four

Having seen Michael into a taxi to catch his train back to Cambridge, William and I made our way home in a very cheerful mood after an excellent dinner. We agreed the play had been thought provoking as well as dramatic and funny, and that Alice had really shone.

'Let's hope it does lead to more work, she deserves it,' said William. 'Must keep an eye open for the reviews – did she say which critic it was?'

'No, but we only need to google review and the name of the play, and we'll find it.'

Next day, I found a review with the headline 'Is this a new star?' It was very complimentary, not just of Alice but of the play. I texted William the link and sent a congratulatory email and the link to Michael who responded almost immediately with a row of happy emojis.

Friday was again a quiet day at the office with no worrying messages and no work crises. I just hoped it wasn't the calm before a storm.

An unusually empty weekend loomed but we were happy to have time to talk to various family members about Callum and to invite some old friends round for a drink and kitchen supper. Although it was great to be so relaxed, nevertheless there was always a niggling feeling at the back of my mind that something would crop up to disturb the peace.

And of course it did. Callum rang on Sunday to say the police had already been in touch and wanted him in London for further questioning at midday on Wednesday. This was a blow, not because it was unexpected, but we hadn't reckoned on it being in London, which meant that Catherine probably wouldn't be there to support him. We agreed Callum could decide on whether to fly down first thing Wednesday or get the Tuesday night overnight train.

I scanned The Times over breakfast next morning and was relieved that there were no articles about Sophia or any drug investigation. At work I sent an email round to the staff to ask if they had seen any comments on the Sophia case in other papers or on social media and was pleased – and rather surprised – that no-one had seen anything. I texted Catherine to tell her about the London summons and ask her advice as to whether he needed someone with him other than a parent.

She called me back to say it was unusual for the interview not to be in Inverness, and that it would be advisable to have a supporter there. She was very sorry she couldn't attend herself. However, she recommended a solicitor she knew of who was experienced in the drug scene and said that she would put us in touch if we didn't already have someone in mind. I thanked her and said I would call her back when I had confirmed her suggestion with William.

Fortunately, William wasn't busy when I rang and explained. After a moment's thought he agreed we should accept her recommendation. He added more cheerfully that he'd already had a chat with Michael about the possible investment in his project, and it did indeed look very promising.

I called Catherine back. She said she would discuss the case with her suggested contact, Byron Davies, and if he was free and willing, she would fill him in on the details so far.

'I'm sure he will want to meet with Callum beforehand. Do you know what time and where Callum has to present himself?'

I confessed I only knew it would be at midday on Wednesday but would find out from Callum. 'If Mr Davies is happy to do this, we'll make sure Callum is here in time for them to meet.'

Catherine said she would get him to call me if he was willing to take the job, and between us we could then decide on a plan.

Before I had time to get back to my work, Callum rang.

'Hi Mum, been thinking. How about I come down today or tomorrow? Be lovely to see you and Dad, and it would be more relaxed.'

'A good idea, if Hamish can spare you. Have you asked him already?'

'Yes, he's fine with it, but I'll have to take the bus into Inverness as neither he nor Ailsa needs to go. I don't mind, though, the buses are reasonably frequent.'

'Good, so fly or train? Remember, Dad and I will be at work all day so there's not much point in getting here much before six - unless there's things you want to do at home, of course.'

'Actually, I did think I might see a couple of friends and,' he laughed, 'look out a change of clothes. I'm getting a bit tired of the few I have with me.'

'Let's say we'll expect you for supper on Tuesday at a minimum but let us know your plans when you've decided.'

I went on to explain about Byron Davies, and that if he agreed to help, he would want to meet up before the interrogation so not to make any too definite plans until he had fixed a time.

'Okay, Mum, thanks for being flexible. Of course I'll tell you whatever.'

'Oh, before you hang up, Bruce sent the link to his gig. Want me to forward it?'

'You're a bit late! Seen it already – watched with Hamish and Ailsa. We laughed our heads off. What a surprise – didn't know Bruce had it in him!'

'Nor us! Anyway, I hope this Mr Davies gets in touch soon so we can all plan a bit. Must go now. Text me your travel decision. Bye.'

'Will do – probably fly down tonight, though, if I can get a seat. Bye.'

He had barely hung up before I rang back.

'Got enough money to pay for the tickets?'

'I'm alright, just about, but thanks for asking. Not spent much up here,' he said. 'There's not much to spend it on!'

'We'll talk about it when you're here. Bye again.'

I only had time to review a couple of documents before my phone rang again.

'Mrs Trenchard? Byron Davies. Is this a good moment to talk about Callum?'

'Yes, fine. Thanks so much for getting in contact so quickly. I believe Catherine Macdonald has filled you in on Callum's situation.'

'Yes, indeed, and I'm happy to help. Although it's clear he's not what you and I would call a drug dealer, making his case incontrovertibly does require some thought, given he's admitted making some deliveries.'

As he spoke my heart sank. Was he preparing me for the worst? I forced myself to speak calmly. 'Do you think you can make that case?'

'Oh, yes.....'

My heart immediately returned to its normal height but sank again as he continued:

'But it's going to be painful for him having to go through the story in forensic detail yet again, and under intensive, possibly belligerent, questioning.'

I pulled myself together before asking him about his experience in this sort of case and what arguments he would use. His answer surprised me.

'I was drawn into the drug scene myself, initially as a mild user when I was just a young teenager in East London, then coerced into being part of the county lines system by threats to tell my parents who had always had big hopes for me, that whole immigrant-makes-good thing. I did well at school in spite of the drug running, but quite soon got caught by the police – all the stuff in the papers about young black men getting stopped by the police is true.

'My parents, bless them, had heard of a charity which helped defend kids like me and thanks to them, my teachers, parents and a remarkably understanding police interviewer, I was given a caution and spared a young offenders institution. The headmaster of my school put me in touch with another charity which worked with kids vulnerable to exploitation, dropping out, petty crime. They used drama to get us to work together, develop self-confidence, cooperate, focus on our futures. Most of us were black, like me, and the effect the drama, encouragement and life-skills support had on us all was amazing. We began to see a positive future for ourselves.

'I was so impressed by the charity's lawyers, and so grateful for all the support everyone had given me, that I resolved to become a lawyer myself. I qualified ten years ago and have concentrated on work with young people like me since then, with considerable success. I hope that answers your question.'

I was silent for a moment as I digested his story, then found my voice.

'Thank you, Mr Davies. I can understand why Catherine put us in touch, and I admire you for taking the route you did. Your parents must be very proud of you. So, how do you want to proceed with Callum? I guess you want to meet him before the police interview.'

'Of course. Is he in London, or still in Scotland?'

'He's coming down tonight if he can get a flight, or tomorrow morning. Probably best if you contact him directly to arrange when and where.'

I gave him Callum's mobile number then asked whether either I or William should be at the interrogation.

'Let's wait until I've talked with Callum and got an idea of how well he'll withstand the possibly tough questioning. I hope that's alright by you?'

Quickly running through my commitments for Wednesday I saw a possible clash, but maybe William could be free if I couldn't.

'I'm sure one of us can be free if needed. May I just say now how pleased I am that you're helping Callum – I'll thank Catherine for the introduction.'

'Maybe you should save your thanks until we've got Callum off his nasty hook! I look forward to meeting him tomorrow or Wednesday morning.'

I made a point of asking about paying his fee, but he said that could wait. We finished the call, and I sat back, reassured that he was someone who would understand the coercion – or in this case, emotional blackmail – which the gangs used as a weapon to recruit some of their runners. I suspected, though, that some did it for the money. In fact, I suddenly remembered reading about a teacher from a school in a tough area who recounted that, when she asked the kids what they wanted to do when they left school, nearly a third of the boys said they wanted to be drug dealers. She didn't think they were joking.

Chapter Fifty Five

We agreed William would go to the interrogation if Callum wanted support as my Wednesday appointment would be difficult to change. Slightly annoyed that there was no word from Callum, after dinner that evening we watched another episode of Yes, Minister, our unrestrained laughter cheering and relaxing us before bedtime.

William was already asleep when I heard the front door open. Sliding carefully from the bed, I was at the top of the stairs in time to see Callum drop his backpack and close the door quietly. I was inevitably reminded of the time not so very many weeks ago when I had stood there and heard him talking angrily to some unknown person about money. How horribly true our suspicions had turned out to be.

'Hi, darling,' I called out quietly as I went downstairs to give him a hug. 'Why didn't you let us know you were coming tonight?'

'Sorry, Mum. No good excuse, except I was in a rush and thinking about things, catching the plane, planning meeting up with friends. I know I should have done but you did say I could come anytime. Sorry again.'

'Forgiven, I'm just pleased to see you. Come and sit in the kitchen for a minute so we don't disturb Dad.'

He followed me as I asked if he had talked to Byron Davies.

'Yup, meeting him at his office at ten on Wednesday morning and we'll go straight from there to the police station.

'Did you get any impression of him?'

'Not really, just made the arrangements.'

'So, what are you doing tomorrow? I hope we'll see something of you.'

Callum looked slightly sheepish as he said he'd arranged to meet one friend who was working at lunchtime, another in the afternoon and several at a pub in the evening. He must have seen my disappointment as he hastily added that he could be home for dinner if it suited us and go to the pub afterwards.

'Suit us!' I said half laughing, half annoyed. 'We were counting on it.'

I went on to ask whether he had thought about having one of us with him for support during the interrogation.

'Yes, please, if you could. I hope it won't be too bad, but Mr Davies advised that I should.'

'It will be Dad as I've got an appointment I can't easily change. Do you mind?'

'Why would I mind?'

He didn't say it unkindly, but it put me in my place! As we went upstairs and said goodnight, Callum admitted he might not be up in time to breakfast with us. Not a surprise.

At breakfast William was amused by Callum's late, unannounced, arrival and full Tuesday schedule. He said he would organise to be free from noon on Wednesday, just needed Callum to tell him where the interview would be. We were scrolling through the news on our phones when William suddenly spoke.

'There's a piece in The Times about drug dealing and it mentions Sophia.'

I quickly found the article. It said the police were investigating a major drug dealing operation and speculated that Sophia's suicide might be connected to it. No-one else was mentioned, for which I breathed a sigh of relief.

Later, at the office, several staff had also seen the article or a similar one in other news sources and made a point of mentioning it to me with encouraging remarks that there were no other names mentioned than Sophia. Apart from that it was a normal work day. Dave had completed his report for Hamish and I signed it off for him to send, suggesting he add a note to suggest Hamish call me to discuss it when he had absorbed the content.

Separately, I emailed Hamish and Ailsa, to tell them about Callum's police interview next day and the Times article. Almost immediately I got a reply from Ailsa saying she would be thinking of him and hoped it would be less traumatic than the Inverness one. Hamish replied similarly a bit later, adding that he hoped Callum would be back soon as he really missed his help on the estate. *'He's a seriously good worker, intelligent and strong – and interested too. Must get lots done before he goes back to Cambridge!'*

I texted my sister and John to bring them up to date. Fi replied quickly, John I guessed was at the surgery. To complete the updates, I also texted Angus and Bruce, both of whom already knew, it turned out. I was reassured that all three boys were in regular contact and clearly supportive of each other.

Callum came home very cheerful from meeting his friends, seemingly unconcerned about the next day's interview, and the three of us chatted over a glass of wine before dinner. William confirmed he'd agreed with the office that he would be out for at least a couple of hours, and Callum gave him the address.

I was surprised when, as Callum stood to leave to go to the pub after dinner, he asked me for Michael Moreton's email and telephone number, saying there was something about the course he wanted to discuss with him. I texted Michael with Callum's details and said the latter would like to talk to him, if that was okay, I didn't know what about. We waved Callum off with admonitions not to drink too much as he'd need a clear head next day.

Callum may have been relaxed, but I wasn't. I was relieved when he came home before eleven, still in a remarkably good mood, just as we were going to bed.

'See you at breakfast,' William said, making it more of a statement than a suggestion as we said our goodnights.

'Yes, Dad. Sleep well.'

Some hope.

At breakfast Callum was subdued, confessed he hadn't slept as well as he would have liked. William and I admitted we hadn't had the best night either, but we all put on the best front we could. I asked if he knew how to get to Mr Davies's office which caused a roll of Callum's eyes as he held up his phone in explanation.

'I hope you get on well with Mr Davies and feel reassured he'll give you the guidance you need. I'll be in meetings most of the late morning and early afternoon, so don't call, just text me as soon as you can to tell me how it went.' My request hardly needed saying.

As William and I left for work, we gave Callum more hugs and good luck wishes. William added that he'd be at the interview by 11.45. As William and I parted at the front gate to go our separate ways, I wished him good luck too.

'I do hope it's not too ghastly, the interview at Hamish's and then in Inverness when they told him Sophia was dead really knocked him for six.'

'I'm sure it won't be easy, but we'll cope somehow.' William tried to sound sanguine as he kissed me goodbye and went to the bus stop, fortunately nearby as he was still slow on his surgical boot.

I walked briskly to my office. The sun was shining which

I optimistically took as a good omen, and I felt better for the fresh air. Knowing I wouldn't have much time – or appetite – for lunch, I stopped at the coffee shop and bought a sandwich.

Preparing for both meetings kept me occupied and the time passed quickly. At 11.30 I took a moment to text both Callum and William to say I was thinking of them, then joined the renewable energy team for an update on a Welsh local energy generation scheme they were working on.

Noon. I forced myself to keep focused on the discussion.

12.30. A surreptitious glance at my phone. Nothing. The discussion continued and, fortunately, required my full attention.

1pm. The meeting ended and I returned to my desk, my sandwich, and my phone. Nothing.

There was only half an hour to my next meeting. Should I text William? No.

1.15. A text from William!

Callum not charged, issued with a caution. Extraordinary turn of events, not sure if C happy or heartbroken. Taking C home, then back to work. Tell all later. Have a good meeting xxxx

Good meeting, my foot! I would have given an awful lot to have been able to go home right then and there, but I could see my visitors being welcomed by Melissa so I put on a smile and went to meet them.

Chapter Fifty Six

I was very glad my visitors came with such an interesting possible project as the discussion kept me from fretting about getting home to Callum. They were two brothers in their forties who had inherited several acres of land in Gloucestershire and were thinking of opening an equestrian centre with some residential accommodation and possibly a café or restaurant. They had a horsey background as their late father had been a successful showjumper, their mother competed in dressage events, and they themselves were accomplished riders. As it was a completely clear site and so could be developed from scratch, they wanted to be as sustainable as possible. They already had several ideas, including making energy from biomass and even a small market garden as there would be so much horse manure to use.

I liked the men and their ideas and called in a couple of staff with expertise in local energy and sustainable building to join the discussion and consider a proposal. The time passed quickly, and I was surprised to see it was nearly four by the time they left.

The rest of the afternoon was free, and I was on top of my to-do list, so I tidied my desk and told Melissa I was leaving early. I had to stop myself from almost running in my impatience to get home.

Letting myself into the house, I called hello to Callum who appeared at the top of the stairs.

'Hi, darling, Dad told me you've not been charged, just cautioned. That's great news! Come down and tell me all about it. Tea? Coffee?'

'Coffee please. I'll be down in a sec, just got to get something from my room.'

It was hard to judge his mood from those few words. I made the coffee, found some chocolate biscuits, and the two of us sat at the kitchen table. Callum's expression was unreadable.

'So, was it very distressing? How many interviewers? Were they aggressive? Was Mr Davies helpful?' I hardly knew know where to start.

'Byron was great, very reassuring when we met beforehand. I liked him, very straightforward. We met up with Dad just before the interview and they seemed to get on well too. I admit I was still very nervous, and the questioning was pretty tough to begin with, but Byron kept the two policemen from overstepping the mark. Dad didn't have to say much but it was great to have him there.'

'What sort of questions were they asking? Did you learn anything about what Sophia was involved with?'

'Mainly it was about how much I knew about her involvement with drugs. I was able to convince them that I honestly knew nothing, that I'd just delivered to the people she told me to. It confirmed my suspicion that somehow she'd got drawn into a fairly major crime gang, but they didn't divulge much. I did tell them that I'd been so upset and ashamed when I realised I'd been manipulated that I attempted suicide.'

I noticed that Callum was close to tears and reached over to take his hand.

'But when did they tell you they wouldn't charge you, just caution you?'

Callum reached into his pocket and drew out a folded piece of paper, crumpled from much handling.

'After they gave me this – it's not the original, they said they had to keep that as evidence.'

He handed it to me, wiping his eyes with the other hand, clearly on the verge of letting the tears fall. I unfolded the paper carefully and smoothed it out. Callum looked away as I began to read.

Dear sweet Callum,
I'm so sorry. I should never have involved you in all this, but I was under huge pressure. You loved me so much I knew you would do anything for me, but I should not have used your love to – I hoped – get me out of a horrible situation.
You need to know I loved you too, maybe not in the way you loved me, but, who knows, in time I might have grown to love you more.
You are a special person and I'm so ashamed to have used you. You won't hear from me again.
I'm so, so sorry. I hope you can forgive me.
Goodbye
Sophia

Both of us were in tears now. Callum moved closer to me and laid his head on my shoulder, his sobs shaking him as they had that day when we went for a walk on Hamish's estate. I put my arms round him and we sat together until, eventually, his sobs ceased.

'Oh, darling,' I ventured eventually. 'I don't know what to say.'

'Maybe nothing, not yet.' He sat up and dried his eyes. 'The police found the letter when they were searching her room for evidence. There was a letter for her parents too, they said.'

'Did you show Dad? His text telling me you were cautioned just said you were very emotional. He didn't say why.'

Callum nodded. 'I showed it to Byron too. He was so nice about it, gave me a hug as big as Dad's.'

'And the police, what did they say?'

'They tried to stay very formal, but I could tell they were sympathetic when they saw I was so upset. In fact, when we got up to leave, one of them gave me a quick pat on the back as he passed.'

'Well, do you think this deserves a drink when Dad gets home, and then a special dinner, or would you rather just be quiet and let it all sink in?' I didn't want to second guess his mood.

Callum reflected for a moment before saying he really wanted a normal family evening, nothing special. 'Although it's a relief it's all pretty much over, I do feel wrung through, would rather be quiet. Maybe celebrate tomorrow? Hamish said he doesn't need me back immediately, to take my time.'

'That's fine, I understand. But is it alright if I give the good news to Fi and the family, and Catherine Macdonald? I guess you'll tell – maybe have told, your brothers?'

'Yes, they know. Byron said he'd be reporting it all to Catherine, but I'd like to speak to her myself to say thank you as she was so nice and helpful. Oh, I've also already texted Hamish and Ailsa. Just got 'thank heavens, great news. Tell all when you're back.' Hamish also said he's got some heavy lifting for me to do next week!'

Callum grinned he said this. He clearly had a great relationship with his employer and hosts.

'I'll talk to both Catherine and Byron Davies too. And my staff. I didn't tell you, but when it looked as if the Sophia and drugs story might be major news, I told my staff the merest outline of your involvement in case your name got into the papers. Trenchard's not a common name and the press would have quickly got to me, so I needed to warn everybody in case there were journalists camped outside the office.'

'How did they take it?' Callum was curious.

'They were great. Said they would smuggle me out of the back door, fetch my sandwiches - I think some of them may be quite disappointed when I tell them it's now very unlikely to happen since you've not been charged.'

Callum laughed.

'That laugh is so good to hear!' I beamed at him, then looked at my watch. 'It's nearly six, Dad should be home fairly soon, he doesn't often work late and I'm sure he's keen to be with you. I'll go and do something about food for tonight, maybe pop round to the supermarket as there's not much in the freezer. Any requests?'

'Something very everyday - sausage and chips – or an omelette? Then ice cream, please.'

'Is that really what you fancy?' Perhaps I shouldn't have been surprised, given the stress he'd been under.

Callum nodded. 'Now, if you don't mind, I'd like to go upstairs and be quiet until Dad gets home.' He stood up and touched my shoulder as he passed on his way out of the kitchen, taking the copy of Sophia's letter with him.

I sat a few moments, absorbing it all, reflecting on the strain of the past weeks. The drug investigation might make the papers in due course, but for now we could all relax. We could put the ghastly time behind us and thank and pay the solicitors who, in my opinion, had earned every penny.

Short shopping list made, I went round to the shops. The sun was still shining, reflecting my cheerful mood. I didn't quite sing as I walked the short distance, but I smiled as I noticed happy things: a child cuddling a hairy dog, two young lovers walking hand in hand, a colourful display of roses in a neighbour's garden, the light on the treetops.

On my way home with my purchases, a bus stopped nearby and William got out – carefully, I noted, as he set his stick on the ground before stepping off the bus.

'Well met,' he said, giving me a peck on the cheek and taking his place beside me as we walked. 'How's Callum? Has he told you everything?'

'Yes. Well, I assume so. He showed me the letter from Sophia. What an extraordinary – but kind – thing for her to have done when she was about to commit suicide. He said there was a letter for her parents too. They must be feeling truly dreadful.' I paused. 'Do you think we ought to write to them?'

'Hmm, I don't know but probably yes. We should ask what Callum thinks. Be very difficult letter to write.'

I agreed. 'I asked Callum what he wanted for supper, should we celebrate, and he said no, sausages and chips! Hope you don't mind, I doubt you had much lunch.'

'No, now you mention it, sounds just the ticket in the circs. Nursery food. Undemanding.'

'That's lucky – and there's two sorts of ice cream for afters, and chocolate sauce. That should keep you happy.'

William chuckled as we turned into our front garden. I told him Callum was having a quiet time upstairs.

'Callum may want to be quiet, I don't know about you, but I could do with a stiff drink after all this. We've time before you start cooking. Suit you?'

I nodded as we went in.

There was no sign of Callum so we sat on the sofa and enjoyed our drinks, running through the trauma of the past weeks, rejoicing that Callum was now safe from prosecution, agreeing that such an outcome would have been totally unjustified, a miscarriage of justice.

I was just thinking about starting supper when Callum appeared.

'Hi, Dad, didn't hear you come in. Thanks a million for coming with me today.' He bent over to give his father a kiss on the top of his head.

'I can't honestly say it was a pleasure. I wasn't as nervous as you, but I felt for you every moment of it. Well done for holding together pretty well when they gave you the letter. We could all see the effort it took.'

Callum didn't respond, kept his eyes down.

I broke the silence by announcing I was going to do the cooking. Calling them to the kitchen when it was ready, I glanced at William with a raised eyebrow. He responded with a half-raised thumb – okay but not brilliant.

It was during that quiet supper that Callum dropped his bombshell. Over dessert I asked Callum casually if Michael Moreton had got back to him, and what he had wanted to talk to him about.

'I wanted to warn him I wouldn't be at his lectures next term – he's such a nice man, I didn't want him to think it was because I hadn't done so well in the exams – or that I didn't like his way of teaching.'

'Oh! Are you changing to different modules? There must be several choices.' I remembered from my studying days.

'No. I don't want to go back to Cambridge next term – maybe ever.'

Chapter Fifty Seven

William and I looked at each other, communicating silently in the way only long-standing couples can, hoping that the shock didn't show on our faces. I gave the slightest of nods to indicate William should respond first, guessing he would control our surprise better than I would.

'That's a bolt from the blue. A bit drastic. What's led you to that decision? Your experience with Sophia, seeing her brother and friends?' William managed to sound very reasonable, not angry or upset.

Callum spoke firmly and clearly, looking up at us both.

'No, the reason is that I've realised engineering isn't what really interests me. I know I've only been with Hamish, working on the estate, for a short time, but even so, it's opened my eyes – and my mind. I love the scenery and the outdoors, but it's not just that. Talking to Hamish and Ailsa, looking around me, realising how in nature everything fits together, but also coming to understand how fragile the environment is these days, made me think long and hard about what I wanted to do with my life.

'Mum, your work on environmentally good engineering solutions is important, and I'm very glad you're doing it, though, if I'm honest, it's small scale. Also, I want to be more hands-on, practical.' Callum waited for our reaction.

I couldn't hold back. 'I have to confess that, as well as being surprised – shocked - I can't help being disappointed.' I took a breath. 'You're very intelligent, you've worked hard to get to Cambridge. I don't think I've pushed you to follow my footsteps. I thought you really wanted to be an engineer of some sort. I was proud to think I might have set a good example of how engineers can make a difference.'

'I don't doubt they can play a very important role,' Callum conceded, 'but I don't think that's the way I want to work, too theoretical, I want to be out there doing things.'

'Like what?' I must have sounded a bit sharp as William gave me a warning glance.

'Well, if Hamish is willing - and I think he would be, there's so much to do – I'd like to stay on with him and learn more, see if it leads me to a particular direction. Could be estate management, or forestry, or even farming.'

I asked him what Ailsa would think about having an employee living with them long-term, and how would he pay for bus fares and outings as Hamish was only paying pocket money. It also flashed across my mind that my earlier – then quickly dismissed - speculation that Callum might be falling for her had perhaps not been so far-fetched.

'I've not had a chance to tell you that Ailsa is engaged and will be getting married early next year.'

That didn't immediately rule out my speculation, though it would have been a very odd way of telling us! I was quickly brought to earth by Callum's explanation.

'She got engaged a few days ago. Her boyfriend came back from holiday and popped the question at the weekend. She was so happy! I met him briefly, liked him a lot. He's another teacher. Anyway, she'll be moving out so Hamish could do with my help even more – especially if Ailsa's cooking lessons continue!'

'That's wonderful news for Ailsa – and, I have to say, lucky man!' William revealed that he had too noticed that she was very attractive, as well as being an excellent cook.

'Yes, great news.' I said, meaning it wholeheartedly, but couldn't resist making Callum justify his momentous decision, continuing: 'It's all very well, the outdoors life, but you've only been on the estate in summertime. You might find the prospect less appealing in winter.'

Callum took this in his stride. 'Fair enough, but that's one reason I said possibly just take a year off, find out if I really wanted to take such a big step.'

I was thinking what more arguments I could apply to dissuade him from such a big step when he continued:

'And on the earnings front, remember Brad, manager of the Castle Hotel? Well, he's been asking if I could do some bar or waiting shifts. I've been putting him off, obviously, while this Sophia and drugs mess was hanging over me, but now it's settled I could help out. If I got my bike up to Scotland, I could cycle over in the evenings when I finished Hamish's jobs. After the summer season, there'll be shooting parties so I could still be useful.'

William nodded approval. He seemed less thrown by Callum's plan than I was.

'But there's even more.' Callum looked a little smug. 'Ailsa has asked whether perhaps I could do some maths tuition at her school. Apparently, some of the children are struggling. They need help before their exams. I think I'd enjoy that.'

It was beginning to seem the odds were stacked against me. Clearly, Callum had been thinking hard about his future, which I had to respect, and maybe a year out would bring him back to Cambridge after all. Or maybe he'd even end up being a maths teacher if this tuition stint worked well. That prospect cheered me a little, Britain always being desperately short of maths and science teachers.

I resigned myself to accepting his decision, telling him I respected it, though I couldn't hide that I was sceptical as well as disappointed. I stood up went over to give him a kiss.

'I'm sorry I took your news badly, but we'll trust you to do what's best for you.'

* * *

Although it's nearly ten years ago, everything that happened that summer is etched in my memory: meeting Michael Moreton in his extraordinary outfit, learning about William's Parkinson's, going to Hamish's estate for the first time with Dave, our concerns at the change in Callum's behaviour, drug involvement and suicide attempt, Sophia's suicide and, finally, Callum's change of direction.

I am enjoying reflecting on all that has happened since then.

A couple of months after Sophia's suicide I spotted a news item about the breaking of a major drugs cartel. Of course I read it, and it did mention her. Clearly, it was serious coup for the police, in the UK and internationally. Poor girl, getting caught up in it, but I had to wonder how; did she fall for one of the gang then find she was out of her depth? We will never know.

Callum did spend the whole year working for Hamish, in spite of the hard winter that year. He then went to The Royal Agricultural University in Cirencester where he flourished, qualified as an estate manager, and got a job as an assistant manager for a big estate in Yorkshire. He moved up its hierarchy before getting a very good job with the Duchy of Cornwall. He even got to meet the King! Although for a while I was still disappointed with his decision to leave Cambridge, I now know it was right for him and am proud that he was brave enough to take such a big step. He's not married, perhaps his Sophia experience has made him cautious, but his brothers recently passed on a rumour that he was dating the daughter of an aristocratic landowner - no name revealed!

Angus introduced us to his Scottish tennis-playing girlfriend - another Fiona - when we went back up to Scotland for a few days with Callum on his return to work for Hamish. We liked Fiona very much, and her interest in the arts opened a new world for Angus so we were glad the relationship survived the termly separations. Once he had got his degree, a masters, and a job in a – rival! – engineering consultancy and Fiona found a job in arts administration, they got married. We were thrilled when they produced our first grandchild, a charmer of a little girl, now nearly four, and I am touched that they named her Agnes Elizabeth.

Bruce has turned out to be the most academic of the three, going on to do a PhD in – yes! - Quantum Mechanics, with Michael as his supervisor. He is enjoying his job in a research company in the Cambridge Science Park. Unsurprisingly, given his work and friendship with Michael, he got to know Michael's actor daughter Alice who, following that debut which William and I saw, has gone on to greater things. She encouraged Bruce in his stand-up side-line, attending his increasingly successful - and sometimes prize-winning – gigs when she could. Just a couple of years ago, he also won her heart! I'm so pleased at the continuing connection with Michael, and I think Alice and Bruce are well suited, but no wedding plans have been aired as yet.

Sadly, William's Parkinson's, although slightly slowed by the new drugs, meant he had to retire from the bank five years ago. As a retirement treat, we all, including Fi and family, went to stay on Hamish's estate. He had followed my and Dave's advice, starting slowly, but the wild camping was really taking off, to the extent he had to turn people away. The youth all camped but Fi, John, William and I opted to stay in the Castle Hotel and were treated like royalty. Hamish spent some time with us, and brought his partner, to meet us. He was an intelligent and charming man about the same age as Hamish - they had met when the young man came on a shooting holiday. Ailsa and her husband came over one evening and we all had dinner together. Great fun and many happy memories.

It was about that time we jointly decided that I would stop work to be with William as he declined, and that I would give up the Trenchant consultancy. With help from the bank, we organised a management buy-out. I have been able to follow their work through up-dates from Dave, Melissa and other staff, many of whom stayed on. They were a very loyal crowd, and I was – am - very fond of them. They have even employed me as a freelance consultant a few times which I greatly appreciated.

Sadly, but maybe happily for him, it's now three years since my beloved William died of a heart attack. It was unexpected and a terrible blow for me, but it meant he didn't have to suffer the long slow decline into helplessness that would probably have been in store. He was so happy that he lived to meet his baby granddaughter. We had a family-only funeral, but an open memorial service. It was wonderful how many people came and how many of them made a point of telling me how much they had liked and appreciated him. Michael was there of course, and was able to report that the investors William had found for his project had come up trumps and real progress was being made in research and production of these new batteries.

Michael has been a stalwart, if mostly long-distance, friend to me since William died, for which I am very grateful. If I am honest, however, I must admit I'm beginning to think it would be nice if our friendship perhaps became something closer. And, happily, I think he feels the same way, but we shall see...

THE END